WELC...

HOPE Y...

PORT NOWHERE is the worst place in the galaxy.
Meet a few of the residents:

Rudof Dyll, scion of the richest family in the galaxy, exiled to the Rock for crimes unknown.

Malik Blayne, tortured, relentless, and determined to save his friends—if he can figure out who they are.

Simikus Giff, a Nicovan with delusions of grandeur.

Tau the Silent, a Human boy reared by aliens, now orphaned by the loss of his tribe.

Charlie Manus, Protectaire's best envirosuit salesman—who wonders what the feek he's doing on the Rock.

Crila Maragorn, a Human/Halsan woman with a dangerous prosthetic arm.

Sha'zreen Glowberreez, Port Nowhere's most famous vidstar—who'd do simply anything for better ratings.

Doctre VanSlyke, for whom the Rock is an endless supply of spare body parts.

Mik'Amr, a local who finds working for the Connies less than ideal.

Jesse Iresson, a dealer in questionable merchandise, searching for truth—but he'd settle for a way off the Rock.

Raeyn Banks, on the run from a past that haunts her, to a future that's looking ever darker.

These and many more are willing—and unwilling—
residents of the Rock.
Are you brave enough to join them?

To Steve, for introducing me to the incredible world of science fiction!

~Diane Thompson

To Scottie and Bruce.

~Charlotte Babb

To my toughest critics: Renee, Kristy and Douglas. Thanks for laughing at all the appropriate places.

~Richard C. Meehan, Jr.

To Jerry, of course and always. To my writing partners-in-crime: you know who you are. And to Barry—I promise I'll get to the bus!

~K.G. McAbee

To my father, Tom, who never doubted me, in spite of myself; and my mother, Angela, who taught me to believe in fairy tales.

~Christopher T. Wilkerson

For David.

~Elaine Corvidae

To my father, the real Nioaka, whose life's teachings have prepared me for this endeavor, to my family for their support and ideas, and to my wife, Diane, whose encouragement, support, and impact on me is as timeless and ageless as the Universe in which I write.

~Steve Thompson

For those what thunk I couldn't right. In joy the book. (Sory they's no pitchers.)

~Jim Johnson

PORT
NOWHERE

Charlotte Babb
Elaine Corvidae
Jim Johnson
K.G. McAbee
Richard C. Meehan, Jr.
Diane Thompson
Steve Thompson
Christopher T. Wilkerson

Mystic Toad Press
Pacolet, SC

Mystic Toad Press
PO Box 401
Pacolet, SC 29372-04001
www.mystictoad.com
Produced and published in the United States of America.

ISBN 0-9752542-2-7

TABLE OF CONTENTS

UNDERWORLD

K.G. McAbee

"Captain, Sir! All present and accounted for, Sir!"

Captain Eversyn winced at the shout, then nodded at Baranin; the young lieutenant was so eager he seemed to be vibrating. Eversyn cast a critical eye over the squad of ten that blocked the corridor, all seasoned Connies looking calm, uninterested and assured, then nodded again. He hoped Baranin wouldn't burst in excitement, but it made Eversyn uncomfortable to see how tightly the boy's hand was wrapped around his blaster.

No one on the Rock was *supposed* to be armed, nobody but the Guard, though that concept had proved more than a farce in the past.

"Good. Inside, triple time. Secure the exits, locate the quarry, surround and stand to until further orders."

"Sir!"

The squad entered the Starview Lounge and followed orders; Eversyn watched them from a strategic position near the main entrance. Quick, smooth, efficient, just as the Consolidated Guard did everything; even Baranin managed to contain his excitement and not shoot anyone.

But it was totally useless, since it was obvious that their quarry wasn't there.

Warnings had reached the wrong ears. Not surprising. It was well nigh impossible to keep anything secret on Port

1

Nowhere, with its endless warrens and tunnels curving back on each other. The high beryllion content of the planetoid itself prevented most scanners from working more than a few meters below the surface, so it had never been efficiently mapped. That's why he'd decided to take the boveen by the antlers and simply show up at the Starview Lounge with a heavily armed squad, hoping Malik Blayne would be there, as per information received.

No luck.

Still, Eversyn never expected to be invited to stay for dinner.

"So, Captain," Rudof Dyll asked, his voice a smooth tenor, the series of silver rings that lined both his earlobes twinkling in the subdued light, "what do you think of our little lounge? Not bad? A bit gaudy, perhaps?" A slender hand, bejeweled to the first knuckle on all fingers, wafted towards the dance floor several meters below, where a number of couples—or in some cases, threesomes or foursomes—were moving in varying degrees of attention and rhythm to soft music. Some few meters below, because Rudof Dyll's table was perched atop one of the several floating balconies that drifted in carefully coordinated random patterns above the floor level of the lounge—now skimming above the dancers' heads, now approaching the transparent dome that protected them from the near total vacuum without, a vacuum that made the stars bright burning lights in the onyx sky.

Captain Eversyn was not happy. Not happy at all. Actually, if pressed, he would admit—but not to anyone else, only to himself, of course, and that in the dark and silence and loneliness of his private domicile—that he was really happy nowhere but behind a desk, bringing order to the chaos of reports and information, then storing that order all neatly away in clearly labeled and docketed files. It was his most secret, secret vice, and it would never do to allow anyone else to know that about him. Being the tall, massive, heavily muscled captain in the Consolidated Guard that he was, everyone took him to be ready at any time with fists or weapons to bring, if not peace, at least some sort of armed détente to any difficult situation.

But Carle Eversyn preferred to deal with paperwork. It was his curse. It was also, though he'd never realized it, his blessing, the means to his constant promotion, and the real reason he'd been assigned to so many difficult and dangerous situations. He had teams of eager fire-eaters under his command, Baranin and others, armed and dangerous Connies who would be happy, with any weapon at hand or bare fists, to break heads—or related organs in non-Human species—whenever necessary to restore the status quo.

But how many of them could write up a concise report, evaluate details, or make deductions from the sometimes sparse information on hand?

Still, the Starview was out of his ordinary haunts. And Rudof Dyll was certainly like no one he'd ever met, in any star system—or nearly out of one, as the rock beneath their feet most certainly was.

The Starview was the most expensive restaurant and lounge on the Rock; no doubt the most expensive Eversyn had ever been in, as his humble upbringing on Garitus Minor Three had seldom provided more than access to the occasional tavern. Even after leaving GarThree as an excited recruit, and his continual rise through the Connie ranks with its concomitant visits to a multitude of planetary systems, he'd not often had the time—or the credz—to visit such places.

But his host certainly had the credz. Sometimes it seemed like half of this damned putrid Rock belonged to Rudof Dyll...or at least, to the Dyll family. And the Dylls didn't mind shelling out some of their vast amounts of credz—more than he could imagine, Eversyn suspected—to keep Rudof in luxurious, extravagant, elegant, ostentatious, sumptuous ...imprisonment here on Port Nowhere.

Captain Eversyn straightened in his lushly cushioned chair, glad that he'd been wearing a clean uniform. He'd have felt even more wildly out of place if he'd had to attend in his usual rumpled drab grey coverup.

He was almost sure he'd lost control of the situation; it was important that he regain it. After all, he was in charge of Port

Nowhere; he was the local commander of the Consolidated Guard. And this man lounging before him was completely under his command.

Then why was he so nervous?

He twisted uncomfortably in his seat. "Uh, this is certainly a very pleasant place, Mastre—"

"Oh, please, no ceremony. Do call me Rudof. Everyone does." Dyll smiled, his thin lips stretching but not opening; with their suspiciously sumptuous red color, the smile gave the appearance of a dagger slash across his pale, narrow face.

Rudof Dyll was dressed in tight yellow breeches tucked into soft, low boots; a frilled, full sleeved shirt of a darker yellow, almost gold, and a vest heavy with embroidery and sparkling with jewels. The yellow-gold tones set off his hair, a deep coppery red, which was scraped back from his long face and imprisoned in a gold clasp, also sprinkled with jewels. His eyes, set behind long, long lashes with tiny jewels on the tips, were a bright green. Rings on his fingers; rings in his ears; one in his right nostril.

Eversyn, without realizing it, sniffed in disapproval. "Very well, then...Rudof. This is a pleasant place to, uh, relax. But I'm at a bit of a loss. Why did you ask me to dine with you? We Connies are seldom asked to social events—especially when we've just searched the place, looking for a known fugitive."

Rudof Dyll's companion said, "Throob," in a deep, reverberating growl that shook the glasses on the table.

"Indeed, I couldn't have put it better myself, dear old thing." Rudof nodded at the Vamir, who sat on his left side and Eversyn's right at the table for four. "In case you don't understand Vamiri, Captain, Algensio just pointed out that I asked you to dine with us for no other reason than the pleasure of your company."

Eversyn eyed the two meter tall Vamir. He—She? Eversyn didn't know much about the species, and decided to let the first gender choice stand until he had more information—he was covered in short dense fur, dark brown with pale streaks that ran up all four of his burly arms, circled his broad chest, and disappeared over his shoulders to run in streaks down his back.

4

No clothing, but a wide belt around his thick middle, just below his second set of arms.

Eversyn wasn't sure, but he suspected that the small whitish things that hung from silver hooks on the belt might be bones...or teeth.

"Ah." He nodded at the Vamir. "Uh, thank you...both."

"Not at all, Captain, not at all. I always enjoy seeing new faces, making fresh acquaintances, and dear Algensio is simply a social flutterby. Not to mention the excitement your little action just created for us! A search, for a dangerous criminal I have no doubt. How positively thrilling." Dyll raised one eyebrow and leaned forward; a waft of scent—expensive, Eversyn knew—enveloped the table and its environs. "And let us be totally honest, as among friends: our scene is just the least bit limited here on the Rock, as I'm sure has not escaped your attention."

"And you don't get off-station much, I believe?" There, thought Eversyn; see what he makes of that little remark. Eversyn knew for a fact that Rudof hadn't left the Rock in more than ten sintinz. That equated to six turnovers in control of the shipping lanes here on the very edge of the galaxy, six counting the coup that had placed the captain in charge less than four standard quintinz earlier.

Six turnovers in government on the Rock; but the Dylls were still the richest family in the galaxy.

"Sadly, no, Captain. I do not. I spend most of my time tending my flowers in my domicile dome. I have quite the collection in my hydroponics sphere; you must come see them. Of course, being so lonely, it makes it all the luckier for me that Port Nowhere has had such a wide and varied selection of...overseers in the past cyks, yes? It at least gives me the opportunity to share the occasional meal with so discerning a gentle as yourself. Here, let me help you to some of this ka'frindi. It's one of the things our little home is famous for, as I'm sure you know." Rudof leaned over the table, picked up a spoon, scooped a greenish blue glob from a small crystal bowl, and plopped it atop the slice of bovsteak on Eversyn's plate.

Eversyn watched in ill-concealed horror as the blue-green goop began to move, spreading over the steak and sinking clearly visible feelers into it.

"You must wait until it gets settled, you know." Rudof smiled. "It releases flavor enhancers and endorphins, but of course you have to eat it before it ends its life cycle—while it's still green, in other words. If you wait until it turns brown, it could make you quite ill."

Eversyn swallowed through a throat gone suddenly dry. He knew about ka'frindi, of course; it was the Rock's major export—the Rock's only export, officially, at least. But he certainly had no desire to put that crawling green stuff in his mouth. Then he remembered who his host was, and picked up his knife and prong with a sigh, sawed off a small bit of the bovsteak, lifted it to his mouth, and forced it inside. He chewed slowly, surprised at the rich taste but not much relishing how the fungus—Lichen? Bacteria?—tried to escape from his grinding teeth.

"Very...good," he said at last, after he'd swallowed and sipped his wine.

"I'm so glad you like it. It's an acquired taste, I must admit, but quite popular on some worlds. The fungus grows on the lower levels here, as of course you know—and, so I understand, nowhere else in the galaxy. I won't mention what it grows on." Dyll smirked nastily. "So, Captain, I suppose you have no intention of discussing who you were looking for just now. Secret Guard business and all that. But perhaps you can tell me this: what are the Consolidated Guards' plans for Port Nowhere?"

"Plans, Mastre—Rudof?" Eversyn coughed. "We're here to keep the peace, of course, and to make sure that the trade routes stay open."

"Of course. We mustn't let the routes close, if for no other reason than to keep my dearest papa happy—and the rest of my family terribly rich. But to be totally honest, Captain, those were the plans for the last, what was it, six or eight new controllers of the Rock? I had hoped yours would be different."

"Throob," commented Algensio around a mouthful of green salad; it was dripping with a red dressing that looked to Everson uncomfortably like blood.

"Yes, you're right, dear fellow," Rudof agreed. "We'd somehow expected more from the Consolidated Guard of Malpairiso Sector, hadn't we? More, at least, than we've gotten from the Red Publicans, or Inversodynamics, or...well, in short, from any of the groups who've—let's be dramatic— seized power here on the Rock in the last few sintinz."

Captain Eversyn tried to slide his chair a bit further away from the Vamir, who chose that moment to grin at him, baring a double row of pointed teeth liberally coated with green and red bits.

"Yes, well, uh...I'm sorry you're disappointed, ah, Rudof. But after all, you're hardly in a position to complain, are you? In fact, not to put too fine a point on it, you and everyone else on the Rock are under my command. My command, backed up, if you don't mind my mentioning it, by my extremely well-armed soldiers."

"Yes," murmured Rudof Dyll, offering another slash of a smile. "That's too true. It's a pity, that. Complaints are useless, yes. Not to mention, you're doing such a good job at...controlling the Rock, too."

Eversyn felt his face going red. "If you mean the smuggling, that's very nearly under control. And the Depths, well, they're just a matter of time."

"The Depths, Captain?" Slash smile. "A matter of time, do you say? The Depths have beaten better men than you, for all your *extremely well-armed* Connies behind you. Think of it, Captain." Dyll leaned forward, holding up a bejeweled finger as he made each point. "One: an endless series of corridors, tunnels and caverns, dug from the solid rock that composes our homey little planetoid. Two: groups of settlers, squatters, the lost and the discarded, tribes of children, hermits, any species you might name and some you cannot, all thronging there in the dank dimness."

The captain opened his mouth, but Dyll continued, not allowing him to speak. "Three: the asteroid belt that surrounds our little home, the ice miners, the smugglers, the pirates. Four:

the countless unknown entrances to the Depths, impossible to find, much less police. Can one man, however many soldiers he has at his back, make even a dent in those problems? I think not, Captain. I think not."

The captain decided to ignore that last statement. "Just because these...barriers have defeated previous controllers doesn't mean that they're unsolvable, Mastre Dyll."

"Throob," agreed—disagreed?—the Vamir.

"Yes, Captain, you speak the true, of course. But these latest little...incidents? That rather nasty explosion at Dock Thirteen? What was the loss there? All those other explosions? And the way those insurgents keep taking over the comsys, sending out those dreadfully unpleasant rants about your own Consolidated Guard, those vociferous complaints about Malpairiso Sector. And after all, you can't even find that pirate or whatever he calls himself, Malik Blayne, can you? Worrying, Captain, for a peaceful, quiet gentle such as myself, I must say. Very worrying indeed."

Eversyn sighed; he could see it was going to be a very long meal.

Rudof Dyll strolled along the wide central corridor towards the connecting airlock leading to the surface and his domicile, the Dyll Dome. The Vamir Algensio stalked by his side.

This was a merchant corridor; upscale, of course, as it was on the actual surface of the planetoid that was home to—that actually *was*, in fact—Port Nowhere. Clothing, jewels, rare imported food and drink, slaves, bed partners to whet the tastes of the most jaded customers; all these and more were just a few of the items for sale.

Rudof yawned at importunate purveyors who tried to capture his attention, unless the item in question caught his attention, as did a string of seven small slave boys matched in height and coloring.

"Yes, yes," he said, cutting short the slaver's description, "but they'll grow at different rates, won't they?"

"Oh, indeed no, honored Mastre," the slaver protested. "They've been carefully selected, and genetically indoctrinated, naturally."

"Naturally," Rudof said, eyeing the boys again; one, the one on the left, had a bruise across his bony ribs and traces of dried tears on his peaked face. "Well, clean them up and send them along; they'll be rather pretty working in my conservatory."

"Oh, certainly, Honored Citizen; very pretty indeed...working in your conservatory." The slaver winked one of his three eyes knowingly and turned away, delightedly calculating his percentage of the sale price.

"Throob," Algensio said thoughtfully as they left the slaver.

"Yes, you're right, of course," Rudof replied absently. "More trouble than they're worth, probably. But what else could I do?"

"Throob," Algensio agreed with a sigh and a shake of his furry head. A wide red tongue rolled out and licked away a few remaining traces of dinner from his chin.

Cutting their way past the rest of the stalls, they reached the edge of Dome Seven and the groundshuttle airlock.

"Dyll Dome," Rudof said, waving a jeweled hand. The lockkeeper nodded eagerly and escorted them through the heavy doors. He ushered them into the shuttle and set the coordinates for them before returning to the corridor, eyeing the huge tip in his hand with satisfaction.

A whirr, a click, and the tiny shuttle sped across its preprogrammed path towards a small pearlescent dome that glistened in the black distance.

The shuttle's path was a twisting one. The surface of Port Nowhere at first glance resembled nothing more than tumbled piles of boulders, some heaped far higher than the huge domes that spotted its surface. But on closer inspection, clear places were hidden amongst the rocks, of sizes varying from a few meters square to large enough for the placement of sizable domes. In the near distance, but crisp and clear through the vacuum, loomed the huge structures of the official docking platforms and trading stations that were the reason for the Rock's existence.

The shuttle beeped twice, gave a last right angle turn, and slowed slightly as its onboard navicomp re-checked the position programmed by the lockkeeper. A few seconds later, it snicked home in one of the Dyll Dome's personnel airlocks.

"Home at last." Rudof Dyll sighed as he unkinked his lanky form from the uncomfortable seat and waved Algensio through the airlock ahead of him, pausing to hit the return button on the navicomp. The shuttle beeped twice politely, and as soon as the inside dome door closed, disengaged and sped back towards Dome Seven.

Algensio stretched all four arms and opened his mouth in a wide yawn.

"Yes, do hibernate a while, dear fellow," Rudof agreed. "I've got to go out again, I'm afraid."

"Throob?"

Rudof shrugged. "No, not as Rudof. Not tonight." He patted his huge companion on one arm. "Don't wait up."

<^>

Rudof Dyll had stripped off his clothes and jewels as he walked across his bedroom, and now stood under a stinging needle-spray of hot water in a shower pod big enough for four. He squeezed a handful of sofsoap from a wall-mounted dispenser and scrubbed his face with both hands, then let the water wash away all traces of makeup. He stepped away from the spray, bent over a basin set in the opposite wall, squirted out a handful of sofsoap from a different dispenser, and began washing his hair. The coppery red color slithered off and into the basin, which caught the organic dye for future use.

Rudof stepped out of the shower pod into a small anteroom that shot out jets of warm air to dry him. Then he stalked into his bedroom.

Naked, Rudof Dyll barely resembled what he thought of as his public image. Tall and lanky, lean but well-muscled, he carried himself straight, head high, and strode confidently around the room—instead of the strolling, slouching, lazy figure that had just left an impromptu dinner party at the Starview Lounge. There was a long laser burn stretching across his back, from the top of his right shoulder to his left hip, and thick white lesions encircled his wrists and ankles—manacle scars, and the kind that were not acquired in a day, but took years to develop. His hair, with the dye washed out, was a dark nondescript brown liberally streaked with white. Brown too were the clothes he selected from a concealed closet set behind a high armoire. It looked too heavy to move—and was, unless you knew the secret catch that shifted it forward. He slid into a baggy brown jumpsuit with zippered pouches, much like the ones worn by freighter crewmembers, and slid his feet into battered boots.

Pausing before a mirror, he reached up and popped out his green contacts and peeled off the jewel-tipped lashes; brown eyes stared out of a narrow face.

Rudof Dyll regarded himself in the mirror, a smile on lips no longer a garish red. "Goodbye, Mastre Dyll; hello, Malik Blayne." The smile twisted into a snarl.

The former Rudof, now Malik, scrambled in the secret closet and retrieved a battered backpack. He hefted the pack as the armoire returned to its former position, then glanced around the room to make sure everything was secure.

The backpack was almost empty. He'd have to fill up on his way down.

Malik hit the palm-lock on his way out the door, strode down a hallway, took a right turn, a left, and stopped in the middle of a shorter hall. Silence permeated the dome, but Malik hadn't got to his somewhat precarious position by taking chances. He tiptoed to the end of the hall, just to make sure that no one was waiting around the corner.

Clear.

It was always clear.

But he always checked.

Malik strode back to the center of the hall, reached up and laid his thumb against an almost undetectable indention near the ceiling. A hatch slid open in the wall near the floor. Malik jerked his hand away, reached inside, scrambled for a bar set in the ceiling, and jumped into the hatch, feet first. It closed behind him with a soft *snkt*.

He kept his eyes shut as he slid several meters down the tube; he didn't like enclosed spaces. At last his boot soles hit an obstruction. He opened an eye—useless in the dense darkness—then fumbled for another indention; in this one, he stuck his other thumb.

An opening beneath his feet—light billowed up around him—Malik slid out.

The room was low and irregular, carved from the very rock of the planetoid itself. There was the faint and ever pervasive odor of mold and fungus. Cases were stacked everywhere, labeled *food, armory, ammo* in seven languages and four glyphs.

Malik filled his pack with a selection of dried foods in polybdalloy packages, strapped a blaster to his thigh, then walked through the cave. After several twists and turns—the cave stretched for some distance and he descended towards the interior of the planetoid with each step—Malik reached a clear area. No crates littered the floor, and here the construction had been done with more care. The walls were straight and true, and he could stand upright without the danger of hitting his head on a jagged protruding rock spike, and walk without dodging boulders. On the far side of the smaller cavern, a transparent cylindrical tube rested on three heavy supports, from the center of which came the constant hum of a life-stasis system.

Within the tube floated the long lean body of a naked man; his russet brown hair, liberally streaked with white, floated in an aurora around his head in the clear gel that surrounded him.

"Good evening, Rudof," said Malik as he checked the dials and filters. "I'm off on a visit to the underworld. I'll send everyone your love, shall I?"

The eyes of the floating figure blinked once, so slowly that Malik had disappeared before they'd made one full circuit.

Malik Blayne stalked a long corridor haphazardly cut from the rock of the Rock. It crisscrossed, intersected, and connected to a multitude of other tunnels, corridors and passageways, some nearly empty, some teeming with all sorts of life; maintenance panels blocked with rusted grates peppered the walls, ceiling and floor. He took what looked to be random turns…but were not.

The combined smells of Humans, dirt, a multitude of other species, fungus, mold, garbage and the general funk of an area that had never seen a sun rose in a miasma so think it was almost as if he had to cut his way through it. It'd been a while since he'd been down the Depths; he had always hoped the smell would become less noticeable as he got used to it, but it hadn't, not so far. He put up with it, but that didn't mean he had to like it.

A turn; up ahead a busy intersection. Malik slowed, then slipped into a cross-passage, ducked behind a pair of L'Taltons; their feathery crests and round, plump bodies effectively shielded him from view of anyone in the larger corridor he'd just left—especially the pair of patrolling Connies in their grey uniforms that he'd seen turn a corner and start his way.

Malik nodded at the L'Taltons, who squawked a polite reply, and headed down a ramp that led from LevFive into the less crowded—and more dangerous—LevSix.

"Mal! My Human! Come in, take load off! Whatcha got for me this beautiful day?"

The shop was a hole gouged from rock on the broad Zeta Corridor of LevSix, sandwiched between an around-the-chrono bar and an inter-species brothel. The proprietor was a shorter than usual—meaning he came barely to Mal's waist—ginger-furred Bansnict named Mrrrow-Gumg, who had delusions of being a five-star merchant even though his shop barely rated a quarter star on its best day.

Not that it ever had a best day, Malik thought as he looked at the sad collection of wares for sale. Hand tools, obviously not of the highest quality polybdalloy, since many were chipped and rusted from the everlasting humidity; MRIs, meals ready for ingestion, the foil packs quite visibly resealed—Mal shuddered to think what they might contain; ragged clothing with unimaginable stains, and piles of the flotsam and jetsam thrown off from the collision of many cultures.

"Nothing for you today, Mrrow. Looking for Tau the Silent. Seen him around the last few?"

Mrrow shook his head, his wide ears widening further and standing taller. "Not for few. What you want with skinny Human boy? Not even good for eating." Mrrow grinned, displaying a mouthful of sharp teeth, several of them beralloy-plated. A long pink tongue snaked out, wiped the corner of one of the Bansnict's green eyes. "That boy trouble. Thief."

"And you're not?"

Mrrow's grin widened. "Merchant. Not same, most times." He gave the wiggle that, in his species, passed for a shrug. "Some times, anyway."

"Well, if you see Tau, telling him I'll buy him a meal at Dhamu's Place on LevSix."

"That place not good food, Mal! Wait." Mrrow reached into his shop—not difficult, as even his diminutive arm could reach almost to the back wall—and pulled out a selection of MRIs. "Here good food!"

"I don't think so, Mrrow." Mal shook his head, grinned to offset the insult to the Bansnict's wares, and strolled away.

Tau would get the message. Flaming Core, he'd probably beat Mal there.

Unfortunately, Mal never expected to get caught up in a minor war on the way to Dhamu's.

He pressed his back hard against the cold rock wall of a minor side corridor on LevSix, his heart pounding, scrabbling almost unconsciously for the blaster strapped to his thigh.

Damn that boy, he cursed silently. *Can't he just meet me at Dhamu's for a sandwich without starting some kinda bov-feek?*

A wall of Connies stretched across the wider corridor a few meters in front of him. They were suited out in riot-control gear: heavy coveralls, thick with blaster-resistant cordion lining; nightsticks with leaded ends; and on hip or thigh, a blaster, ranging from light to heavy.

"Stay calm, citizens," shouted a heavyset woman with a surly expression and the eyes of a straz-head.

What the hell is going on?

"We're not here to interfere with your business," continued the woman, a sergeant by her insignia. "We just want to ask a few questions."

Sure. Just questions...just questions always went with riot gear. Maybe it wasn't Tau who started this.

Malik began to edge quietly backwards, into a maintenance shaft that he could use to bypass the promenade and get to Dhamu's the back way. It was just a couple of corridors over; feek, he could almost smell the toubrew from here...

Across from Malik's position, two spacers came pounding down a corridor—and slammed into the line of Connies.

A Connie swatted his blaster across the face of one spacer, knocking her to the littered floor. Her companion—Malik could smell the fumes of liquor coming off her clear across the corridor—gave a yell and jumped the cop who'd hit her companion.

As if that had been a signal, all feek broke loose. Screams and shouts echoed as a barrage of objects—pipes, bottles, unidentifiable crap scooped up from the floor—rained down on the heads of the Connies.

"We're under attack!" shouted the Connie sergeant.

Good, Malik thought. *They'll retreat, go get reinforcements, and by the time they get—*

"Return fire!"

Blaster fire laced out, catching a man standing a few meters from Malik full in the belly. The man's mouth opened in a blood-filled scream, and he fell to the floor, smoking bowels oozing out like lazy snakes to curl around his twitching torso. A woman, whose right leg had mutated into a charred stump below the knee, was dancing crazily on the other towards a side corridor.

Malik's blaster was in his hand, but he had no real target as smoke and fumes filled the promenade. No use. He had something else more important to do, anyway; warn Dhamu and the others, make sure Tau had made it there okay, then get them all the hell further into the Depths until this bov-feek died down. With any luck, the Connies would bypass the corridor leading to the bar...

Malik raced to the back of the maintenance passage, kicked in an access panel, and with a grunt, squeezed his body into a tunnel half a size too small for him.

<^>

No luck. No damn luck at all.

Connies surged out of the promenade, filling the corridor outside the door to Dhamu's bar, and Malik could see fighting going on inside.

How did they get here so damned quick? He peered down through a ceiling vent, coughing as the smoke and fumes were sucked past him by the huge vent fans. Below him spread a maelstrom of fear and confusion, as green blaster fire and red blasts from older models made crazy stained rainbows of the gray-blue smoke, and faces faded in and out of recognition as rickety circulation fans roared to keep up with the intensified flow of foul air. Screams and protests echoed up to his hidden post; he shook his head and began to wiggle slowly into a narrow passageway that led to Dhamu's storerooms.

"Hey, bov-brain! Over here! You looking for me?"

Damn, damn, damn! Tau's voice. That boy *never* knew when to keep his mouth shut!

Malik slithered back, cursing softly, and crouched over the vent, one hand poised to slam down across the mesh, the other with blaster ready. His brown eyes searched, searched through the confusion below, seeking the lanky figure of the Human boy.

"Yeah, you! You voids couldn't catch a rattu with a block of cheese and two dozen fels!"

There he was! The black castoffs the boy wore faded in and out of focus in the smoke-filled gloom, but Malik could see where he was standing now.

"Can't find your own asses with all your hands and a metal detector—"

What the Core was the boy doing? Was he *trying* to get a face full of blaster?

Malik slammed his empty hand down on the wire mesh that covered the access panel, but the rusty screws held firm for a change. He slammed again, again, and they gave way; the mesh fell on the head of a Connie who had a blaster pointed at Tau. The blaster went off, wide, two meters away from the boy— and Tau turned and ran.

Thank the Core! At least he's got sense enough to—

Half a dozen Connies—apparently deciding that an unarmed boy's insults were a safer bet than scores of angry Deepers with contraband weapons and fists—took off after him.

Malik dropped from the ceiling, cursing fluently, started after them...and tripped over a body. Seconds later, what felt like a steel-toed boot connected firmly with the side of his head...

<^>

A scream.

Malik was pretty sure it was his own.

He jerked up, sick, fighting dizziness, opened his eyes...and at once wished he'd managed to forgo that somewhat less than dubious pleasure.

He sat on an unyielding floor. The room that enclosed him couldn't be near an outer lev, judging from its shape: an opening carved from solid rock in a weird conglomerate of non-Euclidean angles, angles that hurt his eyes. *Something* hurt his eyes, anyway...and his head and his chest and, in point of fact, all the multitudes of him.

Somewhere in the Depths, natch, he thought hazily. *Where else would I be?*

He opened his mouth to complain about the sharp stone that jutted into his back...and watched with varying degrees of calmness as his tongue detached itself and rolled out of his mouth, to pool like a slimy snake in his lap.

Malik snapped his now empty mouth closed as the room shifted around him, the walls changing from grey-green-brown to blinding blue-white. He was no longer in a small unidentifiable corner of Port Nowhere, but onboard a ship—in the control room, no less, of the old *End of Time*. Before him stood Executive OfficerVezmir Zad in all his glory: beefy arms, stocky legs, a chest as broad as the buttocks of a Blender whore, and a face that would make a mother wimmerbat cry.

17

"Blayne!" roared Zad, his face turning an interesting shade of purple as he motioned towards Malik's feet. "What do you mean, coming to the con like that?"

Malik, interested, looked down—careful not to open his mouth and display his tongueless state. His feet, while bare, looked no different than normal; and he often manned the con partially dressed or even naked. After all, the *Time* wasn't a military ship; she was a pirate-rig.

Then he looked again. Yes, his feet were bare; unfortunately, they weren't in their normal position, attached to the bottoms of his legs. Instead they were wandering around loose, as if seeking their missing homes.

Malik could feel another scream building as he watched his feet scrabbling on the deck, which was no longer white but a pale, translucent gray; this new color lingered for a moment before turning black. He wondered what would happen if he opened his mouth to let the scream he was biting back escape, and he wondered too exactly where his tongue had disappeared to—was it lying in wait somewhere, ready to pounce on his defenseless feet?

"Malik?" This voice didn't belong to Zad—and anyway, Malik recalled in sudden clarity, XO Vezmir Zad had died spectacularly and with a great many frozen plumes of blood, just after Maryn Meredi had him spaced out the airlock of the old *Time*.

So the voice didn't, couldn't, belong to Zad…

Then who?

"Malik?"

The voice didn't sound happy. Malik wondered if he should reach out in the darkness that now surrounded him, but was afraid he might lose more parts of himself.

"Here, drink this."

A glass, cold against his lips, poured a burning fluid down his throat. Malik coughed as liquid fire coursed through his body, jerking him unceremoniously back to full consciousness. He sat up, protesting weakly, "What the feek…?"

Crila put one hand—her other one was wrapped in dingy bandages—on his chest and pushed him back down onto what was, he discovered by squinting through the gloom, the floor of

Dhamu's bar. The burly, massive Modajai barkeep himself, his yellow eyes red-rimmed from the smoke that still filled the air, towered over them; dangling from one hand was an ancient Dondaro Mark Five blaster, huge, bulky and sintinz out of date.

How the hells does he even get charges for it, Malik wondered blearily. He blinked and shook his head. "What the...?"

"Yeah, yeah, we already heard that one," groused Crila in her hoarse, I've-tried-to-breathe-vac-too-many-times voice. "Creative conversationalist you ain't, Malik."

Malik gave it another try, his mind as cloudy as the atmosphere. "Where did...?"

"By Bhagnor's scales, you was laying in the middle of a pile of bodies right outside my door." Dhamu shook his head, the light glinting off the grey-green scales that covered it in thick layers. "Them damn Connies ran off and—"

"Tau!" Malik sat up in a blaze of sudden memory...then slumped forward as his head threatened to explode. He took deeps breaths through his mouth, trying not to puke.

"Yes, I saw him run through here, right as that damn riot started outside," Dhamu nodded. "Didn't see what happened to him but the boy can take care of hisself, you know that, Malik. Hells, he's been running the tunnels all his life; ain't nobody knows the Depths like Tau."

"Yah, he does." Malik coughed, fairly sure he wasn't going to puke in his lap, but not willing to risk any credz on it. "But I gotta go check on him, make sure he's all right."

Malik struggled up, checked to see if his blaster was still in its holster, and tried to summon up his second best grin for his two friends. From their expressions, the attempt was a dismal failure.

"I know some of Tau's secret cribs; he'll go to hole in one of them when he can. Thanks for the rescue; I owe you both one."

"You and that boy," Crila sighed as she sprang lithely to her feet, setting her lush mammaries to bouncing. A pained expression crossed her face, only to disappear an instant later.

Mal spared a thought for her injured hand; how had she done it? She'd been fine last time he'd seen her. But he made no mention of the bandages; he knew Crila too well for that.

"One a these days, Malik, one a these days, he's gonna land you in a pile of bov-feek up to your eyes…"

<^>

Captain Carle Eversyn glared at the sergeant who was barely managing to stand upright. Her eyes looked strange; a look he'd seen in others under his command lately. He'd better have the corps physician give them all a check; this damned Rock was probably teeming with all sorts of diseases.

"Well, Sergeant? What do you have to say for yourself? Inciting a riot is not going to look good on your record."

"Yes, sir. No, sir." Voice dull, face blank.

Damn, what was wrong with the woman?

"Sergeant, I sent you to Level Seven to question locals about the whereabouts of Blayne. I did not send you to start a riot. What do you have to say for yourself?"

The sergeant opened her mouth—then toppled to the floor. Her wiry body began to jerk and twist in violent spasms.

Eversyn felt a cold chill shoot down his spine. He slapped a button on his desk.

"Medic! Get a medic in here! Now!"

~END~

SIMIKUS GIFF

Jim Johnson

Simikus Giff sloshed through the waste deep sludge of Port Nowhere's sewage treatment plant. Each hand held a low-voltage prod with which he shepherded the highly prized ka'frindi fungus into the floating collection bins.

He had come to work in Port Nowhere's sewage plant almost thirteen sintinz ago. And he might have lived that miserable period under some illusion of contentment had it not been for a moment of enlightenment during his second sintinz on the job; a moment in which he learned that the slimy film he and his co-workers were forever cleaning from the sludge tanks was not simply sewage scum but rather the valuable ka'frindi fungus, renowned as a food additive for its flavor enhancing and endorphin releasing qualities.

The major export—in fact, pretty much the only export—of Port Nowhere.

From that fateful moment on, the irony of his station in life had not been lost on the Nicovan, and harvesting the valuable delicacy—a mere gram of which sold for more than he earned in a full pay-cycle—had become both the bane of his existence as well as the promise of a better future.

That future, he decided, was just about to begin.

Simikus's work shift would end in another few minz. He surreptitiously glanced around for the plant overseer's patrolling surveillance drone. He caught sight of the floating machine just as it drifted off into the neighboring tank-room.

Now was his chance.

There was only one other crucial detail to confirm. He looked around through the fetid vapors rising from the sludge, his anxiety mounting, until he saw the next part of his plan.

"Ograd!" he hissed. "Over here."

Ograd, another a Nicovan like himself—nearly all of the plant's workers were Nicovan, a laxly regulated, cheap labor force—stopped pretending to herd the still yellow fungus and squinted his black eyes to see through the gloom.

"There you are, Nub," growled Ograd. The nickname referred to that fact that Simikus's left hand was missing its third finger. Simikus grinned, though the expression held anything but humor.

"Be quiet. Come here." Simikus kept a nervous eye out for the surveillance drone as Ograd splashed towards him.

"I want my money now," demanded Ograd without delay.

"Sure, sure, of course," said Simikus readily enough, though he made no attempt to produce the credz. "Does anyone know you're here?"

"Of course not, I snuck in. Nobody will be looking for me for another ten minz, when my shift begins. Now where's my money?"

Simikus twisted his sudden scowl into a smile. "Back here. Follow me." He led Ograd deeper into the shadows behind one of the huge sewage flumes that delivered the Rock's waste to the recyke center. With his face concealed in shadow, Simikus allowed himself a wicked grin as he thought back to the day, just a strechiz ago, when Ograd Paxa had shipped in to Port Nowhere and come to work at the plant; one of the few places that asked no questions when hiring.

They bore a striking resemblance to one another, he and Ograd, more than enough for his purposes. Simikus was hard pressed to view Ograd's arrival as anything short of divine intervention; it was as if he'd been sent straight from the Beryl.

And that being so, Simikus had promptly adapted his plan to incorporate the convenient newcomer.

"That's far enough, I haven't got all day," spat Ograd. "Give it to me."

Simikus turned to face his co-worker. "My pleasure," he hissed just as he jabbed one of his prods into Ograd's throat and activated it.

Ograd went rigid, gagged once, then collapsed into the sludge. Simikus was on him at once, holding him below the viscous filth.

At last Ograd ceased thrashing and floated limply, face up in the sludge. Simikus stood up and checked the time. Five minz before shift change. He glanced back toward the main sludge tank. No sign of the surveillance drone.

"Nub, eh. Thought that was funny, did you?" he asked Ograd's corpse. "Well, it's a pity you're no longer here to appreciate this." Simikus removed a small surgical device from his overall pocket. Acting quickly, before Ograd's tissues began to die, Simikus removed the third finger of the dead Nicovan's left hand. Then, resetting the device, he used it to heal up the wound. "There now, that wasn't so bad, was it?"

As he put the surgical device away, Simikus congratulated himself for having thought of amputating his own finger, which would serve as an identifying mark. He missed the digit, but not for much longer.

Next, he took the prod he had used to incapacitate Ograd, one of many he'd modified over the years for various purposes, and set it to overload. He stuck it in the dead Neek's right hand. Everything was in place. As the prod began to whine, Simikus turned and splashed a safe distance away, into a side corridor.

Sekz later the prod exploded. Sludge and sewage ignited in a rolling wave of fire. Alarms wailed and frightened workers headed for the exits, on to meet the incoming shift in a rush of panicked chaos.

Amid the confusion, Simikus slipped away, leaving the sewage plant and his past behind him...forever.

An ower from now, he would be Ograd Paxa, a Nicovan of means fresh off the transport—registered this time with a hastily, albeit convincingly, forged I.D. packet—come to Port Nowhere for entrepreneurial reasons.

Six levels up, the lift's doors opened Simikus stepped out onto the crowded public mall of the Wayamr commercial quarter—and straight into the broad chest of a Consolidated Guardsman.

"Slow it down," said the Connie.

Simikus felt numbed to the core, as if one of his prods had misfired in its holster and paralyzed him. With a look of disgust, the Connie brushed him aside and continued walking his beat. Simikus watched the officer's back until the burly Human became lost in the crowd.

When he could feel his legs again, Simikus started walking...more slowly this time. "Lighten up," he muttered. "There's no need to get all paranoid just yet. The plan is good, it's working perfectly." He looked around, found the corridor he was looking for and headed down it.

Several turns later, Simikus stopped outside the door of his new home, the pod of Ograd Paxa. Ograd Paxa. He smiled; he would have to get used to using that name from now on. Looking to his left and right, Simikus doubled checked for any passersby. Seeing none, he drew Paxa's finger from his breast pocket and pressed it to the access panel next to the door.

The door to the pod clicked open.

He was in.

Simikus closed the door and immediately reprogrammed the pod to accept his own fingerprint. He then disposed of the lonely digit in the recyke vat. He would be glad once he'd reattached his own finger.

He looked around the tiny dwelling. For a sewer worker, Paxa kept an amazingly clean home. It had been years since Simikus had been inside a room that didn't smell of sludge.

"Well, never you mind keeping this hole in order. By this evening you'll be shopping for something much roomier and a maid service to keep it clean."

Simikus rummaged through Ograd's closet. Ograd Paxa had a surprisingly large wardrobe.

"Five outfits!" Simikus was flabbergasted. Then his eyes alighted on one in particular. "What style! Who would ever have guessed you had such taste, Ograd?" He pulled a dapper coverup from the rack.

Dressed in the dead Nicovan's clothes, Simikus apprised himself in the mirror. The deep yellow coverup with its dark blue piping contrasted nicely with his creamy green skin and black eyes.

"You already look rich," he cooed to himself. He angled his head for one last look at the lobe pointing straight off the back of his skull; nice and shiny. He looked great. He felt great. He *was* great!

<^>

Captain Carle Eversyn read over the incident report as it scrolled across his desktop holoscreen. Unless he was mistaken, there hadn't been any explosions in any of Port Nowhere's sewage treatment plants since long before he'd arrived as head of the Consolidated Guard half a sinz ago. An addendum tagged to the end of the report confirmed what he'd already been thinking, and then some. There hadn't been an explosion in over a hundred sintinz.

He wondered how he should take the incident. On the one hand, it was just the sewage plant, and the Rock had more than enough of those.

On the other hand, this *was* Port Nowhere and everything meant something more than was apparent at first glance.

Eversyn sighed and called his secretary.

"Yes, Captain?" The young Halsan woman's voice practically sparkled over the intercom.

"Please call Mastre Dyll and express my apologies, but I will have to cancel our dinner meeting. Explain to him that an emergency has arisen and duty calls."

"Yes, Sir. Will there be anything further?"

"That will be all, Lisolia, thank you." He clicked the comsys off, then took his standard issue sidearm from his desk drawer and holstered it, picked up his data pad and stylus, pocketed them in his flack vest and headed for the door.

He hated missing his meeting with Rudof Dyll. From what he knew of Dyll—and that wasn't very much—Eversyn was fairly confident that the most influential sentient on the Rock would not take offense. On the contrary, thought Eversyn, Dyll always seemed to take particular interest in his job. Why was beyond Eversyn's ability to grasp. Politeness? Dyll didn't need to be polite to anyone; he was too rich. Sincere curiosity in the routine headaches of the head of the Consolidated Guard's presence on Port Nowhere? *Or perhaps Rudof Dyll simply sees me as an equal.*

That was a comforting thought and it kept him smiling all the way down to the still flaming tanks of the sewage plant.

Simikus Giff was euphoric as he pried the floor plating up and looked inside the secret compartment. Icy air issued from the opening in white, misty swirls.

Although he had already checked more than once and knew himself to be alone in the maintenance corridor beneath the Wayamr district's atmoscyke plant, Simikus nevertheless looked about the shadowy space before setting the panel aside.

Deep within the compartment, nestled snuggly against the coolant pipes, were dozens of frosty vials—each laden with the frozen ka'frindi he had patiently smuggled from the sewage plant.

As ka'frindi, the fungus could have provide him with a comfortable lifestyle—by Nicovan standards anyway—for years to come. But, with the secret he had discovered about the delicacy, instead of comfortable, Simikus was going to be rich beyond his most outlandish imaginings.

He ran a hand across his chilly stash, noting his missing finger. "Ah, yes. Time to fix that." He reached around one of the frigid conduits and brought forth his long absent appendage. Using the pilfered medical device, he thawed and reattached the finger.

"Welcome back, my little friend," he said, flexing the finger until it regained its former flexibility.

Dressed in Ograd's yellow suit, his ka'frindi horde safe, and his finger reattached, Simikus was ready for business. He replaced the floor plate and then quietly stole away from the maintenance corridor.

Captain Eversyn held a rag over his mouth and nose, to filter out the stench of the sewage plant. He had been there less than five minz and already he had reached a conclusion concerning the explosion investigation. A big fat *So what?* It was a sewage plant and the smell was so overpowering that Eversyn could not care less what went on down there, past, present or future.

All he wanted now was to get out of the place.

The plant overseer was short, fat, bald and shirtless... well...shirtless only in a literal sense, since every inch of the man's pallid flesh was coated in...Eversyn did not care to know. The husky Human stood nearly waste-deep in the sludge, apparently without wading boots. He looked up at Eversyn.

"So, what'ch figgered out, Cap'n?" He hocked a loogie, and spat it out.

Eversyn pressed the cloth more tightly to his face and suppressed a gag. Why had he come down here? He could have sent someone else to check into this; Benn, for instance.

"You said...you said that one of your people is missing?"

"Two. I said two."

"You're sure?"

The man snorted and held up three knobby fingers. "I kin count."

All right be quick, give the pretense of an investigation and get out of here. "Let me get their names."

"They was Neeks. I'm 'posed to know *their* names?" The overseer guffawed at the very thought, waving it away dismissively. "Look, alls I wanna knows is what cause the 'splosion. I don't needs to be around here if they's gonna be another one, if you knows what I mean."

"Believe me; I can understand not wanting to be around here." Eversyn glanced around the tank. "You say they use electric prods to herd the fungus?"

"Tha's right. Like this un." The overseer drew a grimy prod from a hip pocket and handed it over.

Eversyn braced himself before taking the cloth from his face and using it to hold the prod.

27

The overseer rolled his blubber-squinched eyes. "Low voltage. Nothin' special."

Eversyn considered the wisdom of using an electrical prod, however low the voltage, while standing in liquid. It was a wonder something like this hadn't happened before now.

He handed the prod back. "Well, if I had to guess, I'd say one of these prods malfunctioned, exploded. That reacted to the gasses in the air, resulting in the fire."

That sound like enough of an answer. It was enough for him anyway.

"I would recommend you have someone perform a safety check on all of the prods. No doubt they could all stand a little maintenance."

The Starview Lounge was one of the places where famous sentients like Sha'zreen Glowberreez and Rock Chipster hung out. Rudof Dyll could sometimes be found there; Core, he probably owned it. No secret there, the Dylls owned half of Port Nowhere. They probably had stakes in the other half as well.

Simikus stepped inside.

The Starview was packed with patrons, its dance floors teaming with dancers moving to the undulating rhythms of the live somasar music that filled the establishment. Simikus felt instantly out of place, as all of the beings in his immediate vicinity hurled a barrage of disdainful glances his way. Nicovan were not popular with the general public. Only a few of his species had ever been accepted into the social upper crust, and those grudgingly.

Ignoring the glaring eyes, Simikus moved deeper into the restaurant. Rudof Dyll was rumored to have his own private table. Simikus hoped the rumor was true. If he could just speak to Dyll, he knew that he could convince the rich Human to do business with him. Nobody was ever rich enough, right?

Simikus looked around; he was growing increasingly anxious. Surely the rumors of Dyll frequenting the place were true. They had to be; all of Simikus's plans hinged on Rudof Dyll. Without Dyll, who else was big enough to deal with

Simikus on the level he wanted? Malik Blayne, possibly, but that man was too enigmatic, too hard to find.

No. It had to be Rudof Dyll.

Just as he was beginning to sweat, Simikus looked up and spotted his intended business partner. Dyll's table was situated on one of the floating platforms drifting over the dance floors.

Though he had never before laid eyes on Rudof Dyll, there was no doubt in Simikus's mind as to who he was looking at. He was so wonderfully gaudy that Simikus could only stare. What wealth, what style! Simikus sighed in unconscious envy as he took in Dyll's loose, frilly shirt, studded with sparkling... jewels? Yes, jewels, by the score. Turning a faint purple with envy, Simikus envisioned himself in such clothing.

As the platform rotated in his direction, he was enraptured by the profusion of glinting gold rings that marched up Dyll's ear lobes, wrapped around his fingers, and there was even a ringlet looped through his right nostril.

The only thing about Dyll's appearance that even Simikus's healthy imagination could not apply to himself, was the red and yellow mane of hair that the Human wore tied behind his head by a golden clasp. Nicovan had no hair. Simikus smiled—well, then, what he lacked in hair, he would simply make up for with additional jewels.

Someone seized him by the arm and spun him about. "What do you think you're doing in here, Neek?"

Simikus winced at the grip on his arm, then gaped up at the huge Modajai. The bouncer was a big as a cargo-lift. Dressed in a skintight singlet, the Modajai was a wall of muscle covered by gray scaly skin. Its face was all square angles and bony ridges.

"Last chance, Neek. You got business here, or not?"

"I... I came to speak to, to Rudof Dyll."

The Modajai scowled and tightened his grip. Simikus felt a tingling numbness seeping into his fingers. "I m-m-mean, Mastre Dyll. I have a business offer in which he may be interested."

The Modajai glanced up toward the hovering platform. Simikus glanced too and found the conveyance parked almost on top of them. He saw the lively face of Rudof Dyll peering down at him quizzically. After a moment, Dyll nodded to the Modajai.

"This way," growled the hulking bouncer as he half yanked, half shoved Simikus toward a set of stairs near the edge of the main dance floor.

Simikus reached the upper end of the steps, and Rudof Dyll's platform drifted over to meet him. Port Nowhere's most powerful inhabitant dismissed the beings that had been his company, all save for an intimidating Vamir, and motioned for Simikus to join him.

Simikus could not believe his great fortune. The Vamir aside, this was a private audience! Simikus sat a little higher in his seat.

"Welcome to the Starview Lounge, my Nicovan friend," Dyll began pleasantly.

Simikus, suddenly aware of the Vamir's skewering stare, nodded nervously at Rudof Dyll. "Um, yes, it's very, very nice. Very posh."

Rudof Dyll's bejeweled eyelashes fluttered as he passed a grin to his bodyguard. "Posh. I can't refute, can I, Algensio?"

The Vamir shook his head, without lifting his gaze from Simikus.

Dyll looked to Simikus, "Again, you're welcome here...not that I have any say in the matter, of course. After all, I'm only a customer myself." Dyll's ornamented face turned away, and Simikus saw that others scattered throughout the lounge were watching closely.

Simikus swallowed the instant unease that turn his heart cold with fear. This was not the reception he had hoped for. He'd expected Dyll to start negotiations at once, not deny that he had any interest in business.

"Um. I, uh...I know where you can procure a large quantity of straz."

Dyll's green eyes widened and he leaned back in his seat. The Vamir had reached across the table, seized Simikus's head-lobe and pushed his face into an abandoned plate of toufood that one of Dyll's earlier guests had left.

As Simikus wriggled futilely beneath Algensio's iron grip, Rudof Dyll leaned in close to his ear and whispered. "Never.

Never, ever speak of such subjects around me in public. Do you hear me, Neek?"

Simikus nodded his head as best he could with his face in a pile of yeasteak. He heard Dyll snap his ringed fingers; Algensio released him.

Cautiously, Simikus sat up straight and found Dyll offering him a napkin, a wry grin on the Human's narrow face. He took it, and slowly wiped the food from his face.

What am I going to do? This is all wrong. What was I thinking? Was I thinking? I've got to get out of here, but how do I do that now?

He laid the soiled napkin on the table, and then Simikus's nerves received yet another jolt; this time a good one.

"You're stupid, but you have nerve, Neek. I like that. You intrigue me. Why don't we go somewhere private and discuss this...merchandise?"

With wary eye on the Vamir, Simikus nodded effusively to Dyll's invitation.

<^>

Eversyn stepped from his shower, clean of the sewage plant, though not feeling so. Two dead Neeks. He couldn't honestly say that he cared, but he couldn't get the fact that no slightest trace of either had been found. The thought nagged at him as he donned a fresh uniform. Things just weren't adding up—the freak explosion, and the missing Neek bodies.

He couldn't make sense of it, and what he couldn't make sense of, he attributed to Malik Blayne. And whereas fifty dead Neeks, much less two, matter nothing at all to him, Malik Blayne was something else entirely.

But if Blayne was responsible for the sewage plant explosion, what he was up to and why was a mystery to Eversyn.

He glanced to his clock on his wall. Oh eight thirty. Perhaps it wasn't too late to have dinner with Rudof. Yes, an excellent idea. He could eat elegant food, discuss his most recent problem...and secretly marvel at the man who was rich enough to eat bov-steak at every meal if he wished.

With a newfound smile on his face, Eversyn left his apartment, and headed for the Starview Lounge.

They were strolling the back halls of the Starview, Simikus and Rudof. *Like a couple of longtime friends!* He could almost believe such was the case, given Dyll's chattiness...had it not been for the Vamir shadowing their footsteps.

"I'm sorry, but I don't think I caught your name, my friend," said Rudof.

"Simi...Paxa. Ograd Paxa."

"Ograd Paxa," echoed the Human. "Hmmm. Sounds familiar, but I can't quite place it." He glanced back to the Vamir. "What about you, Algensio?"

The Vamir shrugged his top set of arms.

Rudof lead them through a door and into a palatial office suite. Simikus could not believe the size of the place.

"This is, uh, very impressive," he breathed.

"What, this? Just an office, dear chap. The office of the Starview manager; he'll be along in a moment. He's a great friend of mine, so he allows me to use it when I need a quiet place to...chat. Do you think it impressive, really? Why, I have bathrooms larger than this."

Wide-eyed, Simikus found his imagination sweeping along, down possible futures in which he himself lived so extravagantly.

"I can see you appreciate good taste," commented Rudof Dyll. "You do realize, don't you, that such a lifestyle might be yours as well?"

"Is...is it safe to talk now?"

"As safe as it gets. Have a seat. I'm sure when Mastre Caravello arrives, he'll be...engrossed with your news," Dyll said as they reached the long, floating band of a desk. He settled himself into a hoverchair cluttered with pillows. Algensio hung back near the door.

Simikus took another one of the hovering chairs and tried to muster his composure.

Silence. Nothing but silence. No one said a word.

Then a door behind the desk slid open and a Human appeared, his plump form framed by the portal.

"Ah, Caravello, dear fellow. Thank you so much for allowing us to usurp your office. Ograd, this is Banastre Caravello, manager of the Starview and, oh my, several other places here and there." Rudof Dyll's lean face lit up in a thin smile.

The chubby Human stood still for the space of a heartbeat, then trotted towards the desk and took a seat.

"Not at all, Mastre Dyll, not at all!" he boomed in a voice three sizes larger than expected. "You're always welcome. Now, what have we here, what have we here?"

Simikus knew this was his moment. If he could get this new Human to accept him as a supplier, he was as good as rich.

"Let me fill you in a bit, Banastre." The smile was still on Dyll's face, but there was quite another look in his eyes—one that had nothing to do with humor. "Master Ograd Paxa here has a little...proposition that he suspects you might have some interest in. Something to do, I believe, with that nasty drug called straz."

"Oh, does he now?" Caravello's chubby face also lit up with a grin. It did not make him look happy. "So now, Ograd— I may call you Ograd, may I not? What's the story on this straz supply?"

"Story?"

Caravello studied him in silence for a moment, and Simikus tried his best not to squirm under the scrutiny. The Human had looked pleasant and cheerful—at first. Now he seemed as cold as the storage space where Simikus kept his ka'frindi. "What grade straz are we talking about? What volume? Who's your supplier? How did you come to know about it, and where is it now?"

Caravello seemed to place more emphasis on the last question, but even in his jangled state of mind, Simikus had no intention of revealing that information.

"It's top grade stuff, top grade." That sounded good, Simikus thought, but Caravello regarded him impassively. Well, if that wasn't enough to interest the Human, the quantity surely would. "I have one hundred and ninety one grams of it."

Caravello's thin brow lifted, and Simikus could feel his confidence lifting with it.

"And where might this impressive amount of straz be now?"

"I, uh, I'm afraid I can't reveal that. I'm sure you understand, honorable Mastres."

A slow smile snaked its way across Rudof Dyll's painted face. "Of course we do, my dear fellow. After all, how healthy would anything be on the Rock without secrets?"

Simikus nodded agreement, smiling until Caravello held out a hand and asked, "Let me see a sample."

"A sample?"

"Come now, Ograd. We're all friends, but not that friendly. Did you think I was going to pay for the product sight-unseen?"

A good point, thought Simikus. Why hadn't he thought to bring a vial? This, if nothing had so far, was going to make him appear the amateur that he was. "I don't have a sample with me. The, uh, the Connies were everywhere so I left it behind."

If anyone in the room was surprised or disappointed by this, Simikus could not tell. "And there is one other thing."

Earrings jingled as Rudof Dyll sat straighter in his seat.

"What?" snapped Caravello, his plump hands braced on the floating desk.

"The 'stuff' isn't yet straz, it's still last stage ka'frindi. That means…"

"I think Banastre knows what that means, Ograd old chap." Dyll cast a quick glace at his bodyguard. Whatever meaning it held was beyond Simikus to read and he felt even more uneasy with his present company. Rudof Dyll only added to his anxiety by smiling sweetly at him and humming a little tune.

Then the Starview's manager said, "So you know the source of straz. Not many have ever learned that little secret. And fewer still are among the living. Isn't that what you've heard, Master Dyll?"

"Yes, indeed I have. Though, to be totally honest, honored sirs, I know very little about the matter."

I'll bet, thought Simikus. At a loss for words, he swallowed hard.

But then, Caravello seemed to shift gears. "One hundred and ninety-one grams, you say?"

"Yes, Mastre."

"Ograd, Ograd, there's no need to call me Mastre...especially when it looks as if we're going to be business partners. I think it only appropriate that you address me as Banastre."

"Yes, thank you."

"Now then, about this sample."

"I...I can go get it if you'd like."

"Forget it. Wipe it from your mind, dear fellow. Instead, I want you to bring me all one hundred and ninety grams."

"All...yes, of course." Inside, Simikus was ecstatic. He was gong to sell it all at once! That meant that he was going to get rich all at once. He could barely contain his sudden exhilaration. "When?"

Caravello glanced at the chrono set in his desktop. "We'll meet here in, say, one ower?" He didn't ask if that would work for Simikus, but the Nicovan didn't care. He was about to become absolutely, fantastically filthy rich.

Just then a soft trilling issued from the desk. The Human pressed a button. "Yes?"

"Sir?" came a voice. "Captain Eversyn is here to see Mastre Dyll."

Simikus's eyes went wide with sudden infusion of fresh panic. The head of the Connies was here? Where they on to him already? Where was the nearest exit?

The manager cast a questioning look at Rudof Dyll; Dyll nodded. "Inform the Captain that Mastre Dyll will be there momentarily." He clicked the intercom off. "The Connies are indeed everywhere, it seems." He grinned at Simikus. "Relax, Ograd. The Captain is an...associate of ours, if you take my meaning." He flashed Simikus a sly smile.

"Ah. Oh yes," Simikus chuckled.

Then Rudof Dyll stood up and stuck out his hand. Surprised by the unexpected gesture, since no one ever showed respect to Nicovan, Simikus stared at the extended hand for a confused moment and then took and shook it.

"My, that's quite a grip for a being so small."

Simikus grinned happily. "I'll be back in an ower."

<^>

"You were absolutely brilliant, a true natural," Simikus commended himself as he hastened through the Wayamr commercial quarter. "And to think of the years wasted in the sewage plants." The very thought caused his cranial lobe to darken in anger. "Well, no more sludge tanks ever again."

Slipping down a narrow alley between a haberdashery and a pastry shop, Simikus opened a rusty hatchway. He passed down into the network of maintenance corridors that crisscrossed below the quarter's main floor. Listening hard, he hurried through a series of turns until he reached the floor plate covering his ka'frindi horde.

He counted the frigid vials as he placed them into the small case he had brought to transport them in. They should still be suitably cold by the time he sold them to Banastre Caravello. After that, after Simikus had his fortune in hard credz, the Human could do whatever he wanted with the pre-straz fungus.

Giddy with anticipation, Simikus started back to the Starview.

Topside again, Simikus hugged the case to him as he crossed the Wamyamr's food court. He ignored the looks of irritation he drew from the motley assembly of species eating at the many tables.

"So what," he hissed to himself, "who cares what they think of me now? In a few minz they'll be kissing my feet."

Just then, one of the many vidscreens around the food court caught his attention. The nightly newscast was on. What was it saying?

"...explosion in the Robiddian sector sewage treatment facility is being investigated by the local division of Consolidated Guard. As usual, the notorious Malik Blayne is a prime..."

Simikus bolted through the tables, hurrying for the nearest exit. The Connies were on to him—but how? His plan had been perfect. Who were they looking for, Simikus Giff or Ograd Paxa? He needed to know, but he had run too quickly and missed the rest of the newscast. Should he go back? No. No, he couldn't do that; there were always Connies in the food court. He would be spotted for sure.

He clutched the case to him. "I've got to get to the Starview, to Dyll and Caravello. They'll help me. They can get me a new ID."

Yes. That was it. He giggled as he ran along the avenue. With the mega-credz he was about to be paid, he could buy more than an ID; he could be genetically resequenced. Why, he could be anybody he liked. The Connies would never catch him, not if he could get to the Starview.

<^>

Simikus ran the rest of the way, and entered the establishment huffing, puffing, and sweating. The place was much busier now, and most of the patrons barely scowled at him as he wove his way though their midst toward the back of the lounge.

As he neared the nondescript door, he noted the huge Modajai standing guard there. The sight of the scaly bouncer caused Simikus to waver involuntarily. He slowed, almost to a stop. The Modajai fixed him with an unreadable stare…before motioning Simikus toward the door.

Looking bolder than he felt, Simikus passed through the door. When the hulking sentry did not accompany him, Simikus regained a great deal of his composure. He was just a few meters from the office, just millimeters from wealth beyond his wildest dreams.

He stopped before the door and let it scan him. There was a pause, then it opened to admit him. Grinning, he stepped inside. His smile of triumph turned witless as he beheld the office's other occupants.

There sat Banastre Caravello behind his desk, flanked on his right by Algensio and on his left by Rudof Dyll.

In a hoverchair on the right side of the desk was Captain Eversyn.

Why would he still be here?

The Connie leveled an inquisitive gaze at Simikus. "Well, well, well; just the Nicovan I've been looking for, or rather one or the other of the two."

Frozen in place, Simikus sent Dyll a pleading look.

"And who might those unfortunates be?" Rudof chuckled to Eversyn.

The head of Port Nowhere's Consolidated Guard produced his data pad and activated it, relating to Rudof the explosion in the sewage plant and the two missing workers. He read off the names. "Ograd Paxa and Simikus Giff."

"Well," broke in Caravello with a smug grin, "this good fellow is neither one of them. He works for me. His name is Wilfor Kudisi."

Eversyn regarded Caravello for a moment, then Simikus. The manager turned his desktop computer screen toward the Connie. "See," he said, "the door scanner even confirms it. Wilfor Kudisi."

Eversyn scrutinized the picture on the screen then studied Simikus. If there was anyone on the Rock with a need for tight, efficient security it would be the Starview Lounge, since everyone—who could afford it—frequented the place. The captain had no reason to question the scan. Still...

"You know what they all say about Neeks. They all look alike," Eversyn said. Everyone but Simikus laughed at the insult. "So I'm sure you won't object if I run a background check on your *friend*."

"Of course not." Caravello's smug grin stayed firmly in place. "I understand."

Petrified, Simikus watched as Eversyn laid the data pad atop the desk holoscreen.

"Don't worry, Wilfor, it's just routine," said Caravello, his tone calm and reassuring.

Simikus nodded meekly, but he was trapped nonetheless. His forged Ograd Paxa ID would be all but useless now, since the only *officially* registered identification he had was as Simikus Giff. He had planned to remedy that detail after he had been paid his fortune. If he tried to run, the Connie would definitely arrest him and run the check anyway.

As he walked the hundred meters to the desk, Simikus became aware of the angular case of ka'frindi biting into his chest. *It's just ka'frindi,* he reminded himself, *perfectly legal.*

Eversyn would simply assume it belonged to the Starview. They served it on their menu, after all.

"Place your palm on the pad," Eversyn instructed.

In utter defeat, Simikus wiped the sweat from his hand and complied. With all three of his eyes closed and his breath held, he waited for Eversyn to slap a pair of sono-cuffs on him.

But he didn't. Simikus half opened one eye. "Is it broken?" he asked.

"My apologies, Mastre Caravello, Mastre Dyll," Eversyn said, ignoring Simikus.

Rudof shrugged and smiled. "No apologies are necessary to me, Captain. You're just doing your job; which, I might add, is more than can be said for your predecessors."

"Indeed, Captain; I completely concur," murmured Caravello.

Eversyn pocketed his data pad and rose. "I hate that I missed our dinner, Rudof. And, unfortunately, I must be on my way again. The more I think about that explosion at the sewage plant, the more it troubles me."

"How so?" Dyll asked. He rose, obviously preparing to walk the Connie captain to the door. A blush spread over the captain's face at this sign of courtesy from the Rock's richest resident. "Do you think the missing Nicovan are responsible?"

"Possibly. But it's just as possible that they're dead and that the real culprit is still at large."

They stopped at the door and Rudof rubbed his chin. "Hmm. Yes, but what could anyone really hope to gain from such an act?"

Eversyn sighed. "Though a motive eludes me, my thoughts keep turning to Malik Blayne."

"Ah, Malik Blayne. Port Nowhere's Most Wanted. Well, I think I speak for everyone when I say that we will all rest more easily once you've caught that criminal."

"I'm doing my best," Eversyn replied as he took his leave.

Simikus's flesh sagged in relief. It was over—somehow.

Now to make the sale and get on with his life of riches. Rudof had returned to his seat and gave Simikus a pleasant look. He motioned him into the chair Eversyn had vacated.

Caravello smiled at Simikus. "I believe we were discussing ka'frindi?"

Simikus handed it to him.

"It's all there," he said. "And by the way, that was brilliant, that Wilfor Kudisi thing. How did you know Eversyn was going to want to check me out?"

Caravello opened the, case, glanced at the contents before nodding to Dyll, then handing it off to Algensio, who closed it up and resumed his station.

"Wouldn't the more appropriate question be, 'How did I know that your true identity was Simikus Giff?' After all, how could I have provided you with a foolproof fake ID without first knowing your true identity?"

Simikus blinked in wide-eyed stupefaction. The Starview manager was absolutely right. But as far as the Human could have known, Simikus Giff *was* Ograd Paxa.

Caravello's smiled grew less pleasant; his chubby face tightened. "Perhaps I am not the one to clarify things for you, Simikus."

The office door opened and Simikus gasped as Ograd Paxa walked through it.

It *was* Paxa! Even before he looked to the missing finger; Simikus had no doubt. "B-b-but how? You're dead! I saw the explosion. I made sure..."

"You made sure of nothing you fool," hissed Paxa.

Simikus looked away, found his eyes locked with Caravello's blue one. "I don't understand. You two know each other?" The man said nothing but instead nodded toward Ograd.

"I work for Mastre Caravello, you void. Didn't you wonder how someone who looked like your virtual twin just happened to show up at the most convenient time for your little scheme?"

"But I thought..."

"You thought nothing. You saw what you wanted to see because it suited your greedy needs. Mastre Caravello's, uh, agents had been onto you for weeks. Did you really believe that only that buffoon of an overseer made use of the sneaky-eye drone? The fool was too lazy to even keep tabs on the likes of you."

"But the explosion?"

"I tossed the prod down the nearest flume; made the blast sound bigger than it actually was. As for the fire; I stayed below the sludge and swam to safety."

Simikus slumped deeper into his seat, shaking his head slowly. It was all over, probably quite literally. "Now what?" he mumbled. From the corner of his eye, he saw Rudof gesture to Algensio. The Vamir circled around the desk and took hold of Simikus with three of his four arms, lifting him to his feet and holding him in place.

Caravello said, "I'm afraid you destroyed some of my employee's property. He wants compensation. I'm sure you won't object."

Ograd stepped closer and Simikus saw that he was holding a medical tool. It looked all too familiar.

"By the way," Ograd said, "my name really is Wilfor Kudisi. But now that my name is registered with your palm print, I'm afraid I'll need more than just a finger."

Simikus Giff stood in the waste deep sludge of Port Nowhere's Wayamr sector sewage treatment plant, more miserable and dejected than ever.

The crackle of the overseer's prod snapped him from his miserable trance just an instant too late. The prod jabbed into the small of his back and the electric charge dropped him to his knees, allowing the filthy mire to splash against his face.

"Pick up the pace, Neek. Half as many hands means you gotta work twice as hard to meet your quota."

41

OUT OF WATER

Charlotte Babb

"You there, Neek! Get me a list of the ten best restaurants in Port Nowhere," Passenger L25 demanded, his Human face tilted so he could look down his nose at the stewardess while remaining seated.

Trillfin Skorm raised her chin, lowering her dorsal lobe to her back, a sign of acquiescence and submission. But she gritted her teeth as her digipods stroked the information into the read-sheet printer. This Human had been more trouble on this one shuttle run than everyone she'd served in a week. He'd wanted a pillow, then he complained about the lighting, and wanted a complimentary globe of water—lots of attention but nothing he would have to pay for.

She brought him the list, cadged from memory—it wasn't worth the time to pull something like that from the comlink.

"Mastre," she said, lowering her lobe again. She added a bit of undulation to make her semi-transparent uniform flow across her banded skin. The Human had been staring her all the way from Dome Seven, asking for some service or another every five minz. It was enough to make her skin crack, and he was rude as well. Everyone knew that Nicovans never complained, never stood up for themselves and never talked back. He took advantage.

Trillfin didn't care about that—part of the job description. She wanted off planet. One day she'd find the mark to take her.

She was pretty sure this wasn't the one, but she played her part anyway.

"Which of these is considered the second best?" He was young, less than halfway to middle age, and not as well-dressed as most of the offworlders who came through Dome Seven. Nevertheless, he had an imperial manner that spoke of privilege and estate, a youngest son, perhaps, hiding out from the family or disinherited, but he probably didn't have the money to eat in the second best restaurant in LevThree, much less LevOne.

"Does Mastre inquire about the food only, the ambiance or the menu?" She tilted forward slightly to show off her chest, which did serve to distract him. He was definitely a mark.

"Food, of course, Neek! All the dancing girls, animascreens, and costumed waiters can't disguise mediocre food." His face reddened. His voice raised enough to catch the attention of some other passengers who had been successfully ignoring him.

"Starview's the best," growled the Modajai trader in R25, his huge, scaled body wrapped in a business toga that cost more than Trillfin would make in a year. "Why take anything less?" His bony face and hard muscle expressed his general disapproval.

Trillfin removed herself from the passenger space to allow them to speak without appearing to listen while she finished the end of shift tasks.

"I have my reasons," the Human said. "What would you recommend, then, for the *food*?" He glanced at the back of the shuttle where Trillfin had disappeared.

"The Crater's good, " said a Vamir lady, her pointed ears aimed at the Human, though she held a read-sheet in one of her four hands while the other three played with her jewelry. "Raw boveen, served at blood temperature. Throob!" The Vamir purred to herself, with a bit of a smile that revealed the sharp fangs behind her furred lips.

"I prefer the Double Dome because they don't use ka'frindi," added a space jockey, apparently Human, but covered in a worn jumpsuit of reptilian skin except for his eyes, which were hidden by shades. "I want to see what my food is and what it really tastes like."

All of them spoke to the Human like he was a Neek, like he was nothing, laughing in his face with their suggestions. The Crater was a LevThree meat market that would eat him alive— maybe literally—the Double Dome was a brothel catering to the most twisted of kinky cross-species entertainment. He didn't seem to realize it though. Trillfin felt a bit sorry for him. He wouldn't last long on the Rock, but maybe his family would pay a ransom for him or at least send him enough credz to roll on. He might be worth the trouble to take care of.

Trillfin sounded the bell that signaled the end of the shuttle ride, interrupting the conversation. "Mastrizes and Mastres. Welcome to Wayamr, the trading post at the edge of the galaxy, where every exotic thing can be found for your pleasure. Please retain your seating until the shuttle stops. File out the doors to the left. Thank you for choosing the Wayamr shuttle service."

The Human looked pale as he pulled his travel tunic around him, facing the door as if it led to the Surface. He swallowed at least twice, but straightened up, listening to more suggestions from the other passengers, each of them a worse choice than the last.

Trillfin decided she would play a tour guide to hustle a few more credz for her trouble. Her shift was over for the cycle anyway, but she wasn't ready to go back to her pod. She'd take him to get a bite from her aunt's clan at the Chow Down. While not even listed on the tourist map, the food was excellent.

Not that the Human would know the difference, for all his arrogance. They didn't get many offworlders there. The clan might enjoy playing with him.

Three Bansnict kits spotted the Human as soon as he got off the shuttle. They crowded around him, their tails twitching and their paws patting him, promising him everything from the best price on straz to their very own virgin sisters—as if any Bansnict understood the concept. If he had any thing loose in his pockets, it was gone by the time Trillfin shooed them away.

"Get out of here, you little thieving furballs!" Trilby screeched, making a supersonic noise the Human could not hear, but which made the Bansnicts cover their ears and yelp. She nicked the load of the one child young enough to pass near her. Although timid and meek, Nicovans had a light touch. She smiled, lowering her lobe to the Human again. "Mastre, if you would like a guide, this one would be honored to…"

"I am quite capable of handling myself, Neek." He brushed himself off and straightened up again, sauntering off towards a tube that would lead him as far away as he could get from the restaurant spiral. She watched him for a moment. He couldn't help hunching his head into his shoulders—a sure sign of an offworlder. None of them appreciated a couple hundred meters of good, solid beryllion overhead.

Trillfin shrugged, forcing her shoulders down to release both her tension from work and her interest in the Human. She went to her lockpod to change clothes. She hadn't gotten much from the Bansnict, a few credz and an ID tag for a LevOne rim dweller—an Ophid. She couldn't use the ID, but she could sell it or maybe get it reprogrammed. Living on LevOne would be one step closer to off-world.

Of course it was also one step closer to being between the Rock and Nothing too.

The credz would buy her a quick meal, so she wouldn't have to cook before she slid into the sleep tank. She took a quick mist, not wasting credz on a full shower, but glad to have her skin wet again. She slipped into her tube robe, which only revealed her species by the ridge of her lobe in the hood. Some of the slave traders were bold enough to snatch a female, even right under the noses of the Connies. Her silver and black skin banding might draw their attention. It was an asset on the shuttle with her transparent bit of uniform, but not outside Main Tube.

She walked through the tube, taking the drop down to the Bubble on the Rim of LevOne. It was a little pricey, but the food was better than average. The Bubble had a dome where she could see the stars. She had tried to get a job there, but they wouldn't hire a Neek. They said she wouldn't get used to the idea of only a skin of polybdalloy between her and Nothing. Agoraphobia, they called it. But when she showed her credz, they let her in soon enough, even if she had to sit near the kitchen, far from the dome.

Trillfin had never been on the surface, the Rock under her feet and Nothing but distant suns overhead, but she knew that was where any future she had would begin. Just working on LevOne was more than almost any other Neek achieved, unless they rode herd on sanibots. She wanted to breathe fresh air and have a chance to learn how the Offal lived and where they got their strange ideas. She didn't want to live and die a Rocker.

She ordered a deep-level fish, pearly white from being raised in the dark tunnels that ringed the reclaiming vats. The large fins were crispy fried; the meat pulled from the bones, arranged in a sunburst on her plate with a tiny dot of blue-green ka'frindi in the middle. She let it grow across the white fish while she ate her salad. It was a special treat, a relief from the usual blocks of sauced toufood she ate in the pod. It might all come from the same plants, but it was nice, as the spacer had said, to see what it really looked like before the ka'frindi spread itself to made the flavors intense, triggering endorphins. She wondered why the Human wanted the *second* best restaurant?

She took a bite of the fish, now veined with ka'frindi. Its flavor spread from her mouth into her face, her ears, even to the far tip of her lobe. No wonder offworlders came parsecs to get ka'frindi. Nobody could grow it anywhere else. If she could manage to get enough of it, she could buy a ticket off the Rock. She stared at the stars outside the dome, leaning into the endorphin mix. If she could breathe space, she could walk naked on the surface between the Rock and Nothing. Equally likely.

She made herself eat slowly. The ka'frindi would only last half an ower before it went into its next life cycle, which was disgusting, but she wanted to spread out the effect as long as she could.

In the kitchen, someone started yelling.

The kitchen door irised as several waiters ran towards her to see what was happening. The same Human was there, struggling with a couple of Fwazeks who were trying to throw him out. They butted his knees with their mushroom-shaped heads, pulling him off balance to bring him down to their height. One of them had a cleaver.

A surge of adrenaline fed into the ka'frindi effect. Trillfin dashed into the kitchen.

"Oh Mastre, Mastre! Please don't hurt Mastre. Please!" She fell to her knees, shoving one of the knee-high Fwazeks aside. She grabbed a fistful of the Human's tunic. The ka'frindi made all her senses sharper: the texture of the tunic, the oily damp heat of the kitchen, the stink of fear from the Human. That smell released some unknown reserve.

She pulled him to her, crying. "Forgive me, Mastre, I let you get lost. I have searched everywhere for you." She made her voice a shrill plea, "Please don't hurt Mastre." She pushed their tentacles from the Human, pulling him to her like a large child. "Shut up," she hissed in the Human's ear, "if you don't want to be an entrée."

The chef, still holding its cleaver at Trillfin's eye level, stared at her. It'd never seen Nicovans join a fight or try to save any but one of their own. Even then, they would usually leave one victim behind to scuttle away themselves.

"He hired you for a guide? He's too stupid to eat." The chef kicked the Human's back. "Let him go. She's probably already unloaded him."

The others let go, their suckers leaving marks on his exposed skin. Trillfin helped him to stand. He was very light for his height. She propped him up as best as she could, her neck under his arm, and took him out the back. They stumbled along the alleyway until they reached the Main. Her food would be spoiled by now anyway. The effects of the ka'frindi were wearing off too.

"I...I don't know what to say," the Human stammered. He had lost all his bravado just about the time he had nearly lost a limb. He seemed to have some trouble breathing too.

"'Thank you' would be a good place to start." Trillfin led him to an overnight warren where he could rent a sleep pod for a few credz. She showed him how to pay for a pod, opening one up to show him the controls.

"I can't sleep in there. It's like a coffin!" He drew his head even closer to his shoulders, like a tortoise. He was very pale, shaking so much that he had to lean against the warren wall.

"What's a coffin?" Trillfin asked.

"You don't bury your dead?"

"I don't understand what you mean. The dead go in the reclaiming vats, if they aren't tossed down a shaft or made into chili." She pressed the controls to close the pod.

He went from pale to green. He slumped against the wall, panting a little, with his eyes closed.

"Are you sick? Who are you?" Trillfin kicked herself. What was she doing here with this offal without a clue? The ka'frindi must have been pretty close to next stage by the time she had eaten it. When would she learn not to pick up strays—an alien stray at that? They always started out cute, then turned into ka'frindi fodder.

He took a few deep breaths, still with his eyes closed. "I'm Jule Emyril, a chef from the Malpairiso sector."

"Trillfin Skorm, Rock Neek."

He opened his eyes. "You are the stewardess." He stared at her.

She stared back. "If you are going to survive your visit, you need a guide. Do you have any credz left, or did the Bansnicts get them all?"

He didn't reach into his pockets, but opened his tunic to feel under his arm. Maybe he wasn't as foolish as he seemed. "Listen, I am sorry about what I called you, and...everything. Thank you. I don't know why you saved me, but thank you."

"Core only knows." Trillfin shook her head at her own stupidity. "You need a place to sleep. You can't sleep out here, not if you expect to wake up."

"Isn't there some kind of hotel? I don't need the best, just..."

"Just the second best would cost me a year's wages. Why are you here? How did you expect to get by?"

"I am a chef, a very good one. I came here to get a job, and to learn how to use ka'frindi."

"Who's your contact?"

"Contact?"

Trillfin sighed again. "You can't just prance in here like you own the place. Nobody's going to hire you unless someone they know vouches for you, especially not to cook." She shook her head, looked him over again. "I wouldn't let you near my food."

"I didn't know." Jule's last tinge of bravado collapsed. "I sold everything I had to get here. On my planet, anybody can get a job in a restaurant, washing dishes or something. It's where you start."

"You're in the Rock now." Trillfin absently scratched her shoulder. In a few owerz, her skin would get really dry. She wanted to get in her tank soon. She ought to just leave this big baby out here for whoever got to him first, but she couldn't do that. He was...a baby. And he did know about things offworld.

"Look, if you can be polite to Neeks, my aunt runs a diner on LevThree. She might let you mop the floor until she decides if you are worthy to clean the grill. I can't promise, but it's the best I can do. I don't have many LevOne contacts. None of them would be interested in you."

"But what's in it for you?" Jule looked hopeful, if still the greenish color of ka'frindi after it turned into the fourth, inedible lifecycle.

"Now that sounds like a Rocker—you might survive here a day or two." Trillfin smiled. "You plan to go back to your world. Teach me what I need to know when I get there. Have you actually lived on the surface?"

"Of course, never in a dungeon liked this. "

She jerked her head towards the tube that led to a LevThree drop. "Walk with me. Tell me about your world." She slipped into her stewardess role like it was warm, salty water.

Jule glanced down the walk way. "It goes down."

"Yeah, it does. We can't afford to live up here, and who'd want to with all the offal...sorry." She lifted her lobe, indicating apology.

Jule sighed. "Okay." He stood, still a little wobbly, his head still pulled into his the neck of his tunic. He followed her all the way down to the drop, his eyes closed, his hand gripping her shoulder. She led him through the spiraling tubes to Aunt Silky's place. He nearly bumped his head on the door arch at the Chow Down. It was a Nicovan place, mostly family with few other species around.

Jule towered over the Neeks, although he was not unusually

tall by Human standards.

"Sit right here," Trillfin said. "Don't talk to anybody."

He hung his head, resting it in his pale hands. She pulled his hood over his head so that he didn't look quite so Human.

Trillfin went to the counter where Aunt Silky sat and spoke to her for a few minz. Aunt Silky clambered off her chair, trudging to the table where Jule sat, followed by Trillfin. An audience of Nicovans began to collect, apparently to see what Trillfin had dragged home this time. They left plenty of space between themselves and Aunt Silky in case they felt a sudden need to leave in a hurry.

Aunt Silky was round and fat, with wrinkled orange and white banded skin hanging from her lobe, from her chin, from any other place that could be seen outside the caftan she wore. Her eyes were orange as well, and sometimes appeared to be ready to fire lasers. She sagged into a seat beside Jule. Trillfin stood behind her.

"Look at me, Sape. I don't know you." Her voice was as deep as a male's, suspicious and threatening. The other Neeks drew back from her another half meter or so.

No Human was as frightening as Aunt Silky.

Jule looked up, not raising his head all the way, peering through his eyebrows at Aunt Silky. Trillfin gave him a tiny nod.

"Don't look like much." She glanced around at the audience. "But neither do they."

The audience took another step away from the door, as that was where Aunt Silky sat.

Aunt Silky turned her attention back to Jule. "She says you can cook. What do you know about Rock grubs? Swimmers? Toufood?"

Jule straightened up a little, keeping an eye on Trillfin. At least Aunt Silky asked him something he knew. "I can make about fifty different things with tofu. How is your toufood different from tofu?"

Aunt Silky turned to Trillfin. "He don't know boveen from Bansnict." To Jule she said, "How many credz you got on you?"

Trillfin risked shaking her head.

"N-n-none, M-Mastriz. The…uh…Bansnicts got it all when I got off the shuttle."

"You see it?" Aunt Silky asked Trillfin. Trillfin nodded. "You get anything from them, then?"

Trillfin reached inside her robe to take out the ID and two credz that were left from the Bansnict. She tried to think of it as an investment, and besides, she couldn't stand up to Aunt Silky even if she were dipped in ka'frindi, or even straz for that matter.

Aunt Silky inspected them. "I know this Ophid. She'd be considerable happy to get this back. Consider this a down payment."

Trillfin said nothing but lowered her lobe as far as it would go. Jule raised his chin as much as he could.

"You think you can learn to be polite?" Aunt Silky asked.

"Yes, Mastriz" Jule followed Trillfin's every move.

"Trillfin, where's he going to sleep. With you?"

Jule's eyes widened. "No, M-Mastriz, I—"

"I didn't ask if you were planning to mate with her," Aunt Silky said. "You got to have a place to sleep but it won't be in *my* kitchen."

Trillfin managed to "He can stay in my pod, until, until he can get his own place."

"All right. Take him out of here. You are responsible for anything stupid he does." Aunt Silky jerked her lobe towards the door.

"Thank you, Aunt Silky, Thank you very much." Trillfin both lowered her lobe and bowed low, her eyes keeping contact with Aunt Silky's. Jule stood up and tried to bow as well, gathering some snickers from the audience.

The audience opened a space for them to leave, but Trillfin heard some of their muttered comments. Someone was already making book on how many more owerz Jule would live.

"Come on," Trillfin said, "I'll come back later to get you something to eat."

Jule slouched behind Trillfin although the top of the tube was plenty tall for him to stand up straight. He had already taken on the "don't hurt me" posture so common to Nicovans. Trillfin was glad. Now she just had to fit him into her pod and find something for him to sleep in on the floor. He probably didn't leave any luggage on the ship, so he wouldn't have anything but what he carried. How did she get herself into these things? She reminded herself that he was from off world, and he knew things she needed to know. Tonight she would start learning.

Once in her pod, she showed him the wetpod and explained about the credz they cost

"Don't go out," Trillfin said. "The door is barred. You'll be safe in here. Mostly just my family outside, but you never know who might show up. Nobody will help you out there."

Jule prowled her minimal kitchen while she gathered some of her clothing to make a pallet for him. He touched everything in the kitchen, rolling it around in his fingers to smell it. She showed him how the cooker worked and had him pay for the extra water from his credz. By the time she had his pallet made, he had fixed toufood for them with a spicy sauce and a bit of slime weed.

"I would never have thought of putting these flavors together," she said.

"This..." He pointed to the slime weed. "...has a very interesting bitterness that blends well with the hot pepper. At least hot peppers seem to be known even in Port Nowhere."

"The hot stuff is ground fire-bug shells. What are peppers?"

Jule peered at his supper skeptically. He shrugged. His face didn't change color this time, although he was beginning to sweat a bit from the heat of the fire-bugs. "Works the same, so it doesn't matter."

"Tell me about your world. Do you live on the surface? Do you have a star? How do you manage all the radiation? Do you have to wear envirosuits all the time?"

Jule smiled. "Most people live on the outside of the planet. Port Nowhere is unusual. We do have a star, Vestia. We call it the Sun. Vestia III has an atmosphere, so the air blocks some of the radiation. We can walk around outside and breathe, play in the water and do all kinds of things. Nobody lives underground, although some of us live in tall buildings that aren't so different from this except that you can see out of them." He glanced around, involuntarily pulling his head back into his shoulders.

"Play in water? That sounds like fun. It must be very expensive, though." Trillfin scratched at her shoulder again. She was ready for bed.

"I lived near the ocean. In the summer, we'd drive down and walk in the surf and go swimming and sometimes just lie out in the sun. It was free. It's great."

"Ocean? Surf?"

"Half of Vestia III is covered by water. It's salty and lots of fish and other things live in it. That's the ocean. It's so big that the water laps up on the land in waves."

Trillfin's imagination had not ever tried to attempt envisioning that much water. After a few seconds, her mind boggled, she said, "Summer?"

"Part of the year is warm, where I live, and part is cold. Summer is warm, winter is cold."

"Why doesn't the government control the temperature? Seems very inconvenient."

"We live outside. We have weather, day and night, summer and winter, rain and fog, dawn and sunset." Jule began to sound wistful.

They finished their meal in silence.

"I'm going to sleep now," she said. "You can sleep on this pile of clothes until we can find you something better."

Jule watched as she stripped off her robe and opened the sleep tank.

"You can't sleep in there!" he cried. "You'll drown."

Trillfin laughed. "No, *you* would, but I won't. You don't have to sleep in a...whatever you called it. Now settle down. Get some sleep. Aunt Silky will work you hard tomorrow. Trust me."

Trillfin slipped into her tank, soaking in the herbal-treated water that had cost her a week's wages. She didn't have anything the Human would know to steal.

Now she had a whole new vision of what off-world what was like. If he didn't follow her advice, Aunt Silky or Bax Tuvalu would eliminate him. He would be worth the risk, if only for the food—the Human could cook. And even if *he* couldn't take her offworld, then soon she'd know enough to find someone who would.

~END~

ENDURANCE

Jim Johnson

The crackly snap of tearing cartilage. A searing heat that radiated from the cheekbones and into the eye sockets. The gushing warmth of a bloody nose.

Half of the arena's audience reeled in mutual agony as their linked combatant's nose broke; they reeled, not in sympathy, but because they literally felt what he felt.

In Kovindi fighting, every one of the spectators was bio-linked to one of the two combatants. Although the sensations were slightly muted, the spectators felt what the fighters felt.

Kovindi was almost always a fight to the death, for a fighter could not surrender unless his half of the audience threw in the drying cloth. But collective surrenders were seldom seen since, as a collective, the audience could endure more punishment than the combatant.

This meant fights usually resulted in one or the other of the combatant's death.

Clutching at their broken-feeling noses, Bharstus Bhogani's half of the audience groaned in pain and anger. Their anger fueled his waning reserves through the bio-link he shared with them. He rallied himself to their collective will and charged at his enemy.

A hulking Modajai with gray, scaly skin and a hard face composed of bony ridges, Bharstus had the physical fortitude of a mountain. He wiped the blood seeping from his nose, then balled his huge fists and charged the Vamir. The felinoid snarled and for the first time in the fight extended its claws. Bharstus didn't break stride; he crashed into the shaggy Vamir, pummeling his four-armed opponent with all of his considerable strength. The Vamir roared while its audience cringed. The Vamir tried to dig its claws into Bharstus's neck, only to find the tactic thwarted by the Modajai's protective scales.

As Bharstus pressed his punishing assault, driving the Vamir to its knees, he was already tallying the night's winnings in his head. This night's prize money would more than double his weekly salary as a bouncer at the Starview Lounge. His facial ridges contorted in a ruthless grin as he opponent crumpled at his feet. The cold grin only widened as the Vamir's audience fell silent.

The fight was over. Bharstus stood straight and calmly strode across the arena to the fighter's entrance in the sidewall.

"Not bad, Bhogani, not bad at all. You only got your face smashed in this time," snickered Toomio from the safety of his booth. A low rumble sounded from deep inside Bharstus's cavernous chest, but he said nothing to the Fwazek. Instead he stood motionless as the Toomio counted out the prize credz, slipped them into a packet and slid the packet through the booth's slot.

"You gonna be fightin' tomorrow night too?"

"I'm working tomorrow."

Toomio shook his flat head. "With fightin' skills like yours, you don't need no other job."

Bharstus took his credz, turned and left Toomio watching his back, as he made his way from the arena offices. Toomio's words went with him. Bharstus had considered quitting the Starview. Toomio was right in a way, but the Fwazek's view encompassed only half of the reality, and that was that few fighters, however adept, ever lived long enough to enjoy their accumulated winnings.

It was early when Bharstus reached the employee entrance underneath the Starview. He rode the lift up to the staff level just below the lounge's main floor and stepped out into the service corridor.

"Hey, Bhogani, looks like you been kissin' an oncoming flutterpod. So who tried to pretty up that ugly mug of yours?"

Bharstus turned to see Chazok; the Starview's senior bouncer. He snarled at Chazok; he had never liked the Rewtem—or any of his species, for that matter. The gelatinous aliens made his scales cringe. How could you fight with something that your fist passed right through, yet once it seized you, once it enveloped you—you could not break free? And even then, it wasn't as though the Rewtem relied on strength, since they had none to speak of. They didn't need it. You either complied, or it smothered you.

"At least I can tell my face from my ass, snot-ball."

Chazok quivered angrily. "Get cleaned up before your shift starts," he hissed and oozed off down the corridor.

Since it was situated on the galaxy-side of Port Nowhere, the Starview Lounge was everything the name implied. One had only to stare up through the establishment's transparent polybdalloy dome to behold the glittering sprawl of the Milky Way—a Human term, but Bharstus felt it an oddly fitting one.

Bharstus was assigned to the front door tonight. Keeping to the periphery, he strode methodically through the steady influx of arriving patrons. He reached the huge, double doors of the main entrance and slipped quietly into the shadowy alcove constructed to minimize the bouncer staff's presence.

And there he stayed, silent yet vigilant for the first hint of trouble. It was early though, few patrons would be inebriated enough to act up just yet. Bharstus allowed his gaze to roam deeper into the establishment, out across the as yet relatively deserted dance floors.

Then he noticed Chazok seeping his way toward the small flight of steps that rose up and over the edge of the main dance floor. The steps terminated in an open mezzanine, its primary purpose being to board and debark the floating table platforms of the Starview's high-class patrons…primarily the establishment's richest customer, Rudof Dyll.

Bharstus squinted as Dyll's platform drifted over to where Chazok waited atop the stairs.

"What is that slime ball up to now?" muttered Bharstus. "So what if I showed up to work bloody from a Kovindi fight. That's no one's business but my own."

Rudof Dyll and his bodyguard, a Vamir named Algensio, both appeared to be listening to whatever trash Chazok was talking. They both glanced toward Bharstus's alcove. Dyll stared for an instant before turning back to Chazok. He said something and the Rewtem oozed away. Apparently Dyll wasn't overly concerned with whatever Chazok had had to say, for the Human resumed eating even as the platform drifted into its slow orbit of the dance floor.

Algensio, however, kept his yellow, feline eyes fixed on Bharstus's shadowy alcove for several long minz.

Several owerz later, at shift change, Bharstus stormed the Starview's back halls looking for that slimy little snitch Chazok.

He found him near the back door of the kitchen, conversing with one of the Human chefs. The Human saw Bharstus first, and his eyes widened as he interpreted the Modajai's body language. He ducked back into the kitchen and closed the door behind him.

Chazok oozed around to face Bharstus. The Rewtem's miniscule eye nodes, incapable of expression, betrayed nothing. "Yes?" he said, calmly enough.

"What were you talking to Dyll about?"

"What business is my business of yours?"

"Chazok…"

"Well, if you must know, we were discussing Kovindi."

"I knew it. Now listen well. If you ever stick your…your…"

"Nose?"

"Kovindi is perfectly legal, but if you're trying to somehow put me on the outs with the boss's best customer, I swear I'll freeze-dry you and grind you into powder."

Chazok seemed to actually consider the threat, as though such a possibility had never occurred to him before. But when he spoke, his tone was entirely friendly. "Bharstus, you're just paranoid. We weren't discussing you. We were talking about your Kovindi opponent..."

"What on the Rock for?"

"...a Vamir, unless I'm mistaken?"

"Yeah, so? I've gone up against several of them before."

Chazok jiggled, a gesture that Bharstus knew was meant for a shrug. "Indeed. I've heard that Vamir can be formidable Kovindi fighters."

"And what business is that of Dyll?"

"None in particular. I was actually asking Algensio if he had ever considered entering the Kovindi."

Bharstus's facial ridges tightened up. He knew Chazok well enough to know that his conversation with Dyll and his bodyguard had not been that simple.

"Now, if you'll excuse, I'm late for my shift." Chazok slid away down the hall, jiggling steadily as he went.

Bharstus watched him go. He would have to kill that Rewtem one of these days. He turned and headed for the exit.

Tired as he was, he decided against going home where he could get a few owerz sleep. Instead, he headed back to the athletics dome and the Kovindi arena.

Toomio was still in his booth.

"Don't you ever leave that box?" Bharstus growled.

"Why should I? This is where the *real* action is." The Fwazek held up a pile of cred chips and let them rain back down into his cash drawer.

"How in the Rock can you spend any of those credz if you never go anywhere?"

Toomio's eyes narrowed appraisingly. "You didn't just come down here to question my frugalness, did you? You looking for a match up? I thought you were working tomorrow night."

"I changed my mind."

"About your job? Finally."

"No. About a fight for tomorrow."

Toomio shrugged. "Well, one of these days you'll decide to go for the big time. When you do, I'll bet my savings on you and maybe then, after you've made me filthy rich, I'll get out of this booth and enjoy my credz."

"Got any Rewtem on the roster?"

"What? Are you stupid?"

"Just kidding. Really, what have you got?"

Toomio rolled his beady eyes. "Bharstus, you know I can't tell you that." He nodded up toward the small monitor-eye that watched his every move. "It's not only against policy, it's unethical."

Bharstus arched a brow ridge.

"So, you want on for tomorrow night. Same time slot?"

"If it's open."

"It's always open for you, my Modajai friend."

The next evening arrived and Bharstus Bhogani readied himself for his bout. He sat in the arena locker room as the three Sloygat attendants assigned to him administered the localized injections of nanotech transceivers that formed the bio-link with half the fight's spectators.

"Done," said one of the four-foot tall, stick-like Sloygat. He shooed his two associates away. "Now for detailed calibration." He motioned Bharstus to the massage table even though Bharstus knew the drill as well as anyone.

"Up your face," ordered the Sloygat.

"Up yours too, twig," Bharstus said as he lay face up on the table.

The Sloygat was oblivious to the wisecrack. Its feet clicked on the hard flooring as it moved to the nearby control board. Bharstus closed his eyes and gave himself over to the ministrations of his assistant.

He heard the clicking of the 'Gat's slender fingers dancing over the keypad. And the massage began.

"I'm going to have to buy of these contraptions for myself," Bharstus mumbled as the invisible force field waves began to knead his hulking frame. Like all of the fighters, Bharstus found the massage to be a great way to loosen up before the match, but he knew that the real purpose of the procedure was to test the integrity of the nanotech transceivers.

The test usually took up to forty minz and, as was his habit, Bharstus used the time to catch up on his much needed sleep. In less than five minz he was out of it.

He was awakened by a distinctly non-Sloygat voice. Instead of a raspy croak that sounded like two sticks rubbing together, the strange voice was distinctly Human. Bharstus opened his yellow eyes and glanced toward the control board. The Sloygat and his two co-workers were gone.

Bharstus sat up and glared at the Human. "Do I know you?" he asked.

He was oddly familiar, at that. He was tall, for a Human, his hair was brown with a bit of white running through it. He had a penetrating, overly confident stare and Bharstus got the peculiar impression that the Human was not the least bit intimidated by him, and yet for all of that, Bharstus couldn't quite place the nondescript face.

The man smiled politely. "The name's Malik Blayne."

Malik Blayne? Bov-feek! The man was reputed to be single handedly responsible for keeping the Connies occupied...and stupefied.

For a fleeting instant it occurred to Bharstus that the reward for Blayne's arrest was larger than anything to be won in the Kovindi arena. But the thought quickly left him when Blayne spoke.

"If you think you can take me, go ahead and try. But just so you know," he drew a Dondaro Mark Five blaster from under his jacket. "I'll punch a hole through your chest big enough for me to escape through." Again, he smiled politely.

"I assume there's a reason for this *visit*?"

"I'd like you to pull out of the fight."

Bharstus barked a hard, sharp laugh. "Or what? You'll shoot me?"

Malik Blayne shrugged. "I'm no murderer and I didn't come here to kill anyone. In fact, let's just say I'm here to *save* a life."

Bharstus slid toward the edge of the massage table, but stopped as Blayne twitched the blaster at him.

"Ah, ah. Keep it parked right there. I said I wasn't a murderer. I never said I was above killing."

"And if I don't back out of the fight?"

Blayne shook his head and sighed. "Two of a kind," he muttered under his breath. Then to Bharstus, "I don't make it a habit of telling other beings what to do with their lives, even if I think they're about to make a mistake."

"Well, I know what I'm doing here tonight, and I'm damned good at it. If you don't like it, tell it to the Core." Defiantly, Bharstus stood up, keeping his distance even though he towered over the Human. "Now, if you'll excuse me, I'm due in the arena." He started toward the door, half expecting to be torn by a blaster bolt.

But Malik Blayne said nothing and did nothing as Bharstus left the locker room.

Outside the door, Bharstus paused. Why had Blayne let him go, especially after going to the trouble of approaching him in the first place? He wondered what his decision to ignore Blayne's offer might mean in the long term; or for that matter, the short. Was this one brief encounter a precursor to future involvement with Malik Blayne?

And if so, was that a good or a bad thing?

He turned back to the door but, as he reached to open it, the staging alarm sounded. Fight time. Well, if Blayne had been seriously concerned with saving someone's life, he should have been more *persuasive*. Bharstus was satisfied. He headed up for the staging area.

Bharstus reached the stairs leading up to the fighter's entrance. He could hear the roaring of the crowd; judging from the tone of their cries, the first fight must still be in progress. Halfway up the long flight of steps, a side door opened and Toomio emerged to join him.

"I don't believe it!" Bharstus exclaimed. "What are you doing out of your booth now, at the peak of the bet placing?"

The Fwazek shrugged its all but nonexistent shoulders. "I'm cashing in."

"What are you talking about?" asked Bharstus. He resumed his way up the stairs, with Toomio at his side.

61

"I've never seen the sort of action I saw taking place on your fight. I couldn't resist. If you win, I'll be a very rich Fwaz. Rich enough to return to Fwazeka and retire to the swamp."

Bharstus scowled. *First Malik Blayne shows up, and now Toomio goes bov-brained on him.*

Noting the scowl, Toomio looked up into Bharstus's eyes. "You are going to win, aren't you?"

Bharstus ignored the question and asked, "What's going on, Toomio? Do you know who just paid me a visit?" The Fwazek shook his flat head. "Malik Blayne."

Toomio's black, beady eyes nearly doubled in size.

"That's right," Bharstus nodded. "Now why would Malik Blayne take a personal interest in a Kovindi fight? Who am I going up against? And don't lie. I know you looked."

Toomio hesitated, and then, before Bharstus could react, the Fwazek dashed up the rest of the stairs with astonishing speed. "I've bet everything on you," he called back down. "So win, by the Beryl. Just win!" And with that the Fwazek was gone from sight.

Bharstus had the unsettling thought that Chazok had entered into the night's fights. *There was no way a Rewtem could be beaten bare-handed, the way Kovindi was fought.* But when he reached the top of the steps and entered the fighter's prep pod, it was not Chazok or any other Rewtem that greeted him on the other side of the partitioning force field.

"Algensio?"

"Bhogani," growled the Vamir.

One bizarre twist after another seemed to be the evening's rule of thumb. "What are you doing here?"

"I'm going to kill you."

The arrogant Vamir was welcome to try. "You make it sound personal, Algensio, but I've never wronged you, never had a problem with you. Am I missing something? Has Chazok put you up to this? If he has, even you know not to trust that slime ball."

The Vamir stared lasers at him through the energy barrier but said nothing more.

The second alarm trilled, declaring the end of the match.

Bharstus turned his attention to the arena floor. A hover-truck was already advancing on the lifeless body of a Talseen, its exoskeleton cracked in several spots, while the victor, a six-legged Coriliun, made its way to the fighter's entrance across the stadium.

When the arena was cleared, the third and final alarm rang out. Bharstus headed along the left curving passage while Algensio went right. They would emerge from opposite sides of the arena.

Bharstus came to a stop at the entrance to the arena floor. The shimmering force field was still in place. Across the way he could see Algensio staring back at him.

What had he done to anger Algensio? Try as he might, he could think of nothing. Whatever the Vamir's reason, it no longer mattered where Bharstus was concerned. Once the force fields were lowered, it was a fight to the death.

Algensio's.

"Pssst."

Bharstus turned to find Toomio peering at him from the other side of ventilation grate.

"Toomio! You knew about this, didn't you; about Algensio?"

"Yes. I wanted to fill you in, but he said he'd flatten the rest of my body to look like my head. You gotta believe me, Bhogani."

With a blur of speed, Bharstus tore the grating from the wall. Toomio squeaked like a rattu as Bharstus yanked him from the duct.

"I don't care about that, Toomio," he said as he dropped the Fwazek to the floor. "What I want to know is why Algensio is willing to get himself killed?"

"You know the Vamir you put down last night, what was his name, Ferinio? Well, come to find out, it was Algensio's clan-brother."

"Bov-feek!"

"No lie. But I swear, I didn't find out until Algensio shows up and gets himself on the roster. How Algensio found out is beyond me."

"Chazok."

"Who?"

"A Rewtem lowlife I work with at the Starview. Doesn't like me."

"He must not be too fond of Algensio either, since odds are you'll kill the poor Vamir. This Chazok character had to figure that much."

"Humph. The slime ball is craftier than I ever gave him credit for."

"How so?"

"Banastre Caravello owns the Starview, but Rudof Dyll has got to have money in it. That means, so long as Algensio and I are in the picture, old Chazok will never be the Mastre's number one."

Toomio nodded. "This Kovindi match eliminates half of his competition...and might keep the other half from working for a while."

Bharstus nodded just as the commencement alarm sounded and the force field deactivated.

"You'd better win," Toomio called after him.

"Don't I always?"

But as he stepped out onto the black, hard packed sand, unexpected, uncharacteristic second thoughts assailed Bharstus. Surely Algensio knew he would be out matched, since only a few Vamir had ever beaten a Modajai; and those few had cheated, using things like undetectable, sub-dermal bio-implants; poison-secretors, usually. Would Algensio stoop so low? Would he care if he were caught afterwards?

Not necessarily, Bharstus concluded, *and does that even matter after I'm dead?*

The force fields powered back up, sealing the fighters within the pit of the arena. Bharstus began the slow walk to the center, noting the tingling sensation as the nanotech transceivers began attuning to their counterparts injected into the spectators.

If Algensio were cheating, where would the implants be, in the hands, the claws perhaps, or his fangs, or somewhere else all together?

Any of the possibilities would be all but impossible to avoid.

He reached the final force field partitioning the center of the arena. Bharstus and Algensio squared off. They stood nearly eye-to-eye.

<^>

The force field crackled between them as the spectators on both side of the arena began to chant for their fighter. Bharstus could feel the influx of power coming through the bio-link, the crowd's enthusiastic bloodlust translating into a hyped up rush of energy.

Algensio would be feeling the same.

Bharstus kept his focus locked on the slitted pupils of the Vamir's eyes, but he was more than aware that Algensio had already extended his claws.

A near deafening alarm sounded and the force field vanished.

The combatants charged one another. The crowd roared its approval as Modajai and Vamir collided. Algensio lunged forward, all four of his arms slashing wildly as he raked his claws down. Bharstus tucked his scale-protected shoulder forward. He drove straight into the Vamir's shaggy chest.

His intention was to knock Algensio back and to the ground but, to his surprise, the Vamir had simply latched on by wedging its claws up under Bharstus's dorsal scales.

Pain stabbed though Bharstus's back as Algensio tried to pry the scales out by the roots. The Modajai bellowed in agony as his spectators did the same.

Bharstus altered his plan. He reached up and seized Algensio's topknot and tore the Vamir loose by the length of golden hair. A gasp escaped Algensio's crowd while Bharstus's contingent went wild as he leaped onto the downed Vamir.

It was clear that Algensio was not the average fighter. The Vamir was Rudof Dyll's personal bodyguard, and Bharstus should have expected nothing but the best. It was time, he decided, to end this fight quickly, even if that meant messily.

He began to pummel the Vamir, telling himself that this was Algensio's own decision, that this was strictly business, strictly Kovindi—when all of a sudden he found himself launched through the air. Algensio, lying on his back, had used his legs to catapult Bharstus away from him.

Bharstus hit the gritty black sand, plowing a furrow into it with his face. Had he looked up, he would have seen the whole of his spectators clutching at their own bloodied faces; an extremely rare reaction to the bio-link.

Bharstus was aware of the blood seeping from his nose and mouth, yet he hardly noticed the pain. Strange, he thought. Bout before he could consider the matter further, Algensio was upon him again.

This time the Vamir's overconfidence would cost him.

Algensio locked his lower set of arms around Bharstus's back, pinning his arms to his side, while using his upper arms to attack his head.

Bharstus slammed his scaled-head backwards, squarely into the Vamir's face. Algensio yowled in pain, letting go of Bharstus and staggering back, stunned.

Bharstus swung about to face Algensio, but his attention was drawn to the stands by the wailing of the spectators. They were on their feet, staggering and stumbling dazedly about, clutching at their faces. Their reactions were far too intense. Conversely, at the sound of Algensio's snarling hiss, Bharstus knew that the Vamir's pain-reaction had been mush less that it should have been.

Just as his own had been when Algensio had turned his face into a plow.

Algensio pressed the attack. Bharstus lunged to meet him. He would run the Vamir over through sheer brute force.

At the last second, though, Algensio veered to one side.

Surprised by the unanticipated maneuver, Bharstus barreled ahead, several paces past the Vamir. By the time he checked himself and turned back, Algensio was already at his side.

Algensio swept upward with all four hands, raking at Bharstus's chest scales. The claws caught, and in the blink of an eye, two of the hand-sized scales were torn away.

For a brief instant, an excruciating blaze seared through Bharstus's body; pain the likes of which he had never before experienced. But then, just as suddenly, the pain mysteriously subsided, becoming a dull aching.

This time, even Algensio seemed to notice the inverted reactions, for he had relented in his attack and was looking up to where Bharstus's watchers were writhing in their seats, clutching at their chests.

"Something isn't right, Algensio. The people shouldn't be reacting like that."

The Vamir looked at him. "They aren't my concern, Bhogani. What matters to me is that you die for killing my brother."

Algensio renewed his attack.

Seasoned Kovindi fighter that he was, Bharstus went for a leg. He dove at the Vamir's left knee, heard it give way as bone and ligament were ripped apart. Bharstus stood and stepped back. He could hear the tormented cries of the Vamir's crowd. Looking their way, he saw what he now expected to see. Every last one of them was either lying flat or hobbling around on legs that felt broken.

He looked back to Algensio. The Vamir appeared to be in little if any pain, but the broken knee refused to work. He was effectively incapacitated.

"It's over, Algensio. I'm sorry about your brother. But this is Kovindi and he knew it, just as you're about to learn," Bharstus said.

He began to move in for the kill.

Just as he came to within arm's reach of the Vamir, the air between them glittered to life as the force field energized. The familiar tingling of the injected nanites died away as the bio-link was terminated.

In an overwhelming rush, the muted pain of the accumulated injuries hit Bharstus like an asteroid. He was unconscious.

"Well, it would have been much easier had you just backed out, but it all worked out and no one got killed." The voice in the darkness of Bharstus's awareness was a Human's voice; Malik Blayne's voice.

Bharstus forced his eyes open, feeling the weight of sedation upon them. "You. How did you do it?" he asked groggily.

"What? The bio-link?" Blayne grinned. "Let's just say that inverting the sensory feed isn't exactly quantum mechanics, but it's my secret."

The drugs were claiming him again, but Bharstus managed another question. "Who…who were you trying to save. Me or Algensio?"

Again with the grin. "Why, both of you, of course."

"I don't…understand."

"Someone had to intervene and, well, Malik Blayne seemed like the maaannn forrr daaa chobbbb…."

The words made no sense to Bharstus as they slurred though his sluggish mind, and then he was out of it again.

Bharstus opened his eyes again and found himself staring at a brown stick. The stick stared at him with its five eyestalks. A Sloygat. Was it the same one that had prepped him for the fight? He couldn't tell.

"What an excellent fight, no? Quite a good one. It was the first time I've seen two winners."

Another Sloygat appeared, leaning over Bharstus, and spoke to the first. "Or two losers maybe, hr hr."

"Hr hr," agreed the first.

Bharstus reached up and, gently for a Modajai, brushed his attendants aside. They chittered at him indignantly as he propped himself up on his elbows. He winced as his chest scales dug into the sensitive skin of the vacancies created by Algensio's claws.

"What's he doing here?" grated someone.

Bharstus glanced to his right and found the Vamir in another pod. Great, he thought. The Vamir was going to carry his grudge outside the arena.

Just then, the room's double doors swung open and in strolled Rudof Dyll and…Chazok.

Forget Algensio. Bharstus wanted a piece of that slimy troublemaker. Mastre Dyll apparently read Bharstus's mind for he waved the Rewtem to a stop just inside the door and then made his way to Bharstus's bed, his plethora of earrings jingling as he did so.

"Ah, Bharstus," said Dyll. "I can see in your eyes that you know the instigator...of tonight's event."

"For someone without one, Chazok sure has one big mouth. I suppose you know then why Algensio wanted to fight me?"

"Ferinio wasn't a child," Dyll said. "And there was no way for you to know your opponent's identity. It was a tragic, to be sure. But I think that with time, Algensio will understand that his clan-brother could have met the same fate at another's hands just as easily. Just as I'm sure that you understand what lies in store for you if you continue to pursue this barbaric pastime."

Bharstus's facial ridges grew taut. "With all due respect, Mastre Dyll, I'm young, I'm strong, and the credz are too good to pass up."

"Well, if it's a question of credz, how big a raise would satisfy you?"

"Mastre?"

"Well, why do you think I sent my friend Malik Blayne down here to stop you two feekheads from fighting?" Before Bharstus could answer, Dyll did so for him. "Because I value the pair of you. Algensio is my trusted friend and bodyguard and you, Bharstus, are the best bouncer the Starview has ever had. I'm sure my old friend Caravello will, shall we say, see reason?"

Bharstus cocked his head. He had never known Dyll's opinion of him. "But what about Chazok? He's the Starview's head bouncer."

A painted red smile blossomed across the Human's pale face. "He *was*, dear fellow. Where do you think your raise is coming from?"

~END~

(IR(LE OF THE BERYL

Charlotte Babb

Crila Maragorn sat in the healers' outer pod, bracing herself against the agony in her left arm. The cut wasn't that bad, no more than a lucky scrape from a Depth dweller's blade that had connected before its owner died.

But it burned like the Core itself, worse than any infection she'd ever seen, burning the flesh black and moving up her arm almost as she watched. The Service Medics just shook their heads and suggested she get her affairs in order. But Crila didn't give up that easily. She'd nosed around every contact she had, from Malik to the old Neek who ran the Chow Down on LevThree. They all said the Ophidia were her only hope.

At least the place was clean, not the smoky, reeking, vaudoo lair she'd expected. She could hear the somasar dripping out its hypnotic music somewhere behind the exam pod.

Nobody would talk to her about how the Snake healers worked, but they all said she couldn't last without their treatment. Finally a green-scaled hand beckoned her to enter the exam pod. Crila steadied herself on her feet before she rose. Even to a healer she would not betray weakness.

The Ophid gestured towards a chair. She said nothing. The humanoid part of her body was only about five feet tall, but her reptile tail was coiled underneath her, eight or more feet of green-scaled muscle and bone. Crila had heard that the Ophidia trained as warriors or bodyguards could launch a venomous strike from twelve feet away. She didn't want to know if healers had the same ability.

Crila sat down and the chair adjusted to her body weight and length. Crila did not release her arm. The Ophid passed her hands over Crila, reading her aura. She took the arm gently and laid it on the arm rest. Though the Ophid's movements were gentle and slow, Crila nearly cried aloud with the pain. It had gotten worse in the minz she had sat, waiting.

"It must come off," hissed the Ophid, her forked tongue flickering briefly over Crila's arm. "But you can survive if you accept treatment."

"Cut off my arm? No." Crila tried to sit up, but found that her center of gravity had moved. The healer held her in place with one finger on her chest.

"Then you die, perhaps a strechiz, perhaps less. When the poison reaches your heart, you will break your ribs in convulsive pain." The Ophid's face was impassive, her eyes dark green with a vertical slit that narrowed as she inspected Crila's arm again. She held Crila's wrist and flicked her tongue again, several times.

The pain phased out, but her hand went limp. Crila did not dispute the Ophid. While they were not trusted implicitly, not one had ever been known to lie. Would Crila give her left arm to live?

Yes.

"How much do I lose? All of it?"

"With immediate surgery, you can save the section above the elbow. In five owerz, we will have to take the shoulder as well. This has been neglected far too long as it is." The Ophid settled back on her tail. "What do you offer in payment?"

"I have credz, of course. How much?" Crila had squirreled away credz that even Malik didn't know about. Cold, hard credz were a girl's best buddy.

"What sort of prosthesis will you require?"

"I would like a hand that works. What, you can't regrow one?"

"This poison makes regeneration impossible. For a mere five megacredz you can have a stump. This guarantees that you will not die from the poison and that you will be immune to it.

In your line of work, however, I would think that a stump would not be an asset."

"How do you know my line of work?"

I know that you are Crila Maragorn, that you work at Dhamu's as a bartender, and that you are affiliated with Malik Blayne, which is how you found your way to me. I have my contacts as well." The Ophid smiled. Her fangs were recessed, but she had enough other teeth to make the smile more threatening than friendly.

Whatever the Ophid had done to make the pain go away was wearing off. Crila was not one to put off making a decision in any case. "Tell me what my options are. I would like to be as versatile as possible."

"I will prepare for the surgery while you discuss your options with my associate." The Ophid undulated out of the exam pod.

Crila tried again to get out of the chair, but found that it would not release her. She also felt a bit groggy, probably from the pain, which began to reach above her elbow like lava in her veins. If time was of the essence, she wished the associate would get its tail back in the pod, now.

An L'Talton waddled in with its feathers ruffled around its tool apron. With its crest a bright shade of orange over its yellow body, it was probably male, but Crila didn't ask. Behind it was a cart of body parts, some humanoid, some mechanical and some that looked like a tinker's wet dream: shiny metals, bright polybdalloy, and some merely skin, scales or fur.

It took a look at Crila's arm and trilled a long whistle. "Bad shape. Cut soon?" Its voice whistled out of its throat like some bad analog recording. This L'Talton had no bedside manner. Most spoke Basica pretty well, and their birdsong language was very complex. They were usually chatty as well, but not this one.

It held out a metal arm, smooth and shiny, like a jewelry display. The arm was about the right size but Crila shook her head. "I need one that will work, not some useless piece of jewelry."

The L'Talton raised its crest and fluffed out its feathers, insulted. "All complete articulate!"

"Will it stand up to bitch-slapping a Vamir?"

The L'Talton's eyes narrowed as it jerked the arm away. "No say want weapon!" It selected another arm, one that would have fit a good size Modajai, with a rocky skin texture to match. It handed the arm to Crila, who almost dropped it. It snatched the arm back, cradling it a bit before returning it to the cart. "No stock. Must build special. Cost more."

"How much is the silver one?"

The L'Talton cocked its head and stared off beyond Crila, possibly listening to some kind of communicator, or maybe just counting on its three-toed, clawed feet.

"You not have credz." It turned to go.

"What do you know about what I have?" Crila struggled to get up again, fighting the chair and the shooting pain in her arm to sit up. She wasn't taking this stuff lying down. "I can get whatever I want."

The L'Talton trilled again, obviously laughing. "Heart comes. She tell." It left, still trilling.

Crila fought a surge of panic. Malik could probably get her anything she wanted, but would he, and did she trust him enough to be in that much debt to him? She'd seen him shaft one of his lackeys who didn't come through on an assignment. Was she valuable enough to him to depend on his getting his investment back?

She didn't like the answers. She hadn't got where she was by depending on anyone else; using them maybe, but Malik was too dangerous to use. She wondered if he had lied to her about the Ophidia, and if he was setting her up or just getting rid of her. Her arm burned now, the pain spreading through her chest and into her head. If this kept up much longer, she would cut her own throat and save Malik and the snake woman the trouble.

The Ophid-came back in with the L'Talton, who pulled a cart full of gadgets, some of which looked like surgery tools and some like a weapons bazaar. Crila again fought the waves of pain to sit up, facing the Ophid at eye level. "If I don't have the credz, why did you come back?"

"To offer you an exchange. You have access to information and contacts that we would like to attain."

"You want me to be your spy? In exchange for my life?"

Crila thought Malik was cold, but then, these were reptiles, heat seekers, not able to generate their own. They were much more noticeable than most species, and more feared. She could be invisible, but an Ophid, never. Her head felt as if polybdalloy rods were being driven through her skull.

"How do you think you will be able to trust me, since you have me in a tight spot?"

"We will be able to trust you, and you will be able to trust us as well." The Ophid reached for Crila's arm. Crila didn't resist. The Ophid lifted Crila's hand to her mouth and with one fang, injected a drop of venom.

Numbness spread along Crila's veins. She relaxed into it, lying back in the chair, preferring death to the searing of the infection. If they wanted her to spy, they wouldn't kill her, and if they enslaved her, she would kill herself. It was a relief, either way. She lay back, waiting for unconsciousness to hit.

The Ophid inspected and cleaned her arm, although Crila could not feel anything. She watched languidly as the Ophid strapped her arm to the chair, and the L'Talton organized the tools on the cart.

In a few minz, the pain was completely gone, but Crila was alert and suspicious again. "What are you going to do?"

"I am preparing to amputate your arm. If you agree to our proposal, now that your pain has subsided sufficiently to allow you to make decisions, then we will fit you with such prosthesis as my associate can show you. The base will be attached to your arm and the nerve connections made during the surgery. You will be awake so that you can learn to manage the prosthesis. If you do not agree, I will merely amputate and you will pay me five megacredz. What is your choice?"

Some of the stuff on the cart looked very interesting. Crila figured that she was pumped full of straz, cut with something to make her feel sober. Still, she didn't want to die even if she had to lose a hand. "Make your pitch."

"We are priestesses of the Circle of the Beryl. We offer you the chance to join us. With what we can teach you, you will be very valuable to us, and we can offer you information to make you very valuable to your employers, whomever you may choose."

Crila knew there was some kind of witch religion among the Ophidia, but she didn't know they took anyone else in. "What's the catch?"

"The initiation is dangerous and requires rigorous training, both mental and physical. Our Circle is not a cult of superstitious stooges. Some initiates do not survive, even among the Sisters."

"And how do you know I'll be on your side?" Crila didn't feel high, and she had taken a hit of straz once before, not by choice. "What if I don't come to the training sessions?"

"We will know. We will remove your prosthesis if you don't appear. Without anesthetic." The Ophid's voice quality did not change. It was matter of face.

The L'Talton nodded, silently.

Crila weighed her options. She didn't want to get by using a stump, and it would certainly be useful to get into their organization. It was a simple choice. "I'm game. Do it."

"I ask again. Do you accept the call to initiation to the Circle of the Beryl in exchange for healing and the integration of the prosthesis and various attachments to be negotiated after surgery?"

"I formally agree, swearing by the blood of my mothers, E!lath'wyn daughter of Vrilakinya daughter of Ree!ayai'inka, that I shall enter the initiation of the Circle of the Beryl in exchange for healing and integration of a prosthesis and attachments to be further negotiated, which will enhance my abilities as a Priestess, when I complete the ritual in service to the Beryl."

At that phrase, the Ophid and the L'Talton exchanged glances.

"I have my sources too," Crila said. "Get on with it."

The L'Talton strapped her shoulders down and her thighs, and put a strap around her forehead. "Fear break chair hold. Strap stay. You safe."

The Ophid floated her hands over Crila's body again, sending a tingling energy that made Crila both very aware and unable to move. She felt the slightest tingle in her mind, learning that the Ophid's name was Heart of the Core, Heart for short, and the L'Talton was called JayRand.

Telepathy was how they communicated!

"Yes," Heart said. She picked up Crila's limp, numb arm and applied a tourniquet. "I am going to bite you again. Do not get upset. You may want not to look. This will be injected into your arm, which will coagulate your blood until I can remove the diseased part. Then we will attach the prosthesis and grow it to your nervous system."

"Do it," Crila said. She decided to watch. They would have killed her by now if that was what they wanted. The Halsan side of her mind was much calmer than the Human part, but she was used to putting it aside until she had time to process its emotions.

JayRand handed Heart a vial of powder, which she sniffed. Immediately she bit into Crila's wrist with both fangs dripping. Even with the drugs and the mind-touch hypnosis, Crila responded. She fought the panic, forced herself to breathe and stared hard at the procedure.

In a moment, Heart had removed her arm with something that looked like a tubing cutter, leaving a clean stump and not a drop of blood. JayRand held the prosthesis up to the stump, adjusting it for fit. When she was satisfied, she gave it to Heart.

JayRand opened a vial of gray powder and poured it on the end of the prosthesis. Heart clamped the metal arm to Crila's stump and removed the tourniquet. She held her hands around the wound and began a whispering chant. JayRand punched a handheld control, aiming it at the prosthesis. Again through the drug, Crila could feel the itch of bio-link nanobots flowing in her upper arm.

"Move your first finger," Heart said. "Don't look! Move your finger."

Although Crila could see the purplish, severed stump of her arm lying dead in the cart, she thought of moving her finger and felt it move, a phantom of the real thing.

"Now the second. Now the third. And the fourth. Stick out your thumb."

At each command, Crila felt her hand coming more to life, tingling as if it was regaining blood circulation.

"Make a fist. Squeeze hard."

"Now spread your hand as wide as you can."

That hurt, but Crila did as she was told. She rolled her wrist and twisted her forearm, all as she saw the metal cylinder lying inert in the arm of the chair.

She looked away from the prosthesis and studied the healers. Heart seemed to be deep in trance, and JayRand focused on the controller. She had not felt the mind touch again, but sensed that they were doing something they did not usually do, that they were spending much mental and physical energy on the surgery. She began to wonder if her original injury had been an accident at all. Why would she be so important? And if she were, why would they allow her into their society? What did they need her for?

The Ophid opened her eyes and stared at Crila. Crila stared back, pulling her Human emotion to the surface to help her focus, bringing up a red rush of anger. The Ophid smiled, and the pain of the surgery hit Crila all in one flash. She strained against the chair and gritted her teeth to keep from screaming. Her prosthesis lifted off the chair arm, as it was not strapped down.

"It works. You have done well," Heart said. "Now if you will allow me to enter your mind again, I will control the pain and help you to sleep while the nanobots complete the nerve connections."

Crila nodded, not trusting herself to open her mouth to speak without screaming.

Again Heart stared into Crila's eyes, moving her hands a few inches above her body. The pain subsided, slowly, like water evaporating from her body after a mist shower. Crila breathed deeply, making her body relax from its arching tension. She remembered her childhood training and worked through each phase, allowing Heart to see her thoughts, at least on the surface. She released the pain as she released her tension.

Finally, Crila sagged back into the chair. JayRand fashioned a sling for her new arm, which appeared to be a polybdalloy cast.

"Not use this cykul," he said. "Come next. More train."

77

"Drink plenty of fluids, no stimulants," Heart said. "Eat protein, plain toufood or even meat if you can. Come here tomorrow and we will discuss attachments and how to use them."

"And the initiation training?"

"We will escort you." Heart nodded to JayRand who released Crila. Heart assisted Crila in getting out of the chair. She slithered along beside Crila as she wobbled out of the exam pod. "You may tell Malik Blaine any of what we have told you, not that he will believe you. When there is need for secrecy, you will know."

"Be careful." JayRand said. Her trilling sounded more like Human speech.

"You did well," Heart said. "You will make an excellent Priestess."

Crila made a shallow bow. "Thank you for saving my life. When the time comes, I will return the favor if I can."

Heart returned the bow. "I understand your sense of honor. It is what saved you."

They had reached the Spiral Three Tube. Heart returned to the healer pod, and Crila made her way to the Chow Down at the top of the Spiral. If she had to eat toufood, she was going to get the best. And Aunt Silky would likely know what kind of fluid would be less than stimulating but better than water.

Then it would be time to find Malik and threaten to kill him.

Dhamu's place on LevSix was full of customers. The entertainment, a percussion-playing Vamir doing tag-team poetry with an Ophid dancer, made just enough noise to make eavesdropping impossible. Crila balanced a tray on her prosthesis to take it out to Malik. She had a piece of her mind to give him along with his order.

She was still getting used to the extra weight of the prosthesis, especially the more mechanical ones. She'd asked Heart of the Core how to increase the strength of the bones that moved it, but Heart only said that the strength would come. JayRand was no help at all, taking her question as an insult to his technical prowess.

Managing her emerging telepathy was difficult as well. She couldn't actually hear the bits of conversation, but she could feel the emotions and catch snippets of thoughts. When the thoughts and the spoken words didn't match, she had to sort through and pretend that she only heard the words. Although he didn't know it, Malik was going to give her some extra practice.

She set her tray on the table and handed him his mug of toubrew. Then she laid her prosthesis on his hand and leaned over just a little to whisper in his ear. She could feel the response of the more humanoid of the customers behind her as her costume revealed more of her legs from behind. Malik resisted the urge to look down her blouse, but she felt the urge just the same. She could not hear his thoughts, but it was possible that he was not thinking at that moment.

She extended a blade from the back of her natural-looking hand. It pointed at Malik's chest where she had more than once laid her head to hear his heart beat. That got a response from him.

"Are you playing, Crila?" Malik's expression didn't change, but his emotional response drew back and looked for an escape route. "Someone could get hurt."

"Someone already has," Crila said, her lips close to his ear. "Me... Did you set me up?"

Malik's turned on the charisma, which wrapped around his mind like an impenetrable wall. Crila could sense nothing of what he was thinking or feeling. He had learned a lot by being Rudof Dyll. He had all Dyll's resources and his own to work with, and he used them, like he was using his physical charm now to envelop Crila's anger.

"I wouldn't do that to you, Crila," Malik said finally, seconds later than an honest answer would have taken.

Just then the music stopped, leaving a note of silence before the general rumble of the crowd returned.

That was a good enough answer for her—lying or not, he had something to hide, and he was able to hide it from her. She smiled, retracting the blade and sending out her own 'come down and see me' vibe. "I just had to know for sure. Drink your 'brew. I'll pay for it."

"No, I can't let you do that."

"It's not up to you to let me do anything, Mal." Crila smiled sweetly, the kind of smile that had razor edges coated with lemon juice, so anyone would feel the slightest edge of it.

Mal noticed, leaning back further from the smile than he had from the blade at his heart. "I didn't mean for you to get hurt."

"Then that makes it all right, doesn't it?"

Crila picked up her tray and turned on one heel to return to the bar. She nearly stepped on the tail of the Ophid dancer who had left the stage for a break. Her arm brushed the Ophid arm, and with the touch Crila caught a burst of thought, emotion and a message so loud that Crila thought it must have been shouted.

Follow me, the Ophid had thought. Her name was Needs No Veil, and she was headed for the wetpod. Crila followed her, her mind still ringing from the message. She dropped off the tray to be ready to use all her tools if necessary. She didn't notice anything else from the folk around her.

The wetpod lounge area was clean, especially so for a place like Dhamu's. He had a couple of Nicovan females who kept it that way. Both of them left when the Ophid came in, not waiting to mark their respect to her or to Crila. The Vamir drummer was already in the lounge. She and the Ophid were a pair, both black and sleek. The Vamir had tiny white hairs through her pelt and a white mark on her chest. Her topknot was very short, but it had a white streak that started from the fur on her face and ran up through the topknot by one ear. The Ophid was entirely black except for her black-slitted topaz eyes, but she wore a white silky veil that covered most of the humanoid part of her body. When she danced with it in the muted light, she almost disappeared under the veil, which would seem to move by itself to the Vamir's drumming.

Needs No Veil reached out to touch Crila's arm again, but Crila drew back. "I can hear you," she said. "No need to beat me over the head."

Then act like it! THINK! The Ophid's expression was neutral, neither friendly nor menacing, at least on the outside, but her emotional state was visibly agitated and orange. *I know your training is not complete, but I have been trying to contact you for ten minz. Your thoughts are like shouting when you speak.*

"Throob?" said the Vamir.

The Ophid nodded. The Vamir placed herself between the door and Crila. Crila stepped back to put the wall at her back. She wasn't sure she could handle an attack from both sides at once.

Calm yourself, Sister. Needs No Veil smiled, careful to conceal her teeth. Her expression was not reassuring, but the emotional impact was calmer, fading from an orange aura to greenish blue.

Crila did the exercise Heart of the Core had taught her to connect with the energy of the Core of the Rock. She could feel the presence of the Vamir, but no thoughts.

What do you want with me?

You were talking to Malik Blayne, threatening him. We do not want him killed.

I wasn't planning to kill him, but I needed to know if I could trust him. Crila gestured with her prosthesis, bringing out the blade. *Now I know.*

Now you know nothing. The Sisterhood wanted you to join us, if possible. Your Halsan blood and training makes you more capable of the mission we want you to do.

Crila noticed that the Ophid's eyes had dilated so much that they reflected green light from the pod. The sound of the thought had changed as well—she wasn't listening to Needs No Veil any more.

Yes, Child! The thought-voice laughed. *No Veil is just the medium this time. You will understand more as you continue your training.*

And the mission then, my Queen?

Protect Malik Blayne.

~**END**~

81

NEVER ERR WITH ONE'S AIR

Richard C. Meehan, Jr.

As an envirosuit salesman, Charlie Manus knew he was the best without having to be told. It was an excellent profession for the times, since most life forms preferred survival in good health versus a gruesome death from atmospheric pollutants. Only a close, feathery, social group known as the L'Talton Assemblage—of all the species on fifty inhabited worlds, planetary constructs, asteroids, and space stations—felt they should not deal with Charlie. For some reason, the birdbrains decided to pay an unholy price to a competitor rather than to him. Perhaps he could change their minds this trip. There had to be an angle he could exploit to loosen their purses. There always was.

As the commuter shuttle swung into low orbit of that hunk-of-rock-in-empty-void known as Port Nowhere, Charlie forced himself to remember that, for the next few days at least, he would be treated like a god. Despite his royal status though, he hated this particular armpit of the galaxy. After all, Port Nowhere, locally referred to as The Rock, didn't get its name from a cereal box. Unfortunately, his employer, Protectaire, Inc., required him to make this semiannual visit to oblivion.

Ah well, at least his first sales call would be the proprietor of his favorite watering hole, not that the simian Modajai was anyone to befriend. The food and drink at Dhamu's Place on LevSix were simply great, even if the locale was more than a little precarious for an offworlder. Just because Charlie's omnipass granted him access to all domes and levels—except the few private domes—he wasn't looking for trouble. It's just that Dhamu's Place was about the only reasonable dive this chunk of gray feek had going for it.

A few owerz later, Charlie found himself in front of that scaled, fish-smelling bulk. Dhamu filled the aisle behind his bar like an oversized wine cork. Despite a few broken teeth and the looks of a cavewoman's nightmare, the Modajai fairly oozed conceit. Charlie had always found that odd, especially considering where the guy lived.

"You're talking like bov-brain, Manus," rumbled Dhamu. "Nobody gets skin cancer no more! Besides, I got scales!" He slapped a grimy rag on the bar for emphasis. "You're just wanting to jack the price. My old suit's got plenty of life yet!"

Charlie eyed him with a "sure it has," thinking that at least the big dope needed a big suit too. With a cajoling timbre, he said, "Dhamu...ah, Dhamu. Surely you are aware of the statutes handed down by the Boss Families? *No one goes outside the domes without protective gear—*"

"*—'cause your life's worth credz to us,*" completed the Modajai grimly. "You're still just tryin' to rip me off."

"Look," Charlie said with exasperation, "your suit counter is already at nineteen seventy-nine owerz and I won't be back this way for another two months." And hopefully never, he added silently. "Dhamu, you have to change it out at two thousand anyway. That's also the rule. Are you planning to buy it from somebody else?"

Dhamu's scales flushed a dusky yellow. He fidgeted with the wet bar towel and let his bloodshot eyes rove his establishment absently. In a burst of fetid breath, he confessed, "I bought my last five suits from you, Manus. I...er...just want change. Nykee came out with whole new sports line."

There it was. A competitor had finally broken into the Rock. Charlie scrambled to pull out the big boys, "You know, Dhamu? You're absolutely right! It is time for you to make a change. You need to get rid of the good 'ole tried and true. What's the use of reliable protection when what you really want is something different? Who needs the comfort of guaranteed defense against the harmful rays of a sun, beryllion dust from the very rock of the Rock, or even a proper air mix? It'll be years before the first signs of cancer shows—maybe on the nose or the forearm. Perhaps a blemish on a lung? Besides, the Boss Families will love to provide medical treatment for you, I'm sure. Your hard-earned credz of a lifetime will go to them!"

Charlie Manus took a deep breath for concerned effect, continued, "But, Dhamu, the worst of it is that the damage is done. The cancer will eat at you like ka'frindi fungus on feek!" Now, give him the Piercing Eye close, thought Charlie. "Dhamu, you're my customer, and my customers are my friends. If you got cancer, Beryl forbid, I'd feel responsible because I would know in my heart that I hadn't done my best to keep you protected, that I had let you go to a competitor offering an inferior 'virosuit. I'd never forgive myself." Charlie stopped talking. Now was the time to shut up, the crux. The first to speak would be the loser.

The overstuffed Modajai squirmed under Charlie Manus's sincere gaze. Doubt flashed in his amber eyes. After a few more bleeding seconds, he groused, "Okay...okay! Send me the same old 'virosuit, Bhagnor-dammit! But just for the record—*friend*—Modajais don't get skin cancer 'cause we got scales!"

Charlie smiled genuinely while pumping Dhamu's thick hand. "Thank you very much. I appreciate your continued business. One last thing though—how about some spare carbon filters? You know how fast you burn through them, Dhamu...."

~**€ND**~

RECYCLING THE DEAD

Diane Thompson

The blade slid easily from the flesh. It was trickier to grasp when his patients flailed about, but the flailing had stopped. Kutof was dead. Too bad; he was only a child.

Dr. Dahn VanSlyke had witnessed more deaths since his arrival at the Rock than in his twenty sintinz in medicine. He had arrived two strechiz ago. No amount of preparation could ready you for Port Nowhere. However, it was the perfect place to test Insta-Limb. It had taken twenty-five sintinz to perfect, five to find a suitable testing facility, and two to find the funds to get to the Rock. Dahn's father's research and development of the medical wonder would become reality here, three sintinz after his death. Once considered an *ogre* by his colleagues, this place so far had been a humbling experience.

VanSlyke arrived with his team and worked twelve cyks to set up his laboratory on LevThree. In time, more space would be needed. For now, a simple laboratory with the basic necessities would suffice. His fellow teammates were more than ready to exit Port Nowhere when their work was completed. No one felt the doctor's passion for Insta-Limb. Albeit a certain cranial overload, he knew that he fulfilled his father's dream, he was ready to get started. The successful development he brought to the Rock was only the beginning. There was much to do here, much he could accomplish. No family—no ties to the off world—medical research was his life.

VanSlyke carefully wrapped Kutof, a Nicovan, in a protective shroud that was saturated with P-200 solution. When satisfied with his mummified wrapping technique, he pushed the gurney inside the holding chamber. Inside were four other cadavers awaiting their donation opportunity. Each in their protective shroud was tagged with species type, limbs suitable for use, and their death date and time.

As Dahn exited the chamber, he checked the readings on the gauge to assure perfect inner environmental conditions. As he logged the numbers onto the chart outside, he heard footsteps outside the lab.

"Doc, we got another here," Kreecher said breathlessly. "It's still movin', but pretty sure it's not gonna make it." He pushed the gurney into the treatment bay.

No doubt that Kreecher had been in the Rock for quite a while, no amount of gore or chaos fazed him. Dahn had met the Vamir a cyk or two after landing on Port Nowhere. He needed an assistant and Kreech, fascinated by the doctor, volunteered. He would also be his first recipient. Maybe a self-serving move for both of them—neither cared.

"No, Kreecher. This one definitely ain't gonna make it." A deep slash to the neck had severed an artery. Pulsating blood from the wound slowed to a gentle trickle. The Modajai gurgled with each respiration, then ceased. Dr. Dahn checked for signs of life and found none. "This is it for now. We don't have time to prep any more." He skillfully wrapped the body as his assistant watched. "We've got to set up for the first case after this," he said without emotion. "Notify the team not to send more until we give the ok."

The Med Recovery Pod retrieved injured persons and transported only the dead or dying to the *Insta-Limb Lab,* the *ILL.* It was crucial to deliver the bodies to the lab within an ower of death. Any delay could create a problem in the implantation of a limb.

"Yes, sir. Yes, sir, of course. I'll tell them to 'pack-a-snack' the rest until further word." Kreecher called the Med Recovery Team on comsys and conveyed the doctor's instructions.

"Thanks." Dahn smiled as he pushed the Modajai into the chamber and closed the door. His only concerns were those related to Insta-Limb; therefore, life-saving measures didn't fit into his plan—death fit. The remainder of the dead and dying would go on to Lev Five to become a feast for the dwellers. This would include those injured beyond donor potential and those who arrived when the holding chamber was filled to capacity. Transported there by way of overstuffed crates, the dead and alive together were packed tightly—a "pack-a-snack." By way of a drop, the filled crates would be sent—much like a catered meal—where the hungry would sort the contents for their delicacies. As savage as it may sound to a Human, VanSlyke had come to Port Nowhere with much acceptance of their way of life.

The doctor and his assistant assembled the instruments for the first case. VanSlyke mixed the P-300, a grainy paste, to its perfect consistency. A basin was filled with P-200 Solution and positioned on a nearby stand.

"Kreech, we're ready. Bring out specimen number two," the doctor said.

"Yes, sir."

Dahn's new assistant and companion looked anxious. Rightfully so, he was about to become the first to undergo the Insta-Limb procedure on Port Nowhere. A blaster hit had taken out the upper right arm above the elbow and the upper left arm twelve centimeters below the elbow. Today, he would become whole again.

Kreecher carefully guided the gurney into the surgical area where Dr. VanSlyke waited. Both checked the tag and confirmed the information to be correct. There were no Vamir donors. Kreech would receive Modajai parts.

This technology enabled bodies to accept limbs surgically attached *regardless* of species. A match was not necessary. The P-200 Solution was a chemical compound that preserved a cadaver when they were wrapped in a shroud soaked with the liquid. The P-300 paste, the same chemical makeup, but in paste form.

He pulled the surgical mask over his face, put on his gown, then gloves. Dr. VanSlyke unwrapped the specimen and

87

immediately began his work. He carefully chose his instruments and meticulously made his incisions. Dahn treated the donor as if a living patient. The skin, muscle, vessels, and bone structure found to be as expected; viable, like living tissues. He amputated the Modajai's arms, scraped away a generous amount of scales, and placed the limbs in the basin filled with the P-200 to preserve them until the recipient was ready. Kreech looked on in awe.

"Get on the table," Dahn said slowly in a monotone voice.

Kreech didn't move.

"GET on the table," Dahn repeated, this time firmly, as he peered over his glasses that sat close to the tip of his nose.

"Y...y...y...yes," Kreech stuttered. He climbed onto the table and looked over at the Modajai cadaver beside him.

"See the mask...there on the tray?" Dahn asked, but continued to work.

Kreech looked just above his head where a tray of instruments lay. Draped over a hook on the edge was a line of tubing and at the end, a mask. It was connected to a black tank with the words Phogonical 3 stenciled on the side in yellow letters. He took the mask, "Yes, got it. Do I put it on now?" Kreecher took the mask in his hand and put it to his face. Not sure how it supposed to fit, he positioned it different ways, but nothing actually fit his broad head. "How, how do I wear this?" he asked.

"Just a min, I'm almost ready. When I tell you to put it on, put it over your mouth, strap behind your head, and start taking very slow, very deep breaths."

"Very slow, very deep," Kreecher repeated and took a few practice breaths. "Dr. Dahn, what is Phog—pho?"

"Phogonical 3. It's going to put you out Kreech. It's sort of like...sort of like anesthesia. You know, the stuff that puts you to sleep when you have surgery. You won't feel or remember anything. Oh, it does other things too, but I won't bore you with all the scientific feek."

"Oh, no sir. You could never bore me. Tell me, what else does it do?"

Dahn smiled, his back still turned away from his patient. "Go ahead and put the mask on." As Kreecher put it on, Dahn turned the valve on the tank until the gauge read five hundred. "Ok, I'll tell you *all* about Phogonical 3."

Kreecher smiled and in a slurred voice said, "Doc, this is some good feek. Think you could fix me up...with a...pretty little Hals..."

When the doctor looked again, he was out. "Well, Kreech, I'm afraid it will take more than a couple of new arms."

VanSlyke shaved away about five centimeters of fur from the Vamir's stumps, then made a careful incision on Kreecher's left arm. He trimmed back the tissue and muscle from the stump until bone was exposed. He trimmed the bone slightly to provide a fresh area to position the new limb. On the tray beside him lay the donor's arms in the solution. Dr. Dahn took a small amount of the P-300 on a spatula-like instrument and smeared across the end of the exposed bone. He then took the donor arm that was awaiting new life and positioned it carefully onto Kreech's stump. With plates and screws into the bones, they were joined. Skilled hands connected layer-by-layer, vessel-to-vessel, muscle-to-muscle, then closed the skin. He repeated the procedure on the other arm. His first Insta-Limb was completed.

Dr. VanSlyke removed his surgical gown, gloves and mask, then wiped the beads of perspiration from his brow.

As the Phogonical 3 was gradually decreased, Kreecher began to gain consciousness. "Hurts...hurts like..." Kreecher moaned.

"It will pass," Dr. Dahn said.

"Soon?"

"Yes, soon." The doctor injected Kreecher with Lispherol. It would block the pain receptors and induce a long sleep. "Move your hands," Dr. Dahn said.

"Which ones?"

The doctor laughed. "All four."

"Sir, I find no humor in this."

"Forgive me. I forgot for a moment that you had more than two."

Kreecher raised his upper arms. He brought them as close to his face as the bandaged limbs would allow. "It worked." He moved his fingers. "It'll take some time to get use to the scales."

"I think you'll adapt," Dr. Dahn said as he gathered his instruments.

"When will I be well?" Kreech asked.

"In a cyk or two. In the meantime, I want you to stay here at the ILL. You will need help for a while."

VanSlyke showed his patient to the small room adjacent to his own living quarters. A small bed and a table were the only things in the cramped space. It was a haven to Kreecher, a safe haven. He laid down and immediately fell into a deep sleep. The Lispherol, a pain med and amnesiac, would last for up twelve owerz.

After Dr. VanSlyke had cleaned his surgical instruments and reorganized the lab, he sat down at a desk in the corner. He opened his journal and began to write.

Today, I restored a life. Not with blood, not with breath. I restored it by completion—no man can function without that. Many must suffer, many must die here. It is because of them, others will be fulfilled. Port Nowhere will gain much from this technology. Here, many lives to me seem hopeless, pointless, filled with endless chaos. They have no realization of normalcy. I will not change that. I must continue on with my research in the Rock. Tomorrow will bring new beginnings, there is no end. —Dahn

Dahn opened his eyes to find he had slept slumped over his desk. He never made it to bed. The past few cyks a blur, he remembered his patient in the next room. He scrambled to his feet, nearly knocking over his chair, and went to Kreecher's side. He found him resting comfortably, but he obviously moved around in his sleep. His bandages were no longer in place. Dr. VanSlyke carefully lifted the arms to assess his handiwork. It looked quite good, no doubt a success.

"Kreecher, can you hear me?" Dr. Dahn asked.

A small slit appeared at the openings of Kreech's eyes. "Unh...unh...I'm...rea...dy," he slurred.

"Ready for what? To get back to work?" The doctor smiled as he watched the arms, all four of them, move. "Look for yourself. What do you think?"

"I've got to…go…" Kreech said with a slur.

VanSlyke bent low to hear, "Go where? I don't understand you Kreecher."

The Vamir opened his eyes suddenly very wide and said, "Gotta go to…to the wetpod."

"I'll help you out, come on." Dahn slid his hands under Kreech's shoulders to help him sit up.

"I can do it myself. I do have two more you know," Kreecher said and laughed a thunderous laugh. He was obviously still looped from the Lispherol but aware that he indeed had four complete upper extremities. "I will be forever grateful to you Dr. Dahn. Forever…" He used the wetpod, then back to his bed. "I'll be ready to work tomorrow, right?"

"Anytime you are ready, but yes, tomorrow you should be ready."

Kreecher looked at Dr. Dahn, "You can teach me this, can't you?"

"What do you mean, teach you?" Dr. Dahn asked as he made a few progress notes.

"That's why you wanted me, a Vamir, I can do more with four hands. I've heard some talk about why you wanted me."

"You forget. You asked *me* for the job."

"Yes, but that is one reason you wanted me, isn't it? I want to learn to help you. I *want* to do this."

"It's not that easy. I've been trained in surgery. I have experience that—"

"So, you didn't intend to teach me, that's what you're saying?"

The doctor sat back in his chair, ran his hands through his hair, then looked Kreecher in the eyes. "Yes, I can teach you. But, you realize, this is a commitment, it will take a lot of time. But, yes, I need someone."

"It took a lot of time to learn for you?"

"The chemical solutions took us a lot of time to perfect. The surgery itself, very basic. Don't get me wrong, it's not a piece of cake."

"Piece of cake? What's a cake?" Kreech asked puzzled.

Realizing his Human slang was not a familiar one, Dahn said, "It's just a way of saying it's not easy, that's all."

"I will learn. I owe you my life." With a look of utmost pride Kreecher said, "Vamiri are loyal, dependable. I am indebted to you."

Dr. VanSlyke nodded slowly, "Ok, ok, just know that we *always* do things *my* way, always."

"Yes, sir."

"Get some rest. Tomorrow you will begin to learn."

Dahn went to his pod, which adjoined the lab, to take a shower. Tomorrow was filled with back-to-back procedures. It was only the beginning. He looked into the mirror. The face that looked back at him was full of lines that told of a life with sintinz behind him. His gray hair laid close to his head from the perspiration the previous cyk. Out loud, he said to himself, "Dad, I wish you were here. It's unbelievable...unbelievable."

~€nD~

INSIDE OUT, OUTSIDE IN

K.G. McAbee

Tau peered through dirty straggles of brown hair at the cell around him. His dark eyes gleamed in his ice-pale face, the right side of which was darkening to faint bluish-purples and reds. The cell wasn't the usual lowlev cave; instead it was sleek, smooth polybdalloy covering the bare rock of the Rock, glinting silvery-grey in the subdued light that trickled through the bars from the outer corridor. He reached out a curious finger and stroked the smoothness, so unlike the jagged surfaces he was used to in the Depths.

Tau had been in plenty of cells in plenty of lock-ups before, but never on LevTwo, never in anything this…was elegant the word? He'd have to ask Crila, or Mal. The RedPubs had got him more than once; the Inversodams at least a ten time, but this was the first time the Connies had got him; he hoped they wouldn't let it become a habit. Still, they'd been a feekin' sight more pleasant than the others; he was barely banged up at all, he thought, brushing a finger over his reddening cheek, though the sergeant who'd tossed him inside had all appearances of a strazzie.

Tau shrugged his shoulders inside the oversized black coverup that swamped him like a firebug inside a cargo bay; he'd slithered out of his battered boots and slid them under the cot that extended from the wall just after he'd been tossed inside the cell. Boots were valuable; he'd never dared take them off below LevFive, even in any of his most secret cribs. And clean water, just sitting there in the flusher, ready to drink; fresh from the recyke tanks, all clear and not smelling like garbage and filled with spores. He liked to paddle his bare feet in the flusher, and bend down to scoop up a drink, whenever any guards walked by. He loved their disgusted reactions.

Funny. Connies were funny. Seven hells, anybody above LevFive was pretty damned funny, he thought. They threw away stuff that he and his tribe would have killed for...or would have, back when he had a tribe.

He reached inside his jacket and stroked the amulet that hung down on his scrawny chest. Bits of crystal, tiny bone fragments, segments of discarded polybdalloy and beralloy, all held together with mismatched wires twisted together; he knew it looked like trash to anyone else, but it was all he had left of his tribe. He remembered Vindi's clever hands when she'd made it...back before she'd been picked up and shipped off-Rock.

All his tribe had died or disappeared, one by one; some picked off by other tribes, many dying from bloody cough or soft bone, a few lost down unexpected shafts, two or three—the pretty ones—snatched and shipped off-Rock for slaves...until finally he was the only one left. He'd decided to die then and was on his way to the Beryl to offer it his life, when he'd stumbled into Crila and Malik Blayne. What in the Seven Hells they were doing there, so deep into the Depths, Tau had never asked. But they'd given him a new tribe and a reason to go on—even if he'd had to fight them both off for almost a strechiz before he'd let them help him.

A rattle at the door to his cell.

"You, void."

Tau grinned at the guard on the other side of the bars. "Yah, you talking at me?"

"Who else, bov-brain?"

"Ah, tell it to the Core." Tau knew his grin was crooked—that bruised cheek hurt—but he had to keep up his well-deserved rep. Mal would be proud of him.

The guard ran her baton across the bars; beralloy meeting polybdalloy made quite the impressive noise. It wasn't the same guard who'd grabbed him; maybe she'd come down from her straz high by now and was rolling and puking on the floor.

"Put your boots on, void." The corporal's broad face split into a sneer. "And wash your face; you're gonna talk to the captain."

<^>

Captain Carle Eversyn sat at his desk, wondering why his belly was doing barrel rolls as if he'd just stepped out of an elevator-tube. Shock. That's what it had to be. Shock. He'd never suspected that Benn—not his second-in-command, not Commander Benita Frohmyn—would do this to him.

But then again, why was he surprised? He'd seen the way Benn handled herself from the beginning.

But to do it to him. What was she thinking? She had to know she'd never get away with it...didn't she?

"Captain?" The liquid tones of his secretary Lisolia fluted over the comm.

Eversyn slapped down the reply button as if it'd just snapped at him. "Yes?"

"Doctor Kwarn would like to see you, sir. He's on his way from the phys-lab."

"Send him in as soon as he arrives."

Carle Eversyn leaned back in his chair, then sat up and shuffled through the pile of read-sheets again. Proof. He couldn't ask for more proof. Why had he never seen it before, never suspected, even after all this time?

Benn, working behind his back, working to take over command, ever since they'd arrived on this damned Rock—and before.

His door beeped and slid open, and Eversyn felt his heart go into hyperdrive.

Doctor Finias Kwarn walked in...followed by Commander Frohmyn. Behind them, a skinny Human boy inside a coverup five sizes too big for him stood grinning like a void, a burly Connie corporal just behind him, her hand on the boy's shoulder.

Eversyn swallowed what felt like several of his internal organs, tried to make his movements casual as he aligned the read-sheets and slid them across into the top-sec slot. No one would be able to access them there except him...although, after what he'd just found out about Benn, he was no longer quite so sure of that.

"Doctor. Commander. To what do I own the honor?" he snapped, settling back into his chair; it emitted a sibilant sigh as the internal nano-bots readjusted to the new body contours.

"We thought you needed to see the results of the tests on Sergeant Naro." Doctor Kwarn tossed a stack of comp-prints on the desk then took a chair without being asked; he'd never been one to respect authority, but it had never bothered Eversyn—until now. "She shows all the signs of being addicted to a powerful narco, something along the lines of zrendor or d'valtir—"

"But stronger, much stronger, sir," interrupted Commander Frohmyn, standing at attention.

She always did that. It irritated the Seven Hells out of Eversyn...but never more so than now.

"At ease, commander." Eversyn watched her intently as she pulled up a chair and settled her compact yet lush figure into it. Her red hair, cropped over her ears—an image of his own fingers in that hair slipped across his mind and he shook his head to dislodge it—looked as if it wouldn't dare become disarrayed without a direct order. She looked just the same as always, damn her.

"Where'd the sergeant get the drug? I was under the impression, commander, that you had control over all imports, legal or not."

"Ain't no import."

Eversyn sat up; amazement dropped his mouth open as his chair nano-bots whined in protest.

"Uh, captain; this boy was in lock-up. Sergeant Naro brought him in, after the...unfortunate incident on LevFive and just before she—collapsed in your office. We think he knows something about this drug."

Damn, did Benn sound...embarrassed?

"Well, boy?" Eversyn snapped.

The burly corporal dragged the boy forward by the collar of his coverup; the stupid grin never left his face.

"This boy is from the Depths. What is he doing on LevTwo?"

"I think, captain, you'll want to hear this…"

<^>

"There." Crila nudged Malik. "See him? He tall enough?"

The woman's voice was a whisper just discernable above the soothing hum of the air-recyke system that murmured through the vent where they sat.

Malik Blayne peered through a crack, nodded down at the single Connie walking slowly up the corridor below them. Just the right size.

"Yah. He'll do."

"Take it slow, Mal. We don't want to end up in the cell next to Tau, do we?"

Her voice was just loud enough for him to hear over the buzz-hum of the fan and no louder; he wondered, and not for the first time, just how she did that.

"Oh, I don't know." Malik shrugged, taking a firmer grip on his blaster. "One way to get to him."

"Yah, if we wanted to get there in a neat little pile of pieces. You got a plan, or we just going to run in, blasters blazing? Cause if that's your idea, you've watched way too many vids, my dear boy."

"I'm not your dear boy, Cri, and I've always got a plan. Shh. Here he comes…"

The Connie, a tall lean male with a shaved head, stopped just below them. The cross-corridor was empty in both directions; nothing but pristine polybdalloy, broken here and there by portals and, just below Malik and Cri's hiding place, a two-meter square vid-screen set into the wall. Malik checked his chrono, then patted Cri on her back and nodded.

The screen, on either side of which they squatted, was already loose. Mal took a firm grip on it, his fingers spread through the mesh.

Below them, the Connie was staring at the vid-screen as a face slowly congealed out of silvery nothingness, like the very beginnings of the universe as it formed out of ions and gasses. A smooth, low, voice—belonging to the famous Sha'zreen

Glowberreez, her dark purple face bisected by a sensuous smile, her hair piled half a meter high—began:

Good cyk, sentients! Welcome to the tenth ower news! But first, a word from our sponsor! Have you entered PNCNN's latest 'My Favorite Planet' contest? Just tell us, in twenty-five words or less, which planetary system you'd most like to visit. Winners receive a free dinner for two in Port Nowhere's most fabulous restaurant, and my own personal favorite, the Starview Lounge. *Who knows? You might even be lucky enough to see me there! Prohibited where void; void where prohibited. And now, the news…*

Just as the last word came from the vid-screens transmitters, Malik yanked up the mesh screen and dropped onto the enrapt Connie below; his booted feet landed squarely behind the man's shoulders and there was a satisfying *thunk* as a head hit the center of the vid-screen. The soldier crumpled to the floor.

"Very neat, Malik my son," Crila said as she dropped to the floor, her knees bending to absorb the shock. She flicked a strand of lavender hair out of her eyes and patted Malik on his back with her right hand—the flesh one. She was keeping her left prosthetic hand carefully in her coverup pocket; Mal didn't dare ask why. She'd only had it a few cyks and the sight of it still made him jumpy as firelice in a frying pan. "Never knew what hit him. Now what?"

"Now we strip him."

"Fun. Let me help. But we'd better drag him out of the corridor first, don't you think?"

A tall lanky Connie with white-streaked brown hair, his head sunk down into the collar of his grey uniform, stalked towards a door at the end of a corridor. As he moved, he read the sign on the door as it rotated through several spectra, thirteen languages and half a dozen glyphs:

Consolidated Guard Headquarters, Sector Three.

Below the title, somewhat smaller languages/glyphs warned:

Termination Possible for Those without Legitimate Reasons for Visit.

The man stopped before the door. One hand held a blaster; the other was entangled in the neck of a coverup worn by a short, wiry woman with lavender hair. The woman was limping and a keening whine came from between her pale lips.

"Don't overdo, Cri," whispered the ersatz Connie as he tapped the toe plate with his recently acquired, Connie-issue boot. There was a *snkt* as the door's internal sensors read the info from the boot-toe insert and recognized it with a cheerful, welcoming *brpt*.

"Heyo, let me have some fun, why don't you?" Crila Maragorn grinned up at Malik Blayne, then slumped into a frightened cringe as the door slid open before them.

Mal tightened his grip on Cri's coverup and yanked her with him through the door. It shut behind them with a satisfied sigh; almost, Mal thought, as if it knew they were well and truly caught.

Mal shook off the image and strode towards a counter that bisected the small anteroom. The Connie corporal sitting behind the counter, broad shouldered and with a head like a cazandor melon, stopped tapping his keypad and looked up when they reached him. His broad jaw tightened in disgust and he snapped: "Your hair is not regulation length and you're—"

Cri reached out her prosthetic hand and stroked the corporal's cheek. His eyes rolled back into his head, a faint burning smell filled the room, and he crumpled across his desk. An immediate whine from the air filters, and the burning smell disappeared as quickly as it had appeared.

"Feek, Cri. That new prosthesis…well, remind me not to piss you off. He dead?"

"Nah. But he'll have a pretty impressive headache when he wakes up; and he might not be as quick to notice stuff like haircuts…or, uh, eating and drinking and such." She sounded almost embarrassed as she carefully unscrewed a finger from her prosthetic hand and slid it into her left forearm through a small hatch near the elbow.

Mal grabbed the corporal and slid him off his chair, then— with some difficulty; damn, they fed those Connies good— parked him in a corner where he was hidden from anyone at the entrance or the single door that lead further into the Connie complex. Then he settled onto the hard chair and stroked the keypad.

On the long screen that made up the entire back of the counter, an apologetic yet dignified 'No Access' was his only reply.

"Damn!"

"Get out of my way, boy," Crila said, shoving him over and settling her rounded butt on half the chair. "Let an expert show you how it's done."

Strokes, stabs, the occasional flick of a prosthetic digit, and Cri had the computer terminal eating out of her hand—quite literally, Mal thought with a chuckle. He'd often wondered where her information came from; this uncanny linking with the keypad told him a great deal about what he'd always suspected—Cri must be a cracker.

"Well, deus my machina, if we ain't the luckiest...Tau just had him a little visit with Captain Eversyn himself, and he's on his way back to his cell. Mal, my son, if we—" she gave a swift flick of a metal thumb and a map appeared on one side of the screen, with two tiny red lights proceeding down a green line that had to represent a corridor; the two red dots were approaching a yellow square, "—wait just outside that door, we'll have Tau in our hot little hands in just under, uh, seven minz. Wait." Cri scrabbled in her elbow hatch, slid a finger out and into its slot on her beralloy hand. "Now. Forewarned is forearmed...so to speak."

Mal groaned and checked his blaster.

<^>

Tau walked as slowly as he dared; the Connie corporal wasn't in a very good mood after their little visit to the captain's office and he didn't see any use in collecting more bruises. But he didn't have to trot, either; heyo, there weren't no Coriliun after them. So he was careful to keep just a slight pull against her hand on his shoulder, and he looked all around as they walked. It paid to remember directions; nobody knew that better than him. Lots of times, he'd saved his tribe by remembering twists and turns in the Depths.

They turned a corner. Up ahead Tau saw a tall Connie with a small Human female at his side. Funny. The woman had lavender hair...

Tau slowed down even more as a pair of armed guards walked past and then disappeared into a door on the right side of the corridor.

"Come on, void," snarled his corporal, giving him a shake.

Tau glanced over his shoulder; nobody. He speeded up, almost pulling the corporal along until they were just opposite the pair he'd seen—and the corridor was empty in both directions...

Let her stand there. Let her sweat. Let her worry. The Core knows I do, and have...

The Core. Damn. On this piece of rock less than three quintins and I sound like I was a Rocker, born in this cesspool.

Captain Carle Eversyn leaned back in his chair and gazed up at his second-in-command. Commander Frohmyn's eyes were fixed carefully on the wall above her captain's head, and her expression was noncommittal, though there was the faintest hint of anxiety about her mouth.

"So, Commander Frohmyn," he said at last. "It seems that, not only have you allowed several members of our team to become addicted to a contraband substance...but you've also somehow managed to lose a very important suspect—to lose him, in fact, within the Consolidated Guard complex, with the highest security rating of anywhere in this triple-damned piece of feek. What exactly do you have to say for yourself?"

"Captain, I—"

Eversyn raised a peremptory hand. "I want to know everything you can find out about this straz drug, understand me? No excuses, commander."

"No sir, but—"

"And I want an all-points on that boy. That was Malik Blayne on the sec-cams, or I'm a Bansnict. So." Eversyn shuffled a pile of read-sheets, slid them into his top-sec slot, then hit the button to open his office door. "I think that's all for the moment, commander. I'll expect a report on my desk by ower seven. Dismissed."

"But...Carle—"

Eversyn looked up, and he felt a violent surge of pleasure at the expression on her face.

"Dismissed, commander," he repeated.

"Sir!" Benita Frohmyn snapped a sharp salute, spun on her heel and marched out the open door. It slid shut behind her.

The silence in the room was deafening.

~END~

OUT OF WATER...INTO THE DEPTHS

Charlotte Babb

Aunt Silky was no worse than any other boss Jule had known. The Chow Down's kitchen was the same too. The food smelled different, but everyone still got hungry at the same time. Jule wasn't allowed anywhere near the preparation process, but he watched and learned as he mopped, washed dishes and dumped the wastes into the reclaim vat. Even the waste was sold, a few microcredz a kilo.

He fed from the leftovers, and they all drank a few globes of Nicovan beer when the cycle was done, which Aunt Silky provided to keep the help from stealing it during the shifts. Nothing new, nothing more than he expected, except that he had hoped to be allowed at least to chop vegetables by now.

Jule's problem was Bax Tuvalu, head cook. Bax had bet that Jule would not live more than a strechiz. He didn't like losing his bet. He didn't like Jule living with Trillfin either. Mating with Trillfin would make Bax an actual member of Aunt Silky's family, a step closer to his owning the Chow Down one cyk. He saw Jule as a threat to his plan.

"Sape!" Bax bellowed. "Get this out of my way."

Jule didn't answer. He wiped the leavings off the cutting board. Bax was making as much of a mess as he could, just to keep Jule busy. Aunt Silky either hadn't noticed the waste, or her reclaim kickbacks had gone up enough to make it worthwhile.

Or maybe she was waiting for Bax to twist himself enough rope.

As Jule approached the reclaim vat, he heard the rhythm knock of one of Aunt Silky's suppliers, a backdoor boy from deep in the Rock. He rapped back a different beat, and got the correct answer. He opened the hatch just enough for the kid's grimy hand to thrust in a net of tunnel fungi from the lower levels.

Jule reached for the globe of water to pay him, but on an impulse, he said, "Wait." Below the opening, he saw a thin, humanoid face with large golden-green eyes peer up at him. He scooped up the scraps and dropped them into the kid's hand, then set the water globe where the kid could reach it. He smiled, nodded.

The face smiled too, then vanished with the water.

Jule picked up the fungi, then turned to see Aunt Silky standing behind him. He raised his chin, exposing his throat, but her expression didn't change from its usual inscrutable disdain. She did, however, nod just a bit.

"You'd better clean those good. No telling what they were grown on," Aunt Silky said. "Bax is busy just now."

Jule bowed, but allowed himself a bit of a smile. Cleaning was only one step below chopping, and chopping was next to cooking.

Bax would be furious.

He brushed each delicate fungus with a soft brush. They called these tunnel lips, not too different from the tree ears that he knew, crunchy without much flavor. His grandmother said they were good for the blood too. He wondered what the kid ate, other than scraps. Tunnel lips weren't nutritious enough to live on, probably too valuable to eat, if they were swapped for water. This was no farmer's market kid; he was a hustler and a survivor, worth cultivating as a guide. Jule would keep some of his food aside for the kid, for the next time he came.

"What the flaming Core do you think you are doing?" Bax yelled as Jule laid the fungi on the drying racks. "Get out here and mop the dining room before the midcyk rush." Bax gestured with his knife.

Jule did not lift his chin to Bax. "Aunt Silky told me to clean these." He finished placing each one carefully so the air would circulate properly. Then he grabbed the janipod and mop, and headed for the front.

Jule was glad to see Trillfin when she came back from work every cykul, talking of who had come and gone on the shuttle. He told her about all the gossip that came through Aunt Silky's, whether it made any sense or not—Charlie the envirosuit salesman had come by. Aunt Silky threw him out but not before he managed to make a deal with Bax. A mangy-looking Bansnict had brought a container of chapaw and delivered some message that Jule hadn't managed to overhear while he was bussing tables. Trillfin knew most of their names, and sometimes even told Jule stories about them. Jule told Trillfin about the kid and the tunnel lips. But Trillfin wanted to hear his stories about his home world. She was like a little girl hearing her first fairy tales.

"They dig holes in the rock and put dead people in there and leave them?" Trillfin shuddered. "Nasty. And what a waste."

Jule hadn't tried to explain embalming. As dirty as the Rock was, Trillfin had never seen soil. Local farming here was done on slurry—not clean, reclaimed sludge like the official food producers used, but home grown, composted from…he didn't think about that. If he died here, he hoped Trillfin would throw him down the nearest lava vent and not reclaim him. But he would get off the Rock before that happened, out where he could see sunlight and blue sky again. He hadn't learned what he came here for, yet.

The part that Trillfin liked best to hear about was day. She had seen the stars through a dome, but she could not understand the daylight and sunshine.

"What do you mean, it gets light and then the lights go off? The lights stay on all the time unless there's a powerout or a quake."

"Vestia III is like most planets. It revolves around a sun, so every cykul it rotates, with the sun shining only on one side.

The light side is called day."

"I think the Rock rotates, but I never figured that it mattered." Trillfin shrugged. "I have heard that sometimes you can't see the Galaxy from the domes. Business goes down."

What Trillfin refused to listen to was his description of the ocean, miles and miles of open water, water to swim in, water she could breathe while she was awake, water with light shining through it. She would laugh at him when he would try to tell her about it.

Trillfin would be as out of water on Vestia III as Jule was on the Rock. She was making him a home here. He might even take her with him when he left. But now he needed to know more—something that would let him get past Bax, something only he could do to show Aunt Silky.

"What's in the Depths?" Jule asked Trillfin one evening. "Who lives down there? How do they survive?"

"I'm not taking you there, if that's what you're after," Trillfin said, her eyes showing white all around her pupils. "It's dangerous. They'd slice you up for a sandwich with your eyeballs on the side."

"Kids live down there, don't they? The ones who bring the tunnel lips and the slime weed?"

"Most of them die kids too. As soon cut your throat as look at you. Some of them wear the teeth of the ones they've killed. It's tribe magic." Trillfin shook her head. Her voice took on a stern, *because I said so* tone: "You are not going down there." For a moment she even looked like Aunt Silky. She wasn't nearly as dumb as she acted sometimes—none of the Nicovans were.

Jule smiled. "Of course not. I just want to know about them. So I'll know what not to do. Where not to go."

"Don't go down." Trillfin said. She wouldn't talk to him for the rest of the evening. She climbed into her sleeper early and closed the hatch with a sharp click.

Jule missed the next opportunity to talk to the kid from the Depths. Bax was taking a break when the kid knocked on the hatch, so he took the bag of fungi. He also opened the globe of water and drank half of it before he gave it to the kid. He tossed the globe through the opening, so the kid would have to chase it. Bax tossed the bag at Jule, not caring if the fungi were bruised in the process.

Since Aunt Silky had allowed Jule to clean them once, it was beneath Bax to do it now.

Jule swore under his breath. Now the kid wouldn't trust him at all. He'd made an impression, though. The mushrooms were large, firm, the best Jule had seen. So the kid was hungry. Jule would find a way to feed him.

Bax wasn't making it easy. He had stopped making more of a mess than was necessary. Maybe Aunt Silky had said something to him, or maybe he was bright enough to know see that he didn't need to provide a reason for keeping Jule on. Jule tried to keep out a bit of his own supper for the next time, but Bax made sure everything was scraped into the reclaim vat. Bax personally counted the water and beer globes every time, too; not that he didn't take one with him now and then.

Jule figured that Aunt Silky was waiting to see how he would handle Bax, but until Jule got sick she ignored them both.

One shift, as he was mopping up, Jule noticed that he was sweating, even though he felt cold. It was all he could do to drag the janipod back towards the kitchen after the dinner rush. Aunt Silky called him to come up to her perch by the cashbox.

"You look bad, even for a Human, Jule. How do you feel?" Aunt Silky put her digipods against his forehead. "No fever. No color. How long have you been here?"

"Four quintinz, I think. I'm just tired."

"No, you're sick. Leave the mop there." Aunt Silky pulled Jule's sleeve up and looked at his scrawny arm. It was greenish white, like fish belly. "Go home. I'll be around later."

"I'm fine, really." Jule's eyes struggled to focus on Aunt Silky's face. He leaned heavily on his mop handle.

"I don't know much about Humans, but something is wrong." Aunt Silky let her words soak into Jule's brain. "I don't know what it is—we don't use ka'frindi. Maybe you don't know good fungi from bad. Spores, maybe."

Jule's head was already swimming. "Whatever you say,

Aunt…" He couldn't quite get the words to come from his head to his mouth. The last thing he remembered was clutching the mop handle to steady himself.

Bax could see Aunt Silky and the Sape talking in the dining room. The Human had finally had enough of the tunnels spores and rock dust to get sick. Bax had been feeding the poisons to him all along, even going off LevThree to get raw beryllion. He'd rented an envirosuit from Charlie Manus just to go into a tunnel where the tunnel lips were fruiting. The Sape hadn't been here long enough to be immune to the spores. There was no way Aunt Silky would shell out enough credz for a healer, if she even figured out what the problem was.

As Bax watched, Jule collapsed, taking the mop and janipod with him. The Chow Down was as good as his. No Neek would challenge him for it, whether he mated with Trillfin or not. He took his time coming out when Aunt Silky called him to carry Jule back to Trillfin's pod. By the time he had cleaned up a little, she had three other Neeks carrying him.

"You're in charge while I'm gone," Aunt Silky said. "Keep an eye on the dining room."

Bax raised his chin, as much to hide his expression as to show respect. Everything was falling his way.

But he noticed as Aunt Silky left with the Sape, she took the cashbox with her.

He heard the rhythm knock on the back door. The kid had brought more tunnel lips. He rapped out the answer on the door and raised it just enough for the kid to slide in the bag. This time the kid held onto the bag, jerking it back until Bax laid the water globe down and stepped out of reach.

The kid slung the bag across the kitchen floor and snatched the water globe. Bax hit the button to shut the back door, but it did not close before a puddle of stinking yellow liquid ran inside.

The kid had marked the door.

Bax swore. Now he'd have to clean up both the dining room and some kid's piss from his kitchen. When he finally got to the fungi, they too were ruined—bruised and rotten. Jule would pay for that if he lived, and Silky would if Jule didn't.

Jule woke up with a blistering headache. His veins felt like they held molten lava. He could not lie still, but moving was torture. He moaned a little, but the sound reverberated through his head. Even breathing hurt.

"Lie still!" thundered from somewhere outside him. A drop of burning liquid touched his tongue, adding thirst to his misery. He tried to suck more of it, and it came, each drop growing cooler and more refreshing as he was able to take it in. The fire in his body began to solidify into simple pain. He passed out into cool, blessed darkness.

He opened his eyes to see his body lying on the floor of Trillfin's pod. Trillfin was kneeling beside him. She laid a wet rag soaked in green slime across his forehead. Most of the rest of his body was soaked in green slime too. It looked like his only chance to get off planet was going to be without his body.

He turned to look behind him. Another...Spirit? Soul? Consciousness?...floated in the air behind him. It was a Snake-Woman, twice his height, but coiled, almost like some reptile guru meditating. It could see him. It glanced back at his body, nodding towards it.

He looked back at himself again. He didn't know how to get back in his body, and he didn't want to feel the pain again. The Snake-Woman pointed at him and then to his body. He moved with the arc of her finger, feeling a flash of pain as he entered his body...and then nothing.

When he came to again, the fire had cooled to a dull ache. He chanced opening his eyes a slit. The face he saw was Human, not Trillfin's. He tried to speak but could only croak.

"Hush," the face said. The face was familiar, but he couldn't place it

Something cool dripped into his mouth. He sucked at it, expecting to pass out again, but this time he stayed conscious. Jule opened his eyes further. He was in Trillfin's pod. He didn't see the Snake-Woman, or Trillfin. It was darker than usual. Trillfin might be in her sleeper. He risked stretching his hand. It was only stiff, not painful.

"No. Be still." The face had a soft voice, but it was high-pitched, like a child's. "Silkymomma say be quiet. Drink. Rest."

"You're the fungus kid." Jule said. He tried to lift his head, but the pain came back, and he saw red galaxies before his eyes. Jule moaned.

"Learn hard," the kid said.

"Talk to me," Jule said. "Tell me your name and why you bring us the tunnel lips."

"Stupid Sape. Silkymomma give water."

"What's your name? What do I call you?"

The face grinned, now looking childlike instead of serious. "Slime. Me Slime. Silkymomma pay me much water to watch you."

Jule slept and woke, slept and woke, sometimes to find Trillfin and sometimes, Slime. One day both of them were there, and they pulled him up to sit in a chair for a while. They made him choke down some plain toufood—nasty stuff with nothing to give it flavor.

Trillfin laughed when he complained. "Hasn't eaten in a strechiz, but he fusses about the food." She sprinkled a tiny pinch of firebug shells over Jule's plate.

He smiled, even when the heat flowed from his mouth all over his body. His pain nerves felt burned out, and the firebugs were only a bit of warmth.

Trillfin got up from the table. "I have to go to work. Slime will stay with you. Try to sit up as long as you can, but don't do anything else. No cooking."

Jule nodded. He knew he wasn't going anywhere yet. "Thank you for taking care of me." He nodded at Slime too. "Both of you."

Trillfin patted his head and his cheek, where his beard was more than stubble. She said nothing as she went out the door, locking them in.

"How much water is Trillfin paying you to stay with me?"

Slime shrugged. "Not talk business. You not part of deal."

"What will you talk to me about?" Jule leaned back in his chair, already tired from sitting up. "How did you get your name? How do you survive here?"

"Why you care? I live here. Not you. Why you here?"

"I want to be a great chef. I have heard of ka'frindi and how it makes everything taste so very good. I want to know how to use it, how to grow it."

"That easy. Feek and wait."

Jule's stomach wasn't up to the mental image his brain produced. He swallowed again. He was glad he hadn't tried ka'frindi yet.

Slime grinned at him. "Want know more?"

"What do you eat then? You can't live off of tunnel lips."

"No. Good thing. Silkymomma buys." Slime grinned again.

Jule told his stomach not to listen. "So, what then?"

"Bugs. Grubs." Slime grinned at Jule's expression. "Any trade. Any steal. What people give, if can eat." Slime stretched, leaned back against the wall. "I feed tribe. Tribe feeds me. You no tribe. Why you leave them?"

"I don't have a tribe." Jule's head began to swim. He clutched the edge of the table to keep himself vertical. "Help me to lie down."

Slime was very strong for such a young kid. He couldn't be more than ten or eleven. He helped Jule lie down and tucked him in. Jule struggled to keep his eyes open.

"Slime, bring me some of what you eat, if you can, and let me cook it for you."

"Stupid Sape." Slime grinned as Jule slid back into dark sleep.

<^>

Bax cursed under his breath. He forgot that he had cooked all the tunnel lips. The kid hadn't shown up for more than a strechiz, not since he'd marked the back door. He certainly wasn't going out to look for lips, but he didn't want to have to explain to Aunt Silky why the firebug curree didn't have any crunchy bits in. The Sape hadn't been back to work in a strechiz either, but he wasn't dead. Aunt Silky had been away from the Chow Down more than Bax could remember since he was a child. Maybe that was a good sign, maybe she trusted him to run the place—except that she always took the cash box when she left, and she never left except after the midcyk rush.

Bax had to take the credz from the few customers and make his own change. Nobody dared stiff him, and even he didn't dare take too much off the top of the tab. When his friend Simikus came by to see if he wanted a drop of straz, Bax didn't have enough cash to spare for it.

Bax scrubbed his grill and cleaned the back, still trying to see how to get rid of the Sape, since it looked like he would recover. Maybe if he did some cooking, Bax could sabotage that. Or maybe Bax could find him another job, one where Jule would find himself on the hot end of a lava vent—like toufood popcorn down the Rock's throat.

When Jule awoke, Slime had brought him a bundle of slime, creepy crawlies—grubs, roaches, and newts—and some small tunnel lips. Slime fed him one of each thing at a time. Jule would roll it in his mouth, or chomp or suck out the juice as Slime suggested. Each time, Jule would wash out his mouth with water. Slime watched as Jule closed his eyes and just ate, not looking at, but just tasting. Finally Slime picked up a cockroach, fishing it out of the jar where he had imprisoned it.

"Cook these," Slime said, "use lava vent, if hot, or a grease-wick. No cook—you sick."

"Do you cook anything else?"

"Most bugs. Some worms. Me know which." Slime shook his head. "Eat wrong, you die."

"All right," Jule said. "Help me up and we'll see what we can do with them."

Slime helped Jule up to a chair, then scooted him over to the cooker. Slime pulled the head and legs off the roach and Jule showed him how to hold it against the heat source. In about a minz, the bug gave off a nutty smell. Slime smiled.

"Taste that!" he said.

Jule closed his eyes again and gingerly took a bite. It was crunchy, with sweet creamy center, like a bonbon. "All we need is some chocolate," he said.

"What chocolate?"

"A plant on my home world that is bitter unless you mix sweet with it, but when you do, it has a wonderful flavor."

Slime grinned. "You know how I get name Slime?"

Jule shook his head.

Slime took the last bit of the bug Jule was still holding, dipped it into the container he brought that was filled with a brownish slime, and handed it back to Jule. Slime nodded. "Eat."

Jule shrugged. He popped the whole thing in his mouth and chomped it. It was good—sweet, creamy, bitter and even a little salty. Not exactly chocolate, but he'd eaten chocolate that didn't taste this good. He smiled.

"Yes! Good! You the first one to try. No one else like but me" Slime grinned. "You ask ka'frindi? It stage two. This stage one. Straz stage five."

Jule looked in horror at the brownish slime. As he watched, it began to turn blue-green.

What had Slime said about ka'frindi?

Feek...and wait.

<^>

The second strechiz after Jule had been carried out of the Chow Down, Aunt Silky came to see Jule in person. She brought some toufood and some other things in a mesh bag which she left on the table in the kitchen.

Jule stood up when she came in, raising his chin to her. He was still a little weak, but Trillfin allowed him to get up and do some simple cooking and cleaning up. She hadn't let him pay Slime either water or credz, only letting Jule learn from Slime or teach him. Aunt Silky was obviously footing the bill.

"Well, Jule," Aunt Silky said, calling him by his name for the first time. "I hear rumors that you think you can cook. Show me."

Jule bowed, much more correct in his posture this time, keeping eye contact and his chin up. "What is your pleasure, Mastriz?"

"None of that LevOne lip with me, boy." Aunt Silky nodded

curtly. She sank heavily into the chair. "Show me something quick and simple, something none of the other choke-n-puke pods around here serve."

Jule nearly panicked, knowing what few ingredients Trillfin kept in her kitchen. He had certainly not been allowed to buy supplies, not from the local Nicovans, and they couldn't afford anything from offworld or even from LevThree merchants.

In the bag was a block of toufood, some slime weed, a couple of tunnel lips and several kinds of dried bugs and fungi. Some of it he had used, and some was completely unfamiliar. He opened each container, smelled it, closed it. One container of slightly reddish powder had no smell, so he crumbled a bit of toufood and sprinkled a few grains of the powder to taste it. It was hot and sour, like a vinegar made of habaneras. He heated a bit of oil in a pan, sprinkled the red powder in the oil, then sautéed a handful of crumbled toufood. He chopped some tunnel lips and slime weed while the toufood soaked up the flavored oil, then stir fried them, with a bit more oil. The color was appealing, reddish toufood with green slime weed and white tunnel lips. He took out some toasted roach crème that he and Slime had saved from their last cooking venture and spooned a dollop of it over the slime weed, making a bit of a presentation. He considered pulling a knife through it for even more style, but remembered who he was cooking for.

No LevOne stuff here—just choke-n-puke.

Jule handed the plate to Aunt Silky with another bow. It had taken only three minz to cook from start to finish and had used few ingredients—cheap ones at that. He watched her from the corner of his eye as he pretended to clean the kitchen area—he had been well-trained not to make a mess as cleaning up a mess was not what a cook was paid for.

Aunt Silky inspected the dish, smelled it, mashed up some of it with a prong. She finally took a bite, rolling it around in her mouth before she finally chewed it up and swallowed. She drank from a globe of water she had brought along, and went through the whole ritual again. Her face did not change expression. She neither smiled, gagged, spat nor frowned.

Jule took on the Nicovan "don't hurt me" posture and simply waited.

"Now," Aunt Silky said, after her third bite. "Take the same things and make something else, something that looks and tastes different."

Finally Jule felt at home. He had done this assignment as an apprentice. The key was to use a different order of cooking. He started with water and slime weed, then tossed in two big dollops of roach crème, making a soft sauce. He mashed the toufood into a paste and mixed it with the slime weed, all soft, creamy and slightly green. He sprinkled the tunnel lips with the hot & sour powder then placed them on the creamed slime weed without cooking, mostly for color and texture rather than taste.

After the first bite, Aunt Silky nodded her head. She began to eat, first from one plate, then the other, comparing. "Bax tried to kill you, you know," she said, "and he didn't know you could cook. What's Slime been teaching you?"

"He's showed me good stuff and bad, what to eat, what to cook first, what to leave alone." Jule tried to sort out everything Aunt Silky said, what it meant, and what it meant now.

"I haven't eaten roach in more cycles than I can count."

Jule didn't answer. He didn't look at her either.

"I came up from the Depths," Aunt Silky said. "I've lived off toasted roach, tunnel lips and slime weed. This is cuisine where I come from." She put her prong down by her plate and took another swig from the water globe. "Can you do fancy cooking too?"

Jule nodded.

"Tried working with ka'frindi yet? Did Slime bring you some?"

"We—we grew some," Jule said. He didn't know what Aunt Silky knew, and he didn't want to tell her anything she didn't want to know. "Yes, I tried it."

"Then you know why I don't use it."

"No. Not really."

"Do you know about straz?"

"Yeah. I've heard of it. A later stage of ka'frindi. A drug. Very addictive."

"You had a pretty good dose of it, or rather, the stage just before it. It nearly killed you." Aunt Silky handed him her plates. "If you ever try straz, it may kill you outright, or you may just be a mindless strazzie the rest of your short life."

"So what do I do now? Sign a warrant on Bax?"

"There's no law down here, not for the likes of you—and us." Aunt Silky pushed herself up from the table. "You'll have to face him down. I've got a lot invested in you. Make it worth my while."

<^>

Three cyks later, Aunt Silky let Jule make a bit of toufood soup and served it to the bravest of her clientele. They liked it, even though they said it would never be as good as Aunt Silky's recipe.

Aunt Silky told Jule, "That's because when I make it, I spit in it."

Bax continued to cook during the midcyk and lastcyk rush, and Aunt Silky hired another Nicovan to clean up behind him. Jule came in early to cook for the fourth shift meal and to make preps for Bax. He would leave just as Bax came in and go back to Trillfin's to process the things Slime and his tribe brought in: toasted crème, fried grubs with firebug or hot-and-sour coating, and other kinds of take-along, packaged food.

Word began to get around, and the early cyk rush began to be the cred-maker. The Chow Down's reputation improved so much that even some non-Neeks began to show up, including the legendary Malik Blaine.

Aunt Silky took Blayne's order herself that morning and delivered it. She took a seat beside him while he ate. No one could hear what they talked about, even though every ear was aimed in their direction.

Bax came in for his shift about half an ower early. Jule was finishing chopping some grubs as the oil heated to fry them. He had all the condiments filled—firebug shells ground, tunnel lips dried and sliced, and a vat of slime weed soaking in hot-and-sour juice, which had become a Chow Down favorite.

Bax put on his white uniform and apron—some things being the same all over the Galaxy. He hadn't said anything to Jule since Jule had come back to work. Jule didn't know if Aunt Silky had talked to Bax, but Jule just stayed out of his way, just did his own job.

And he made sure he didn't eat anything that Bax cooked.

Jule heard Bax coming up behind him. Bax was large for a Nicovan, heavy-set, and his solid footfalls raised the hair on the back of Jule's neck. Jule spun around, knife in hand. Bax stood behind him, glowering.

"You won't live out the day, Sape," Bax said. "Make your peace with the Core because you're going to see Her."

"Then you'll have to show me the way," Jule said.

He'd known the fight was coming since he had met Bax. Jule was stuck between Bax and the cutting counter and the grill with no maneuvering room. He had length of reach over Bax, but Bax had weight advantage, more space to move in and, Jule hoped, less experience and slower reflexes.

Bax took a step closer. Jule crouched a little, his knife ready to pierce Bax's belly if Bax made a jab towards him. His knife hadn't cut meat in a long time. Something about steel craved blood, and Bax's would do.

Bax feinted with his left fist, jabbing with his knife. Jule saw the movement, ducked right under the fist and slit Bax's apron at elbow level. Now Jule was in the open kitchen, and Bax was against the grill. No blood showed on the apron, so Jule hadn't connected with him. Bax was more agile than he looked.

Jule could hear some commotion in the dining room, but he was focused on Bax. The sounds were far away and not important. Bax turned and seized the oil pot and slung it at Jule, the arc of the brown liquid flowing in slow motion from the edge of the pan as Jule jumped back, slamming his hip into the reclaim vat. The steaming oil splattered across his stomach, soaking into the layers of cloth in his apron instead of frying his face. Jule backed toward the back door, limping slightly where he had hit the vat, but luring Bax across the oil-slick floor.

Bax charged toward Jule, bellowing in rage. Another sound came through to Jule, the sound of a female screaming something, but he couldn't make out what it was. He let Bax get up some momentum, then he dodged down and right, towards the dining room door. He picked up a flicker of movement on that side and rolled under another blade. He stood again, between the open door where a waitress stood yelling, scanning for any other assailants. Bax turned to follow Jule, lost his footing and fell, just as the other Neek reached him. Bax clutched at the other Neek to steady himself and then threw him against the back door. The second Nicovan slumped to the floor.

"Bring it on," Jule said.

Bax glanced at the door by Jule's hand. A man had appeared there with blaster drawn.

"Get out of my kitchen!" Jule hissed. He swung at the man who stepped back into the dining room. Jule was tired of bowing to Neeks, and he wasn't going to back down to another man. This was his fight and it was past time to have settled it.

Bax circled around him, trying to get between Jule and the door, his feet still sliding from the oil. He made a rush at Jule, his knife by his hip ready to slice its way through Jule's short ribs.

The oil did him in. Bax slid just enough to be off balance. Jule sidestepped him, driving his own knife into the Neek's ribs just as Bax's blade glanced along Jule's shoulder. Jule twisted his knife and jerked it out, both to deepen the wound and to get his weapon back.

Bax was bleeding now, but he did not slow down. His eyes seemed glazed over—Bax was on straz! He couldn't feel the pain yet, but he would be slower. Jule would have to stay out of his reach, or disable him...or kill him.

He'd known it would come to this, one way or another.

Jule went for Bax's arm, aiming for the wrist, to make him drop his knife. He missed. Bax was too quick. Jule heard the other Neek behind him just in time to dodge, but the other Neek's blade slit his sleeve and his arm.

"Stop this!" thundered Aunt Silky.

Bax glanced at her. Jule grabbed his cutting board and threw it at Bax, clipping the side of his head and dazing him. The other Neek dropped his knife and backed up to the tunnel side back door, pressing the exit button.

When the door opened, the passage was full of children, Slime and his tribe. Each of them held some kind of weapon—

118

sticks with pieces of polybdalloy or rocks tied on, knives, and pieces of machinery. The Neek collapsed and covered his head.

Bax rushed towards Jule again. Jule dodged towards the back door, leading Bax towards the tribe. He held his blade low. He only had one more good swing left in that arm before it went numb. Bax held his knife high, to slash down when he reached Jule. Jule swung up and across, slicing Bax's neck, but Bax's swing caught Jule's arm and broke it. Jule dropped his knife, his fingers reacting to the pain. He jerked away from Bax, trying to keep an eye on the knife, ready to grab it with his other hand.

Blood poured from Bax's neck. He looked surprised. He couldn't breathe. He put his hand to his throat as if he were choking. His eyes crossed. He fell backwards into the tribe. A multitude of small hands took hold of Bax, dragging him into the tunnel.

Jule picked up his knife, looking around him for more assailants. Bax's friend, still cowering, began to crawl out the back door As if from a distance, he could hear people screaming, Aunt Silky yelling, all kinds of commotion. The door to the dining room was blocked by Aunt Silky and the man. Jule closed the back door.

"Now what?" he said to Aunt Silky. His adrenaline faded to let the pain take over his awareness.

Aunt Silky frowned, looking at the mess in the kitchen. "I'm going to have to pay another healer, and hire a cook, too. That's what!"

~€ΠD~

INITIATION

Charlotte Babb

Crila Maragorn flexed her left arm in balance with the right, making precision moves that caused the aiming light to describe intricate arcs on the walls of her pod. The prosthesis on what was left of her left arm was heavier than her right arm, and it was taking a lot of practice to keep herself in balance while she practiced the dance moves that would be required during the ritual. The dance was intricate and not designed for a person with feet instead of a ten-foot reptilian tail. The Sisters had modified her steps and even created a solo part for her. Everything they did was music and dance and art: always a performance. She wondered if they ever let their hair down—not that they had hair on their scaly skulls.

She was used to using the prosthesis at work, tending bar at the Starview Lounge. She could balance a tray of drinks or stir the most delicate tinimar to the satisfaction of the most fastidious customer, even better than she had done with her flesh arm. Her new arm was very responsive. She had even begun to feel some tactile sensations from its surface due to the bio-link nanobots that the L'Talton had used to attach it.

She stepped and turned on the ball of her foot, swinging her prosthesis around for momentum, making the rotations that would have been her wrist and hand mimicking a snake's head. It was a beautiful movement when Heart of the Core did it, but her arm only made light dance on the wall. Again she felt the difference, the exclusion. First she was Halsan/Human, now a non-Ophidian dedicant.

Crila had to give the Ophidia credit, though, and not just because they could crack her accounts, even her most well-hidden accounts. Every training session she had attended had brought her another attachment for the prosthesis. JayRand seemed to delight in developing them. She had projectile weapons, injectile weapons, power tools, even a cache of nanobots and an interface with built-in programs for drilling, comsys cracking and brute force bio-linking. What she did not have after eight sintinz of training was a mission or an understanding of exactly what the Circle of the Beryl wanted from her.

While the Ophidia had never been known to lie, they were not known for open and aboveboard negotiations either. But they had her caught in a net that supported her as much as it held her captive; she was in too deep not to play along. Malik Blayne had pumped her for information, and she had told him everything she knew, but it amounted to nothing.

Dripping with sweat, Crila wiped her face and went to her water pod to take a shower. She could shut down the prosthesis with a thought, closing it to keep the inner workings dry, although it seemed impervious to anything it had been exposed to so far.

She felt very alone. Malik just wanted her to spy on the Ophidia, as no one knew much about them. The Ophidia wanted her to spy on Malik and Core knew who else. She didn't like being between the Rock and Nothing, and that was where they both had her.

Crila was blindfolded as Heart led her down the spiral tube to the place of initiation. She could hear Heart's scales scraping softly against the smooth rock and JayRand's claws clicking. She extended her aura out as far as she dared, as they had taught her, but she felt no other presence until they entered a large open space, thick and musky with smells of smudging incense, anxious bodies, steam, sweat and probably some kind of psychotropic. A somasar played on her right, great streams of water flowing across its catch basins as well as tiny fountains and trickles, which made a most ethereal music. She had grown to like it during her training rehearsals, as it put her almost immediately into a light trance state, one that enhanced her awareness, but kept her emotional responses in check until she needed them. When Heart stopped, the trio was nearly in the center of the great pod, judging from echolocation. JayRand removed Crila's blindfold, brushing her face with her feathered fingertips.

A glance told Crila that she had about twenty fellow initiates, mostly Ophidia, but one other Human, a pair of gray-banded L'Taltons and a golden-skinned Velantran. All recruited, she supposed, as she had been, although none of them had her obvious mechanical enhancements. But why? How many spies did they need? Surely their secrets would be spread across the Galaxy with so many outsiders let in.

If the outsiders survived to tell the tale.

Heart and JayRand began to strip Crila of her jumpsuit. They had not told her what to expect except for the dance, but she did not resist. It would not be the first time she'd been naked in public, and there was no one who would likely be that interested anyway. Her sponsors passed their hands and feathers over her body, clearing her aura. They draped a veil of translucent fabric over her body, just as each of the other initiates was being veiled and prepared. The veil draped to her feet and just skimmed her fingertips. It would not get in the way of her dance steps. Crila's veil was a pale, shimmery green, while the others were in shades from lavender to deep blue: symbolic of the water of emotions, the flow of energy into the psychic centers. Crila had always been a quick study, even if she didn't see the point of what she was being taught. It was better to learn to parrot a bunch of nonsense than to have her prosthesis removed—abruptly, and without anesthetic.

Heart and JayRand faced Crila, staring into her eyes. She could not focus on both, so she gazed back at Heart. A whispery thought came into her mind. "When the time comes, reach for us with your mind. We will be here."

All the sponsors withdrew from the center circle. The music on the somasar changed as attendants changed the water flow and moved the basins. It became more tinkling, as monotonous drops fell at different intervals of time and timbre. A drop that fell onto a gong made a deep reverberation that started the pattern that Crila had learned for the dance. Without any signal, she began her steps. The dance would take her around the circle. She hoped the other initiates were doing the same. She hated to dance with folk who had two left feet, if only metaphorical, and who had no rhythm.

As the dancers moved in a serpentine spiral, priestesses gathered around the edges of the large cavern. The smell grew stronger with musk as the dancers undulated towards the center that opened down to allow a colored mist to escape. Crila first thought that they would be forced into its depths, but in moment, she saw a dais rise from the floor. It supported a pillow on which reclined the largest, most fearsome Ophid she had ever seen. She was glad she had practiced her dance until she did it in her sleep, or she would have stopped dead in her tracks, disrupting the whole pageant.

The Ophid was at least sixteen feet long, and probably eight feet in diameter at her hip. Her cloacal opening was not covered, as Heart's always was. It was opening and closing in rhythm with the music, its wet depths exposed. Her head was covered with something that moved, snakelike, an ancient medusa in the center of the spiral of dancers, each one dancing ever closer to her.

Crila knew that the last position of the dance left her neck and shoulders exposed as she lay back across her heels. She began to get an idea of what the Ophid Queen would do. She pulled her mind back into the dance, because it was too late to change her mind now; too much lava had flowed behind her to go back up that shaft.

She whirled and made the sight on her prosthesis describe infinity on the walls of the pod, intricate patterns that were reflected from glazed tiles on the walls and sparkled in the water in the somasar. One by one the dancers spiraled into the center and knelt, facing away from the Ophid Queen. The somasar had started to run faster, and the dancers breathed in time with the music, their chests heaving under their veils.

Too quickly it was Crila's turn to whirl in place and sink to her knees, first stretching her arms ahead of her and her rear end toward the queen, then raising up and leaning back, her back rigid and her arms balanced at her breasts. She leaned back so far that her head rested on the dais. She waited for the end of the dance, when the somasar become deathly quiet.

A hissing noise came from the priestesses who watched the ritual, partly an affirmation of the dance well done, but something more. The sound built into a force field as the priestesses began to clap their hands in a slow rhythm. Crila could see the Queen moving slowly from her pillow, but she could not see what she was doing. Someone screamed, and the hissing increased in volume. The somasar chimed in, keeping only a rhythm like a heartbeat in every pentatone, soft high drops and tinny middle drops and rattling deep drops as water dripped on metal basins.

In her turn as the tension increased, the Ophid slithered over Crila's head, her opening on one side, and her fanged mouth on the other. Crila had never smelled anything like that, but her humanoid side wanted to be somewhere else, anywhere else. The queen put her hands on Crila's shoulders, holding her down, and struck, sinking her fangs deep into Crila's neck, going right through the veil.

Crila's back arched further. This was poison, deadly and administered deeply. She had at most, a minz to react. She thought of JayRand and Heart, reaching out for their minds, for the answer to what to do. She fought the panic that raced through her, speeding the poison to her brain and heart. They had trained her for this, even though they didn't tell her why she must stay in this position and go deeply into trance. She called to them from her own heart, from her own body and mind, as she felt the venom burning through her veins. Her whole body burned like it was being covered with lava. But she breathed deeply and kept her mind steady.

"Yes," Heart breathed, "go deep into trance."

Crila could hear her words like a voice in her head. Crila made herself breathe deep in the rhythm of the music. She relaxed her back and her limbs, and she spoke mentally to the healer pair, "Help me."

She could hear Heart's voice speaking and JayRand's trills, but she saw a vision of red fire becoming a green liquid, refreshing and life-giving. Crila focused on the flowing green fluid that ran through glass tubing and from there into her veins, quenching the fire and healing her body where the venom had seared it. As each minz passed, she heard more voices in her mind, voices that encouraged her, like hands holding hers, stroking her as they would a female in laying.

Next to her she heard screaming in her ears, but she put that from her mind. She had no antidote to the venom, and would not know how to use it if she had it.

"You cannot help her," JayRand trilled. "She must do it herself, and if she cannot, we will put her out of her pain quickly."

"Listen to all of us. Use our energy," Heart said.

As Crila reached out to her healers, she began to see the whole community, the names and the energy signatures of each priestess, including the giant Queen, who in this energy space seemed only like an old Human woman, one who cried for her great-grandchildren who were dying in the circle. She saw the heart connection of Heart and JayRand, the bond that the L'Talton needed to survive provided by the Circle. She heard the mental cries of her sister initiates, and called out to them, in her mind or by her voice, she did not know.

"Use their energy. Change the poison! Change it in your mind!"

The Ophid beside her stopped writhing and lay limp below the dark purple veil she wore. One by one, the voices of the initiates joined the Circle, encouraging the others, or dropped out, never to be heard again. In an ower, all the initiates were Sisters of the Beryl.

Or they were dead.

Keening started in the Circle around the dais, lamenting their lost protégés, keening for the loss of life, wailing in release of grief and banishment of the spirits of the dead to the Beryl. The dais raised further, the columns supporting it set apart to reveal a chamber of lava below. Each dead initiate was taken by her supporters, her throat cut and her now blackened blood caught in a bowl. The body was wrapped carefully in the veil, like a child in the egg, and then dropped into the lake of fire below.

The blood in each bowl, four of them, was poured together into a large chalice. The sponsors of each initiate put a finger in the bowl, first touching the middle of their foreheads, then licking the blood with their forked tongues. The new sisters, raised to their feet and braced by their supporters, did the same, and then the chalice was passed among all the circle. What was left was drunk by the Queen herself, writhing against the poison she had herself injected into the initiates.

All the priestesses wailed and moaned, hissed and clapped themselves into a trance, sending energy through each other and to their Queen, to help her and them transmute the venom.

At the Queen's signal, all sound stopped, and the cavernous pod echoed with silence. No one moved, not a finger, not the tip of a tail nor the fluff of a feather.

"My daughters," came the words from the mind of the Queen, "my new daughters and those who have survived the ritual yet another time. We are here together. Let us remember our mother, she who leads us and guides us, never leaving us alone as we are never far from our sisters. We have returned our sisters to Her who could not stay with us this time. May they be blessed and return soon to us, strong in the ways of the Circle."

The Queen continued, after another minz of silence. "Let us now name our new sisters, so that we can share with them our knowledge and ways, while we share with them our meat."

Each team of sponsors led the new sister to the front of the dais where the Queen, Likes to Laugh, could inspect them as their veils were removed. The Queen spoke a name to each one aloud, in the hissing speech of the Ophidia, but each sister heard it in her own head.

Crila's new name was Gives More Than Was Taken. She inclined her head in acknowledgement.

Queen Laugh did laugh, her fangs retracted and her tongue wriggling like a worm. "Your spirit is very strong, Gives More. No one has ever offered energy to someone else while she herself was not out of danger. We are honored to have you as our sister."

"I too am honored, Great Grandmother." Crila said, in her mother's native Halsan tongue, using the honorific for the eldest female in the tribe. "May I have permission to list myself in your lineage under these two who have brought me here?"

"Yes. Now go eat, and prepare yourself for your first assignment. There is much to be done, and you will be our ears and eyes in places we cannot go unnoticed."

"As you wish," Crila said.

She knew the Queen's heart, as she did Heart's and JayRand's. She would never be alone again, and while she would never repay them what they had given her, she would never be obligated to another again.

~END~

ERR ONLY ON THE SIDE OF AIR

Richard C. Meehan, Jr.

The sales meeting with that damnably stuffed shirt Eversyn—*Captain* Eversyn to you!—had not gone well. Charlie swirled the russet fluid around his glass, rum neat as they used to say, as he contemplated his failure to get the all important envirosuit contract extension. It was quite the appropriate drink for his current mood, a favorite beverage of Ancient Earth seafaring pirates. After all, everyone on this stone heap thought he was one. Pirate, that is. Sometimes he even believed it himself. Well, that's what he got for selling envirosuits. Everybody needed one; nobody wanted to pay for it; least of all, *Captain* Carle Eversyn of the Consolidated Guard! Malpairiso Sector was in deep bov-feek with that one protecting their interests. How could he possibly *not* renew a 'virosuit contract when more than half his troops required them? Nykee had to be horning in on his business. They just had to be—

"What's up, Charlie?" Crila, the one-handed barmaid at Dhamu's Place, plopped her other hand, the prosthetic one, on the simwood bar as if to demand an answer. At least she was using her fake hand and not one of her assorted interchangeable sharp instruments.

Charlie Manus simply bleared at the luscious half-breed over the rim of his glass. He didn't really want to talk to anyone just now, not after his too recent and quite substantial loss. Of course, formidable lilac-skinned breasts heaving out of a tight halter required a few seconds of attention before sinking a gaze back into the depths of any drink.

"Okay Manus—so you don't want to talk. But if you think you're gonna swish that drink around all night taking up space, you've got another thing coming. Bottoms up and have another, or move on!" A small group of mushroom-like Fwazek chattered loudly over the clink of glasses and other conversing patrons. "I'll be there in a sec, squash-heads!"

"Leave me alone, Cutie Pie," slurred Charlie. "I'm not in the mood."

"DHAMUUUU!"

The blocky Modajai lumbered over. "Is Manus bothering you again, Crila?"

A weighty fist slammed down next to the barmaid's forearm prosthesis. Charlie could have sworn Crila's breasts jiggled from the impact. He tried to lock eyes with the huge Modajai, but had to settle on the rippling pectorals instead.

Dhamu rumbled, "Crila's busy, Manus. Get another drink or get out. I got to pay for that new 'virosuit you sold me, and she ain't your type no way."

"How do you know what my type is, Dhamu?" bristled Charlie. "Lavender happens to be one of my favorite colors."

In a whoosh of movement, Crila replaced her fake hand with what appeared to be a sickle with a razor edge. Charlie briefly wondered what she would actually use that accoutrement for when he suddenly found the tip poking under his chin. "R-R-Rum—NEAT!" he yelped. The pressure left as quickly as the fuzziness in his head.

"That's better, my Human *friend*." The barkeep clumped on to handle the yammering Fwazeks next.

Crila pushed a two-finger glass at Charlie with her now-replaced false hand. "Are you gonna tell me what's eating you, or do I have to call Dhamu back again?" Her compact athletic body pressed against the bar, or rather, her mammalian origins.

With a sigh, Charlie gave in. "It's that *Captain* Eversyn. He wouldn't renew his detachment's suit contract today. In fact, I couldn't get him to take his stiff neck out of his file drawers. He kept talking about overcharges and quality issues. Crila, you've known me for years—have I ever cheated anyone?"

"Is that a loaded question?" Crila quirked her ample lips into a sidelong grin. After a moment, she must have realized Charlie was serious. "It's not a matter of cheating, Charlie. Do you really want to know what people think? Mostly, they're jealous. The way you've got an omnipass, for instance. Nobody gets one of those unless they're either extremely well connected, work for the Connies, or the Boss Families. You waltz in a few years back as the only envirosuit peddler we've ever had, and plop, that old Connie Captain Jolly, Eversyn's predecessor, up and crams one right on your lapel! Word gets around about stuff like that, Charlie. People get edgy."

"But I'm not a cheat, Crila!" Charlie was many things, he admitted that, but in his dealings, he was clean. Otherwise, he wouldn't be the best in the business. "Do you have any idea what Protectaire will do to me when I tell them I've lost the contract for all those Connie 'virosuits?"

Crila sighed. "I'm gonna give it to you between the eyes, Manus. Take me, for instance. I've never been to LevTwo in my whole life. All those fancy living quarters, swanky restaurants, glittering rich folks like Rudof Dyll...people hate you, Charlie. They hate you because you have what they will never have—freedom."

She had his attention, at least the portion that wasn't sinking back into inebriation after the brief adrenalin boost from the sickle deal. Freedom...freedom from what? People were jealous of *him* because he could move about Port Nowhere taking his life in his hands whenever he chose? Jealous over an omnipass that did nothing to guarantee his safety as an outworlder in this mini-Hell? These yokels could all go tell it to the Rock! If they only knew how his company forced him to call on this airless damn asteroid for political reasons and strategic corporate growth...the fact that the Rock was the jump point to the Andromeda Galaxy...how Protectaire cared nothing for lives, only profits...they'd shove him out the nearest airlock. Feeling lightheaded and more than a bit reckless, he asked, "You've never been to LevTwo, Crila?"

Crila fixed him with her radiant violet eyes. "I just said I hadn't, Manus. Don't rub it in, okay?" He skin deepened a shade toward purple in annoyance.

Insight pounded around Charlie's sloshing skull. "How'd you like to go...with me...for lunch tomorrow at the Starview?"

The Human/Halsan woman looked stunned.

~€ND~

H€R€ B€ DRAG⊙NS

Elaine Corvidae

The second-born of her litter smelled death in the tunnel.

She paused, ears pricked forward, and listened intently. From far away, she heard the drip of water as moisture collected on the rocks and ran down in silver beads. From closer by came faint whimpers, as of some hurt thing. Other than that, all was silent.

The thin threads of phosphorescence clinging to the rock were all the light her sharp eyes needed to pick out the details of the tunnel. She lowered her head to the ground, scenting and sighting for any sign of danger. But there was nothing, save for the whimpering and the smell of death.

The source of both was not far. Just around the next bend, the dead thing lay, surrounded by a pool of congealed blood. It was not far gone in rot, so the second-born of her litter moved cautiously, in case whatever had killed it lingered. Beside the dead thing huddled something alive, and it was from this that the whimpering came. Strange, that whatever had killed the dead thing had not eaten it. Strange, too, that it had left something alive.

She moved closer, investigating the live one with her nose. It was in need of cleaning, and beneath the stink of waste she detected the sour smell of hunger. It was small and bare-skinned, with hair only on the top of its head. Large-eyed and

132

short-muzzled—a young thing, she decided. Not only prey, but the easiest prey of all.

And yet...

For a long time, she wavered above it, oddly torn. Then, with a sudden, fluid move, she scooped it up in her arms and raced away, leaving the dead thing behind.

Tau hauled himself up over the uneven rock that lined the inside of the airshaft and peered out through the grate. Sporadic light flickered in his eyes, strobing wildly as a transport rumbled between him and the bright-whites. The air stank of oil and metal, and if he'd had his eyes closed he would have known he was on LevFour just by smelling it. Refineries here, or so he'd heard. Up-levs used their machines to chew up the Rock, looking for Core knew what, then brought it here to melt and shape.

The rock rumbled under his hands as another slag-filled transport grated past, and he shivered, instincts insisting that any shaking at all meant a cave-in. *Maybe I ought to just head out?* But hells, he'd checked Dhamu's already, and Mal wasn't there, which meant no free meal for Tau. There were easy pickings here on LevFour, though, and he couldn't leave just because he didn't like the place, not if he wanted to have more in his belly than air.

He popped the grate, then paused, waiting for a passing slag-hauler to cover his movement. No need to let the Connies know just where he was going in and out from, after all. He touched his necklace, the only thing he had left of his tribe, for luck, because he always did that when he had to deal with other Humans. His other talisman, the one wrapped up in heavy cloth and stuffed down his coverall in just about the last place cops tended to want to look...that one he left alone. For the day when he needed help real bad, he figured.

The hauler came by, and he was out and had the grate back in place in a blink. Hands in his pockets, he walked off, all innocence, nothing to see here. No one was nearby to watch, anyway; the haulers and the transports could look after themselves. Give you a nasty shock if you tried to touch one.

He'd seen it happen once—some toothless pup didn't believe the stories and tried to jump up on one, maybe to steal some of the stuff in the back, or take the wiring, or to just wreck it for all Tau knew. It'd fried him good, then run over him when his body fell jerking in front of its treads.

Yeah, the machines could take care of themselves, but even so nobody in charge on the upper levs ever quite believed it. So there were always some kind of guards hanging around, keeping an eye on things and bored as bov-feek. These days that meant Connies, but it didn't really matter. They were all the same, far as Tau was concerned.

A hiss of annoyance escaped him as he came up on the guard station. A couple of pups had already beaten him there and were busy entertaining the two Connies. Haulers whipped back and forth, and as they approached, the Connies would throw something—usually food, but on real good days it might even be credz—in front of the oncoming machines. The kids ran out into the path of the haulers, snatched up whatever had been thrown, and ran back the other way, ideally before they got flattened.

Or ideally for the pups, anyway; Tau figured the guards always kind of hoped somebody would get run over, because otherwise where was the fun?

As he came up, though, he could see these pups had no sense of finesse at all. Just ran out and grabbed the stuff and raced back, no showmanship, nothing to keep the Connies interested. Back in the day, when he'd had a tribe, a couple of them would distract the guards with their antics while somebody else came up behind them and cleaned out their pockets.

Well, there ain't no tribe now. Ain't nobody but me, and I can't be in two places at once.

So he waited until one of the guards tossed something, then shoved the pup who was about to go after it out of the way. Tau ran out into the path of the hauler—then did a handstand. The prize was part of a sandwich roll, so he scooped it off the floor real quick with his tongue while he tried to keep an eye on the approaching hauler. It roared down on him, fast and indifferent, like some kind of mold-brained grass-eater, and he stayed balanced on his hands, pushing it....

At the absolute last minz, he sprang out of the way. The air off the passing hauler blew his stringy brown hair into his face, and he could feel the heat of the metal through the fraction of space that separated them. The Connies roared with laughter, and one of them even clapped, something that almost never happened. Grinning broadly, Tau took a bow. They'd want him to do more—they'd throw something a lot better next time—

A heavy hand clamped down on his shoulder, spinning him roughly around. Startled, he found himself staring up into a face that looked like it'd had a few close encounters with the front of a hauler itself.

"You, boy," said the man, leaning in so that Tau could smell the booze on his breath. "You're Tau the Silent. And you're gonna help us out."

The second-born of her litter laid the tiny, squalling thing on the mossy nest in the center of the den. The others had come, drawn by the sounds and the unfamiliar scent. The third-born drew closer, and pursed his mouth into an expression of happiness.

"You have brought back food," he said.

She snarled and struck at him with her front claws, so that he backed away. The abdomen-shredding claw on one back foot tapped out a warning against the stone.

"This is not food," she growled, and showed him all her teeth.

Their mother moved closer, smelling the creature. "Why have you brought it, then?"

The second-born had no answer. She wavered, uncertain in the urges that gripped her. "It's a baby," she said at last.

It was not a good answer. Young things were weak, stupid, or both. There was no reason for her not to have eaten it already.

But her mother seemed to understand. She had been brought to this place long ago, already full of pups, and had escaped into the dark. But the moonlit world of her birth haunted her stories and sang yet in the blood of her children.

"You have no mate," she said. "No young. But your heart desires these things. You wish to make this youngling into your own pup."

"It will die," said the first-born. "Better to eat it now."

"No." The second-born of her litter moved so that the youngling was beneath her belly. "It will not die. I will not allow it."

"If you wish," said their mother, and that settled it. She ruled their pack, and her word was their law.

Satisfied, the second-born lay down beside her new pup and began to clean it with her tongue.

"Is it a life-bearer?" asked third-born.

She snuffled at it; it made an odd sound and flailed its limbs wildly.

"I don't think so," she said uncertainly, but who could tell for certain with such a strange creature? But her guess pleased third-born, who was not a life-bearer either, and he began to clean it as well.

"You got the wrong guy," Tau said, and gave them a smile that showed all his teeth.

"Flas? What's going on?" one of the Connies called.

The goon with the combustible breath answered without looking away from Tau. "Nothing! Me and Klon are just having some fun on our time off, that's all."

This didn't sound too good to Tau, who didn't want to know what an off-duty Connie's idea of fun might be. "You're looking for Tau, right? I just seen him down on LevFive—"

Flas smacked him hard enough to make his ears ring. "Shut up."

Another hand closed on the nape of Tau's neck and began dragging him along. "Let's take this somewhere more private," said the woman who was doing the dragging. Klon, probably.

"I'm telling you, you got the wrong—"

This time he got a good kick along with the slap, so he shut up fast. They dragged him stumbling away from the main area and down an unfinished side tunnel. His face met a wall of freshly-broken rock, and the sharp edges cut his hands as he tried to keep from falling.

"We know who you are," Klon said. She was just as ugly as her partner, and Tau considered telling her so, but she was also twice as muscle-bound, so he thought better of it. "We heard about you, boy. They say you know the Rock like nobody else."

And that was the problem with having a rep, he figured. Sometimes it got you in places you wanted to be, and sometimes it got you places that you didn't, and there was no knowing which beforehand. So he grinned again, flashing his teeth. "Oh, so you need a guide? Why didn't you just say so, Mastriz, Mastre? Reasonable rates, no bone breaks, that's my motto—"

"You're doing this for free, void," said Flas. "And any funny stuff, and you'll be doing it dead."

Tau thought about pointing out that he couldn't do much of anything dead, but they didn't seem open to that kind of deep thought. "And this place I'm taking you? Want to tell me where it is?"

Klon smiled. "Why, you're taking us to the pirate treasure, boy."

First-born was wrong; the child did not die. Second-born regurgitated food for him each time she returned from the kill, and fed it piece by piece into her new son's mouth. He grew stronger, and in time began to move about on all fours, climbing over the backs of the adults, grabbing their ears, and giving them no peace. Soon enough, he ran about on two legs, but he was descended from some loose-jointed climbing kind and could not run as fast as they.

In other ways as well he was disabled, and at first it made her sad. He could not smell all that they could smell, although his eyesight was very sharp indeed. And though he learned to speak easily enough, his mouth was not formed as theirs, and he could not say the words clearly. Even so, they were used to him, and understood, and she did not think that he ever realized that deficiency.

Most distressing of all, though, was that his ears were nothing but stationary flaps to either side of his head. This lack made it hard to tell his moods and frustrated them all no end. But ultimately it was with this that her son first showed his cleverness, for he began to use one hand, crooking two fingers in an imitation of ears. He held them forward, or back, or at half-mast, and so compensated for his handicap. So proud of him was she that she hunted his favorite prey and regurgitated it all for him.

"The what?" Tau asked, figuring he must have misunderstood.

Klon hit him this time, and did it a lot harder than her partner. The taste of blood filled his mouth, and he spat weakly.

"The pirate treasure, void," she snapped.

His head was starting to ache pretty good by now, which maybe was why he made the mistake of trying to reason with them. "If I knew where any pirate treasure was, I wouldn't be doing handstands in front of a toothless hauler for food, would I?"

"Don't play dumb, bov-brain. You can't outsmart us." Flas stabbed a finger in Tau's general direction, but he was too drunk to get real accurate with it. "We heard all about how old Captain Grusel found him an alien with a skeleton made of solid gold, and how he hid the skull someplace deep inside Port Nowhere."

Tau groaned inwardly. That story'd had hair on it when the Rock was young. He thought about telling them that it was just a dumb legend, the kind of thing only pups and mold-brains believed, but decided that they'd probably just pound on his face some more if he tried.

"Heyo, you got me!" he said, and gave them another smile full of teeth. "I know where it is all right. I was just waiting for the right time, cause it's too big for me to get out alone."

"Bad luck for you," Klon said with an air of satisfaction. "Now get moving. We're in a hurry to get rich."

Second-born ran through the tunnels, her strong legs digging claw into rock with every stride. Ahead of her was the prey, the stink of its fear drawing her after it. It fled, surprisingly nimble for its size, but she could hear its breath rasping as its strength began to give out. Even if it had not tired, the end was not far off now.

The prey stumbled just as it reached the ambush. Her siblings and mother sprang from the shadows to either side, soundless and quick. Third-born came at it with legs extended, and the killing claws on his feet tore into its belly. It screamed its death-cry as innards spilled out, but first-born silenced it with a crushing bite to the throat. It twitched once or twice, then went still.

"We are strong together," said their mother, as was tradition, before she began to tear away the prey's coverings.

Second-born went to the nearby crevice where she had put her son before the hunt began. It had taken him a long time to learn the most important of rules: to stay where she put him, still and silent as the stone itself, until she returned. But now he did it correctly every time, and she was proud of him.

Although too young to join the hunt, he was big enough now to share in the kill directly. He clambered out when she called him, all awkward limbs and ragged topknot of hair, and they made a place for him at the kill.

"I love you," she said, and licked some of the prey's blood from his face.

Tau's mind raced as he led the Connies to the drop that would take them to LevSev. If he could just get them into the tunnels, maybe he could shake them. Problem was, they'd had just enough brains to bring lights with them, which would make it harder to slip away into the dark unless he was really quick. And of course, if he was going to be able to slip away at all, he'd have to make them trust him enough to relax, which didn't seem too likely.

As soon as they got on the drop—which Tau almost never rode, at least not on the inside—Klon shoved him against the back wall.

"Check him for weapons," she said.

Flas pulled out a Connie scanner, and Tau wondered if he was supposed to be using it off duty. The knife hidden in Tau's boot lit it up, of course, so they yanked that out and took it.

"That's all the metal on him," said Flas. "'Cept for that dumb piece of jewelry. Wonder if we could sell it?"

Tau felt his heart beating hard, and it was all he could do not to put his hand over the necklace. But Klon just snorted. "Worthless. Leave it where it belongs—with the rest of the trash."

Kill thief, Tau thought, but kept the insult locked behind his teeth.

But their check had given him an idea. When the drop bumped to a halt at LevSev, they got off, and he took a quick look around. They were a good run away from the busier places like Dhamu's, but for a moment he still clung to hope that they might run into Mal by chance. But there was no sight of anyone except for a pair of L'Taltons going off in the other direction.

"All right, vat scum, get moving," Flas growled. Or tried to—Humans didn't growl too well, so far as Tau was concerned.

"Hold up—I gotta piss," he said.

"Well, hurry it up, then, or we'll cut it off for you."

He went to the nearest convenient wall so that his back was to them, and unfastened his coverall. Hoping that they weren't paying too much attention, he slid his hand inside and found the thin string around his waist and the heavy cloth bag that hung from it. Going on touch, he slid out one of the two sickle-shapes inside and hid it in his sleeve.

Guess I need that luck now.

"Hurry it up!" Klon barked, and he quickly refastened.

"Okay, okay! This way," he said, and started walking.

Second-born's son grew taller and taller, until he was all long, gangly legs and arms. Soon, she thought, he would be able to hunt with them. He would never be as fast as they, but she thought that he might hide in a side-tunnel or alcove while they drove the prey towards him. If he stepped out ahead of it, it would at least pause in surprise, while the rest of them came up on it like dark wind.

But that was still in the future, for he was yet young. And during the sleep-times, when they all lay in a warm heap, and her son nuzzled sleepily against her, she silently wished that he might remain a pup forever.

<^>

"We've been walking for owerz in these damned tunnels," Flas groused.

The light from the Connies' lanterns showed a pair of faces flushed and sweating from exertion. Although they hadn't been in the Depths for long by Tau's estimate, their broad faces were already getting grimy, and their boots were caked in muck.

They were taking a rest break beside one of the many shrines that showed up at the junctures of some of the more heavily-used tunnels. Somebody had carved out a niche in the wall and set a crude stone figure inside of it. Offerings filled the little niche: bits of wire twisted into jewelry, the sole from a boot, pretty rocks, even an L'Talton feather. The Lady of the Stone was supposed to prevent cave-ins, bad air, soft bone, and lung rot, although Tau had never seen the slightest bit of evidence that she did any of it.

He wondered if either of the tribes who routinely fought over this bit of corridor was watching them from hiding now. He didn't doubt they knew he and the Connies were here—if nothing else, the Connies had been making enough noise to wake the Core. But laying low when there was trouble around was something they understood—he did, too, and didn't blame them for it.

"Almost there," he said encouragingly. And then, just for show: "So, since I'm taking you to the treasure and all, how about splitting it with me, huh? Just a little cut?"

"Sure," Klon said, and then laughed at her joke. Flas joined her, and they passed a flask that smelled like it was full of whiskey back and forth.

Kill thieves, he thought again. *Carrion eaters.* And wondered if they had ever meant to leave him alive, even if there had been a treasure to lead them to.

When they were done drinking, Klon made a menacing gesture in his direction. "Come on, boy, we don't have all cyk!" As if they hadn't been the ones sitting on their asses, drowning whatever brain cells they had left.

He led them on. As he had promised, the destination he had in mind wasn't much farther. It was a cramped little tunnel well off any of the main branches, and the walls leading to it were covered in ghost marks. Tau kept waiting for them to call him on that, but they didn't, and he realized that they didn't even know what the marks meant.

At last, he stopped, and pointed towards a tunnel that split off from the one they were in. It was low enough that an adult Human would have to go inside bent over, and the walls were festooned with fungi of multiple species.

"There it is," he said, and showed them his teeth. "Just waiting for you."

Death came in the midst of their sleep-time, when they were least prepared.

The scrape of a foot on rock woke second-born, and she lifted her head sharply. The scent of one of the many things they hunted came to her, but this time it was mixed with the smell of eagerness rather than fear. She came instantly to her feet, and the rest of the family woke as well.

"Hide," she told her son, and he ran to the back of their cave and wedged himself in behind a rock.

First-born took a wary step towards the cave opening, her head bobbing up and down as she tried to catch the scent. The rest moved in behind her, prepared to defend themselves against prey suddenly become bold.

Light exploded in the dark cavern, brighter than any second-born had ever seen. Fire sizzled over her skin, and she heard herself scream. First-born fell to the ground, her body twitching even as blood poured out of the gaping hole in her chest. Third-born shrieked, clawing at his eyes.

Only their mother attacked, perhaps because she had known what it was to be hunted long ago, before she had been brought here. She leapt towards an unseen target, her great talons ripping down like scythes. But then the light came again, and she collapsed as well. A moment later, third-born fell beside her.

The creatures who had killed her family advanced into the cave. Despite her pain and her wrenching grief, second-born knew that she had to protect her son. Coiling the powerful muscles of her legs beneath her, she launched herself at her enemies, letting out a throaty roar that shook the stone above them.

And then the light came again.

<^>

"There?" asked Flas suspiciously, hunkering down and peering into the low tunnel.

Tau nodded. "Yah. See how well-hidden it is? Nobody'd think to look in a little place like that, would they? But it isn't little—just at first, anyway. Then it opens up real big, and the golden skull's in there. Sitting on an altar, kind of."

He'd figured out a long time ago that the trick to lying was giving just enough detail to make it sound like you knew what you were talking about. Both Connies nodded eagerly at his fantasy, and he knew he had them. "But, uh, you better let me go in first."

They'd probably planned on sending him in first themselves, but having him *ask* for it aroused suspicion even in their booze-soaked brains.

"Why?" Klon demanded.

"Well, uh…you just better," he said, and did his best to look vaguely guilty.

"It's a trick," Flas muttered, peering at him through watery eyes. "I'm going in first."

"But—"

"Shut up!" Flas cuffed him upside the head. Tau put on a sulky expression and jammed his fists in his pockets, curling his fingers around the sickle-shape inside the left one.

Flas dropped down on his hands and knees and started crawling into the low tunnel. "Damn, it stinks in here! Must be all these creepy things." He reached out and brushed one of the fungi, as if clearing it out of his way.

The round fungus popped with a soft, sighing sound, releasing a cloud of black spores directly into Flas's face.

The Connie made a disgusted noise and started to draw back—then stiffened. A horrible, choking sound came from him, and his body suddenly convulsed. Flailing limbs hit more of the fungi, triggering the release of even more spores, and within seconds a creeping black cloud was drifting from the tunnel opening.

Klon just stared at her convulsing partner for a moment, her mouth hanging open. Then, with ugly realization dawning on her equally-ugly face, she spun towards Tau.

"You little—!"

He lunged towards her, slashing down as hard as he could with his mother's killing claw. It tore through Klon's cheek, laying open the flesh to the bone. A combination of shock and pain made her jump back—and into the growing cloud of spores.

Tau didn't wait to see what happened. He turned and ran back the way he'd come as fast as he could, holding his breath just in case a stray spore had found him. But once he'd turned a few corners, he stumbled to a halt, lungs heaving.

Behind him, all was silent, and he guessed that Klon had succumbed as well. By now, the puffer spores would be germinating in the warm, wet environment of the Connies' sinuses. Within a few owerz, they would have sent threads up into whatever brains they had. If condition were right, the Connies might even briefly regain motor control, although they'd be nothing more than shambling zombies for the next few weeks, until the fungal threads had finished digesting them slowly from within.

Thought they were predators. But they weren't smart enough to remember that everybody's prey for somebody—something—else.

There was blood on his mother's talon, so he carefully cleaned it off with the corner of his jacket. When he was done, he pressed it gently to his face, breathing deeply in a futile attempt to catch any last, lingering molecules of her scent.

But there was no smell on it but his own, so he regretfully replaced it in its pouch with the other one.

The child huddled in the darkness for a long, long time, waiting for his mother's signal to come. But he had seen her fall, and so his wait was one of absolute terror, filled with the ultimate fear of any young thing, that its parent will never wake up. Eventually, when his thirst had grown too great for him to be still any longer, he snuck out of his hiding spot and into the cave.

His family lay stiff and cold, and the stench of blood and rot filled the air. He did not understand why they were dead, or why those that had killed them had not fed. Crawling to his mother's side, he lay down by her and began to cry.

Time passed, how much he did not know. But at last a light came into the darkness. A child much like him hunkered in the cave opening, looking wonderingly at the carnage. When it saw him, it came closer and spoke. But its words meant nothing to him, nor did his to it.

It took him by the arm and pulled, and he knew it wanted him to leave. But he screamed and clung desperately to his mother's body, begging her to wake up.

Because he knew, deep in his heart, that if he left with the other child then he would never see her again.

The other spoke in its incomprehensible language again. Eventually, it seemed to realize that he didn't understand, because it sighed and took something from its pocket. The thing looked like his family's killing claws, but it was straight instead of curved. The stranger took its not-claw and pressed it against his mother's toe, just below the great talon, and he saw the flesh part.

Then he understood. Growling and showing his teeth, he snatched the not-claw from the stranger. Once the stranger had backed away a little, he bent over and gently, gently removed first one talon, then the other. Clutching them both to his chest, he stood up and went to the stranger.

Although it could not speak to him, it patted him gently on the arm with a clawless hand, before finally leading him away.

~€ND~

(ATCH OF THE DAY

Jim Johnson

Benita Frohmyn moved with a blend of confidence and caution through the rough stone passageways on the lower fringes of LevOne. Dressed in the ragged clothing and tattered cloak of a pilgrim-turned-straz head, she passed anonymously among the addicts and cutthroats whose little hell this was.

At a bend in the tunnel, Benita slowed her pace and listened. A moment later, several inebriated Fwazeks staggered into view, jabbering in their nonsensical sounding native tongue. She watched the short, disk-headed aliens as they passed her by, seemingly oblivious to her presence. When they had gone, Benita resumed her journey and not long after reached her destination.

Grey-green smoke issued from the rock-hewn entrance; the only advertisement Grajink needed to attract his clientele.

Grajink was no Banastre Caravello, and the place he ran was no Starview Lounge. Grajink's business, however, was almost certainly the more profitable of the two.

Straz dens almost always were.

Before entering the den, Benita stuffed a pair of nasal filters up her nose. It took a moment to get them positioned just right. She closed her eyes, wincing ever so slightly as she felt the nano-fibers expand throughout her sinus cavity, weaving their protective barrier.

Drawing the smelly hood of her commandeered cloak over her head, she entered the warren. Little to no effort had gone into the straz den's configuration. In fact, other than the dozens of darkened alcove-like booths etched from the porous, black stone walls, everything appeared to be as nature had crafted it: a maze of lava-born tunnels running and winding in every direction.

Straz heads in various degrees of burnout occupied every available nook. The more conscious among them occasionally took note of Benita's passing, but she wondered if her presence actually registered in their frazzled minds.

In spite of her filters, Benita could not entirely escape the invasive reek of straz. Thick tendrils of straz smoke twisted in the half-light. The narcotic haze made her skin itch, but she refused to oblige it by scratching. She continued deeper into the den.

Finally, tired of looking for an unoccupied booth, Benita stepped up to the nearest one and drew back the shabby, firebug-eaten curtain. A gray-green cloud of smoke billowed out. When it cleared sufficiently, Benita peered into the booth.

"Hey!" snapped one of its occupants, a Bansnict.

"Shut up and move out," Benita ordered in her most authoritative tone.

"That's good advice, Sape," the Bansnict growled. "Follow it yourself."

"That wasn't advice, shorty. That was an order." Benita reached into the gloom and seized a fistful of the alien's chest hair and started to yank him from his seat. She was stopped when something too large to be the Bansnict's hand locked onto her wrist. She gritted her teeth as the grip tightened.

"Don't I know you...*Human*?" The voice, though unfamiliar, was deep and resonant. *A Vamir?*

As if in answer to her question, she felt herself drawn into the booth. Halfway over the small tabletop, a face appeared before her, materializing from the smoke and darkness like some phantom.

Definitely Vamir, she realized, but not just any of that four-armed, felinoid species. She recognized the unmistakable scar tissue that covered half the Vamir's face, including the empty socket of its right eye.

"Hello, Walgraf," Benita offered. "You seem to have healed up rather nicely."

Hatred like the fires of the Core itself burned in Walgraf's remaining eye. The Vamir only hissed maliciously, while his Bansnict associate snickered with glee.

"You know this Sape, Wal?"

Without releasing Benita from his grasp, Walgraf turned his eye toward his friend. "This Sape wench tried to kill, Grrr-Vreng. Tried, and failed," he said, looking back to Benita.

"If I had meant to kill you, Walgraf, you'd be dead. Just like the rest of your gang. You were in the wrong place at the wrong time. You know that as well as I do, so get over it and consider yourself lucky to have come away with only a cosmetic injury."

With a roar, Walgraf shoved Benita backwards, out into the passageway. As she slammed against the unforgiving wall, she saw the booth's curtains part as the Vamir, in a burst of straz smoke, launched himself at her. From the booth, Grrr-Vreng's snickering became a cackle.

The gap between them was small, and Walgraf was fast. Benita was faster. The passageway and the booth erupted in a flash of white light. Walgraf yowled in agony as he crashed to the floor at Benita's feet.

The smell of singed hair actually overpowered the stench of straz. With one foot, Benita nudged the huge Vamir onto his side. He groaned, but it was clear to Benita that he was unconscious. The stun blast she'd hit him with had burned off the hair of Walgraf's face and upper chest. She reset her DM-8 to kill and holstered it.

The stirring of the booth's scorched curtain drew Benita's attention just in time to see Grrr-Vreng as he attempted to sneak away. "Where do you think you're going, *snict*?" But the Bansnict didn't stop, and Benita let him go. Stepping over Walgraf, Benita settled into the booth and waited. It didn't take long.

Scarcely two minz later the sooty green smoke choking the passageway eddied aside as a pair of avian figures—their

feather crested heads bobbing in unison as they moved—
approached the booth. Benita settled back into the unforgiving
contours of the rock-carved seat as the two L'Taltons settled in
opposite her.

Benita made a show of checking the time before turning her
full attention to the new arrivals. "You're getting slower in
your old age, Grajink."

The male L'Talton clucked once and blinked his shiny
black eyes. "Within the contexts of our species, Commander,
I'm only half your age."

Benita smiled indifferently.

Grajink looked past his mate, Rijink, to where Walgraf lay
in the passage, still unconscious.

"Speaking of age, Commander, one would think that you
would have developed a better set of social skills by now."

Benita shrugged. "On top of needing a seat, I also needed to
get your attention. Besides, Walgraf and I are old friends. He
understands."

With her impatience evinced by a ruffling of her breast
feathers, Rijink cut to the chase. "Why are you here,
Commander Frohmyn?"

Benita leaned forward, her eyes laced with menace. In a
voice more hiss than whisper she said, "Better wise up
fast...both of you. If I wanted my name and occupation
broadcast through this bov-pile you run, I wouldn't be dressed
in these Core-accursed rags. The next time either of you
addresses me by name or rank, I'll blast you both to atoms."
She finished her warning by drawing back her cloak to reveal
the DM-8 hidden therein.

Seemingly unflustered, Grajink held up his talon-tipped
wing-arms. "Seeing as I am not yet being feasted on by vermin,
this must be a social visit." He cocked his head, focusing his
left eye squarely on Benita. "Might I assume that you are here
to finally partake of the house specialty?"

"You know Sapes," squawked Rijink, "they'd rather
destroy things than build them. Maybe she's here to kill
someone."

Grajink shook his head. "She hasn't killed either of us...yet,
my love."

"The both of you, shut up already," Benita said at last. "I'm here for information."

Grajink's crest collapsed against his skull as if a Modajai had slapped it down. His beady eyes narrowed to wary slits and when he spoke, his voice was a low warble. "Information can be a dangerous commodity," he said. "Deadly in the extreme and expensive...very, very expensive, at the very least."

Benita noticed the fleshy corners of Rijink's blunt beak twitch greedily with anticipation. She ignored her and said, "Well, I'm not packing any extra credz, and as Walgraf is breathing, you can see that I'm not in a particularly murderous mood today."

Rijink shook her head. "You seem to have misunderstood my husband."

Before Benita could reply, Grajink interjected. "No, she hasn't."

Rijink blinked several times in obvious confusion. "But she just said..."

"What our Human friend said and what she meant are two different things, my love."

Benita decided enough time had been wasted. She leaned across the table and, to Rijink, said, "Now sit there and keep your beak shut."

Rijink chittered angrily from the back of her gullet until Grajink placed a restraining hand on hers, at which point she wisely settled down.

"As I've already said," Grajink began, "information can be a dangerous and costly thing. And not just to receive, but also to supply. So, if you aren't willing to kill or pay to get it, what incentive do I have to risk my tail feathers to provide you with any? That is, assuming I even possess it in the first place."

Benita leaned back in her seat, confident. "For the record, Grajink, I never said I wouldn't kill for what I wanted." She savored the subtle flurry of uneasy blinks that passed between the L'Taltons. "There's an ancient adage, Grajink, that says 'you scratch my back and I'll scratch yours.'"

Forgetting herself, Rijink looked at Benita then Grajink. "What the Core is that supposed to mean? Is that some sort of Sape thing? I can't believe..."

Rijink's beak snapped shut in mid sentence as Benita slid the DM-8 partially from its shoulder holster. "I'm talking about obstacles," Benita said. "As an officer in the Consolidated Guard, I have them. And you, Grajink, as a straz pusher, have them."

"What is she trying to get at?" Rijink ventured cautiously.

Without looking to his mate, Grajink said, "Rivals. She's talking about rivals, Riji. In her case, I suspect she means Captain Eversyn."

Benita nodded.

Grajink continued. "Now be quiet, Riji. Go on...Benn. I'm listening."

With a last warning look at Rijink, Benita shoved the DM-8 back into the holster. "Give me the name of your chief competitor's supplier and the location of his or her base of operation, and I'll see to it their business gets crippled."

For a moment no one spoke. Then, Grajink said, "All in the name of your obstacle, Carle Eversyn?" The L'Taltons eyes gleamed with blatant admiration.

"My back is itching, Grajink. How about yours?"

Dressed again in her uniform, Benita drove her Guard-issue bubble car through the narrow thoroughfares of the Wayamr Commercial District. She was only vaguely aware of the squawks, growls, hisses, squeaks and yells of the pedestrians scattering before her vehicle.

Approaching Grajink had been a good choice. The L'Talton's information felt right; it felt reliable. The fact that the info had necessitated her coming here only served to increase Benita's sense of confidence in its validity.

She was approaching her destination. Benita began paying closer attention to the flashing neon holo-signs earmarking nearly every shop front along the way.

When she spotted the gaudy red-and-yellow *Protectaire* sign, Benita whipped the bubble car up onto the white polybdalloy sidewalk before the establishment's front entrance. She stepped from the car and at once tugged her uniform into compliance. She ignored the scarcely concealed glares of the district's shoppers as they were forced to sidestep her car in its illegal parking spot.

Benita unclipped her data-pad from her belt and called up the Guard's file on *Protectaire's* Port Nowhere sales rep, one Charles Richard Manus. She skimmed the man's bio and criminal record, then shook her head.

Manus had no serious violations on record—but she noted numerous indicators of legalese light footing.

From all indications, the enviro-suit salesman was not above bending the law in the pursuit of reasonable profit.

Be that as it may, Benita thought as she returned the data-pad to her belt. *If Charlie Manus is good enough to serve as the Consolidated Guard's sole supplier of envirosuits, he's also good enough for what I need.* In fact, the salesman's links to the Guard would only further tie the outcome of her plans to Eversyn.

Inside the shop, Benita found herself unexpectedly impressed by the sheer number and variety of new and used envirosuits on display. The suits were arrayed across the shop floor, along its walls, and even overhead, all of them supported by small anti-gravity plates.

"May I help you?"

The voice caught Benita off guard. She turned to find herself being addressed by Charlie Manus himself and not some flunky assistant sales rep. It struck her then that there was no one else in the shop. Apparently, Charlie Manus didn't care to split commissions.

Benita took quick note of the man's attire and saw how much more it said about the man than did his Guard file. The suit—certainly what had once been called a business suit—was like no other Benita had ever seen outside of archival history disks from her academy days.

It was a gray, faintly sparkling, two-piece outfit consisting of nondescript slacks and jacket. The jacket actually had *buttons.* No one but the impoverished scum from the Depths wore buttons. And who would want to hassle with such an archaic means of fastening one's clothing when there were so many more practical means such as zip-line or grab-strips?

And then there was the thing hanging around the man's neck. Gaudy and luminous, there were tiny red-and-yellow *Protectaire* logos dancing, bouncing and tumbling across the strip of cloth. It was an absolute eyesore.

Benita squared her shoulders and straightened her back. "I need a deep water regulator for a G-428 envirosuit."

Manus tilted his head ever so slightly. "A Consolidated Guard regulation suit model. Hmmm."

Benita watched as Manus steepled his fingers and touched them to his chin. He seemed to be wording his next remark carefully, Benita thought. She observed his eyes as they fleetingly panned over the rank insignia affixed to her uniform. She noted the telltale glitter of...respect? Yes, more than likely that was it. Speaking directly to the Rock's number two Guard officer, Manus was bound to be impressed.

"A deep water regulator," Manus echoed. He motioned her to follow. "A rather unusual request." They stopped before a recessed wall display that was labeled *Envirosuit attachments and accessories*. The salesman pressed and held a button and, one by one, the attachments moved into and out of view.

"I can't recall the last time anyone wanted such an attachment, what with all the Talseen, Uffu, Mezuklen and other aquatic species handling most underwater affairs. I realize I'm..."

"...being nosey?" Benita finished for him.

Manus drew his finger from the button. "I'm sorry. I..."

"If you want to know what I want the regulator for, just ask."

"Er, uh, well, all right, but only because I want to provide you with the best product for your specific needs."

Benita stared though the salesman until he uncomfortably asked, "What do you need the attachment for?"

Benita smiled pleasantly and said, "None of your damn business."

The salesman's business smile faltered for an instant, but he quickly recovered. "Ah, here we go," he said. He pointed to the display. Benita looked to see the short, bronzalloy regulator in the display window.

"*The* G-428 regulator," he said, as his fingers danced over the showcase's control panel.

What had Manus meant by emphasizing *the*? Benita tried to decipher the blur of information flashing across the screen but it was too fast to follow. "*The*?" she asked.

"In more ways than one, I'm afraid," the salesman confessed.

Benita felt her facial muscles tighten like knots.

"According to my files," Manus said, "it appears that, over the last fifteen quintinz, the Consolidated Guard ordered so few of the regulators in question that *Protectaire* simply decided not to restock my inventory.

"As unfortunate as it is, these things do happen. After all, everyone knows how expensive trans-galactic shipping costs are. If a product does not sell, it is not restocked, thereby freeing up freighter space for more lucrative items."

Benita folded her arms across her chest. "I only need one."

The salesman pressed another button; something inside the showcase clattered. "And I only have one. This is the only G-428 deep-water regulator in stock." The transparent face of the display slid aside. Manus reached inside and plucked out the regulator.

Benita offered her hand but the salesman hesitated, actually hesitated, almost clutching the regulator to his chest. Grumbling, Benita held out her right wrist, containing her subcutie.

Three minz and a hundred twenty credz later, Benita was once again behind the stick of her bubble car harrying the pedestrians of the shopping district. For a moment her thoughts were preoccupied with the feeling that the envirosuit salesman had swindled her. No, it wasn't just a feeling; it was a certainty. For the life of her, she just wasn't sure how she'd been cheated, nor did she have the time to go back to learn.

She would deal with Charlie Manus later. She would teach the man his proper place in the scheme of things where Captain Benita Frohmyn was concerned.

<^>

During the next few minz, Benita directed her bubble car down a series of increasingly dilapidated side tunnels, following them further and further from the relative safety of the upper levs. By the time she reached the humid, unlit passages of the Lake District, hers was the only vehicle in sight.

Benita pulled over to the side of the tunnel and put the bubble car in park. She keyed up the local map—such as it was—and got a fix on her exact position—such as it was. Next, she input the data Grajink had supplied her.

"Computer, composite the current map with the data I just gave you, then show me the resulting map."

Benita watched as Grajink's information was integrated with the local map. As the map began changing to reflect Grajink's additions, a satisfied smile lit the darkness of Benita's face. The ancient access port fit the map exactly where Grajink had said it would.

Benita restarted the bubble car and followed the map to the access port.

<^>

Benita stepped from the bubble car, the sound of her boots on the dank stone echoing away down either length of the tunnel. She dug a flashlight from behind the seat and flicked it on. She panned the beam over the glistening walls, and almost cried aloud when the light revealed the gray metal discrepancy of the access port door.

"Grajink, your days of dodging the law have come to an end."

Benita hurried to the car and snatched out the enviro-suit she'd stowed there. Quickly, she donned the suit and activated the helmet. The clear membrane oozed up from the suit's collar, solidifying into a protective shell that entirely encased her head. Next, Benita took the deep-water regulator and snapped into place at her throat. Lastly, she slid her DM-8 into the holster on her suit's thigh. She was ready.

Beyond the port's first door, Benita found the base of a rust-whittled ladder. She gave the first few rungs perfunctory tugs, testing their strength. Confident that they would support her weight, she scaled them. When she reached the top of the ladder, she found herself in small room filled with an assortment of corroded computer banks and a series crumbling valve wheels and levers.

Directly across from her, she spied the top of a second ladder well. It was sealed shut, its iris looking like a solid sheet of red flaking metal.

Why, by the Core, hadn't these idiots used polybdalloy or some other rust proof composite?

Benita looked at the rows of rusty levers. Most looked as if they might snap into dust at the slightest nudging. She tried to read the labeling at the base of each lever but time, with the aid of water and fungus, had obliterated the text. Even if the levers could take being thrown, there was no telling what using them might do. *For all I know, I could drain the lake right on top of my head.*

Benita moved to the second ladder well and prodded the hatch with her foot. She scraped away several flaky layers of rust before deciding it was too much work. She stepped back, drew her DM-8, took aim and blasted the hatch. It exploded in a gritty cloud of metallic rain. The resulting hole was more than wide enough to let her pass. She peered down through its still-smoking edges. Her suit lamp glinted off the water far below.

She double-checked her new regulator, and started down the ladder.

At the bottom of the wet-well, Benita entered warm water and swam upward through a narrow access tunnel. It was just as Grajink had promised.

"A water trap, just like the ones used in plumbing sinks on a starliner," the L'Talton had said.

And, just as Grajink had also assured her, the other end of the wet-well was not sealed off. She emerged from the narrow tunnel into the sort of claustrophobic blackness only outer space and deep water can create.

More of Grajink's words—words of warning—passed through Benita's thoughts as she swam straight up from the lake's long forgotten entrance.

Don't bother using your lights. It'll be too dark to see for at least a hundred meters.

"If you're saying I'll need to conserve my battery, Grajink, don't worry. I'll only be down there for a few owers," Benita had said.

Both L'Taltons had clucked at that. "You bov-brained Connie Sape," Rijink had blurted. "In the deep lake, a light source will bring every whale-fish down on you like a junkie on spilled straz."

"I see," Benita had said, just before she blasted a whole through the female L'Taltons head.

Grajink's eyes had doubled in size but he had had the wherewithal not to react.

"Not only did she call me a Connie," Benn had pointed out to the shocked L'Talton. "She had a smart ass attitude. She should have learned how to show respect to her superiors, Grajink. She might have lived longer."

Dowsing her suit's light, Benita continued toward the surface of the black lake. After a short while, she paused in her ascent. She raised her left arm and keyed in a command on her wrist pad which activated her suit's heads-up-display. The HUD appeared on the inner surface of her faceplate. It was a map of the lake—also provided by Grajink—and on it were highlighted several points of interest to her plan.

Benita took her bearings, angled herself toward her first destination and started in the new direction. In the distance, above and to her left, the pitch black of the deep began to yield to a soft illumination. Faint and fuzzy at first, the pale light grew in intensity as Benita swam. Shapes began to emerge within the glow. A cluster of multifaceted constructs clinging to the craggy face of the lake-wall: Cluster City, home of the Uffus.

As she swam to within thirty meters of the geometric village, Benita became aware of small dark forms flitting through the water between herself and the city. Sentries? Probably. Benita refrained from drawing her DM-8 as she pressed ahead.

All at once, several of the lake dwellers swam at her from every direction, encircling her, each training a small blaster on her. Without looking around to count, Benita could see at least four of the furballs. But there were more, possibly double that number.

True to Benita's recollection of the Uffu, not one of them was more than half a meter tall. Each had a furry, fluke-tipped tail, which they used to ply their murky domain. Their heads were large and round and nearly split in two by a wide, blunt toothed mouth.

Benita knew that this was a make-or-break moment in her plan. Grajink believed that his rival, a Rewtem named Molvox, bought his straz from someone working out of Lake Karkonita. Who that someone was, Grajink couldn't—or wouldn't—say. But the L'Talton had insisted that the lake's Uffu workers were the ones Benita needed to speak with if she were going to learn the secret of Molvox's source of straz.

The foremost of the Uffu swam a bit closer, never relaxing his aim, and motioned Benita to follow. The tiny alien turned, its body wriggling gracefully from side to side as it swam. It didn't wait to see that she followed; it didn't have to as the remaining Uffu formed an escort phalanx around her.

They entered Cluster City through what appeared to be a standard, if somewhat small, airlock. Inside, Benita waited for the lock to drain before deactivating her helmet. Just as the last of the water trickled from the room, the eight Uffu shook the water from their fur. Benita's short cropped hair was instantly soaked.

"Feek!" She blurted.

The eight Uffu froze, their almond eyes upturned and fixed upon her, low growls emanating from their cavernous mouths. If they were offended, tough ka'frindi; Benita was offended as well and she wasn't about to apologize to a bunch of knee-high furballs.

The apparent leader stepped closer to Benita and craned his neck to meet her gaze. "What are you doing in our lake?" he demanded in startlingly clear Basica.

"Greetings to you too," Benita said. She waved a hand around the airlock, causing her diminutive captors to flinch. "Am I getting the special treatment or are you always this rude to you guests?"

One of the other Uffu, a bluish one, piped up. "I say we toss *It* back in the lake, Ka'Noa. Toss it back without *Its* helmet."

Ka'Noa snarled. "You do your job, Su'Veya, I'll do mine."

To Benita, Ka'Noa said. "Until I know why you're here, Sape, you go no further. And if I don't buy your reason for being here, Su'Veya may get to have his way."

Benita pursed her lips. It was time to get serious. She unzipped her envirosuit and peeled back the upper left portion. At the site of her uniform and her rank insignia, the Uffu gasped as one.

"I'm here on official business," Benita said.

"What business do we have with the Consolidated Guard?" Ka'Noa demanded.

Benita indicated the weapons the Uffu were sporting. "First things first, Ka'Noa. It's illegal to aim weapons at an officer of the Guard. Have your friends put away their toys and then we'll talk."

Ka'Noa seemed to consider, then to a yellowish Uffu said, "Ee'Rivo, collect the stingers and return them to the lockers." When the weapons had been gathered up, Ka'Noa dismissed everyone but Su'Veya, who remained in the lock while the other Uffu disappeared through the inner lock door. When they had gone, Ka'Noa motioned Benita and Su'Veya through the same lock and into an intersection of corridors beyond.

Benita was left alone in a pyramidal room where she waited. And waited. And waited.

The Uffu had not confiscated her DM-8; apparently they were not quite as willing to cross the Consolidated Guard as the one called Su'Veya had acted. Benita was about to draw her weapon and start blasting for answers when a section of the wall before her opened at chest level. From the opening a shelf of sorts intruded upon the room. A moment later, an Uffu Benita had not yet seen ambled onto the ledge; as a result, he was eye to eye with her.

Without a moment's hesitation, the Uffu launched into a lengthy introduction accompanied by a flurry of wild hand gestures.

160

"Welcome to Cluster City," she said. "Your arrival is most unexpected. However, given your important ranking in Port Nowhere's Consolidated Guard, you are hereby granted an audience with His Excellency, the Most Exalted One, Father of the Lake, Wisest of the Wise, Friend of the Sacred Whale-fish, Clan Chief of the Lake Karkonita Uffu, His Majesty Yee'Mora."

Just as the herald finished speaking, a second Uffu trotted onto the ledge. He was sporting a short, twisted scepter that looked to be made of coral. The herald bowed deeply to the new arrival and stepped to the side. The chieftain had a sleek black pelt accentuated by patches of white fur around both of his yellow eyes.

Trying to keep from laughing out loud, Benita bowed to the hairy little monarch. When she stood straight, Benita found the scepter practically in her face. She scowled, yet somehow kept herself from brushing it aside.

"What business do you have in my lake, Human?" Yee'Mora demanded.

He was direct if nothing else, thought Benita. Hopefully he would appreciate the same trait in others outside of his purview. "I'm here by order of Captain Eversyn to investigate straz trafficking."

Yee'Mora blinked repeatedly as he lowered his scepter. He exchanged looks with his herald and spoke something in Uffu.

For a moment, Benita watched and listened. It was a moment too long. Even as she heard the snap-sizzle behind her, she felt the stinging warmth of the stunner between her shoulder blades.

The first thing Benita became aware of was darkness. Her head felt as though it had been stuffed with Rock dust. She heard the creaking of a swaying rope and then several clicking sounds.

With a good deal of effort, Benita managed to force her eyes open. Everything was swaying in a most nauseating way. She turned her head in an effort to orient herself. It was then that the creaking sound and the swaying made sense. She was strung up by her feet, which also explained her heavy headedness. She could see that her hands were tied and that her DM-8 was missing.

Click-clack. Click-clack. Click-clack. Benita twisted her body toward the sounds. A Talseen. She watched as the huge, two-meter tall crustacean clattered towards her across the metal deck plating. Talseens were common enough on the upper levs of the Rock that they rarely drew attention, but here in the Lake District they could be found by the thousands.

The Talseen stopped a meter from Benita; its nine stalk-eyes waved to and fro as it regarded her. Benita could just make out the clan symbol etched into the side of the Talseen's shell. She didn't recognize it nor could she decipher the glyph. As a result she wasn't sure who she was dealing with.

The Talseen spoke. Its voice, originating as chattering and clicking from its mandibles, was translated into Basica by the multi-purpose harness attached to its under-shell: the same sort of harness worn by most Talseen, as it also supported the auxiliary arms the Talseen needed to more easily function outside of their own communities.

"The last time I saw a Sape down here in Karkonita was over thirty dekquins ago."

"I'm sorry, I didn't get your name," Benita said with a shrug of her shoulders, hoping to distract the Talseen's roving eyes with the movement, while she fingered the back of her belt for her knife.

"Vaskar. Lake Warden Vaskar."

"Well, *Lake Warden* Vaskar, you aren't exactly running a five star resort down here."

The Talseen took a step closer, its artificial hands opening and closing rhythmically. "I don't like trespassers, especially meddling trespassers, in my territory. And more than that I don't like Sapes, especially Connie Sapes."

Benita felt the hilt of her sona-blade but she waited to draw it. Vaskar was still too far away.

"I guess that means that Captain Eversyn's suspicions about straz trafficking from down here was right on the credz."

The Talseen's eyestalks froze. Then, without a word, Vaskar raised its giant natural pincers and lashed out at Benita.

The first claw snapped tightly on Benita's thigh, the second claw glanced off her shoulder as she twisted away.

In that brief moment, Benita pulled her knife. Before Vaskar could react, Benita flipped the blade in her bound hands, activated it, and severed the rope that bound her wrist. Vaskar released her thigh, raising both pincers to strike again. But even as the Talseen did so, Benita reached out and seized hold of a bundle of Vaskar's eyestalks. Vaskar tried to scamper away, but Benita held fast.

"Stop!" cried the alarmed lake warden.

Benita wasn't listening, nor was she giving quarter. She stabbed the sona-blade to the hilt into the fleshy gap between the Talseen's dorsal and ventral shells. She maxed the blade's intensity and scrambled the crustacean's brain.

It took at least two minz for Vaskar to stop shaking. In the interval, Benita slashed the rope that held her up by her ankles and crumpled to the deck. When the feeling returned to her feet and legs, Benita stood and looked around. She was on a pier on the underground lake's surface. She looked down at Vaskar who, being essentially lobotomized, lay a listless lump at her feet. Thankfully, he was the only other living thing in sight.

Using all the strength she could muster, Benita slowly pushed the unresponsive Talseen over the edge of the pier. When the subsequent splash failed to draw anyone else's attention, Benita peered over the edge into the clear water. Vaskar was sinking into the blackness of the depths.

Just then three great white shapes swam into view. Whale-fish. The blind albino leviathans, each at least ten meters long, circled the helpless Talseen. Then one of them opened its enormous mouth and swallowed the Lake Warden in a single bite.

"What a way to go," she said to herself as she moved away from the edge. There was no doubt in her mind that somewhere around—or in—this lake was the major straz source Grajink had told her about. The only thing left to do was to figure out how the operation worked, sabotage the investigation in such a way that Eversyn took the blame, and to get back to her own Lev in one piece.

There was no sound, no tingling of the sixth sense. Benita simply turned to find herself no longer alone.

"You?" she exclaimed, bringing her sona-blade up as a reflex.

The blade flew from her hand, batted away.

And then Benita herself was sent hurtling through the air. She flew backward, off the pier and into the clutches of the cold lake. Blinded by the swirl of bubbles created as she broke the surface, Benita fumbled to activate her helmet, but could not find the button.

She kicked for the surface but struck her head on something solid above her: something white and pasty. It moved away, but even as it did so, Benita glimpsed a pale movement to her right, and another below her.

The latter shape overtook her, filled her field of vision like an oncoming ground-shuttle. A rent appeared in the whiteness. The whale-fish had opened its mouth.

The last of Benita's air escaped in a gargled scream as the jaws closed around her.

~END~

OUT OF THE MOUTH OF THE BEAST

K.G. McAbee

It was between shifts in Dhamu's bar. In a place that had never known day or night, in a bar that never closed, it was almost impossible to find privacy and quiet. Almost, but not quite. The work shifts set up to keep the infrastructure of Port Nowhere ticking along, with some marginal degree of success, provided a certain ebb and flow of customers in all the establishments on the Rock, from the lush elegance of the Starview Lounge to the lesser known—to the up-dwellers, anyway—places like the Chow Down, the Blender, or Dhamu's.

Malik stared out over his table, checking the clientele. Against the far wall—rough and carved from the Rock as were most places below LevThree—four L'Taltons perched on stools around a table, sipping the weak pale toubrew that Dhamu brewed in the back room and clucking softly to each other. One, a neuter by the orange-gold color of its breast feathers, reached over from time to time and groomed its pair-mate's crest; one of the others—by their red-brown crest, those two were females—scrabbled in a flat bowl for bits of toasted toufood and tossed them into the air for its pair-mate to catch in its beak.

Aside from the L'Talton pairs, the only other occupants of the bar Malik could see were Crila and himself, and Dhamu behind the bar. He didn't count Tau the Silent, who, after polishing off three huge sandwiches and two glasses of beer, was stretched out on the padded bench beside him, snoring in quiet content. And Dhamu didn't look much more awake as he pushed a dirty rag in concentric spirals across the bar's stained polybdalloy.

Not that the burly Modajai ever looked more than marginally interested in what was going on around him; Kovindi fighters, even those who, like Dhamu, made it out alive and with enough money to find another profession, were seldom the same afterwards. Vicious fighting to the death could really take it out of even as tough a race at the Modajai.

"Cred for your thoughts, Mal my son?" Crila Maragorn took a drink of beer and winced at the taste.

"They're not even worth half a micro, Cri. And if you'd rather have brandy or—"

"Nah, beer's good enough, even if I do know what Dhamu uses to make it. Brandy makes me chatty." She took another drink as if to prove her point; this time the wince was just visible. She tossed a forelock of lavender hair out of her eyes; they matched the lavender shade, though the blue-green streaks that ran though them, and her pale skin, showed she was part Human as well as having Halsan in the mix.

What else was in her background, Mal wondered as he examined the small yet lushly figured woman who sat across from him. She was dressed in a brown spacer's coverup open to show a halter, and boots that had seen better days. Except for the forelock, beaded with tiny bits of obsidian and garnet, that persisted in falling into her face, her hair was cropped short. The right hand that held her beer glass was flesh; the other one was hidden beneath a glove, but Mal knew it wasn't meat. He'd seen the damage that hand, with its various prosthetics, could do. Recently, in fact; she'd wiped a Connie's mind blank and knocked him to the floor with just a stroke of one finger. Not that her other hand was useless; he'd seen her bounce unruly spacers out of Dhamu's when she was working her shift. Cri liked a peaceful bar, and never minded cracking a few heads to get it.

"What makes *you* chatty, Mal?"

Malik looked into her eyes and felt a power that he could not explain. *Those damn Ophids; what'd they and their crystal do to you, Cri?*

"Saved my life is all. Why? Worried I'll walk around inside your head and find out some stuff you don't want me to know?"

Malik opened his mouth to reply—then realized he had not spoken aloud. "Hey; don't do that. It's as creepy as one of Tau's cribs down in the Depths. I always feel like something's watching me just out of sight. And since when did you get telepathic?"

"Since, oh, just lately, I guess. Or maybe I always been, and what the sisterhood did was just to show me how to tap it. But don't worry, Malik; I can't really see into that blocked off head of yours. I just pick up bits of flotsam, crap that floats around on the surface, like scum on top of sewage."

"Thanks—I think. That's a relief." Mal didn't know if he believed her, but didn't see what he could do about it if she was lying. He'd known Cri for, damn, it must be nearly eight sintinz. He trusted her...as much as he trusted anyone.

"Nah, you're not a trusting soul, are you, Mal?"

"Will you stop that?"

"Sorry, son. It's just that you're, uh, broadcasting pretty strong right now. Something is, you should pardon the expression, preying on your mind. Want to talk about it?"

"No. Yes."

"What I thought." Crila nodded. "Whatever you tell me won't go out this hole, unless you give me leave. So talk. Get it off your mind."

Malik took a long drink of his toubrew, then set the glass down with precise care. He looked down at Tau, whose snores had gotten louder, and pulled his jacket further up over the boy's shoulders. A dirty toe peeked from the boot that just missed kicking him when Tau jerked in a dream.

A dream. Was it a good one? Could a boy like Tau, who'd lived in the Depths all his short life, *have* good dreams? A full belly and a safe crib; those were his ultimate in joy. Tau had been off to throw himself into the pits when Mal had found him; lost his family, then lost his tribe, the boy had said, and didn't want to live any more.

Malik knew what that was like; losing the only thing you had and not wanting to go on.

"So tell me about it."

Crila's voice was soft, soothing; no commands, no orders. Mal sighed, looked down at the table and saw his past in the interlocking rings of spilled beer.

He didn't think he'd be able to talk about it, but once he began, the words flowed out like the babblings of a strazzie.

"I was created in a lab, Cri. Can you imagine what that's like? To be grown like food or ka'frindi, on feek and chemicals? To know that you're nothing but an expendable piece of meat? I know. I knew from the beginning. They all made sure I knew…"

Doctre Xandrino stalked into the lab and I shuddered and hunkered down in my cage, just like all the rest of us test animals. Well, all but two of us. Number Three, in the cage next to me, just lay on his back in his own filth, moaning softly. He couldn't throw off the latest disease they'd given him; his skin was peeling off all over his body; bones were already showing through the skin of his arms and legs, and his eyes were black pits, sunk back into his head. Three wouldn't last much longer, unless the Doctre decided to save him instead of watching the progress of the disease to the end.

Sometimes he did that; sometimes he brought us back. Two had been brought back a handful of times, but his mind wasn't there any more; he just drooled and snarled most of the time when I tried to talk to him, or whined as he licked his water bowl clean and thirsted for more. Four; well, Four had been gone for a while. The last we'd seen of him, he was strapped to a gurney and being rolled out the door. There were screams; we hoped they weren't his.

We were probably wrong.

So it was mostly One and me; I was Five. We were cloned from the same tissue, and we were test animals to see what the original tissue could stand; what pain, what disease, what damage we could live through, thrive through.

It hadn't always been that way for us. Once we'd had training; we'd lived in rooms and slept in beds, instead of on crumpled piles of fiber in polybdalloy cages. We'd been taught to read, so we could study the family our tissue had come from.

Family. That was the most alien concept, at least for me. One had understood it, or said he did; Two also, before his mind went. Three had tried to explain it to me; he'd always been quicker than the rest of us, before the diseases had eaten his brain away and left nothing behind.

Family. Related—that meant they shared DNA, of course; that much I could understand. After all, each of us had identical DNA strands; we'd been grown from the same tissue, in the same vat. That seemed normal, seemed to make sense.

But the part about living together, sharing...love. Alien. Too alien for my mind to grasp.

But that was before Doctre Xandrino took over the labs. There had been a change in power, somewhere, somehow; we never found out what had happened. Just, one day, the Doctre arrived and took over. He wanted to see what we could stand, so he could inform the real one—the one with the family— what his body could take. That's what we were, he told us; spare parts for Rudof Dyll.

I didn't much like Rudof Dyll, even if he was me, or I was him. Why wasn't he in a cage, puking his life out or drooling, brainless and empty?

Doctre Xandrino paused before Three's cage and spoke softly into his portable comsys. I knew techie terms; I could read, and listen, and remember. I didn't know for how much longer, though; only One and I were still aware.

"Subject Three appears unable to withstand the ravages of the beldon-zeta bioengineered virus. It would be an interesting study to bio-link his brain with one of the other test subjects, to collect more precise data. Yes. Note that Subject..." I held my breath. "...One should undergo bio-link procedures in—" he paused, as if gauging how much longer Three might live, "—at ower seven this cyk."

I looked up at the big chrono on the wall across from my cage. It was ower four already. One didn't have much time left. Bio-links would kill one side of the link, if the other one died. And it didn't look like Three had much time left either.

That would leave me, and Two. How long would it be before I was drooling and whining in my cage beside him, I wondered?

Not soon enough to suit me.

A warning klaxon brayed over the door leading from the lab. Doctre Xandrino dropped his comsys; I couldn't even hear the clatter it made as it hit the floor, not over the sound of the alarm. I watched at the Doctre strode towards the door; his lips were moving so I know he was cursing, but no voice could compete with the klaxon.

The door burst open before the Doctre had taken more than five steps. A man, burly, bulky, zipped into an enviro-suit with the hood thrown back, stepped inside. He held up a hand; the other had a blaster in it, pointed squarely at the Doctre's chest.

The alarm cut off. Through the ringing in my ears, I heard Xandrino splutter: "What is the meaning of this? Guards! Guards!"

"Ain't no guards no more." The intruder grinned a silvery grin; he had more beralloy teeth than real ones. "Me and the voids has just took care of the guards. So calm down. Your little place has been took over. Now; what we got here?"

This wasn't asked of Xandrino, but of another envirosuit-clad figure who walked into the lab behind him. An arm reached up and pushed the hood back; a long nose wrinkled as the air from the lab hit it.

"Stinks in here, don't it?" asked the burly man. "Want I should just burn it all while we loot the rest of the 'cile?"

"It's a lab, Kllurt. Lab-or-a-tor-y. There are probably valuable drugs in it." The newcomer was female, with short curling black hair that framed a brown face. "We are pirates, you know; when are you going to learn what pirates do? We steal anything of value, remember?"

"Hah. Joke. Then what, cap'n? Kill the lab boy here, toss the animals in the recycler, and see what we can find?"

"Better idea, Kllurt. Good boy, you're learning. So go to it."

"I think you'd best get out of my lab," began Doctre Xandrino in a placating tone, since there didn't seem to be any guards. "I'm sure we can some to some agreement that will satisfy us all. Come out of this stink and into my office, and we'll—"

A broad beam of red-orange blaster fire, and the Doctre fell to the floor, his head cut neatly from his body. The blast was so quick that I could see his eyes fluttering as his brain took the last few seconds of life to realize it was over.

"Kllurt. Sloppy. Now look at that mess."

The captain shook her head at Kllurt, her tone chiding. She stepped with care over the still twitching body. Kllurt kicked the head with one massive boot; it rolled under One's cage. One had caught the edges of the beam, I saw; he was lying still in the bottom of his cage, smoke rising from his chest.

"Zantz, what'd they do in here?" She was looking down at Three; he looked back up at her, but there was nothing left in his gaze but pain. She raised her own blaster, somewhat smaller than Kllurt's; a pale yellow needle beam shot out and Three sighed as he died. A tiny red-rimmed hole leaked blood. Two whined and giggled, reached through bars and dabbled a finger in Three's blood, then licked it. Two was always thirsty.

The captain gave a disgusted sound and used the blaster's needle beam on him. Two grinned at her as he died.

Then she turned to me and raised her blaster.

"No...please."

My voice was rusty from disuse. But most of all, I was amazed to find out that I didn't want to die. Not want to die? It was all I had wanted for too long.

The burly pirate stomped over and stood beside his captain. He pointed his blaster at me.

"Feek, this one talks. I thought they was all just vat-born testers, spare parts. Want I should blast him?"

She looked down at me. I didn't recognize that look in her eyes; I didn't remember ever seeing it before. I learned—much, much later—that it was called pity.

I also learned how seldom the captain allowed herself to feel it.

She leaned closer to my cage; I watched her long nose wrinkle in disgust and realized how filthy I was, how much I must stink. But the rest of them, even Doctre Xandrino; they were stinking even more right now.

I looked up, met green eyes. They were the last things I was ever going to see, I knew. I was glad they were so beautiful. I'd almost forgotten beautiful, in my time in the cage. Almost forgotten a lot of things.

"Do you have a name?" The captain's voice was strong, but not harsh.

"Fi—" A fit of coughing took me; the smell of burned flesh wafted past as it was sucked into the recyke-sys. I could taste the copper of blood in the back of my throat. "Five."

If I'd ever had another name, and I was almost sure that I had, I couldn't remember it.

"Five." The captain stood straight; she was almost as tall as Kllurt. She looked around the lab. "Only three others in here. Shouldn't you be Four?"

"They took Four. He was strapped to a gurney. We never saw him again." I hadn't spoken so many words in a long, long time.

"So."

For a long moment, the captain just looked at me. I watched those eyes. I wanted them to be the last sight I'd ever see.

Then she holstered her blaster. "Kllurt, get the rest of the crew busy stripping this place. I want everything of value stowed away in Hold Seven so we can get off this planet. They must have auxiliary guards somewhere in orbit; we need to be loaded and gone before they arrive."

Kllurt gave a sloppy sort of salute and turned to go.

"And Kllurt? Send Quarneon in here."

"What you want with the medic, cap'n? You hurt?"

"No. But our newest crewmember needs some attention. Now go."

<^>

172

Crila reached over and patted his hand. "I think I like your pirate captain, Mal. What was her name?"

"Maryn Meredi." He'd said it. He hadn't been able to say it for so long that the relief was overwhelming. "She had her medic fix me up, then put me in a stasis tube. Next thing I knew, I was all well."

"Where's Captain Meredi now?"

Malik turned up his glass, swallowed five times, and set it down empty. He looked at his friend, who smiled back at him, pity in her eyes. He recognized it this time.

"Dead. Maryn's dead, Cri."

"Oh, I'm sorry, Mal. What happened?"

"I killed her."

~END~

(OΠfID€Π(€ GΛΜ€S

Christopher T. Wilkerson

Round I: Deal, Duck, & Cover

"Okay, so let me get this straight, Mastriz...Ny'storae, is it?" Jesse Iresson exhaled heavily. "You're the curator of this—what was the name?"

"Axhal," the blue woman offered.

"Axhal," he continued, "Emporium of Antiquated Delights. A museum?"

She nodded once.

"A museum. And you want me to, how did you say, *acquire*," he pronounced the word delicately, as if it tasted vaguely of brown ka'frindi, "seven crystal vials of this...narissum?"

The blue head nodded again.

"And that is what, exactly?"

The Yruldhi "woman," for want of a better term, nodded once more, gravely, either missing or ignoring the dubious tone that modulated just under the surface of Iresson's voice. She was humanoid at least—as far as he could tell—although these days that certainly wasn't saying much, and stunningly beautiful, in the harsh and pristine way of a distant glacier. And she had four of the most perfectly proportioned breasts he had ever seen in his—my God, was it seventeen, now?—sintinz of

174

dealing with the ever-revolving freak-show that was the artifacts trade in the Malpairiso Sector.

Leaning forward until her lower breasts rested lightly on the edge of the table, Ny'storae removed her matte-dark glasses and bored into Jesse with solid-black eyes as dark as the shades she had just removed. "You have a rep for being reasonably reliable and at least somewhat discreet. And we have a rep for being generous…with both reward and punishment, as appropriate."

Jesse was liking her less and less, no matter how many tits she put on the table. He studied her porcelain-smooth, azure face, the delicate lips tinged faintly green, her inky black hair—he assumed it was hair, and tried not to look too closely—pulled tightly back and held by bronzalloy clasps. This was not a customer with whom to screw around, he decided. So, for the direct approach, then.

"I don't deal in narcotics," he said. "Of any kind. It's never worth the unholy feek-storm it inevitably calls down."

She leaned back slightly and smiled. Jesse almost grimaced, in spite of himself.

"Of course not," she intoned, as smooth as temple chimes, "and no one here would ask you to. We just want the perfumes as…souvenirs, for our patrons."

"Patrons?"

A pause. Perhaps she was annoyed by the question? Jesse couldn't be sure.

"As I told you over the vid-com, Yruldhi do not distinguish between history and mythology the way…Humans do," she tried to hide the scorn in her voice, and failed. "Wherever we settle, we make it a priority to preserve the lifeways of our ancestors as best we can. That includes at least one reconstruction of our lost temple. The requirements are…exacting…and tend to be expensive. We make up some of that expense by operating a modest 'museum,' as you would call it."

"Charging an equally modest fee for tours?"

Ny'storae shot him a warning glance. "Our…heritage…is extremely important to us, Mastre Iresson."

Again, Jesse wasn't exactly sure just what to make of her hesitation.

But then the timbre of the woman's voice changed abruptly, becoming conspiratorial, almost gossipy: "Besides," she smiled, "the elderly tourists do get such a thrill from our mock-rites. Coincidentally, the sacrifice reenactment ceremonies are quite a spectacle for the senses...for *all* the senses."

Did she wink at him? Could Yruldhi wink? She let out a languid sigh. "You really should indulge, as long as you're here."

Iresson let the invitation linger awkwardly over the grimy table. The two sat immersed in shadow at the back of the bar— the Tunnel Rat Tavern, he remembered from the sign on the heavy beralloy door to this dank hole-in-the-rock. Made sense. Everybody in the Rock was a tunnel rat, especially down this low. Pale smoke wafted random bits of conversation, and some tart, unidentifiable odors, past them.

How the hell did I end up in the belly of some overgrown rock-beast at the ass-end of the galaxy? Jesse wondered for the fifteenth time that cyk.

The TRT was cut out from a side-passage off one of the main thoroughfares of LevFive—the beginning of the end of civilization, and for most offworlders stupid or godforsaken enough to find their way this deep into the gullet of the Rock, the last place they'd ever see. Jesse had walked into some of the most vicious underworlds in the sector—and lived to walk out again. He was well accustomed to the kind of stink-hole that so often functioned as a temp base for traffickers of questionable merch or sensitive info. Still, Port Nowhere was something else, more than just same-feek-different-asteroid. The desperation here clung to his skin like an oily sheen, coated his teeth when he talked. *How long does it take this rock to digest a grown Human?*

Not a question he really wanted to answer. He never should have taken a meeting this far down, especially on his first trip to Port Nowhere. But his client had insisted, had left explicit instructions for bypassing basic security and making the stomach-churning drop straight to LevFive. And the money was just too good, and too urgently needed, to ignore. So here he sat, acquiring a layer of slick grime and trying not to gag in the cloying air of the Tunnel Rat, as his would-be client worked to seduce him with anything besides solid info.

His face, however, betrayed none of his frustration and disgust, and the moment wore on heavily.

"Well," Ny'storae finally continued, her features gliding fluidly back into their businesslike demeanor, "can you acquire the vials?"

Down to the bottom line. This was a bad idea, of course, but that had never stopped Jesse before. "I'll need three strechiz. Half the cred in advance, the rest on delivery. And," he leaned forward for emphasis, "keep my name out of your database."

The woman rose, unfolding several of her intricately jointed legs—not so humanoid after all, apparently—and smoothing the lapels of her dark, polyester suit. "Your terms are acceptable. As far as I'm concerned, we have an agreement."

"Yes."

"Here." She handed him an unmarked packet. "As you stipulated, half in advance. And we'll expect to hear from you in three weeks." She rotated away from the table and began to scuttle off past him towards the exit, then paused. Without completely turning back, she spoke over her shoulder: "Or to read of your untimely demise in the holo-news."

She was almost to the door when it exploded.

Jesse hit the floor instinctively, ducking forward and rolling to put the table in between him and the sound of the explosions that popped now in rapid succession behind his back. *Flare grenades, damn!* he swore to himself, his eyes already stinging from the first flash of harsh, white light. He felt the other flashes through the exposed skin of his hands and face. Screams rippled through the crowded bar, blending with muffled sounds of bodies hitting the floor, the walls, odd tables, each other. All his instincts shrieked at him to run, to get the hell out, but he knew better than to tear off in some random direction before he had any idea of what was happening around him. The flares seemed to have stopped, so he risked a quick glance around.

He opened his eyes and panicked—he was blind! No, it was just dark in the bar, he realized, to his great relief. Whoever'd attacked had cut the local power supply. He shifted to face the entrance to the bar. What dim light there was came from the flickering husks of the flare-grenades, smoldering in the greasy fluids that pooled on the floor. Most of the tables were overturned, and armed humanoids were moving through the crowd, hurling people to the ground and holding them there at blaster-point. The assailants looked to be concentrated at the entrance, a good thirty meters from where he hid. Between the darkness and their bulky uniforms, Jesse couldn't make out any details about them. He saw no sign of Ny'storae anywhere near the club's entrance.

Behind him now, a faint clicking noise caught his attention over the snarling of the uniformed humanoids and the whimpering of terrified patrons. Still crouched under the table, he turned around just in time to see five or six dark, polyester pant-legs scurry around the far side of the bar and vanish. Barely suppressing a snarl of his own, he shifted as silently as he could to get his feet under him. *Gonna have to make a run for it,* he realized, swallowing hard. Taking a deep breath, he hurled himself out from under the table and launched towards the corner, just as the screech of rending beralloy echoed from the other side of the bar.

He was spotted instantly. He could tell because pulse blasts blew holes in the bar a hair's breadth from his head, and then took out chunks of the flooring at his feet.

"Dammit," he growled, "I'm getting too old for thi—argh!"

A pulse grazed the back of his right shoulder, just as he cleared the bar and turned the corner, ripping through the multi-pocketed boven-hide vest that had been his field uniform for nearly seventeen sintinz and cutting a shallow trench into his shoulder blade.

On the far side of the bar, he spotted the outline of what had probably been a secret door before a certain blue demon—he made a mental note to curse her some more as soon as he got out of there—had dislocated it from its track in her hasty escape. Behind him, he could hear the soldiers, or guards, or thugs—whatever they were—thumping after him, shouting what probably translated to "Freeze!" or worse and trampling squawking civilians to get to him. He ducked through the damaged door and dove around the nearest corner he could find, hoping to lose himself in the gurgling, multi-headed crowds of LevFive.

It wasn't terribly difficult. Humans were by no means a majority of the populace down this far, but neither were they so rare as to attract undue attention, especially ones who looked as rough as Jesse now did. After several long minz of brisk walking, he glanced back over his shoulder. He could still hear a shout or two, but by now he'd become part of the anonymous mass of moving flesh that circulated through the main passages of this level. And this far below the surface, he imagined, nobody would've seen nothin', especially if asked rudely by some armed uniform.

Passing a polybdalloy-plated bulkhead, he checked his reflection as inconspicuously as he could manage, hoping with moderate desperation that he wasn't so completely banged up as to stand out from the crowd around him. He could ill afford to be rousted by some overzealous beat-guard, if they made it down to this level. Nor did he relish the idea of presenting a tempting mark to any ganders or raptors who might be cruising for fresh, usable meat that looked too weak to put up much of a fight. His reflection met him not quite halfway, on both counts: he looked like refried ka'frindi on hammered bov-feek.

Well, nothing unusual there. What really demanded attention was the slowly expanding dark stain on his tan tunic, spreading down the sleeve from his right shoulder. He needed to find a place to patch himself up, and quick. So he started walking again. He had no idea where to go, but he obviously couldn't stay here. Though at least he had a packet of fresh credz tucked securely in his vest. Right. Fresh cred from a client he'd love to throttle.

Another client. Another deal. And these days it seemed like he always needed the work. Of course, he'd gotten a bad vibe off this Yruldhi from the first. Now he'd been shot up, again, and he was probably already in some official database of fugitives from justice. Again. And this time, all within twenty-four owers of docking.

"Yeah, sure, we have a deal, lady," he mumbled under his breath.

On the other hand, maybe he was jumping to conclusions. Perhaps the overzealous, blaster-friendly renovations of the bar actually had nothing to do with Ny'storae. Her story had seemed harmless enough, as far as it went. But the thought only lasted an instant. Then Jesse came to his senses. *Sure, they all tell me a nice, harmless story,* he groused to himself, wincing in pain—his shoulder was really starting to sting. He glanced down at the dark stain that soaked his sleeve. *But somehow, thegodsdammit, they always forget to mention this part.*

Round II: Some Fur, Some Scales, and a Green-eyed Girl

Fighting off familiar pangs of distress that tugged at the fringes of his mind, Jesse worked to make out the holo-signs of shops and businesses while navigating the currents of bodies surging around him. Lots of bars. Several pawn brokers and assorted import-export dealers. More than a few marquees he found untranslatable; some of those included vivid, full-color anatomical diagrams of Humans, other sentients, and some creatures he couldn't identify. Perhaps the storefront of a street-doc, showing who and what could be treated?

Hoping for a little discreet medical attention, Jesse paused at the nearest such sign. A quick glance through polybdalloy front windows, however, suggested these places really offered the wayward traveler a very different type of attention, from whatever species the customer might desire. *Well, that's one thing that never changes, no matter what rock you look under,* he snorted.

He was about to move on when he realized something wasn't right. There was a small side-tunnel just past the brothel, and he moved toward it, being careful neither to hurry nor to go too slowly. As he neared the alley, he finally felt it— a soft tugging at his trouser pocket. Without a word, he grabbed behind him with his right hand, latching onto a furry limb, and twisted around the corner into the tunnel. He had no clue what he'd caught, but he slammed it up against the rock wall and held it there by its throat. He snarled at it viciously as it gasped and wheezed.

"Look, pal," Jesse growled, "I am not in the mood to get mugged to day, do you understand? I'd just as soon dice you up and eat you, but your carcass'd be worth more to me on the open meat market!" Jesse hadn't realized quite how much rage had been fomenting beneath his thoughts until it came out. The creature was short, maybe a meter from head to toe, and covered in bristling fur. Its long, writhing tongue flailed about helplessly as Jesse pressed his elbow harder into its neck. Seeing real terror in the creature's eyes, he held it to the wall for a moment more, then set it down, still keeping its wrist in his iron grasp.

Instantly, the thing tried to flee.

"Oh, no you don't," Jesse jerked back on its arm, perhaps a little too hard.

The creature yelped.

"You're not going anywhere."

Giving up the struggle, then, the little beastie held still, but its eyes searched frantically for some way out of its predicament. Seeing none, it looked back up at Jesse and waited.

"That's better. All right," Jesse spoke calmly now, "You want me to let you go?"

It gyrated its head so vigorously its pointed ears flapped against its skull.

"Good. I'll make you a deal. You take me to someone who can patch up a blaster wound," he glanced down to indicate the blood on his sleeve, "with *no questions asked,* and I'll let you stay in one piece. That sound fair?"

The thing shook its head again.

"Okay. Let's get going, then."

With Jesse in tow, his fingers still locked around its wrist, the creature scurried from the alley, weaving in and out of the crowd. Jesse quickly lost track of any landmarks and had to resign himself to trusting his furry prisoner. After enough twists and turns to make him feel more than a little dizzy—or was that loss of blood?—the diminutive pickpocket led Jesse into a dimly lit passage that was several tunnels removed from the main public zones. Echoes of distant voices reached Jesse's ears, but he couldn't place them. There was no one in sight. His guide led him to a scarred and dented beralloy door at the end of the corridor. With its free hand, it tapped out a complex rhythm on the sensor pad to the left of the door. A panel in the top of the door slid open, and a pair of large eyes appeared. They did not look the least bit pleased.

"What kind of bov-feek is this, Paz, you little son of a bottom-feeder?" a voice like grinding stones bellowed. "You know the rules—no outsiders, and definitely no *offal!*"

The little creature growled at the glaring eyes above. "Mhartom, don't you make me climb up there and hurt you!"

Jesse nearly lost his grip on little Paz, trying not to laugh. But apparently the creature was being serious. A moment later, at any rate, unseen gears hummed to life, and the metallic clang of large bolts moving back reverberated through the alley. The door swung inward.

Paz looked over his shoulder at Jesse. "Well," he sighed, "come on in. I hope you'll appreciate how much you're gonna cost me, offworlder." He growled again.

Given the thing's size and round, furry face, Jesse might have mistaken the sound for purring. Might have, that is, except for the cold menace in the creature's narrowing eyes.

He met Paz's menace with some of his own: "Perhaps you'll remember that the next time you think you've found an easy mark in some newly-arrived 'offal,' fuzz-ball." That got him another growl as they crossed the threshold.

It took a moment for Jesse's eyes to adjust. As dimly lit as the corridor had been, this room was darker still. Small, portable glowbz barely illuminated an area that had probably been designed originally for cargo or inventory storage, judging by the heavily riveted beralloy bulkheads in varying stages of corrosion. Crates and boxes of all descriptions lay scattered about the room. Some of these had been covered with layers of tattered blankets in rich, garish colors and now passed for furniture. There was a holo-viewer against the far wall that looked to be six or seven generations out of date. A thin curtain partially hid a narrow doorway in the far right corner, diagonally across from the entrance he'd just come through. That was the only other exit Jesse could see.

Damn, he thought. *What a cozy little trap.* He exhaled slowly. *Damn, damn, and double-damn.*

Paz gyrated free of Jesse's grip and scuttled towards the curtained doorway. "You wait here, Human. Mhartom?" He looked past Jesse to the corner behind the door, then nodded meaningfully at Jesse. With flash of fur, he disappeared behind the curtain.

In answer to Paz's unspoken command, a deep, grating sound began to rumble behind Jesse. Before he could turn and look, a rough shove pushed him farther into the room and clear of the outer door, which Mhartom closed the rest of the way, the mecha-bolt lock clanging back into place with metallic finality. Turning just in time to see this Mhartom step out from the shadows, Jesse swallowed hard.

What stood before him appeared to be a mountain...or at least a rather sizable chunk of one, somehow detached and animated in black coveralls. But Jesse quickly amended his first impression, as he realized the thing's rocky texture was actually a covering of rough, grey scales accented with ridges of bone. At a height that easily cleared two meters, scale and bone now towered over the Human. Heavy brow ridges did nothing to hide the displeasure in the being's glare.

"Mhartom, I presume?" Jesse hoped the cockiness in his tone was more convincing than it sounded to himself.

He looked about the room again. Still only one exit, and though he had a clear shot and thought he could make it before this behemoth caught him, he had no idea how much worse might await him on the other side. And he wasn't exactly at his full strength right now, anyway. He scratched at his beard, looking for the right opening gambit.

"Love what you've done with the place," he offered.

Mhartom remained unmoved, blocking the main entrance, so Jesse planted himself on the nearest makeshift chair. He gestured toward the ancient holo-viewer with his good arm.

"So, how many stations you get on that thing?"

Silence like granite, as the question hung in the air. Mhartom's personality was apparently as warm and friendly as his appearance. The giant didn't even seem to be breathing, though Jesse mused that he had no way of knowing if that were normal for whatever species Mhartom was.

"Let me guess," he said, still fishing, "you're *not* the mouthpiece for this organization?"

That seemed to get a rise out of his host. At least Jesse thought he noticed a brief widening of Mhartom's eyes, a slight shift in his stance. In a heartbeat, however, the bony features resumed their original expression, or lack thereof.

Well, that's something I might be able to work with, given time, Jesse thought.

Right now, however, that was exactly what he didn't have. In fact, discovering one tiny, potential crack in Mhartom's façade did precious little to improve this steaming, lumpy, festering, seemingly bottomless feekhole of a situation. Jesse silently composed several particularly creative curses for Mhartom's demeanor, his scales, and his possible parentage. After that warm-up, he progressed to cursing the room, the holo-viewer, his would-be mugger, and the blue-skinned, polyester-clad, she-demon that had dangled a quick score in front of him a week ago, thus tricking him into coming to this gangrenous, pus-soaked, running sore of a port in the first place. He was just about to get to his own parents—wherever the hell they were—for bringing him into this pox-filled galaxy to begin with when the curtain across the room drew aside and the girl walked in.

Jesse assumed she was a girl, which, granted, was always a dangerous practice, and especially so on a day like today. But still. She was humanoid, about two-thirds his height, with a slight frame and exquisitely delicate features. He would have taken her for *sapiens,* but for her lustrous, golden-metallic skin. Inky black hair fell straight to her shoulders, framing high cheekbones and slanted, oval eyes that flashed a bright, fiery green, even from across the dimly lit room. By Human standards, she looked to be barely more than a child, perhaps just beginning puberty.

Jesse stood up, suddenly feeling very old.

She walked right up to him and poked him in the chest. "You should have your mind washed out," she accused. "Just be glad Modajai," she waved her hand at Mhartom, "can't hear things like Velantra can."

Jesse was nonplussed. The effort of trying to fit her words into any of this increasingly bizarre picture must have shown on his face, because the girl suddenly dropped her mask of righteous outrage and giggled. She looked over her shoulder to where Paz had followed her into the room.

"Looks like the Sape's been caught with his mental trousers down."

More giggles.

Jesse was suddenly struck by a disturbing image of this girl-child actually pulling down his trousers. The thought was so powerful he had to look down to make sure he was indeed still clothed, despite the fact the girl hadn't moved at all in front of him.

Now feeling old *and* humiliated, he could only stare at her mutely.

She giggled again.

He finally found his voice. "Now wait just a damn minz. That was you, just now—the...image...?"

She affected a wide-eyed innocence.

Then she winked at him.

"Oh, no...oh, no, no, *no!* You stay the hell out of my brain, kid!" He didn't have time for these ridiculous games. His shoulder was killing him; in fact, his upper arm was going numb.

Mhartom rumbled deep in his chest and took a step towards Jesse, balling up his fists. Jesse moved back from both girl and beast, but held onto his indignant rage.

The girl stepped between Mhartom and Jesse, still snickering. "Oh, Mhartom, you really must learn to relax just a bit." She took his massive fist in her slender hands and massaged his fingers open. "There. Now, as for you," she turned to Jesse, "I'm tempted to let Mhartom here use your bones for drumsticks, after the way you roughed up little Paz."

The fur-ball yipped his assent, but before Jesse could speak, the girl went on, "Then again, if the little bottom-feeder tried to pick my pocket while I was still bleeding from a run in with the 'stalkers, I'd prolly want to beat his ass, too." She paused, as if considering the idea. Her brow furrowed. "Of course, if Bla'ag Thul's got his pet monkey-thugs after you," the girl said to herself, "who knows how much you might be worth? Hmmph." She eyed Jesse and shrugged.

Obviously, there was no way he was going to figure out what was going on here, so Jesse gave up trying. "Look," he began, "I'm sorry if I hurt your little friend there, kid—"

"I'm *not* a kid, Sape!" Green fire flickered in her eyes.

Jesse held up his hands, palms out, hoping the gesture would indicate his desire for a truce. He was starting to feel seriously light-headed. "Listen, the fuzz-ball promised to take me to someone who could patch up a pulse blast wound. I don't think it's too deep, but it hurts like hell, it's getting worse just standing here, and I can't go tooling through these tunnels with a shirt soaked in blood—it attracts all the wrong kinds of attention, you know?"

He paused for a moment, eyeing her carefully before continuing. *What the hell?* he reckoned. *Let's roll these dice.*

"I mean, if there *is* any law down this far, they'll figure me for the wrong kind of people faster than 'Tiny' here," he nodded at Mhartom, "can say 'What's the password?' I doubt they'd care about your pick-pocketing gig, but I'd hate to have to tell them about any off-world smuggling operations they might not have noticed, yet."

The green fire in the girl's eyes paled noticeably. She recovered well enough to shoot back: "You'd be lucky to make it back to Boulevard. You couldn't possibly find a Connie down here, and even if you did, none of them would listen to *you!*" Her voice was confident, but Jesse saw she was still pretty shaken.

He pressed further. "And I guess there couldn't possibly be any other players down here who'd care at all that some punk-amateurs were cutting into their action?"

She looked from Paz to Mhartom, and back to Jesse. Their eyes locked. On to her now, Jesse struggled to keep his mind blank, despite the blood loss and his mounting frustration. The effort required was massive. But just when he felt his strength ebb, the girl-child looked away.

"Come on," she addressed them all. "We're going to Grandmother's house."

Round III: Over the Edge and Into the Rock…

Grandmother's house was, of course, no more a "house" in the sense that Jesse used the word than any other dwelling carved out of the bare rock, but by the time they arrived, he was past the point of quibbling over such semantics. The journey was to him a miasmic blur of garish lights and faces, punctuated frequently by equally garish odors, splattered across a throbbing backdrop of dissonant noises—at least one of which was his own ragged breathing. Paz and the Velantran girl led the way, but it quickly became apparent that if Mhartom didn't carry him, Jesse wouldn't make it to their destination.

He'd held out as long as he could, in the interested of trying to stay alive, but his wound and, more distressing, the continued loss of blood had him in seriously bad shape. If he didn't get to a medic soon, he would have to bother with one at all. He was quite sure, as he faded in and out of delirium, that a post-mortem meat-processor would be appointed for him.

So it was no surprise that, without having noticed a doorway or portal of any kind, he found himself at Grandmother's house. He realized they were there when suddenly the noise dropped away and the vivid brilliance of the outer corridors was replaced by soothing shadow.

He forced his eyes to focus, and as they adjusted to the darkness, some details emerged. Rugs and tapestries covered much of the floor and walls of a huge chamber. Little effort had been made to carve and sculpt the rock; instead, the décor followed the natural contours of the cavern. Statues, paintings, holograms, and live models filled every available niche and cranny, each softly illuminated by small glowbz, lending the place a museum-like quality. But it was the most thoroughly intimate museum Jesse had ever seen—full, but not cloying…hypnotic, but not dizzying…vibrant, but not manic. Despite the expansive area and the abundance of priceless artwork, the place had the organic, welcoming appeal of a quaint parlor.

Somewhere in the shadows, Jesse heard the trickling of open water, but he couldn't pinpoint its location. The sounds intertwined with the faint melodies of a somasar.

"Carry me in, boys—let me get a look at this void!"

The booming voice shocked Jesse out of his reverie. It was followed by several vigorous grunts and what sounded like some creative profanities in a language Jesse did not speak. Then the owners of the voices moved into the nearest light.

Jesse's mouth dropped open. Borne aloft on a jewel-encrusted palette by four of what he now recognized—thanks to Mhartom—as Modajai was an enormous Human woman. Her enormity filled the cavern around her. It overtook the muscular, scaly bulk of her litter-bearers. It filled Jesse's perception to the exclusion of all other thought. In all his travels, in all his wanderings through one bizarre warren or haven after another, and in all his surreal dealings with characters who defied categorization or description, it had never occurred to him that a Sape could amass such…well, *mass*. He was, rather obviously, at a loss for words.

The Modajai litter-bearers deposited their charge, amid wrenching grimaces, before Jesse and his escorts, Paz, Mhartom, and the Velantran girl whose name he still didn't know. Breathing loudly, they then melted back into the shadows. Even in his weakened state, Jesse knew better than to assume they were gone, however.

Grandmother—for the woman before him could be no one else—leaned forward slightly—or perhaps she just exhaled—and squinted at Jesse. Her eyes all but vanished. Long moments passed before she moved again.

Eventually, she took a deep breath and sighed dramatically. "You'd best get him to the Doc," her voice resonated through the chamber, rattling Jesse's ribcage. "He don't look none too good."

Then she locked her gaze upon the Velantran and squinted again. "This better be worth my while, Razhu!"

The rumble of her words reverberated long after Jesse finally blacked out.

<^>

"Ah, there we are. Coming around at last, meat?"

Jesse kept his eyes closed and gritted his teeth. The high, screeching voice had been assailing him for some minz now, and each word brought him closer to outright violence. Which, all things considered, was probably the stupidest idea he'd ever entertained—his dalliances in the green-light district of Terra-17 notwithstanding. Moving further into consciousness—whether he wanted to or not—he took several deep, ragged breaths. His bones felt gelatinous, and he barely had the strength to keep his lungs expanding and contracting. But if he didn't say something soon, he knew that beralloy-rending voice would rake his last good nerve, and that would be it. He'd either have to talk, or take his chances at lashing the owner of that voice to death with his jelly-arms—while lying flat on his back, to boot.

I'm definitely getting too old for this, he moaned to himself.

"Nonsense! You're not even old enough for me to call you 'kid!'" A new voice. A giggling voice.

Oh, no. Not her, again.

"Hey, watch it, offal! We coulda letcha just bleed out and harvested your meat for some quick cred."

Well, that's true, he thought. He opened one eye. Light lanced through his brain like a las-knife. *Damn!*

"Easy there, junior," Jesse croaked. "That last line felt a little forced. You want to sound angry, not hysterical." He closed his eye again.

The screeching voice returned with a vengeance: "There he is, charming as I assume he always was. Razhu, you may go inform Grandmother that the procedure was a rousing success."

Jesse winced. *What the hell's he talking about? All he had to do was patch up a flesh wound and get me some fresh plasma.* He tried opening his eyes again. More las-knives, but he decided to play through the pain.

"Look, doc, I appreciate your services. How much do I owe you?"

The doctor—a gnarled and wizened figure that could perhaps have started life as Human, but now seemed an extension of the rough-hewn cave-wall behind him—clucked his tongue against his one, prominent tooth. "Tsk tsk, not to worry. Grandmother's taken care of everything."

Jesse resisted the urge to let fly an extended barrage of curses. *Oh, this is gonna cost me,* he screamed silently. Then he sat up, and screamed very loudly.

"Easy there, son," the doctor crackled. His voice was like claws shearing beralloy. "Take it slow. Gotta get your rock-legs back, you know?"

"What did you do to me?"

"Nothin', nothin'. Nothin' but save your life, that is."

"But it was just a pulse-blast! Yeah, I lost some blood, but—"

The doctor's stony face turned grim. His voice dropped an octave: "Now look, son, you just relax, or I'll dose you with something that *will* relax you. I saved your life, and that's all you need to know."

Jesse met the doctor's hard glare and realized he was, in his present condition, quite outmatched. "Sorry, doc. It's been a...a hard day."

"Yeah, so I'm told." The little man busied himself tidying up the miniscule cleft in the rock that apparently served as his office, waiting room, and surgical theatre. "So I'm told," he trailed off, muttering.

Jesse found his vest on the table beside him, along with a fresh, clean tunic. His muscles screamed in protest as he put them on. *Maybe I can salvage something from all this,* he thought.

He cleared his throat gruffly. "So, doc, if I were to slip you a couple of credz, you think you could do me a small favor?"

The doctor whirled around. "I don't peddle medz unlegal-like, don't care how much cred you got drippin' off of you!"

"No, no—you got me all wrong," Jesse soothed. "It's just that I'm new here on the Rock, and I could really use a little info. That's all." Jesse met the doctor's eyes steadily, his face a picture of humility and contrition.

The doctor harrumphed. "What kind of info?"

"Ever hear of something called 'narissum'?"

"Hmm, can't say as I have."

Damnation, Jesse thought. *Just can't catch a break!* He sighed.

"Tell you what, maybe if you do hear mention of it, or if someone else comes asking you about it, you could let me know. I'd be very grateful..." He reached into one of his vest pockets for the credz he'd gotten from Ny'storae. His fingers found nothing. Ignoring the pain of moving so quickly, he frantically searched the other pockets. Nothing!

The doctor harrumphed again. "Just what I need—a nice, fat handful of offal gratitude. You spacers spend too much time in the void, if you asked me..." He turned away, still muttering into his dingy lab coat.

Jesse stood up, exerting all his will not to cry out as his joints and muscles shrieked their protest. He had no idea what this alleged doctor had done to him, but for the time being, he couldn't afford to care. Right now, he needed to find his new "friends" and have a little talk with them. And once he had his credz back, he was back on his ship and off this damned rock, if it meant he had to claw his way back up to the surface with his bare hands.

At least, he noticed as he made for the exit, the searing pain in his muscles had died back to a dull, constant ache. Just the same, he steadied himself on various tables and instrument stands as he passed through the lab. He tried not to notice the noises—and in some instances, actual glances—that came from various jars, beakers, and cages along the rough-hewn walls. The door to the outside was a circular, beralloy hatch centered about waist-high. Stooping over, Jesse paused before climbing through.

Looking back over his shoulder, he addressed the back of the dingy lab-coat that hunched over a flickering com-screen next to the table where Jesse had lain: "You're right, I suppose, Doc. You did save my life." Jesse swallowed hard. "Thank you."

The lab-coat seemed to straighten a little bit, but quickly hunched back over the screen, muffling whatever reply the Doc might have mumbled.

Jesse cleared his throat. He pitched his voice as cold and rough as the surface of the asteroid. "But if I find out you did anything else to me along with it, you won't be able to find a hole in this place deep enough to hide from me."

He let the words fall flatly into the narrow lab, holding just a moment to make sure he was heard before twisting the hatch open and crawling outside. It closed behind him with a clang as he stepped down into the corridor. Startled by the sound, he turned to see a solid wall of bare rock. The cover was so complete that, for an instant, Jesse honestly believed he must have been mistaken to think there was a door there at all, much less a laboratory.

His surprise only lasted a moment before he shoved it forcibly from his mind. Too many other things to worry about right now, anyway. *Like getting my credz back from that kindly old crime boss. "Grandmother," my ass!*

Jesse had taken three determined steps when it hit him: *Where the hell am I?* The corridor was unfinished rock, dimly illuminated by random patches of soft-glowing lichen. Passageways branched off to his left and right, quickly disappearing into thick shadows. Rage, frustration, and despair each put in a serious bid to overwhelm his thinking. He fought them all down, taking deep, even breaths.

When he had his emotions in check, he offered a silent thanks to his old Masters at the Academy. He'd often wondered what they'd have to say about his unique interpretation of the concept of fieldwork. A wan smile flickered at the edges of his mouth, despite the impossibility of his present circumstance. *"Once the aim is identified,"* he recited to himself, *"completion becomes a simple gesture of will."*

Jesse sat down, resting his back against the rock wall. Perhaps that's what had turned this past cyk into such an unmitigated catastrophe. He had not been clear about his aim in coming to Port Nowhere from the beginning. At the time, he'd convinced himself he needed the money. Of course, the creditors who owned his ship had helped to convince him of that, too. But he'd gotten out of a thousand tight spots before, and he'd never had to break his own rules about whom he'd take as a client and whom he wouldn't, either.

Everything—everything—about this Yruldhi woman, this Ny'storae, had set off mental warnings he'd spent his entire career—if you could call it a career—trusting. But there was something else about her, too. Something enticing... All her talk of her race's long-lost homeworld, of the remnants of her vanished, vanquished culture seeking to rebuild whatever pieces they could of what they'd lost... *That's* what had hooked him, what had gotten him to agree to a meeting deep inside of a port he'd never seen, at the very outermost edge of civilization—against every screaming instinct he had.

Jesse actually chuckled out loud at that last thought. He may have been out of the Academy for a [decade], but he could never escape himself. Whatever else he'd become, he would always be, at some level, that scrawny, wide-eyed dedicant, seeking initiation into the Mysteries of Origins, looking up at the pin-pricks of light flickering in the night sky and wondering where his people came from.

But right now, there was a bloated old woman holding the only few credz he had to his name and way too much control over his life, and she needed dealing with. Time for him to do what he did best, and turn this insane menagerie of characters and their hidden motives to his advantage—somehow.

He stood up. *Okay, I've got my aim,* he thought. *I suppose now I just have to "will" myself back to Grandmother's house?* He was about to add on some choice profanities for his old Masters' infatuation with abstract—and, in his opinion, utterly pointless—axioms, when the shadows to his right giggled.

Razhu stepped into the emerald glow of the nearest lichen, smiling but attempting to look cross at the same time. "Where have you been?" she chided. "We've been looking all over for you!"

Jesse blinked at her, twice. He was no longer surprised by anything that came out of her mouth. "What's the problem? I just stepped outside for some fresh rock."

A cascade of giggles. She reached out and took his hand. "Come on, I have to get you back to Grandmother." The girl tugged at his arm till he followed her down the passage. "We've been worried ever since you disappeared from Doc's."

"What do you mean, since I 'disappeared'? I just walked out the door."

193

She sighed elaborately. "You can't just 'walk out the door' when you're at Doc in the Rock! The Doc has to put you back out himself, or there's no telling where you'll end up. It's security, see—the Connies don't seem to approve of unlicensed, unmonitored med-practitioners, so the Doc has to make sure they can't find him."

Jesse couldn't resist it. "So, he hides *underground?*" he joked.

Razhu rolled her eyes at him. Jesse stuck his tongue out at her in reply.

"No," she lectured, "he's *in* the rock. Doc-in-the-Rock. You want to see him, you gotta go into the rock, too. And when you're done, you come back out of the rock, wherever the Doc puts you. You *never* just jump out the back hatch! What if you stepped out into the Core?"

Jesse thought for a minz, as she hurried him through several twisting corridors. "If it's that random, how did you find me?"

Razhu didn't answer. She squeezed his hand tightly and pulled him behind her through a wide archway that opened onto the main Boulevard of LevFive, not too far from where Paz had tried to rob him. Several minz passed as they dodged and wove their way through throngs of street traffic, eventually turning off the main thoroughfare into a maze of back alleys and connecting tunnels. They came to a stop in front of a plain, metal door. A placard above the door was marked in several languages. The ones which Jesse could read all said *Granny Khouri's Fortunes, Etc.*

The girl looked up at him and grinned. "I'm glad you're one of us, now." She slid the door open and dashed inside before Jesse could respond.

Round IV: Fortunes for Sale or Rent

Jesse hesitated for a moment before following Razhu into Grandmother Khouri's hole-in-the-rock fortune telling shop. Staring at the sign above him, he couldn't help but reflect on the coincidence of the situation. Mere moments after declaring his intention to confront this 'Grandmother'—whoever she was—here he stood, outside her door, his aim completed. Completely coincidence, of course, but it did give him pause.

He hadn't thought about his old Masters much at all in the past ten sintinz. In fact, he'd tried to forget as much as he could of his former existence, before he'd wised up and accepted the harsh realities of living. He scratched his beard. The damned Academy had taken seven sintinz of his life, used him like the mindless tool they'd fashioned him to be, and he'd been all too happy to let them.

He took a deep breath and let it out slowly. *Well, I still say to hell with their mumbo-jumbo,* he thought, angry that the old feelings had come back to life so perniciously, and so unexpectedly. *It'd be just like those bastards to have planted some damned delayed program in my brain. But it's my brain, godsdammit, and I'm gonna use it to get my credz, get back to my ship, and get the hell off this rock!* One last deep breath to pump up his uncharacteristically shaky confidence, and he slipped through the doorway into Grandmother Khouri's waiting parlor.

The scene inside caught him quite by surprise, though upon reflection, he had to admit he'd had no idea what to expect. This place was nothing like the hazy images of artwork and shadows he remembered from his first encounter with Grandmother. A narrow entranceway opened into a brightly lit chamber. The ceiling and walls were finished in sleek polybdalloy and outlined a space that was easily a hundred square meters. Modular polybdalloy partitions divided most of the area into individual cubicles, each with varying combinations of Comsys equipment: ear pieces—or other organ pieces, for non-humanoids—vid-screens, holo-viewers, all cutting-edge tech.

At the front of the suite, right in front of where he'd entered, a wide space was left open, and it led up to a reception desk. Behind the desk sat a gracile, purple-skinned humanoid. He looked to be the Human equivalent of a teen-ager. He also looked to be bored out of his mind.

Seemed like the place to start, especially since Razhu obviously hadn't waited for him to follow her in—she was nowhere in sight.

Jesse walked straight up to the desk. "My name's Iresson," he said.

The purple boy cocked his head to one side and stared at him. A universal gesture that Jesse translated as, "And that means *what,* to me?"

"I'm here to see Grandmother."

The boy cocked his head to the other side.

Jesse gritted his teeth. He didn't have time for this. "She has some credz for me," he pressed.

The boy perked up slightly. He made a guttural, coughing sound; Jesse thought the kid might be choking on something, as the noise got louder and the boy began to shake. Then the kid opened his mouth and exploded into a barrage of harsh, hacking laughter.

Jesse seriously considered giving this void a crash course in public relations. He'd just clenched his fists to deliver his first lecture when he caught a glimpse of fur speeding towards him on the floor.

Paz bashed into Jesse's knee and instantly began to climb. In a heartbeat, he whipped around Jesse's legs, swung across his back, came around his shoulder, and perched eye to eye with the Human, one claw gripping Jesse's collar and both feet anchored in the pockets of Jesse's vest. He then glared at the man—who glared back—for a long moment, absently licking one of his huge eyeballs clean.

When he finally spoke, he bared his front teeth. "Where the hell have you been?" Paz demanded. "Never mind. Don't care. Just come with me."

With that, he leapt into the air, landing several meters away, and took off through the maze of cubicles towards the back of the office complex. Jesse shot a withering look at the purple punk behind the desk, then ran off after Paz.

He caught up with the little pickpocket in front of what appeared to be a real wood office door. Jesse reached out to feel its texture; if it were synth, it was one of the best synth jobs he'd ever seen.

Paz tugged on his pant-leg to bring him back to the present. "Come on," he said. "Time to talk business!"

Inside, the office was paneled in the same exquisite synth wood—Jesse just knew it *had* to be synthetic—as the door. The paneled walls were lined with bookshelves full of replicas of old-fashioned books. Jesse could scarcely believe what he was seeing—he hadn't seen this many real books in one place since the Academy. On the far side of the room, a huge synth wood desk stretched nearly the whole width of the office. Behind it loomed the expansive frame of Grandmother, a deep scowl filling her face as her immense bulk filled the back of the office.

Jesse stared at her for a moment, glancing from her to the door he'd just come through, then back to her. *How the hell did they get her in here?* he couldn't help wondering.

Grandmother didn't give him much time to ponder the matter, though. She leaned forward slightly, spreading onto her desk. "Jesse Iresson, humph."

Not sure if it were a question or not, he answered, "Yeah, that's me."

"That your real name?"

"Of course, it's my real name." What was she getting at?

She snorted. Her face, Jesse thought, resembled a figure-eight: a round forehead over a rounder jaw, held together by squinty eyes that were too small for her face, let alone her whole body. The fact that her iron-grey hair was pulled severely back from her face did nothing to help the image.

She snorted again, and reminded Jesse of mythological monsters from several different worlds. "Nobody uses real names in the Rock."

Now she was calling him a liar? "Look, I'm not 'in' the Rock. In fact, I never had any intention of staying on this rock as long as I have. I came back here to get my credz, which you or one of your buddies here," he glanced down at Paz, who shrugged, "lifted while I was out cold." Jesse took a step towards the great desk.

At once, he noticed two large Modajai partially concealed in the shadows behind Grandmother. *Oh well, it's too late to back down, now,* he thought. He stabbed a finger in her direction. "Just give me my money, less whatever the cost of that lunatic doctor was, and I'm gone." He let his arm fall slowly back to his side. "You'll never have to deal with me again, and you can get back to whatever it is you do, down here."

A long moment passed. Jesse couldn't even begin to read Grandmother's face.

At last, she said, "Come here."

"What?"

"Come here, to the desk. I'm going to tell your fortune."

This time, Jesse snorted. "You're full of fee—"

Both Modajai growled audibly and stepped forward. Grandmother waved them back with an enormous hand.

She focused on Jesse. "Come here, boy."

Jesse did not like the way this was going. His instincts were screaming again. How much deeper was he going to have to dig himself in, before he could think about digging out? Still, he didn't appear to have much choice but to keep playing along, at least for now.

He walked slowly forward until he stood directly in front of the desk. Grandmother's eyes bored into him from within the folds of her face, and he had the uncomfortable sensation of being strip-searched. Jesse watched her face as she examined him. This close, he could tell she was clearly as Human as he was, despite her incredible dimensions. She had just as clearly seen many more sintinz than he, and the times had left their marks on her. He'd learned to read those marks on his clients' faces—sometimes the hard way. In the lines around her eyes and mouth, he read experience, more than a little pain and hardship, shrewdness, and ruthless pragmatism, but no outright cruelty.

At length, Grandmother grunted what might have been her approval. "Give me your right hand," she commanded.

Jesse hesitated only a moment before complying.

"Now," she said, "Let's see what's written here…" she trailed off, apparently lost in concentration.

"What?" Jesse prompted.

She dropped his hand and stared into his eyes. "Here's the way it's going to play out, see. You're broke, you got no credz, and you owe me for your Doc in the Rock bill, among other things." She went on gruffly before Jesse could interrupt. "But don't you worry. I got a friend, topside, on LevOne, owns a trinket shop for high-class tourists, and he needs somebody to run the place, somebody humanoid. Apparently, the average tourist tends to be put off by the Coriliun understanding of 'courtesy' in customer relations."

Jesse lost all semblance of patience. "Are you mad, you gargantuan bovine? *I* owe *you?* You robbed me! You cleaned me out, and now I'm supposed to take some bov-feek job in some damned tourist trap to pay off what I *don't* owe you in the first place? Forget the credz, you keep 'em! The hell with it. To hell with the docking fees—I'll blast my ship straight through the port dome if I have to, but I am *gone!"*

Both Modajai guards came forward from behind Grandmother's desk, but Jesse was already turning to head for the door. He was about a meter from the exit when Mhartom stepped into the doorway and planted himself like a stone.

Well, so much for the righteous-indignation approach, Jesse thought, turning back to face Grandmother and her bodyguards. *Only one card left to play.* He absolutely hated having to throw everything he had into one gambit, one he had no reason to believe offered any hope of keeping him in one piece, let alone paying off. But a quick tally of his alternatives came up somewhere between zero and nil.

"I'll tell you what's really going on here," he said. He pitched his voice low, keeping his tone even, so that each word rode a current that said: *this is the bottom line.* It was the voice he used to close his deals, or to inform a client his rates had just doubled due to that client's lack of cooperation, faulty info, or similar idiocy. "You could give two bov-feeks for whatever credz I allegedly 'owe' you for the Doc, or anything else. That story's about keeping up appearances—namely, the appearance that you don't help anybody for free. I understand that. It's business. In this case, it's also hooey. But it provides decent cover for what you really want, doesn't it?"

"And what is it that I 'allegedly' really want?" She mimicked his tone, shooting for condescension, but falling short and sounding merely petulant.

Jesse stared her down for a brief moment, measuring just the right length of time before continuing. "You're the kingpin—'scuse me, the queenpin—of a third tier, grey market smuggling outfit, doing most of your business offworld, but providing a handy outlet here in the Rock for out-of-town acquaintances who need to make things disappear. Hell, maybe even if they need to make people disappear. These lower levels have got to be perfect for that. Not to mention the convenient supply of sentients down here whom no one would ever miss, should some offworlder want to purchase something more exotic than last sintinz' outdated techware."

Grandmother's eyes had lost much of their squintiness. "Who in the name of the Core told you that?" She glowered at Paz, then at Mhartom.

Jesse chuckled, affecting casual disdain. "Please, didn't 'Tiny' there and the little thief," he nodded towards each of them, respectively, "tell you how we first met? I busted the fuzz ball trying to pick my pocket, and I convinced him to take me to a doctor. First stop on the way was one of your unmarked, and I'm sure untaxed, warehouses."

"Humph." Her glowering shifted back to Paz, who was working very hard to become invisible.

Jesse pressed the advantage. "And let's not forget all the reproductions and facsimiles of pseudo-classical artworks with which you surrounded yourself when these two and the girl brought me to you, in your little museum. Oh, don't worry. It was some of the best imitation work I've seen. But imitation, nonetheless."

Grandmother's patience was obviously wearing thin. Her ruddy face had paled considerably, and the index finger of her left hand tapped ominously upon the polished woodgrain of the desktop. Her words were terse: "What's your point?"

Time to bring it on home, Jesse told himself. "It seems pretty clear that you've had enough of being third tier. You're dyin' to break into the second, maybe the first tier of the import-export business. Maybe even get into full on black-market goods and piracy, I don't know. But all the big time players run on the upper levels, and you got about as much chance of getting up there as you do hopping over that desk and dancing a jig, don't you?"

All the color that had drained from her face came flooding back. She was just about at the breaking point, Jesse could tell. But he couldn't let her break just yet, not if he wanted to get out of this.

"Take it easy, now," he soothed. "I'm just sayin' it's pretty clear that you don't need me to work off a few credz of debt in some trinket shop. What you *do* need is a Sape face on the top levels who can put a semi-respectable front on your more...creative...business endeavors, right? Maybe move some 'specialized' merch in or out quietly, interface with the various high rollers who breeze through the port and might make valuable customers." He paused. "Or easy marks.

Jesse paused again, to let the implications sink in. "And if that's the only way I'm getting out of this room," he glanced at the three Modajai who effectively had him surrounded, "let alone back up top, in good health...well, I guess I can live with that."

He had no idea if he achieved the nonchalance he was going for with that last comment. There was nothing for it but to wait out Grandmother's reaction.

It was not precisely what he expected. She laughed. Just a chuckle or two at first, but that soon crescendoed to full on, gut-shaking guffaws.

"Name of the Core!" she exclaimed. "Razhu said you'd be worth talking to, and by the Beryl, she was right!" She pounded a considerable fist on the desk. "What can I say? We're getting muscled out down here in the Depths. Bla'ag Thul's thugs are everywhere, and the old days of local operations, keeping everything strictly in the Rock... Well, you just can't make a living like that, anymore." She shrugged. "What can you do? The only place to go is up. The folks with the real credz never make it down this far, and as you so politely observed, I'm not as mobile as I used to be."

Jesse wasn't sure exactly how to respond to that, so he tried diverting her focus. "You've certainly got plenty of sentients working for you. What I can't figure is why you'd go to such trouble just to strong-arm me into helping?"

"I got hardly no good sapiens on the payroll, is the thing, see? And, heyo, that's the key—nobody takes us Sapes seriously, especially when it comes to the mean end of this business. Other species see us as too soft to be a threat, and our Sape tourists and up-lev types are so laughably thankful to find some of their own kind in a place like this, you can put damn near anything past 'em."

She thought for a moment, then went on. "Listen, Iresson, I think we understand each other now. You know I got the muscle to make whatever I want to happen, happen, at least down here. And now you also know that I need your help. Why don't you make this simple for both of us?"

He had to admit, the exchange had gone rather well, given the circumstances. He was specifically glad to have had his conjectures about Grandmother and her organization confirmed. Jesse was a big fan of knowing exactly where he stood. He nodded. "Okay, I'm in—for now. I'll give it a stretchiz, no questions asked. After that, after I get some idea of what I'm able to move for you, and how much it's worth, then we'll negotiate my split."

Her slitted eyes widened for a split second, and Jesse wondered if he'd gone too far, but then she smiled and said, "Fair enough. Mhartom will take you topside. He'll pose, for now, as your assistant. I'll have pass-codes arranged to get you through the level checkpoints." Her smile faded. "Don't disappoint me, Mastre Iresson."

Jesse nodded. *Right,* he thought. *No problem. Just don't expect me to play your damned puppet one minz longer than it takes me to reach LevOne!*

Round V: The Way the Game is Played

The journey up from the labyrinths of LevFive was unremarkable, which as far as Jesse was concerned was quite remarkable, in light of his first eight owers since arriving at Port Nowhere. Mhartom escorted him to and through each security checkpoint with an efficiency that bordered on rudeness. Each time they left a level, their codes were checked by stern-faced Connies; likewise, each time they entered the next level up. No one asked them any questions, although they did draw some quizzical stares, particularly as they worked their way through LevThree suburbia to find the secure-node that would jump them straight up to LevOne.

Mhartom did not speak. He barely made a sound. When he did, it was little more than a grunt as he less-than-gently nudged Jesse in the direction the Modajai wanted him to move.

Jesse, for his part, was glad for the silence. He studied as much as he could of the levels they crossed, though obviously their chosen route did not allow for much sight-seeing. There was, in his thinking, a stark beauty to the colossal machinery he glimpsed on LevFour, underscored by the equally stark absence of people. A sharp contrast to LevFive. In his Academic days, he might have called it "surreal," but nowadays such poetic reflection didn't last long before being shoved aside by more immediate concerns. LevThree, on the other hand, could have been lifted out of any number of worlds Jesse had worked.

A suburb is a suburb, he thought, *even if it's subterranean.*

He saw nothing of LevTwo; when he asked one of the Connies at the LevThree exit point what to expect there, the woman looked up at him sharply and summoned her partner, a tall, fur-covered creature with four powerfully-built arms extending from under his uniform. The first guard double-checked Jesse's passcode. When it cleared, she mentioned something about LevTwo's being a secured level and told him to move along and take his Modajai with him. Mhartom bristled at that, but Jesse led him into the lift as quickly as possible. He knew better than to indulge his pride around local police, even if his "assistant" didn't.

After the door slid shut, Mhartom growled, "Vamir."

"You know that guy?" Jesse joked—he'd had his own dealings with the species before.

"That's what they're called, the four-armed, hairy slime-eaters."

"Guess that makes our buddy Paz a two-armed, hairy slime-eater, huh?"

"No, he's a Bansnict."

Jesse said, "Oh," and wondered if the same genes that made Modajai large, grey, and scaly also blocked their capacity for humor.

When the lift door opened onto the bustling, cosmopolitan lights and rhythms of LevOne, Jesse almost offered a silent thanks to the Masters, but he caught himself in time.

"Well," he looked up at his stone-faced companion, "We've made it to the big-time."

Mhartom glanced down at him coolly, remaining silent.

Jesse stepped from the lift. "I'm just sayin', don't let it go to your head."

The Modajai followed him out, then took the lead, turning left and moving quickly into the flow of foot traffic headed for one of the prime tourist districts. Jesse took a deep breath and followed, jostling his way into place just behind his guide.

He normally couldn't stand crowds, but at this moment it was all Jesse could do to hide his elation. *This is gonna be even easier than I thought,* he told himself, even as he forced his outward expression to remain calm.

Every few meters, lanes of pedestrian traffic formed crossroads; people moved in and out of the flow with hypnotic intricacy. Perhaps five minz went by before Jesse was surrounded on all sides by total strangers. He could still see Mhartom's back, a meter or two ahead of him, his shoulders set in concentration as he navigated among the smaller folk around him. The lunk did not seem to notice the increasing distance between them.

A few minz later, a large group of sapiens merged into the lane. Jesse fell off his pace even further, and soon all he could see of Mhartom was the back of his head, apparently floating upon a sea of people.

At that point, Jesse ducked to the side and headed back towards the lift as fast as he could without standing out from the other travelers. He passed the lift and the security node, moving straight into the domed tunnel leading to the hangar bay. Up here, Port Nowhere didn't seem all that different than any other space port. The domes were spacious, everything was clearly labeled in multiple languages, and finding one's way was just a matter of navigating the crowds and watching one's step. In no time at all, it seemed, he'd made it to Hangar Seven.

He went straight for the lock-pod compartments, glad he hadn't broken all his personal rules since coming here. First thing he always did in a new port was to rent an extra pod, under an assumed name, for emergency supplies, one of which was a cheap envirosuit, in case he had to go through an open hangar. His good suit was in the pod rented under his actual name, but that's the first place the heat would look, if the heat were ever on.

Which, right now, it was, definitely. Hopefully, in this case, old Granny Khouri hadn't yet been able to track down exactly when he arrived, or precisely where his ship was berthed, but that could only be a matter of time.

The pod was right where he'd left it, which wasn't too surprising, as the rows of pods were carved out of the solid rock and fitted with secure, polybdalloy doors. Of less certainty was whether his key-code would still open it—fortunately, it did. Good to know at least some bit of luck was still with him. At some point, if he made it out of here, he'd have to ask himself if he shouldn't consider a career that wasn't quite so dependent upon random moments of luck.

Donning the suit as quickly as he could, he double-checked all the seals and closures, then made for the airlock that led to the hangar proper. Just a few hundred meters to Berth 42, and he was back on the *Pathfinder* and the hell away from this lunatic-infested chunk of cosmic gravel.

Hangar Seven housed the hundreds of small, personal craft on temporary layover for business or pleasure. At least, the ones whose owners didn't know the Dyll family, or invest heavily in the Connies' security fund. Jesse passed by ships of all shapes and descriptions, from middle-class vacation models for the wage-slaves who'd spent lifetimes scrimping for retirement to sleek sports models, scaled to be barely larger than the wanna-be astro-trash who flew them to impress the real moneyed crowds. One of the former occupied Berth 41, blocking his view of his own ship until he came around to the front of the berth.

When he cleared the travel-home ship, he stopped cold, too stunned to move.

The berth was empty.

No *Pathfinder,* no ship of any kind! Just empty space and filthy rock flooring.

Jesse stared at where his ship wasn't for a full minz. But rage soon overcame dismay—which was good, because it kept him from panicking—and he dashed back the way he'd come to find whatever docking official was on duty. The checkpoint station was just inside the airlock that led back to the LevOne domes.

"Officer!" Jesse shouted, forgetting himself, the com-speakers in his envirosuit overloading. Instantly, he regretted it, but there was nothing for it but to press on. "Officer," he said more calmly. "Forgive me for interrupting you, but there seems to be a small mix-up, and I was hoping you could help me."

The official was a broad woman with curly black hair framing her round face inside her envirosuit. "What seems to be the trouble?" she asked, with all the enthusiasm of a salesman who'd just been asked for a refund.

"It's my ship—"

"You don't say?"

Jesse forced himself to remain even, fighting down the urge take her by the neck and fling her bodily from the asteroid. "I docked in Berth 42 about nine or ten owers ago, paid for a full cyk."

"And?"

"Well, if it's not too much trouble, I'd really like to know *where the hell my ship's gone!*"

That seemed to get her attention, if not her sympathy. "The craft's name, sir?"

"The *Pathfinder.*"

She turned to the holoscreen built into the station desktop. "One minz, please." She scrolled quickly through various menus and manifests. Then she paused, her eyes widening, and looked straight up at Jesse. "Uh, would you wait right here for a moment, please, sir?" She moved to a comsys link and punched in a dial-code. Her voice dropped to a whisper as she spoke into the com-link.

Jesse couldn't make out what she was saying at first, but he thought he caught mention of his ship. Then he distinctly heard the name Khouri, followed by the word stolen.

Damn! he swore to himself. *It's a setup!* But where could he run?

He had just convinced himself that it didn't matter, that the important thing was just to get away from the hangar, when two large figures loomed up on either side of him.

"We're going to have to ask you to come with us, sir," said the one on his left, a Vamir.

His Modajai partner added, "Thank you for your cooperation."

Jesse tried indignation: "What the hell is the meaning of this? I want to know what you cretins have done with my ship, and I want to know now!"

"Your ship," the first Connie chuckled. "That's rich, you void! You steal Grandmother Khouri's personal yacht and then demand to know where it is!" Both guards laughed. "Okay, tell him where 'his' ship is."

Connie Number Two shook his head. "Well, you can't be too careful—apparently there's thieves out jackin' people's cruisers." More laughter.

"*Grandmother's* ship is in impound, where it belongs," said, the Vamir, sobering up, "until one of her people comes to sign it out with her passcode, of course! Now—"

Whatever Number One was about to say next died in his throat. A huge explosion rocked the hangar, knocking all three of them to the ground, which buckled and shook, even as sirens blared out throughout the dome.

"Security to Bioportal Gate 19! Security to Bioportal Gate 19! Med-team to Bioportal Gate 19!" boomed over the hangar's public address system.

Jesse wasted no time. He was on his feet and tearing for the portal back to the main domes of LevOne before either Connie could get back up. He reached the airlock and juked through, ducking aside to the rows of lock-pods to throw off his rented envirosuit. It would only slow him down and make him an easy target once he got back to the market districts. Hurling the flaccid suit to the far end of the corridor, he rushed back down the tunnel tube to the main level.

He stepped into a mad scene: waves of Connies and civilians all running in a thousand directions at once. Sirens screamed unintelligibly overhead. Jesse looked around for the thickest crowd of bodies and headed straight for it. Ripples of little Pazzes—Bansnicts, Mhartom had said—churned around his legs. He just knew he'd have been completely relieved of all goods and funds, in this confusion, had he not already been flat broke. But at least he'd be damn near impossible to spot for the moment, and maybe he could figure the next move to get his ship back.

His thoughts were shattered by two huge, scaled hands, which clamped down onto his shoulders and lifted him forcibly from the crowd.

"You got bov-feek for brains?" Mhartom thundered over the roar of the commotion, setting Jesse down away from most of the confusion. Paz and Razhu flanked the Modajai, and all three stared at Jesse expectantly.

"What?" Jesse was sailing right past his breaking point. "Your precious Grandmother had me arrested for stealing *my own ship!* So don't give me any of your self-righteous condescension, you fungal-sucking rock-head! I've had enough!" He heard Mhartom growl. "What," he was on a roll, now, "you want to take a swing? Fine. Here's my favorite head—why don't you rip it straight off my body, and I'll never have to look at your ugly face again!"

Mhartom raised a clawed hand, and Jesse wondered if his bluff were about to be called on him.

"Mhartom." Razhu's soft voice somehow carried over the din surrounding them.

The enraged Modajai looked down at her. He slowly lowered his arm.

"Now," she continued, "Jesse, you know what you're up here to do, so why are you worried about your ship right now, anyway?"

Jesse could scarcely believe his ears. She sounded so reasonable, and for a moment, he had to think to remember why he hadn't followed Mhartom like he was supposed to. Then a more important question struck him: "How in the hell did you three find me in this chaos?" He gestured at the manic crowds, the overhead sirens.

Paz sniffed. "Well maybe you're not as clever as you think, running straight for the hangar where you left your ship." He glanced side to side, then leaned in towards Jesse. "Or maybe, maybe the good doctor made you a little easier to track down. Grandmother likes to protect her investments, you know." The Bansnict laughed a harsh, rasping laugh.

Jesse's rage swelled again. He felt his face go crimson. Then he felt a cool hand on his. Razhu took his hand and held it gently.

"Come on," she said quietly. "You can settle up with Grandmother about that later." A sly gleam crept into her eyes. "There's not much that's really all that permanent in the Rock, anyway. But for now, you're here, and you're one of us. So you can't get to your ship right now. Don't you always make your way by playing the hand you're given?"

Jesse got the uncomfortable sensation that she was more familiar with his thoughts than he was. He took a deep breath, let it out slowly. "Okay, so what's the move?"

"Come with us to Emyl's shop," she said. "He's waiting for you. We'll help you get set up, me and Paz and Mhartom." She led him by the hand towards the main thoroughfare. Paz and Mhartom followed behind.

Razhu winked up at Jesse. "We might stick around up here for a while, too," she teased. "I think Grandmother wants us to look out for you."

"Yeah, I'll bet she does."

Paz came up on Jesse's left. "You know, Sape, there is a chance we could actually stand to make some large credz, if you're as good as Grandmother seems to think you are."

"He is," Razhu assured.

Jesse cleared his throat. "Okay, so where exactly is this 'trinket shop,' anyway?"

"Tried to show you," Mhartom rumbled from behind him. "Down the main passage, by all that new construction."

"Yeah," said Paz, "they're putting up some kind of weirdo museum or temple, or something. Don't know what it's s'posed to be. 'S weird, whatever it is."

"Temple?" Jesse grabbed the Bansnict by the shoulder and turned him around. "What temple?"

"'S a funny name...like Eckle, or Oh-h...er...somethin'."

Jesse was ready to lift the Bansnict in the air and shake him, when Razhu squeezed his hand, pulling his attention back to her.

"Axhal," she said. "The temple's called Axhal."

Jesse let go of Paz and slowly straightened up. He walked on in silence for a while, letting the words settle in.

At length, he looked down at the diminutive Velantran and said, "You know, Razh, this may not be such a bad hand after all."

~END~

THE LITTLE SLEEP

Steve Thompson

It was, as always, boring. I was bored, and with no end in sight. I was working the spaceport again! There was the usual constant inflow of all types of species and people coming to the Rock for one reason or another, but mostly it was the *other* reason that I enjoyed.

My name is Mik'Amr and I'm a Sergeant in the Consolidated Guard on the Rock. I was pulling a four-two in the spaceport security section of the Rock. I mouthed off to the lieutenant, and now I'm monitor jockeying for the next forty-two owerz.

"Damn!" I muttered under my breath. "I'm stuck up here again."

"Sir?" answered the Consolidated Guard 1 recruit—commonly known as CG1 or just Cog1—sitting next to me.

"No. Nothing, Cog1; just thinking out loud," I replied.

The Communications-Link panel in the spaceport security booth was alive and chattering—as always, it seems, when I'm stuck up here. Over the speakers of the com-link panel came a cry for help, from another Connie squad; they were in distress, a patrol stuck in a firefight on one of the low-levels.

"Get some damn help down here NOW!" yelled a Connie over the comsys.

My insides were starting to tighten up. I could hear the sound of disrupter discharges in the background noise, as well as the screams of wounded and dying guards.

"What is your location?" asked the calm voice of the Connie com-link dispatcher.

I could feel the sweat running down my back; it made my back itch and I couldn't scratch it. Moreover, feek, was I getting pissed.

"This blasted envirosuit! I hate these things!" I said.

"Sir?" asked the new Connie recruit again.

"Shut up, listen, and try to get the location of that fight," I shouted.

"Yes Sir!" piped the recruit.

The speaker came alive again.

"LevThree!"

Jumping to my feet, I keyed the comsys, and yelled, "Activate your damn perim-fields!"

There was a pause...and then the comsys erupted once more into a barrage of sound. I heard the Connie guard issue orders to his subordinates to activate their perim-fields.

The dispatcher came back on and informed the group under fire that reinforcements were on the way; it would be there in a matter of moments.

I sat back down, wiped the sweat from my brow. I glanced at the array of monitors on the spaceport security console—nothing. "It was good while it lasted." I muttered.

"Sir?" asked the recruit again.

"Oh, shut up!" I snapped.

"Yes, Sir."

One good thing was for sure, though; I didn't have to scratch my back any more.

I turned back to the monitors and checked the readings on the influx of species. All normal and no reportable biohazards, the console readings were reporting.

Then, something caught my eye; a small sentient with what appeared to be a soft downy fur covering across the body. I zoomed in the security camera for a closer look. The sentient looked to be about one meter tall, with delicate features, except for the large, protruding optical orbs that seemed to reach almost entirely around its head. I looked at the biomonitor to see what kind of species this was. It reported that this was a Gordoffian.

"That's just great!" I exclaimed.

"Sir?" asked the recruit again.

"That's all we need right now."

"What's that, Sir?"

"Did you catch that species that came in through the bioportal."? I asked.

"Yes, Sir. What about it?"

I turned to look at the new recruit and asked, "Don't they teach you new guys anything in the academy?"

He turned to look at me, sat up straighter in his chair, and answered, "Y-Y-Yes S-s-sir! They did, sir!"

"That's a Gordoffian, an inhabitant of the planet Gordoff in the Lictorone system. The planet is located in the twelfth spiral of the galaxy. The inhabitants of the planet Gordoff are all females."

"How do they...they..."

"Screw?"

Blushing, the Cog1 answered, "Y-yes S-sir."

"They don't, you moron, they're asexual. Did they not teach you anything in the academy?" I asked. I turned to look at the console again. "I tell you what, why don't you go down and escort the young 'lady' to the security briefing pod. I want to ask her what brings her to our humble planetoid."

The Cog1 jumped to his feet, snapped back, "Yes, Sir!" turned on his heels, and marched to the door. It opened before him and he exited; the door closed behind him with a whooshing click.

"You know good and well what the Core is going to happen when he goes down there, don't you?" asked a hoarse, throaty voice behind me. I turned to see my long time friend Nioaka standing there, staring at me with those five small beady eyes of his protruding from what appeared to be two small twigs sticking out from a tree branch.

Nioaka is a Sloygat, a species that resembles an ancient plant species called *tree*. He specializes in language interpretation, or as the depth dwellers call it, *langspeaks*.

213

Nioaka stands just under one and a half meters, and is bipedal, with what appeared to be roots that are actually his feet.

"What?" I asked, holding out my hands in front of me with palms up.

"You know what!" Nioaka snapped back.

"Hurry up and get your twiggy rear over here, let's watch what happens."

"Oh, you're bad, you son of a Neek."

Grinning, Nioaka willowed over to the biomonitor.

Motioning to the Cog1's chair, I offered, "Have a seat, Noak, take a load off."

"Very funny, bum-gap."

Laughing, I mocked, "I forgot, you don't bend too good."

I glanced back to the biomonitor; the recruit was just walking up to the Gordoffian. I pointed to the monitor. "Watch his reaction, Noak, he doesn't have his helmet on! See, his blood pressure is already going up. His heart rate is increasing. I wonder if he's got a woody yet?"

I grabbed my side with both hands and almost fell out of the chair, I was laughing so hard.

Nioaka offered up his hand in the ancient universal signal of close intimate contact.

"Why don't you eat feek and bark at the Core?" retorted Nioaka.

"Always with the negative waves," I snapped back.

Composing myself, I motioned to another new recruit to take over the monitors. "I'm going down to talk to the new arrival; you got the con."

"Yes, Sir!" replied the new recruit.

"Come on, Noak, get the lead out!"

"Very funny, Mik, just keep it up and I'll..."

"You going to club me, again?" I interrupted.

"Eat feek," snapped Noak.

"Touchy, touchy," I replied.

I grabbed my helmet and made my way to the briefing pod in security. Spaceport was a wide-open area about 300 meters across the circular dome, with a retractable roof to provide scenery for the Rock's *guests*. Connected to the spaceport were twenty arriving and exiting gates; each gate has an attached bioportal, which scans arriving species for a variety of diseases and contraband. The different species emerge through the air lock and pass through the bioportals for scanning. If contraband or a biohazard is detected, the specimen is immediately escorted to the appropriate pod for dispositioning. If contraband is detected, the specimen in question is sent to the briefing pods for investigation/interrogation of the circumstances, while biohazards are sent directly to the medpods for curing.

We made our way to the briefing pod door. I looked over at the Cog1; he looked flushed and was sweating profusely, standing, or should I say leaning next to the door. His hands were shaking, and when he wasn't leaning, he hopped from one foot to another. I stepped up to him and pointed my finger in his face like a father would point and scold a child.

"Next time, Cog1, do your homework. If you're going to work the spaceport security booth, always, always do your homework! A Gordoffian exudes strong pheromones that affect humanoid males and females."

"Y-y-yes S-s-sir." The Cog1 sighed, then said through gritted teeth, "May I be excused, Sir? I don't feel too hot."

"On the contrary, Cog1," Nioaka said, "that's the whole point, isn't it? You *do* feel hot. Don't you?"

"You're excused, Cog1." I shook my head.

"T-t-t-thank y-you, S-s-sir."

The young recruit took off down the corridor, almost at a dead run.

I couldn't control myself anymore; I leaned against the corridor wall and laughed so hard I slid down to the deck.

Nioaka kicked me; those woody legs of his hurt. "Compose yourself; you're a sergeant in the Consolidated Guard, you should know better. Try to act more professional."

"I bet you he's headed straight for the brothels as we speak; and besides, you know you were laughing too, I see your branches shaking. So, don't you dare try to tell me to act more professional, you son of a birch." That started me laughing all over again.

215

"Eat feek," snapped Noak. He turned to the pod door and keyed his security code. I put my helmet on and entered the room.

With my intercom sys turned on, my voice sounded eerie and foreboding, adding to the image. "I'm Mik'amr and this is my side-stick, Nioaka. I mean langspeaks-expert Nioaka."

Nioaka cut his eyes over to me in a menacing glance.

The Gordoffian was sitting behind the briefing table. Her arms were crossed over her two large breasts, and she was scanning the room. She looked up at me with those black-in-black eyes. They were so large that I could see my reflection in them. It was unnerving. She opened her mouth to speak and what came out was a series of melodic notes that had a kind of singing/chant-like cadence.

At least that is how it sounded through the intercom sys on my envirosuit. I really hate these things.

"Noak, this is you." I stepped back out of the way.

Nioaka stepped up and stood with his branch-like palms up, he greeted her with a universal sign of peace; he held up his right hand, curled back his digit tendrils until the first two remained up in "V" configuration. She smiled and returned the gesture. She again opened her mouth to speak and another series of melodic sounds came out.

"What'd she say, what'd she say?" I asked.

Nioaka just stood there and listened to her, taking in everything she had to say. After she had finished, he answered her in her in own language, and turned to me.

"What'd she say, what'd she say?" I repeated.

"She said that her name was Ka-Mir, and that she came to the Rock to see a Captain Carle Eversyn."

I rolled my eyes. "Cap'n Eversyn! Oh! That's just great!"

"You going to let me finish or you want to wait till you sleep to figure it out?" snapped Nioaka.

"Okay, Okay, go ahead, finish."

"She said that she was looking for Carle Eversyn, in order to facilitate a trade agreement with her planet and Port Nowhere," said Noak.

"I can only wonder what kind of trade agreement that Eversyn wanted to set up with her, and her planet. Probably the kind of trade that happens down on the lower levs."

"She seems to me to be very intelligent and likable, but ..."

"But what?" I asked.

"Will you let me finish a sentence once in awhile, you piece of depth void!"

"Sure, sure, go right ahead."

"Well, as I was saying. She seemed to be very intelligent and likable, but ..."

"You've said that already."

"Eat feek. She said she was going to Headquarters to propose to him, to ask him to marry her. That is apparently how the Gordoffians secure favorable trade agreements with other planets."

"You're feeking me, aren't you? You're just trying to get me back for chopping you."

"No, really, she is going to ask Captain Eversyn to marry her," replied Nioaka.

"This *is* news. This is shaping up to be a very exciting day indeed. I can't believe that Captain Carle Eversyn will be getting married," I muttered.

The idea that Captain Eversyn was marrying anybody was ludicrous, but this was astounding news, I thought to myself.

"What? You know I can't hear you when you mumble and have that blasted helmet on. Speak *up!*" exclaimed Nioaka.

I turned back to look at Ka-Mir, again my intercom sys making a muffled, muted rendition of my voice, and asked, "Do you have any ideas on how I can communicate with her?"

"Yeah, live three hundred sintinz," replied Nioaka, poking me with his branchy tendrils.

"Son of a beech," I snapped.

"What?" asked Noak.

"Nothing!"

"I wish you would stop that!" said Noak.

I turned to look at Noak; his eyes were twitching back and forth. Those eye movements never cease to unnerve me. That gave me the Core creeps, even after all these sintinz of being friends and partners. "No, really, we need to wrap this up so that we can spring this on Cap'n Eversyn. I'm sure he'll be happy to meet his new bride. But, first I feel that I have to run this through my superiors."

"Oh, you're bad, you know that Commander Frohman's gonna hit the dome."

"Serves her right. Besides, we have to finish this. Now, how in the Core do I communicate with this, uh, specimen?"

"Sure...yeah...I can see that you're getting testy again."

I crossed my arms over my suit and glared. "Just tell me how to talk to her," I said through gritted teeth.

"All right, I tell you... Let's take her down to headquarters, and we'll implant her with a comchip."

"That'll work," I replied, surprised I hadn't thought of it myself, "but first let me notify headquarters and tell them what's going on. I'm sure that Eversyn will want to spruce up a little before his new bride arrives."

"Eat feek," replied Nioaka. "Laugh it up while you can, Sape!"

The intercom sys in my envirosuit snapped and crackled to life.

"Get me some back-up to the spaceport arrival dome now!" shouted the Cog1 in charge of the security section.

"What in the name of the core are you yelling at, Cog1?" I asked.

"There's been an explosion in the arrivals section of the bioportal Gate Nineteen!"

"What's the damage?"

"Right now, Sir, I don't know," the recruit replied.

"I'll go take a look. You stay calm and notify the dispatcher. Then get some reinforcements up here to contain the passengers and restore some order."

"Yes, Sir," replied the recruit.

I turned to Nioaka, "Noak, we got some business to take care of."

I glanced at the guard on the Gordoffian, "Keep her here and for the Core's sake don't let her out of your sight."

"Yes, Sir!" replied the female Connie guard.

I could feel the sweat running down my back again. *Damn, I hate it when that happens,* I thought. My back started to itch again. *I hate these blasted envirosuits.*

"Come on, Noak, we gotta go!" I said, "I can't work in this thing." I reached up and unclasped my helmet and laid it on the table in front of Ka-Mir.

I reached out and grabbed Nioaka, picked him up and started out the door.

"I wish you wouldn't do that," exclaimed Nioaka, "it is so embarrassing."

"I can't help that you're too slow. Shut up and enjoy the ride."

The door opened, *swoosh*, and with Noak tucked under my arm, we were out of the security booth.

But just as we stepped out, the whole world shook with what could only be described as an earthquake. If it were not for the fact that the Cog1 in the security booth had reported an explosion at Gate Nineteen, that is what I would have thought, but instead it was yet another explosion.

"Corporal Dviess, stay here with our guest while we check this out." I commanded.

"Yes Sir, Sergeant!"

I ran to Gate Nineteen. There was complete pandemonium, Humans and other species alike were screaming and crying out in pain. The area was filled with smoke and several small fires had been started. Numerous bodies and body parts had been strewn about. There was a fur-charred Vamir holding a stump where his arm had been just a few moments ago; on the ground in front of him was what left of his arm, still twitching.

"Noak, get on the comsys and order a med-team to Gate Nineteen, have 'em bring the meat-pod too. We have several dead."

"Yeah, right away!" replied Nioaka.

I bent down, took hold of part of the Vamir's tunic and ripped a strip off to tie around the stump, to help stop the bleeding. Green blood everywhere. *I hope you don't have any diseases, you furry void,* I thought. The Vamir just sat stunned and holding the stump where his arm used to be. I tied the tourniquet around the fur-singed stump. I looked up into his eyes and tried to talk to him to get him to focus and help me.

"Noak, help me!" I cried.

"What do you want me to do?"

"Hold this tourniquet in place while I find something to tighten it up with," I said. I looked around the area, and found a piece of polybdalloy, that looked as if it used to be part of the gate itself. I grabbed the piece, slipped the polybdalloy into the knot in the tourniquet, turned it slowly tightening it, watching the blood slow, and finally stop.

"Noak, hold this right here."

Nioaka held out his hand and inserted one of his branchlike fingers into the tourniquet knot to temporarily hold it in place. I tore another piece of the Vamir's tunic and tied it around the upper part of his arm to hold the tourniquet in place.

"There, that should keep it from bleeding some more," I said.

"Here comes the med-pod," replied Noak.

The medical team arrived and loaded the Vamir onto the floating gurney. They worked on him, running medical scans and administering further first aid to help stabilize him for transport to the MedSec on LevThree.

"We'll take it from here, Sergeant," remarked the med-tech.

I stepped back and looked around; other med-techs had arrived and were attending to the injured. "Who in the name of the Core did this?" I asked.

Nioaka stepped up to me and presented me with a charred, smoking part of what used to be the bioportal. On one end of the charred piece was a series of distorted marks about three centimeters long and a millimeter wide. The areas around the marks were blurry and muted. It looked as though the cell structure of the polybdalloy material had been disrupted. The blurred areas resembled marks made from dragging a spoon through toufood leaving furrows in the pasty foodstuff.

"Noak, old oak, what do you think of this?" I asked.

With a quavering voice Nioaka replied, "Th-Those remarks are not necessary to conduct this investigation."

I looked up to see Nioaka shifting and reshifting his feet and wringing his hands. "What's the matter, old friend?"

"N-Nothing. I'm fine, Sape!" Noak said in a voice edged with tension.

"Blast it, you better tell me what in the name of the Core's your problem, stickman!"

"I-I got to go!" cried Noak with a voice raw with terror. Nioaka started walking off and I saw it. One of Nioaka's legs was smoldering, small wisps of smoke coming from his thin, treelike, right leg.

"Medic!" I yelled.

I grabbed Noak's right leg and looked around from something to put out the smoldering fire. Frustrated that I could not find anything to smother the fire, I started to pat it out with my hand. The medic arrived, saw what I was doing, opened his medbrief, and retrieved a small container with an aerosol top. He pointed it at Noak's leg and squeezed the trigger under the top. A fine stream of white foam erupted from the tip, coated Noak's leg, and spread out. The fire was out. All that was left was a small, thin trail of smoke and steam. The medic waited for a moment then reached into his brief for another instrument. This time the medic came out with another aerosol container type, pointed the tip at Noak's foam covered leg, and sprayed his leg for the second time. The mist that came of the beralloy container hit the foam, and instantly the foam disappeared and so did the char marks of the fire. The grimace on the Sloygat's face had disappeared, replaced with a look of relief. Nioaka let out an audible sigh and relaxed.

With a calm, professional voice, the medic asked, "How do you feel now, Sir?"

"I'm fine, now," replied Nioaka.

With a mischievous grin I said, "You had me worried there for a minz, old shrub, I thought you were really going to go up in smoke this time."

"Eat feek, Sape," snapped Nioaka.

"Torchy, torchy," I sniggered back.

"Comsys, this is Nioaka. Send a CGSI team to Gate Nineteen immediately," ordered Noak.

I picked up the piece of the polybdalloy that I had dropped earlier, re-examined it. "Noak, these marks look just like a disruptor blast," I said.

"Where are those Core voids getting the disruptors? We're the only ones allowed to carry them," exclaimed Nioaka.

"I don't know. I'm going to get Eversyn involved," I answered. I hit my comsys button, "Dispatch, link me with Captain Eversyn." There was a short pause and my comsys erupted with the sound of Eversyn's voice.

"Eversyn here."

"Cap'n, this is Mik'Amr," I responded.

Eversyn's voice was professional, and matter of fact, "Yes, Sergeant, what it is?"

"Cap'n, we have an explosion at Gate Nineteen in the spaceport and we've found some evidence that indicates a disruptor blast."

"You're positive?"

"Yes, Sir. CGSI, *Consolidated Guard Scene Investigations*, is enroute to the scene to conduct the investigation and collect more evidence. We should know in a little while," I answered.

"Mik, find the voids responsible for this and let me know," Eversyn boomed. "Is that Sloygat with you?"

"Yes Sir, as always."

"Good, maybe this time he can keep you out of trouble. Eversyn out!"

A click and the link went dead.

With an arch smile, Noak asked, "Are you going to stay out of trouble this time, Mik?"

I shot Noak an icy look, then turned and started to look around again for clues.

"Oh yeah, next time you decide to start smoking again, I'll let you burn and then notify your next of kindling."

"Eat feek, Sape!"

The CGSI Team arrived and I showed them the area that I thought was the epicenter of the blast, and they set to work gathering information. I turned to Noak. "Noak, let's go get the guest and escort her to the Cap'n, I'm sure he wants to meet his new bride-to-be."

"Oh, you're bad," he replied.

We started toward the lift, boarded and headed back to the security booth that held Ka-Mir.

<^>

When we arrived back at the security booth, the doors were hanging off of their sliding track. It looked as though they had exploded outward, only there were no signs of an explosion. One door was hanging from its slide hinge mechanism, but the other did not fare so well; it was lying down on the deck, cracked, with the wires from the sensor device still sparking. We carefully stepped into what was left of the booth to find the guard unconscious. I rushed over to her and felt for a pulse. It was weak, but steady.

"She'll live. Get a medteam in here to see about the Corporal." I commanded.

Nioaka hit his comsys button and called for a medteam. "Eversyn's going to be pissed when he hears you're the one who lost his new bride-to-be."

"You're right, Noak. I'm in trouble...again."

~END~

ERR FROM AIRLESSNESS

Richard C. Meehan, Jr.

With rum surging through his system, Charlie realized that he may have made a mistake. When Crila Maragorn asked Dhamu for time off to go with Charlie on a lunch date to the Starview Lounge the next day, the big Modajai looked as if he would pound them both. He had done just that to an obnoxious Fwazek only a short while ago. The mushroom-shaped creature had been hauled off by his comrades, looking for all the asteroid like a bov-pile. Charlie had too much work to do and didn't need that kind of grief.

"What? Is my food no good now, Crila?" grumbled Dhamu.

"Of course it is," Crila mollified. "Heyo, just let me have some fun!"

If Dhamu could have crinkled his brow ridge, he probably would have. "I know what you call fun. Maybe I'll go get Mal. He'll fix you good."

Dhamu's Place had always served reasonable food along with good drinks. That's why Charlie headed there first when the commuter flight dropped him off for his routine sales visit. "Dhamu, I promise I'll bring Crila back safe and sound. How about I give you a free 'virosuit replacement filter when I pick her up tomorrow?"

"Jus' remember, Manus," grumbled Dhamu, "any harm comes to Crila, I'll send Malik Blayne to collect your privates so's I can grow ka'frindi on 'em." A level of concern flitted through the Modajai's yellow eyes. "And don't you forget to bring the filter, neither."

Every sales trip to the Rock for the past twenty years Charlie had frequented Dhamu's Place, but he had never seen this side of the enormous Modajai. Could it be…tenderness…for the little barmaid? Charlie used his favorite sales close, "You know me, Dhamu. Have I ever steered you wrong in all our dealings together?"

Dhamu harrumphed.

<^>

Next day, Charlie collected Crila at Dhamu's Place in a rented flutterpod. He normally used the two-person vehicle to impress clients, since only the ultra-rich had any form of individual transportation. It made a better impression than simply walking through the maze of grimy caves and moist tunnels within the locale of the spaceport.

Besides, getting from Dhamu's to the Starview Lounge was a complex series of twists, turns and elevation systems, not to mention checkpoints where Charlie's omnipass would be required. Legally traveling from LevSev to LevTwo was a privilege granted to a small number of beings.

With Crila stuffed into a shimmering gold knee-length dress, which accentuated the lavender of her skin, hair and eyes, he couldn't imagine making her walk. She'd come out looking like a bruised banana. Even with white streaks in her predominately lilac short hair, Crila was stunning!

"Eyes up, Manus," she warned.

However, Charlie noticed she granted him an optimum view as she bent to enter the deep red flutterpod. She was certainly aware of her effect on him. He forced his knees to haul his body around to the pilot's seat and folded himself inside. No one ever said these flutterpods were roomy, but right now, the closeness was an unexpected delight. What surprised him even more was that Crila had managed to attach an appliance to her left forearm that looked like real flesh. If he hadn't been acquainted with her from Dhamu's—and once having a 'virosuit specially made for her…ah…unique requirements— he would never have known she was missing her left forearm.

225

Dressed in a formal deep gray business suit, conservative throughout the ages, Charlie commanded the pod to transport them to the Starview for their luncheon reservation. The ovoid conveyance lifted a few centimeters off the cavern floor, accompanied by a telltale resonance, as if a thousand butterfly wings gently beat the surrounding air. It moved off at the pace of a fast walk.

"So...Charlie. What's on the agenda?" Crila's voice held the roughness of years of barroom repartee, or perhaps the daily second-hand smoke had damaged her vocal cords.

The timbre of her voice was the only mar Charlie could notice—not that he was searching—it's just that it was such a subtle shame for anyone with a taut body like hers. He caught himself wishing for more time to hit the autogym himself.

"Heyo, I'm talking to you, pal!"

"Oh—ah—sorry, Cutie Pie."

"Manus, you call me that again and you'll take me back to Dhamu's, pronto."

"Feek, are you *beautiful*!" Charlie knew it was the wrong lingo before it rolled off his tongue.

"Okay, bov-brain. Turn this fancy crate around—right now!" Crila's eyes bored into Charlie like lazdrills.

Charlie withered. "I...I'm sorry. No offence. But you are...ah...easy on the eyes?" He cringed at his choice of words, but instead of flailing him, Crila seemed to soften.

The mauve tone of her cheeks lightened as she spoke, "No. It wasn't you, Charlie. It was me." She let that comment hang on the air between them for a breath. "I'm not used to anyone treating me to such...flattery. Just get us to the restaurant, will ya?"

One last checkpoint at the LevTwo airlock was all that remained between them and the sumptuous meal to come. As the flutterpod glided smoothly up to the guard station, a lanky young Human with crimson hair fairly leapt in front of the vehicle.

"Halt!" A white-gloved hand shot out in the ancient universal sign for *stop*.

The pod had already come to rest automatically. Charlie wondered why the Connie was acting with such stiff formality. Maybe he was just new. That had to be it.

Crila breathed in his ear, "Charlie, don't call me by my real name. Make something up if he asks."

That startled the salesman. He glanced at Crila searching for an explanation, but it was too late for further talk. The Connie was already at his side. Pods required no doors, since climate was fairly constant inside the Rock, if humid. Unfortunately, that meant no privacy either.

Grasping Charlie by the elbow, the guard asked him to step out of the vehicle. Once he unfolded from the pod, Charlie discovered his nose only came up to the Connie's shoulder. The name over the breast pocket read, "Lt. Perry Baranin."

"Sir, please stand still for an identity check." Lt. Baranin produced a handheld device and commenced to waving it slowly up and down. "According to the dynascan you are one Charlie Manus, envirosuit representative for the Left Galactic Arm division of Protectaire, Inc. Is this true?"

"Yes, Lieutenant. May I ask why we are being detained?"

"No sir."

"Then, may we enter LevTwo now? My...ehem...date and I are running a bit late for our reservation at the Starview."

"Sorry, sir. My orders are to detain anyone attempting to enter LevTwo from the lower levels. Your flutterpod is registered to a rental agency on LevThree. You must remain here until cleared by Captain Eversyn himself."

Charlie's temper flared. "Son, do you know who I am?"

"You're Charlie Man—"

"No, no. Not that part. If you'll read your scan more thoroughly, you'll see that I possess an *omnicard!*"

The lieutenant dutifully read down the scan again. Charlie new exactly when the young Connie found the notation about the omnicard—his eyes bulged. It was a pleasure to see someone else squirm for a change. Usually Charlie was the one on the hot seat as he tried to sell his merchandise.

Lt. Baranin snapped off a salute. "I—I'm sorry, sir."

"It's alright, young man. Now, may we continue on our way?"

227

The lieutenant appeared to battle something internally. Indecision washed back and forth several times across his face before he choked out, "You may go, sir. B-but your... aaah...companion will have to remain here until Captain—"

"That's not acceptable, Lieutenant!" Charlie forced calm back into his voice with some difficulty. It was time for another sales pitch. He leaned in close and spoke in a confidential hush, "Lt. Baranin, this is my first date with the lady here. Can't you gimme a break? Just look at her." He waved in Crila's direction, while his other hand pressed a hundred-cred note into the guard's.

The experienced barmaid obligingly leaned forward into the lieutenant's view, offering up for his eyes the fullness craved by most young Human males. "Can we go now, dear," she effervesced. "We're going to be late. And I'm starving."

The lieutenant was agog; dumbfounded.

"Lieutenant? Hello there. May we go now, please? Let's not keep the lady waiting."

The lieutenant managed to string a few words together. "Y-yes. I...ah. Why, I suppose so. I'll just get the airlock." His bulging eyes followed the pod as it flitted on its way. The hundred-cred note was nowhere to be seen.

At last, the flutterpod arrived at the illustrious Starview Lounge. A rotund little man in a maroon bellhop ensemble offered a hand to Crila as she unfolded onto the red carpet which lead up to the ornate double polybdalloy doors. Charlie issued a few quick commands for the flutterpod to find itself a park.

"Greetings Mastriz, welcome to the Starview. And you, Mastre."

This sort of high profile work was a bit unusual for Banastre Caravello, owner of the Starview, thought Charlie. Of course, few knew that Rudof Dyll also had his bejeweled fingers in this particular pie. That fact alone meant anything could, and sometimes did, happen here.

Working up a bit of nerve, Charlie found Crila's hand with his own. To his chagrin, he had grabbed her prosthesis. Bov-feek! There was nothing for it but pretend everything was fine! He felt a trickle of sweat creeping down beside his ear; his necktie seemed to tighten like a noose.

Crila, on the other hand, so to speak, did not seem to notice the envirosuit salesman's discomfort. She was apparently enchanted by the extravagance of the Starview. Caravello had just pushed open the double doors to allow them a first glimpse of the galactic arm through the domed ceiling. No matter how many times Charlie had witnessed it, the sudden panorama after time spent down-lev was always breathtaking. For a LevThree bar worker like Crila, who spent all of her time inside hollowed out stone, it must be nearly euphoric to see so much unrestrained space both above and within the lounge.

"Come inside Mastre...Mastriz, and fill your bellies with your heart's desires," soothed the restaurant owner. His arms were gently bidding them to enter.

As they past the main doors, Charlie happened to notice a Modajai bouncer, rust-colored blood drizzling from a broken nose, standing at attention inside a boxed alcove. Obviously the alcove was built to minimize the impact of security forces on the ambiance of the famous eatery. The ploy hadn't worked.

"Oooh, look, Charlie," said Crila. "There's Rudof Dyll. See? He's eating at a table *on* a floating platform!"

Although Charlie normally would have thought *whoop-dee-do* over the dandy-on-a-disk, his date's bubbling excitement seemed to flow into him. Her fake hand had tightened uncomfortably, and still he found himself gaping in wonder at one of his oldest and most bejeweled customers.

"Mastre...Mastriz?" Caravello was still steering the couple. "Here is your table. I hope you enjoy the view for which we are so well known. Your servitor will be with you shortly." After drawing their chairs—lady first, of course—the stuffy man left them amid the aromas of exotic spices and dishes.

Moments later, a Human waitress in a jet cocktail skirt and frilly white blouse appeared. "Good evening. My name is Wyonitra, and I will be serving—what are *you* doing here?" She put a hand to her mouth, amber eyes rounded. Her attention seemed for a moment to have locked on Crila, but settled on the salesman.

Charlie's cheeks burned. "Uhmm, no need to make a scene, is there, Wyonitra?" He wondered why the waitress found his presence so surprising, since he ate here quite frequently. A pair of feathery L'Taltons at the next table, who had cocked their heads at the exchange, went back to pecking at their bowls.

The waitress recovered, "Oh—I'm sorry sir. It's just that you're so...*famous*. Yes, that's it—famous!" Her eyes flicked to Crila and back.

"Well, let's get on with the ordering, shall we?" Charlie was still miffed over the delay at the LevTwo airlock. He didn't need a mooning waitress to louse up the rest of his date. Yet, something about the way Crila had ducked her head at the waitress's approach...that's it...they knew each other!

"Would you like to begin with a cocktail? We have the House specialty of course, an alcoholic punch containing a single droplet of Adonis nectar, served in a chilled goblet. We call it Draught of the Gods. Umm...delightful."

A glance at his date and Charlie nodded, "Two of those would be fine."

"Good choice, Mastre. While I have them prepared, perhaps you would like to consider the midday entrées?" The waitress pressed something under the edge of the round obsidian table and a full-color menu sprang to life in midair. "Take all the time you need—everything is good. However, tonight's special is boveen filet, marinated for two days in our famous sauce, with a dot of ka'frindi on the side. You also have a choice of two vegetables. I'll return if a few moments with your drinks. Place your order at your leisure by simply touching the menu." With a final glance at Crila, the waitress filtered away between tables.

The salesman could plainly see that he was right. More than twenty years of practice at reading client's faces told him those two women definitely knew each other. Crila would not look at him. Instead, she was about to try and redirect his attention. It was like reading a tabloid, all emotional impact and no substance.

"You can see the stars in the tabletop, Charlie. Look." Crila pointed with a purple-coated fingernail. Her hand must have brushed across the menu, for the smell of fried fish wafted up Charlie's nose. The virtual menu item had enlarged and was rotating slowly, a golden slab of some sort of finned delicacy well presented.

"That's nice," said Charlie noncommittally. He could tell Crila was not going to be forthcoming about the encounter with the waitress, and suspected the rest of the meal was going to be rather superficial too.

The drinks came, with Wyonitra pretending to fuss over laying prongs and other eating utensils, napkins and so forth. "Do you need anything further, Mastre? Mastriz? No? Well, I'll bring your meal out once you have made your selection then." She left.

As Charlie suspected, the meal was rather subdued despite the fantastical zest of boveen steak laced with ka'frindi. Crila made no reference to the waitress. In fact, he couldn't get her to say anything much beyond how pretty the view was, or how Dhamu would love to see it someday.

As they finished their last bite of flame tart for dessert, a rush of perfumed air wafted over their shoulders. Charlie turned to see Rudof Dyll hovering abreast their table with the usual glint of mischief in his eye.

"Halloo, there!" cried the dandy, his frilly shirt dribbled with the bright orange of a flame tart's sweet topping. "Good, aren't they?" He popped the last of a tart in his mouth and licked his fingers.

Dutifully, Charlie plastered on a smile. After all, Dyll was a top customer. "As always, Rudof, your food is beyond compare."

"Yes, yes. Well, you're right, of course." Dyll flipped an arrant wisp of golden hair back from his forehead. Earrings glinted in the muted spotlighting. "And who is this enchanting woman you have with you tonight, Manus? I didn't realize you knew anyone quite so luscious."

Charlie cleared his throat. "This is Cri—OUCH!" His leg exploded in pain.

"Crouch, did you say? That doesn't seem very fitting for this beautiful creature. What's wrong old boy?"

The salesman stopped rubbing his assaulted shin and was glaring at Crila. Her pursed lips told him she didn't want her real name known here either. "Ehem. Rudof Dyll, I'd like you to meet...Camiele A'gorn."

"Charmed, I'm sure," Dyll lifted Crila's fake hand to his lips, hiding the remnants of a quirky smile. "Charles, I have a bit of business to discuss before you go. Care to join me?"

"I haven't paid out yet," said Charlie.

Rudof Dyll placed his hand on the couple's table and said, "No charge." A faint voice rose from the black surface as Dyll retracted his palm. *Yes, Mastre.* "Now, you're all taken care of, Charles, old chap. Come along, you two love birds." He hid a teetered laugh behind his manicured fingers.

A blush of mauve deepened Crila's cheeks as the two of them climbed aboard Rudof's floating dais. His private table was already set with two more chairs and sparkling goblets filled with cracked ice and pristine water—a delicacy in itself. The dais lifted gently above the lounge without so much as rippling the water's surface. Patrons below watched them enviously.

"Now, Charles, down to business," said Dyll. "I need to place a rather sizable order for more of those Model D1A1 Type III Envirosuits—oh my." He batted his mascara eyelashes in thought. "I can't use *those,* can I?" He glanced furtively at Crila.

How could this be? Dyll recognized Crila, too! It was all over his powdered face. A tinge of jealousy zinged through Charlie that even a pouf like Dyll seemed to know more about his own date than he did.

"...I say, Manus, old boy? I'm talking to you!"

Dyll had ordered 'virosuits off-planetoid before. If Charlie wasn't careful, he would lose this sale. He pasted on his business persona and set the personal quandary aside, "Model D1A1 Type III's—right. Why can't you use them?"

"Oh my, haven't you heard? Lynn...no...Finn...no...Benn. Yes, Benita Frohmyn. She was Captain Eversyn's second-in-command, you know. Tsk, tsk. Poor girl. Pretty too. What a shame."

"What's a shame?" Charlie's attention was totally focused on Dyll now.

Dyll leaned in conspiratorially. "She was wearing one."

"Wearing one what?"

"Why, silly chap, a Model D1A1, of course!"

Charlie gripped the table edge. He could tell when someone was about to impart bad news—

"In the belly of that damn big fish."

What in the Core was Dyll talking about—

"Her envirosuit failed, my, my. And she *died*."

Charlie suddenly felt ill. He glanced at his companions. Questions spun around his mind so fast, he couldn't get a grip on one so he could ask it.

"No, no, no, dear Charles. Not here. Not on the dais. Let me get you to my private lavatory. We can talk business when you're feeling better." Rudof Dyll's hand reached for his tabletop controls just as a message flashed across its small monitor. "Oh my," he flung his ringed fingers into the air, "that dreadful bore Captain Eversyn wants to see me. Well, I suppose there's nothing for it but to dump you off. Here we are now. Off you go."

Charlie and Crila found themselves at the upper deck of the Starview, helped by Banastre Caravello to exit the floater. The man sure gets around, thought Charlie. This level held the restaurant's private offices, which were off limits to all regular patrons. It had been years since he had been up here.

"Banastre will show you out, by way of the facilities if necessary. Charles, do get back with me soon about those envirosuits, will you? Banastre—do take care of my friends. Good of you to come, Charles. Nice to meet you... Camiele A'gorn!" With another sideways grin accompanied by a dainty wave, Dyll dropped out of sight.

"Mastre and Mastriz, would you follow me please?" Caravello walked them through a couple of portals, past some of the most lavish offices Charlie had ever seen. "Will either of you need...refreshing?"

Crila took a few steps as if she knew where she was, and then paused. "Charlie, would you take me home now? I have things to do before work tonight."

~END~

SURFACE TENSION

Charlotte Babb

"The Chow Down? Yes, Mastre, I know where it is," Trillfin Skorm said, for the tenth time today. "Take the drop by the Crater on the Main Tube to LevThree. You can't miss it. Don't get out of sight of the drop, though."

Jule Emyril had made a name for himself *and* the Chow Down. People came down from LevOne and even LevTwo to sample his cooking. But neither he nor his Nicovan roommate, Trillfin Skorm, had the credz to get off world. It was all they talked about when they went home. They had long ago stopped pretending that Jule would get his own place—why waste the credz? Trillfin overheard Aunt Sulky tell someone that they were a sad couple: they didn't know they were in love, they weren't able to mate and make a family, and they'd never get off the Rock.

One cykul when Trillfin woke up and slid out of her sleeptank, Jule was already awake, waiting for her.

"Trill, I'm going up to LevOne!" He didn't even wait for her to dry off or get into her robe. "Aunty has a job for me, cooking for some Offal. Finally, I have a contact!"

Trillfin stretched and flapped her gills to close them. "Aunty has the contacts. Do you get paid or does she?"

"Can't you be happy for me?" He had lost the offworld

slouch, as the weight of the rock ahead no longer bothered him, but he sagged in a Nicovan posture of defeat.

"Sure, you know I am, but with Aunty, credz are thicker than water. What's the deal?"

"I don't know all the details, but I'm supposed to go up today to meet them, and Aunty said you could show me the way. It's your cykul off, right? Then you could go with me, maybe as a guide and help me talk to them. Please?"

"Fix me some food, Sape, and let me wake up." Trillfin recycled the water in her sleep tank into the refresher, then picked up her best robe to wear into the LevOne residential district, one that she knew only by reputation. Aunty had put Jule up to this, as he still couldn't navigate half a level away from the Chow Down without a guide. He just had no sense of space. She wondered if all Offals had flat-thinking.

She smelled something good from the kitchenette—not that she had the ingredients Jule was used to working with in the restaurant, but he could make something good out of raw toufood and rock fungus that grew in the tube three spirals up. She didn't know why he knew it would be good. But that was his talent. Maybe this would be their ticket out. And he still wanted her to go along too, not just as a guide. She always had the thought that this was just an arrangement, a comfortable one for both of them, but just temporary until something better came along. And she had hoped that nothing would.

She sipped the hot, fishy broth that he made to energize them in the morning, and had a plate of scrambled toufood with bits of green stuff sprinkled over. She never asked what it was. It was good, and she told him so.

"Of course I'll go with you to the place." She rubbed his head with her hand. "Now do you see why I insisted we spend credz on that new robe? Your offal stuff just wouldn't do for them."

"You were right." He stood up and paced, two steps across and back. "Can we go soon? I don't want to be late, or get all worked up before we get there."

"All right. I'm ready." Trillfin smiled. "You're getting worked up and we haven't left yet. She swallowed the last bite of toufood and swigged the broth. They never had leftovers—it saved on recycling credits.

She led the way, playing the Nicovan servant for the Human Mastre Chef.

"Now remember, you're a Sape—I mean, a Human. You look people in the eye, and you demand what you need to do your job."

He laughed and shook his head.

"No, I mean it. I've even heard you talk back to Aunt Silky, and you are still alive. No Neek would ever do that."

At that Jule straightened up, stretched his neck out and tucked his chin. He showed no sign of submission or meekness, and even gave Trillfin a few orders to get the practice.

"Find us the quickest route, Trillfin," he said. "I must not be late." At first, he sounded petulant and whiny, but his confidence and his imperial manner returned to him. He began to swagger just a bit, towering over Trillfin.

She dropped her chin and stared up at him across her eyesocket ridges while they stood waiting for the LevOne drop tube, Trillfin whispered back to him, "Don't get too used to that, Sape. I know where you sleep."

He grinned. "I wondered how much of that you would take."

At the LevOne landing, a Consolidated Guard checked their identification and the invitation Jule had to enter the residential area. His patron was to be Mastriz Zabayaba. The Connie gave them directions, along with orders not to stray from the prescribed path.

"Up there they pay for security and protection," the Connie said. "They get it."

"As is right," Jule said. Trillfin said nothing.

They climbed a spiral through several turns, the closest to the surface that Trillfin had ever been. When they found the address, it was an airlock. They buzzed the owner, allowed their palms and retinas to be scanned by the Iron Eye and gave it their invitation. In a few moments, the door opened and they were admitted.

When the air pressure equalized, the door ahead of them opened into an incline of luxury neither of them had ever seen. Free running water cascaded down ledges to create tinkling waterfalls between growing exotic plants with multicolored leaves and flowers, all in shades of teal, cream and burgundy. Insects made chirping and singing noises. Jule was impressed, but Trillfin was amazed.

How could someone waste so much water?

"Trill, think," Jule said. "The water is recycled. They just pump it through, over and over. They may even use the plants to clean the water so they don't have to buy water."

"Can you imagine having credz enough to own your own water?"

Surely people that rich could spare enough to send a couple of people off world. But would they?

When they had climbed what seemed like two spirals up the winding path, they came to another airlock. This one was smaller and different, with straight vertical lines and only a curve at the top. It made Trillfin uneasy. It just didn't look right.

Jule walked right in as soon as the doors slid open. That too was different, but Trillfin had no choice but to follow. She stood in front of Jule, remembering her role as his servant.

But when the second door opened, she shrieked.

She was standing between the Rock and Nothing.

Nothing but space. Hard winking stars and the spiral that was the Galaxy.

Nothing.

A polybdalloy tube had been built across the surface of the Rock to the dome of Mastriz Zabayaba. Soft light illuminated the craggy mountains and rocky plain. In the distance was the peak of the Beryl, the fabled green crystal that had been grown before Port Nowhere was built. But all Trillfin could see was the Nothing of the stars in the airless sky.

She ran out of air to shriek with, yet she still screamed.

Jule grabbed her around her waist to hold her. "Trill, Trill baby, it's ok. It's just the stars. That's where we're going. Trill, to the stars." He turned her away from the sight to face him. "Hush, now, it's all right."

He shook her just a bit, gently, to get her attention. He closed her eyes and her mouth, and stroked her lobe to calm her, holding her against him. Then he held her head back and force-breathed into her mouth. Most of the air came out of her gills, but some went into her lungs.

She gasped and started to scream again.

He covered her mouth. "Trillfin, no. Trill, it's all right," he crooned over and over. Finally he tried another tack. "Shut up, you stupid Neek and do your job!"

He'd always read where the man would hit the woman to get her attention, but he couldn't do that. He had got her attention, though, as she was staring at him, her anger working through her agoraphobia. He had a small globe of water—everyone carried one. He fished it out of his robe and splashed it in her face. "Breathe!" he said. "Breathe. You can do this."

"You better not ever speak to me like that again," Trillfin gasped. Her eyes had focused on him and her voice had gone almost as deep as Aunty's.

Jule relaxed, just a bit. "Now, we are going to walk along the surface, and it is going to be all right. Look at the floor, and it won't bother you." He took her hand and led her into the tube. "Remember how I couldn't sleep in a pod? It's the same thing."

Trillfin stumbled after him, her hand locked in his, and her eyes closed. But halfway through, she jerked her hand back. Jule tried to grab her hand again, but she shook her head no. She wasn't calm enough to talk, but she stomped in front of Jule and led the way, staring first at the far airlock and then a bit at the time, up at the peak of the Beryl, and then, up at the stars.

By the time they reached the airlock, she had almost begun to breathe normally, and her robe was dry. And she was staring at the massive spiral of the Galaxy.

"By the Core," she whispered, "it's beautiful. It *is* the Core."

"Yes," Jule said. He stared at the spiral too, even after the airlock opened. Trillfin pulled him in.

He smiled at her, and she smiled back. When the third airlock opened, it was filled with the musky scent of snake. It was guarded by an Ophid, ten feet of yellow and white reptile, the first four of which formed the body of a woman covered with scales except for her face, her arms and her chest, which were covered with armor.

She held a needle laser at waist level and raised herself up to meet Jule eye to eye.

"We do not allow Neeksssss here," she said, her orange, forked tongue flashing out to sample their smell.

"Express my regrets to your Mastriz, then, as I will not work without my companion." Jule turned on his heel to face the airlock. Trillfin turned also.

"Foolish Human!" She hissed to herself, "A redundancy. Wait here." The Ophid slithered away.

There was no where else to go, as yet another door blocked both their return to LevOne and to the dome.

"Jule, no, you…" Trillfin whispered.

"Hush." Jule smiled. He had regained his imperial manner, but not the bravado that had brought him to the Rock.

"But you can go back," Trillfin stood trembling. People didn't turn down jobs on LevOne, not where the owner had its own water and a handful of Nothing. "I can stay here."

"Hush. You have to get used to the surface before we can live on Vestia III." He stroked her lobe. "Just how many Human offal chefs do you figure they have applying for this job? How many have Aunt Silky's stamp of approval?"

They turned back around when they heard the scrape of scales on the polybdalloy.

"Mastriz will see you. Your…*companion*…may follow."

~**€ND**~

BETWEEN THE ROCK AND NOTHING

K.G. McAbee

Vurp nodded at the list in his hand. He licked the tip of his stylus with a thoughtful air then checked off two more items.

"Good," he said, and the slow boom of his voice rumbled like thunder. "She be happy this."

His voice bounced off the walls of the irregular enclosure, its outer perimeter a bedraggled conglomeration of semi-defective dome sections and out of date atmo-seals. Outside, there was nothing; literally, nothing but vacuum. This tiny jagged asteroid, his home base, had just enough gravity to make loading his ancient shuttle and his even older runabout easy...and keep him from floating out of his pod during sleepshift.

Vurp shuffled towards the airlock, his boots sending up clouds of dust as he made his twisting and turning way through piles of this and heaps of that and mountains of other.

"That's Mastriz Zabayaba, not 'she', you bov-brain!" squeaked Dingul. He rammed the stylus in his pocket and grabbed a harpoon, shook it at Vurp's cloudy reflection in the side of a polybdalloy crate. "We've got to make sure that the containment field is stable right now this very minz as ever was. Come on!"

Vurp ignored Dingul, put the harpoon down, and continued with his check list. Only after all the items were marked did he place the list on a hook near the air lock and began to tug on his enviro-suit.

"Hurry up, why don't you?" Dingul snapped as he tested the seals and drew a deep breath. "She'll be waiting! It's time— blazing Core, it's past time to haul ice!"

<^>

Mastriz Zabayaba strolled down the walkway that linked her domicile dome to her private spaceport and cargo bay. Her Ophid bodyguard, Strikes Without Mercy, slithered beside her.

"Always on the alert for danger, Strikes." Zaba nodded at her employee in satisfaction. "Good. I pay your circle enough for an armed cadre of Connies."

"Isss my ssserviccce not sssatisssfactory, Mastrizzzzz?" An orange forked tongue snaked out of Strikes's mouth and sampled the water-laden air.

The riot of plants lined either side of the three-meter-wide semi-cylindrical walkway was interspersed with the occasional pool containing small yellow, green or orange swimmers. The Mastriz looked around in pleasure, her wrinkled face aglow.

Nothing showed wealth like water. And nothing showed water like free-standing pools and growing things.

A soft hiss from Strikes reminded Zaba that she'd been asked a question. No use irritating the Ophid for no reason.

"Your service is excellent, Strikes. But you've got to stop scaring away the Neek female and her Human pet. He's a damn fine cook. It's hard enough to find anything fit to eat on the Rock, without you giving the only decent cook I've found heart palpitations about his mate."

"Neeksssssss are nassssty…"

The sharp - beep-buzz of an alarm ripped through the walkway like a blaster, cutting off Strikes in mid-sibilance.

"Finally!" snapped the Mastriz. She speeded up, her thin legs whipping the skirts of her robe into a frenzy. "That fool promised me ice two cyks ago! And this time it better not be mostly air and sand."

They reached the end of the walkway. Through the transparent airlock door, the Mastriz could make out a squat figure, its cheap enviro-suit covered in multi-colored patches.

"I wish he'd invest in a new suit," the Mastriz muttered as she hit the button to cycle the airlock door. A hiss of equalizing pressure and the heavy door swung open.

Vurp Dingul stepped into the pressurized walkway and reached up to remove his helmet. His gloved fingers moved with the ease of long practice as he slapped and prodded the various seals, then pulled the helmet off.

"Mastriz Zabayaba," Dingul squeaked, one eye keeping a nervous watch on the Ophid bodyguard. "An honor to see you, as always."

"Honor," Vurp echoed.

"We've brought you ice, the finest ice to be had, with no rocks or sand or shards or, or, anything that's not, uh, well, ice. It's very tasty, clean, most clean, and, uh, full of the best, the very best, uh..." Dingul ran out of superlatives.

"Ice," agreed Vurp.

"And about time too!" snapped the Mastriz. "No, no need to come any further in."

Vurp Dingul's smell, a combination of unwashed body, refurbed envirosuit, body wastes recycled ten too many times, and just the faintest undercurrent of dirty socks, made her even more eager than usual to get the little Human out of her domicile and back in his ship. "I'll come out and check the cargo myself."

"Mastrizzzz..." Strikes hissed, but Zabayaba waved an airy hand. The Ophid didn't have a suit that fit her, and besides— what could possibly happen in a cargo bay with no one in it but Vurp Dingul and some load-bots?

The Mastriz shucked out of her robe and, dressed in little more than a skin-tight coverup that made her look like an animated skeleton with lavender hair, slid into her own envirosuit. It was the finest model, guaranteed by Protectaire against vacuum, noxious gasses, carnivorous fungi, and disease-infected spores. She made a mental note to get with Protectaire's local rep, Charley Manus, next time he was by: the suit's filter-sys was definitely not proof against Vurp

Dingul's reek. She could still smell him. Manus would whine that she was eating into his profits...but he'd no doubt throw in some extra filters, free of charge.

Mastriz Zabayaba hadn't got rich on the Rock by overlooking any way possible of getting freebies, or even almost freebies.

Take Dingul, for example. He was totally insane; he was alone so much out in the asteroid belt that trailed behind Port Nowhere, he had split into two personalities, just so he'd have someone to talk during the long, dark stretches of time. His insanity didn't interfere with his ice-finding abilities, though; Vurp Dingul had a nose for ice. And Zaba took—had always taken—full use of his unusual talents.

Like now, for instance.

Dingul put his helmet back on and they entered the airlock together. After it cycled, Vurp stood aside and motioned her into the bay. It was little more than a crater with a retractable translucent cover; once a craft was inside, a dome slid closed in case it was necessary to pressurize. In the case of Dingul's delivery, it was the best possible storage facility—very cold and very dry.

In the center of the crater sat Vurp's runabout. It was squat and stumpy, little more than an engine with a minute control room sitting on top of it, all balanced on three projecting stanchions. Since the ice was transported inside a large net that attached to one side, Vurp didn't need to worry about cargo bays or elaborate storage systems.

Zaba rubbed her gloved hands together; her cargo bay was more than cold, it was frigid, and her suit's internal heaters whined in protest at the abrupt change from the warmth and humidity of her walkway. But the cold was worth it; the pile of ice chunks was growing. Her load-bots removed fragments from the cargo net that hung from Dingul's dilapidated ship and stacked them neatly—as neatly as possible, anyway, considering their odd sizes and shapes—against the near wall, where the ice would be handy for the melters.

It took a lot of water to keep Zaba's plants growing. It took a lot of water to keep her slaves alive. It took a lot of water to impress on everyone else just how rich she was.

Not as rich as Rudof Dyll, of course. But she was getting there...

Most of all, it took a lot of water for her favorite dish, swimmers in slime-weed sauce. Not that the dish itself used water; but she had to keep the fish somewhere. She certainly was not going down into the Depths to hunt them herself.

Vurp Dingul left the load-bots and trotted over to her; he put his helmet against hers. His comsys must be out of order—again—she thought as she boosted her own system's sound pick-up.

"Mastriz is happy with the ice?"

Zaba nodded once, mouthed 'It will do', and turned toward the airlock leading back into her plant-lined walkway. *These old bones are really beginning to feel the cold*, she thought. *About time for another rejuve...*

A faint sound, muffled by the low pressure, came from behind her. She turned.

A load-bot was trundling towards her, a jagged piece of ice balanced on one long extensor, the other empty. It was off balance and its sensors were iced over, she could see; so badly iced over that it had no way of perceiving that she was standing right in front of it. She stepped aside, and bumped into Dingul. They tripped over each other, landing in a pile of flailing arms and tangled legs—

Right in front of the lumbering load-bot.

The massive bot strode inexorably forward, forward, forward. Zaba watched its impassive sensor array, twinkling red and yellow as light bounced off the ice crystals that covered it, grow larger, larger, ever larger, until it filled her view.

"Mastriz!"

A pair of arms encircled Zaba. She felt herself being dragged across the rocky surface, her feet bumping on projecting spikes. The arms around her were so tight she could barely breathe, and her suit's onboard computer, noting her distress, upped the air mixture. A faint hiss sounded in her ears as the arms loosened abruptly, dropping her with a thump onto the ground.

She watched the load-bot trundle over the very spot where she'd just been lying, its treads pressing rocks into the sand.

A clang against her helmet. Vurp's slow deep voice asked, "Mastriz hurt?" Dingul at once began an almost indecipherable chatter. "The Mastriz did not get damaged, I hope, I hope? She is well and unharmed and without tears in her suit and there is no blood or whatever the Mastriz's species uses for blood? Come and let me help her to her warm place."

The arms seized Zaba about her scrawny middle again, and once more her suit whined in protest as her entire bottom portion was cut off from support-sys. The crater tilted and twirled around her as she felt herself hoisted up and plonked across Vurp Dingul's shoulder.

The airlock cycled and they were inside the walkway. Strikes was slithering back and forth, dismay on her face and bloodlust in her eyes.

Vurp set Zaba down with great care, and helped her detach her helmet and get out of her suit. Dingul was still chattering, but since he hadn't removed his own helmet, she couldn't make out the words.

Then the words made no difference, as they were cut off when Strikes wrapped the end of her tail segment around his waist and lifted him a meter off the floor. Flailing arms and legs made no impression on the Ophid as she began to squeeze.

The Mastriz watched in some curiosity as Dingul's face grew darker and darker. Then she raised a hand.

"Put him down, Strikes."

"But, Mastrizzzzz…"

"Now."

With a petulant hiss, Strikes dropped the little Human so hard he bounced.

Dingul scrambled to his knees, snatched his helmet off, shook his head and took a whooping breath, then another.

Behind the Mastriz, an echoing crash seeped through the double doors - of the airlock, muffled by the pressure differential. She turned.

The iced-over load-bot had dropped its piece of ice and had started back for another. Unfortunately, it was unable to tell a chuck of ice from the less than pristine right side stanchion of Vurp Dingul's runabout.

A crunch. A teeter. A crash. And the Dingul runabout tottered sideways on its remaining two legs and fell, with a louder crunch.

Right on top of four extremely expensive, top-of-the-line load-bots.

A cloud of dust rose, mercifully blotting out the scene of destruction.

Dingul, who had yet to rise to his feet, sank instead further down into a frightened crouch. Strikes hovered over him, the tip of her tail lashing in expectation; her face beamed in anticipation.

"Sssshall I rid you of this Human, Mastrizzzz?"

Mastriz Zabayaba thought about it seriously for a second...then sighed. "No, Strikes. If he's dead, how will he repay me for all this damage?"

"But-but-but-but...it was not my fault, not at all, not my fault at all, not mine or Vurp's."

"Not our fault." Vurp shook his head once in agreement.

Zaba tried to hide her smile. She'd been trying to find a way to keep Vurp Dingul on the Rock. She had plans for the little Human.

Pity about the bots. But this little accident wasn't going to be a waste.

Not a waste at all.

~€nD~

TAU'S STARS

Elaine Corvidae

Raeyn walked quickly, head down, unable to hear anything over the frantic beat of her heart. *Calm, calm,* she told herself desperately. And: *No one knows.*

But that was a lie. Someone *did* know, would have to know by now. She'd jettisoned the manacles the first chance she'd gotten...but that would only mean her disappearance would have a slight air of mystery, as opposed to absolute certainty.

But they might not look here.

Perhaps. This wasn't called Port Nowhere for nothing, after all. Any fugitive with even a small amount of sense would head towards the inner planets and try to lose herself there. Perhaps even return to Hermia 12, try to rejoin the shattered pieces of her old life.

Except that was the first place they would look, when they found the bodies. When they found her gone without a trace. And maybe, when they didn't find her among the inner planets, they wouldn't keep looking. They would write her disappearance and the deaths off to an attack by rival pirates, or parties unknown.

Raeyn shivered and tucked her hands up under her armpits for warmth. She'd arrived in Port Nowhere only last cyk, on a transport that didn't ask any questions so long as its passengers had enough credz to buy silence. She'd tried heading towards Level One, but they *did* ask questions, and she'd decided not to push things. The same thing seemed to be true of Level Two. When she'd finally gotten up the courage to talk to someone and ask where she could find a cheap place to stay, they'd pointed her down here.

To Level Six.

I can't stay here.

In some places, the walls were covered or patched with ceramic and polybdalloy. But for the most part, they were bare rock, reminding her of the tons of asteroid above her head. The air was moist, and the stinks of mildew and rot mingled with the smell of cooking food and exotic spices. It turned her stomach and made her want to close her eyes and pretend that she was somewhere else.

This is only temporary. Soon enough, I'll have saved up enough credz to see the stars again. I'll buy a new identity— certainly someone in a place like this can cook up a good ID.

The crowd around her was like a crash-course in xenobiology. Sentients of all descriptions glided or hopped or walked or glorped past. Many were scarred, or talked to the air, or huddled in the shadows making deals with one another. Vendors sold wares from shops carved out of the rock, and Raeyn would be willing to bet that half the stuff was stolen and the rest was contraband. Whores of every kind flashed scales or fur or skin, or whatever it was that enticed their particular species, or at least caught the eye of another.

Well, even if the setting was odd, the inhabitants were familiar, as a kind if not as individuals. The daughter of Haverdo Nosta and Nel Banks had spent most of her life on the wrong side of the law, after all.

Just never…in a hole. Buried alive.

She had to get back among the stars. She had to; that was all.

<^>

Raeyn opened her eyes.

After almost two cyks of walking, she'd finally resigned herself to the fact that she couldn't afford anywhere to stay. The transport had taken too much out of the credz she'd stolen from Sanctiblan. Anonymous travel didn't come cheap, and she'd paid well for the privilege of stepping into Port Nowhere without any official record of her arrival.

Truthfully, there were one or two places she might have been able to stay. She'd seen plenty of brothels in her unplanned tour of the station, and even though she wasn't pretty, her body would get her a bunk at least.

But she hadn't escaped Sanctiblan to give away her freedom to some pimp instead.

Luck had been her friend for a change. In her wanderings, she'd found an access tunnel that didn't seem to go anywhere in particular. The only light came from the small glowb strapped to her wrist, and it showed her only slime-coated stone. It had seemed as safe as anywhere else, at least to her tired mind.

And now, something had awakened her.

She lay very still, trying to decide what it was.

A nightmare?

A distant noise?

No. There was a nearby sound, the whisper of what might have been breathing, so faint that she wouldn't have heard it at all if not for the preternatural silence of the tunnel. The shadows seemed to take on weight and substance: a shape half-perceived and half-imagined.

Something tugged on her left boot.

With a cry of fury, she snapped her leg blindly in the direction of the thief's face. She felt the hard sole of her boot connect with flesh and heard a startled yelp. Adrenaline burned through her, and she scrambled to her feet, switching on her wrist cone as she did so. The beam of light showed her a crouching figure, nothing more than a shadow. She had the impression of skin so pale she could see the veins underneath, enormous black eyes, and stringy brown hair. Then her attacker was moving, trying to slide away from the light, like a cockroach in the dark.

She launched herself at him, swinging with her fists. But this time she lacked the element of surprise, and he ducked under her blows. Wiry arms wrapped around her legs, tripping her up so that she fell heavily to the ground. Fury gave way to sudden panic—he had her down, could crawl on top of her if he wanted. The flash of metal at his throat caught her attention, and she grabbed the necklace, trying to wrap it around his neck and strangle him before he could hurt her. Within seconds, they were both rolling in the muck on the bottom of the tunnel.

"Get away from me!" she shouted. Her knee connected with his thigh, hard enough to bruise, although she missed her true target.

"I'm trying to!" he gasped, scrabbling at her hands at his throat. "Let go, damn it!"

"Did you hear that?" asked another voice, deeper and farther away. Raeyn's attacker froze instantly, and she did as well, fighting to catch her breath.

"Sounded like it came from that way," said another voice. "Some tunnel rats, probably."

The white light of the cone illuminated the face of Raeyn's assailant. Human, as far as she could see, maybe her own age although it was hard to tell with all the grime on him. He wore a battered coverall, with a jacket over that, and maybe several layers under it for all she knew. He had the long hair of a dirt-kisser; most spacers kept theirs short enough to fit under an envirosuit helmet without hassle. Well, she amended, at least spacers who routinely needed to put on envirosuits because they were boarding blown ships to snatch the cargo.

"Kill that light," the boy whispered, so low she could barely hear him.

For a moment, she hesitated, torn between the unknown threat of whoever was investigating the noise they'd made, and the known threat of the thief. Hoping that she hadn't come all this way just to get her throat slit in the dark, she flicked off the glowb, and plunged them both into night.

Gods, but it was dark. She couldn't see her hand in front of her face, and she felt the vague flutters of panic starting in her belly. The sound of boots scraping rock seemed somehow louder once her vision was gone.

"Come on," the boy whispered in her ear. "We got to move, or else they'll trip over us."

"I'm not going anywhere with you," she hissed back.

"Look, I'm sorry I tried to steal your boots. Wasn't anything personal, was it?"

He sounded honestly bewildered, and for a moment she almost wanted to laugh. But then she remembered standing on the bridge of the *Sunslayer*, watching the vids while the ship they'd just ransacked became a ball of fire, and her parents looked fondly into one another's eyes. That had been business, not personal, and she'd never even had to question it.

But it's sure as hell personal when it's happening to you.

"All right," she muttered.

<^>

Raeyn soon discovered that there was light in the tunnels, after all. Threads of phosphorescence showed here and there, many of them widely separated. Their light was incredibly dim, less than that of a candle, but just enough to give her a glimpse of tunnel walls that had been roughly hewn from the rock and then left unpolished. As they passed one glowing light, she leaned closer and saw that it came from some sort of fungal growth.

It was not the only life form decorating the tunnels; there were many others, from delicate lichens that looked like lace, to bloated growths bulging from the walls, to things that oozed from the ceiling like strings of multi-colored snot. The air was moist and close, and if possible smelled even worse than that of LevSix.

The boy led her through a twisted maze of passageways, some of which sloped down, others of which went up. They split off, rejoined, or ended abruptly with no rhyme or reason that she could discern. Within minz, she had to admit that she was thoroughly lost.

And maybe that was his plan from the start. Lure me down here, into this...whatever. Maze. Where I can't easily escape; where I'm in his power.

I won't be taken alive. Not again.

They climbed down a narrow oubliette, which had hand-and-foot-holds cut into the slick rock of the interior. Once at the bottom, Raeyn stopped and planted her feet. "Where are you taking me?"

The boy was nothing more than a shadow among shadows. "A hide."

251

"Who were those people?"

He shrugged. "Don't know for sure. Seen them around though, and those that I've seen with them, I don't see again. Slavers, maybe. Maybe worse."

"There isn't worse."

He shrugged again. Annoyed, she switched on her glowb; he blinked in the sudden brightness. He was short and small-built, not much taller than she.

"And why are you taking me to this hide? Twenty minz ago, you were trying to steal my boots."

His mouth twitched into a close-lipped smile. "Said it wasn't personal, didn't I? I see somebody who don't belong down here sleeping in a tunnel, I figure I'll just help myself to whatever they've got before someone else does. That's how it goes."

"So why help me? Why not just run?"

He frowned, picked a rockflea out of his hair, and absently crushed it. "Well…you got a mean fist, but they probably got guns and worse. If you want me to take you back, I will."

"Of course not." She hesitated, not know what to do. "I…my name is Raeyn," she said at last.

"Tau."

"Where are we?"

"The Depths." When she didn't react, he sighed and scuffed the floor with his boot. "You're from one of the uplevs, ain't you?"

"I'm not from Port Nowhere. I'm from…from the stars," she finished lamely.

To her surprise, he actually laughed. "I ain't some pup to go believing in things like that."

For a moment, she didn't understand what he meant. Then she did, and it made even less sense.

"What do you mean? Stars aren't something you believe in—they're there, right in front of you!"

"I ain't never seen one," he said, still grinning, as if he thought she was putting him on but he didn't mind it too much.

"But surely…I mean, other people come here, don't they? People from other places?"

252

"Maybe. I heard more say they wanted to leave, though. I figure it's the same as those who say you go to some good place when you die. Just a story to keep people hoping for something better and distract 'em from what they really got."

"But...where do you think new people come from?"

"Port Nowhere's a big place, ain't it?" he said, and now there was the edge of annoyance in his voice. "Look, we can't just stand out here in the open jawing. You got anywhere to go? Know anybody here?"

In the open? This narrow tunnel didn't even approach "open" as far as she was concerned.

"No."

"Then take your chances, or else come with me. We get to my hide, you can tell me all the kids' stories you want."

She started to scowl, then realized that she wasn't in any position to take offense. So what if he called her a liar? She'd been called worse things. She *was* worse things.

He turned away and loped off into the dark. Afraid of losing sight of him, she cursed silently and hurried after. In the light of her wrist glowb, she saw that he moved with a quick, easy gait, his head turning as he scanned the environment around him continuously. Something white on the tunnel floor caught his eye, but he barely even slowed as he scooped it up. He pinched it in two, popped half in his mouth, and offered the rest to her.

A grub. Oh gods, he's eating some kind of grub.

The gorge rose in her throat, and she shook her head. "N-no thanks."

He shrugged and ate the rest of it, licking the gooey residue off his fingers.

They passed through a twisting confusion of tunnels, diving deeper and deeper into the Depths. As they went, the growths on the walls grew denser, as if fewer people passed this way. White marks began to show up here and there on the few clear spaces on the walls. It was a single symbol, repeated over and over again, but not one that she recognized.

"What does the writing mean?"

"You mean the ghost marks?" Tau asked, sounding vaguely surprised that she didn't know. "Means this passage leads somewhere that somebody died. Cave-in, or bad water, or some such. People see that mark, they head the other way."

"We don't seem to be heading the other way."

He gave her that close-lipped smile again, and she suddenly realized what it reminded her of.

Predatory species did that, species where showing your teeth was a threat, not a reassurance.

"Can't fool you," he said dryly. "That's cause I know what's down here, and it's worth the risk. Look, I ain't lived on my own this long just so I can fall down a shaft or smother in bad air, so don't worry." He paused and seemed to think a minz. "But if you ain't with me, then don't follow the marks."

At length, the passage they were in seemed to run out without going anywhere. The ceiling dived down, until there was nothing but a narrow throat of stone, too small even to go through on hands and knees.

Raeyn stopped, certain that he had tricked her after all, but Tau simply flopped down on his belly and started to wriggle inside.

Claustrophobia hit her, and she closed her eyes. "I can't do that."

He stopped and backed carefully out.

Oh gods, it's too small to even turn around in there. You'd get stuck, and you couldn't move, and you'd die, I can't do this I can't...

There was some kind of nasty slime smeared all over his jacket from the narrow walls of the tunnel. It seemed like the only clean thing about him was his eyes, large and dark as the spaces between the stars.

"Why not?" he asked, as if he considered her hesitation incomprehensible.

"Because I can't. I won't fit."

His eyes swept over her figure, and it was all she could do to suppress a shiver. But if he liked what he saw in any way other than the purely practical, it didn't show.

"Sure you will. You ain't skin and bones, but you'll fit."

She swallowed hard. "I can't," she said again, this time in a small voice.

He looked at her contemplatively for a few minz, then nodded, as if he'd agreed on something with himself. "How about this way?" he asked, and started to feed himself back into the narrow tunnel. But this time he went feet-first. When only his hands were still visible, he beckoned to her. "Come on. Take my hands. You ain't gonna get stuck."

She'd thought that killing Sanctiblan and running away had taken courage.

But that had been nothing at all compared to what it took to follow him into that constricted tunnel. The stone seemed to press down on her, as if the whole weight of the planetoid was gathering itself to crush her. She held her arms out in front of her, her fingers trapped securely in Tau's, and wriggled her body like a worm. *Oh gods, just think about the stars. When I get away from here, I'm never going to set foot on a planet again. Or if I do, I'll have a big villa open to the ocean, just like on Hermia 12.*

Fortunately for her sanity, the tunnel wasn't long. They popped out the other end, tumbling a couple of feet to land on a thick mattress of what looked like some sort of moss.

Is this what it feels like being born? she wondered, and had to suppress an hysterical laugh.

"See? Told you," he said, with another of those grins.

Limp with relief, she rested on the moss for a moment, trying to wipe some of the slime off her clothes and hair. Tau rolled away, scrambled to his feet, and vanished for a moment into the darkness. She heard the scrape of ceramic on rock...and then the light came on.

The lantern was dimmer than her wrist glowb, but less directional, and revealed the space around them like the opening of an eye. Moisture gleamed from the rock, enhancing its vibrant colors. Rusty red swirled into obsidian; dark gray streaks banded washes of milky white; and garnets speckled a green so deep it was almost black. The stone flowed and twisted and humped, molded by geological forces beyond her understanding into fantastical forms. The ceiling was hidden in shadow, but she caught the faintest glimpse of crystals that reflected the light back. And it went on...and on...a huge cavern, a fairytale kingdom hidden in this place of eternal night.

Tau lifted his lantern, and the shadows shifted, revealing a new host of wonders. Her mouth all but hanging open, Raeyn climbed to her feet and took a cautious step into the cavern. The glint of water caught her eye, and she saw the edge of a lake. The water looked clear and pure, and her mouth suddenly felt horribly parched. She started towards the lake edge—first a drink, and then she would scrub away all the slime and filth of the tunnels, all the slime and filth of her life....

"Don't," Tau said, grabbing her arm.

She looked at him in surprise. His face was grim, mouth set into a tight line.

"The water's bad. That's the reason for all the ghost marks."

"Are you certain?" she asked reluctantly. It certainly *looked* all right, so clear that she could see the sloping bottom.

He pointed to the shore. "You see the white stuff there? The mineral deposits on the edge and bottom? Makes the water poison to drink."

It seemed horribly unfair, like a trap baited with sugar. Her disappointment must have showed on her face, though, because he turned away and started off towards the nearest cave wall.

"Don't worry," he called back. "I got supplies here. I'll get you something to drink, okay?"

His supplies were cached away in a narrow slot between rocks, which looked like just another shadow to her until he probed it with a metal bar.

"Checking for bugs before I stick my hand in," he said, which made sense.

The gods alone knew what horrid things might be nesting down here.

They had their dinner, such as it was, on the shore of the poisonous lake. "Tell you something most others don't know," he said, and held out a huge piece of fungus. "Just sink your teeth in and suck, all right?"

She took it doubtfully but did as he asked. The taste was foul, and she almost spat it out, until she realized that her mouth was filling with liquid. Startled, she swallowed and shot him a questioning glance.

"They store water. Purify it, too. If you can find these, you'll never go thirsty." His face took on a wistful look. "My mom taught me that."

Raeyn felt a sudden twinge, although whether it was longing, or rage, or even hate, she didn't know. She didn't want to think about her parents, because even memories of the good times led inevitably to memories of the bad ones. To eyes glazed with straz-hunger, to rough words and shouts, to the slow disintegration of everything they had ever been.

"I lost my parents, too," she said once she'd drained all the moisture out of the fungus.

He nodded and handed her what looked like a strip of dried fish. She decided not to ask—probably better that she didn't inspect their meal too closely.

"Did they die?"

"Might as well have."

Tau bowed his head, his curtain of tangled, brown hair hiding most of his face from her. Only his mouth showed, the lips soft and mobile and pale as the rest of him. "I had a mom, and two aunts, and an uncle, and a grandmother. Granny said she came from somewhere else, just like you. She must have been from a really big cave, cause she talked like you could just run and run without ever having to go around a corner or nothing. Maybe you came from the same place?"

"I don't know. What was it called?"

"Home."

Raeyn couldn't help but smile, even though she knew he hadn't meant it as a joke. "Then maybe I am from the same place after all."

<^>

Tau lay wrapped in a dirty blanket over his multiple layers of clothing. The faintly musty smell of the moss he'd gathered to make a soft nest filled his nose, and he thought it was about time to change it out, before it got anymore infested with bugs than it already was.

He closed his eyes for a moment, just enjoying the sound of another person breathing. Her scent lingered on his clothes from when they'd fought, clean and a little spicy, and he enjoyed that, too. Damn, he'd been lonely, ever since the last of his tribe had given in to soft bone and died in another one of their hides. Vindi'd been so bad at the end that her coughs had literally broken her ribs, and she'd died in agony. Not the way he wanted to go, for sure.

And he'd thought that maybe he'd get used to being alone...except that he'd never been alone before in his whole life, and it was harder to adapt than he'd thought it would be. That was why he'd let Mal feed him and stuff. But Mal had his own business, didn't live down here, and so Tau pretty much stayed lonely.

She don't belong down here, either, he thought. His jaw still ached where she'd kicked him. Damn, that had been stupid— he'd forgotten one of the first things his mom had taught him. Lots of prey, especially big prey, would kick behind it when you were running it down. If they ever found a boveen or something like it—not that they ever had—she'd been adamant that he wasn't to get behind it, or else its hooves could break his face or worse.

And so, like some stupid pup young enough to still have his dinner regurgitated for him, what had he done?

But what was done was done, and you learned from what you lived through, or else it killed you the next time.

The sound of Raeyn's breathing changed, and he propped himself up on his elbow to check on her. She was sleeping way over near the lake, like she still didn't quite trust him even though he'd shared his food with her. Maybe people where she came from didn't put much store in that bond, but it meant something down here.

He could see her even with the lantern turned off, just like he could see everything that put out heat, no matter how dark it was. It hadn't seemed odd when he was growing up, but after his family was killed and the tribe had taken him in, he'd realized that none of them could do it. When they'd taught him how to speak their language, they'd told him he was Human like them.

At the time, he hadn't even known what that meant.

Raeyn was lying on her side, her face buried in her hands, her shoulders shaking silently.

258

"Are you all right?" he called. When she didn't answer, he sighed and slid out of his nest.

She didn't look at him when he sat down by her. He didn't really know what to do to make her feel better. The memory of his mom licking the tears off his face with her warm tongue came back hard, making him ache inside. She hadn't understood tears, but she'd understood he was unhappy, and she'd sure understood comfort.

"It's all right," he said, but he said it in his family's language because that was still the one that meant kindness to him. "Our bellies are full, and all the prey is asleep, growing fat for tomorrow. All is safe, and your..."

Your family is around you, that was how it ended. But it wasn't true in her case, or his anymore, so he shut his mouth fast.

Raeyn sat up, wiping her face and blinking at him. "What? I don't understand what you're saying."

Her voice trembled, and he felt bad for her.

"Just that...that it's okay." He smiled at her encouragingly before he remembered she couldn't see him. So he touched her hair lightly, as a substitute, but she jerked back.

"Sorry. I didn't mean to scare you."

"What do you want from me?"

She sounded lost and bewildered, and he felt even worse. "Just somebody to talk to," he said.

The light at her wrist came on, and he blinked rapidly as his eyes adjusted. He could see colors better in regular light; her coppery hair leapt into clarity like a sudden spark.

But fire was bad—you never knew when a spark might ignite gases down here, blow you straight to the Core, or suck all the air out of a closed tunnel and leave you to suffocate.

That ain't a good omen, he thought with a little chill.

"Look," he said, trying to take his mind off it, "I been thinking, and I might be able to help you. I got a friend, Mal, up on the official levs." He waved his arm vaguely over his head. "He's got all kinds of connections. Might be able to set you up with a job."

She stiffened, which wasn't the reaction he'd expected. "I won't work in some brothel."

Just the thought of her working some place like the Blender or the Double Dome made him feel weird inside. He didn't like it, not at all, and he bared his teeth before he could even think about what he was doing.

"Didn't say that, did I?"

"No." To his surprise, she even smiled a little, but it was a sad smile. "You didn't. I'm sorry, Tau. I just...I'm just tired."

Something about the look in her eye told him that she meant the sort of tired you didn't get over just by sleeping. It was the kind of tired you got from looking over your shoulder every day, from fighting for every moment, the kind that ate up your heart from the inside until there was nothing left.

He knew how that felt, maybe too well. It had dragged him down after his tribe had died, until it seemed like the only sleep that would cure it was the sleep of death. But Mal and Crila had stepped in and caught his attention, got him interested in living again. And he figured maybe he could do the same for somebody else.

"Get some sleep," he said. "And then we'll go up to Dhamu's and find Mal, okay?"

<^>

What damn time is it? Raeyn wondered. And: *How long have I been here?*

Tau apparently worked only off the chrono in his own head. And maybe, given that he was used to long stretches with no light, no chronos, and no shift changes to regulate his sense of time, it was even somewhat accurate. But Raeyn just felt disoriented and cranky, her body unable to decide whether it wanted to sleep or wake up.

They circled around to Dhamu's bar for what seemed like the twelfth time, although in reality was probably only the fifth. When Tau had led her up out of the Depths to Level Seven—or LevSev, as he called it—she'd assumed that he already had some kind of pre-arranged meeting with this friend of his. But it quickly became obvious that his only real strategy was to look inside to see if Mal was there, then circle around what seemed to be a marketplace, shoplifting everything in sight.

Then it was back to Dhamu's to start the whole cycle over again.

Don't complain, she told herself. *Things could be a lot worse. Although if he gets us caught by the Connies and locked up for theft...*

"There," said Tau, the first word he'd spoken in owerz, and cut off into the bar so abruptly that she stumbled trying to keep up with him.

The bar was dim, and clientele from various species sat at booths or at the bar. None of them gave either her or Tau a second glance, which immediately endeared the place to her. Tau threaded his way through the free-standing tables, then slid into a booth across from a man who had been eating alone. As Raeyn hesitantly followed suit, scooting in beside Tau, the man looked up...and her heart almost stopped.

It had been years since she'd seen his face, and even then it had only been on vid. The *Sunslayer* had crossed bows with another pirate outfit, and a few shots had been exchanged. But her parents had always insisted that she know their rivals, the ships and the crew both, from the captain down to the galley cook. And she knew this man.

Malik Blayne.

But he's dead—or supposed to be.

Oh gods, what if he recognizes me? She'd grown up a lot in the last few years, but that didn't mean he wouldn't know her.

But if he did, he kept the reaction well hidden. "Tau," he said in a gruff voice that she liked immediately. "Who's your friend?"

"This is Raeyn. She's from the stars." Tau grinned, as if he'd said she was from never-never land. "She needs a job."

"Does she?" Malik's brown eyes studied her, and she could see the sharp intelligence lurking in their depths. Tau seemed to take people as he found them; this man, she suspected, did not.

A Velantran waitcreature approached with a bored look on his face. Either the people who tended this bar where incredibly non-inquisitive, or else had already seen everything at least once before.

"Two more sandwiches and two globes of beer," Malik said.

261

"I don't have any credz," Raeyn told him, her nerves thrumming with the effort to keep her voice level.

"Of course not. None of Tau's friends have credz," he said with a smile that took years off his face. "Come to think of it, I didn't know Tau had any other friends."

Raeyn frowned—it seemed a harsh thing to say.

But Tau just grinned. "She's new down here."

The beer was awful, but better than Tau's fungus. The sandwiches seemed to be made out of fish, liberally coated with a heavy sauce that also tasted fishy. Her distaste must have shown, because Malik nodded in the direction of the sandwich. "Eat it. The sauce is made from fish livers. For the vitamin D."

"Oh," she said, taking in the implications of that.

He leaned back and folded his hands in front of him. "Now, why don't you tell me what sort of job you're looking for?"

She told him what she thought was safe, and hoped he didn't notice that her collection of skills were exactly the kind that someone brought up by pirates would have. While they talked, Tau put away two beers and two sandwiches at an astonishingly fast pace—then slumped over against the wall and promptly fell asleep. That, more than anything else, convinced her that he must truly trust Malik Blayne.

Now if only I could know whether Blayne deserves that trust. Damn the luck. Just when everything seemed to be going so well...

But he hasn't recognized me. Not yet. With any luck, he won't.

That still doesn't mean I can trust him.

When she was done, Malik nodded thoughtfully. "I might know someone who needs some technical expertise. Tell you what. Come back here tomorrow with Tau, and I'll let you know for certain, all right?"

She nodded warily. "And what's your cut in all of this?"

Malik smiled wearily, and she saw all the lines around his eyes. "I do favors for my friends. And they do favors for me. Tau has lent me a hide once or twice, when I needed to stay out of sight for a while."

She felt something harden inside her, although she couldn't say why. "If you're tallying favors, then this goes on my account. Not his."

He sighed, and the lines got deeper. "I'm not tallying anything, girl. I don't have enough friends to do that."

<^>

Malik sat alone at the booth for a while after they'd left. When the Velantran came to clear the table, he shook his head and picked up the globe Raeyn had drunk from.

"Tell Dhamu to put it on my tab," he said, and the Velantran just shrugged and left with the remaining dishes.

When he was gone, Malik held the globe up to the light. The lip-print on it would yield more than enough skin cells for him to run a DNA profile on her. Or, rather, for "Rudof" to do so, since it would be some of the Dyll billions paying for equipment fast enough to snag the important markers and make a match.

It wasn't that he didn't trust Tau. But the truth was, Tau was at the age where males could get spectacularly stupid over anything with a pair of tits. And although Tau wasn't entirely Human—Dyll's machines had been hard at work decoding his genes, too—he was Human enough for the hormones to be there, maybe keeping him from thinking as straight as he ought.

A girl with no past that she'd admit to wasn't as suspicious in Port Nowhere as it might be somewhere else. Half the people on the Rock had come there for the sole purpose of disappearing, either from their families, or from governments, or from whatever boogeyman haunted their nights.

But Malik hadn't stayed alive this long by trusting blindly, and he wasn't going to start now.

<^>

"Damn," said Malik quietly.

He sat in his private office in the Dyll Dome. The window in front of him looked out onto the conservatory, where green plants waved and bobbed gently in an artificial wind. Brightly-colored birds flew about like jewels; fine nets that were invisible from a distance kept them from smashing into the Dome's transparent sides. The scene was meant to be the vision of a lost paradise, carefully replicated from the gardens of what had been Rudof's home before he had been exiled here.

Whether the gardens had been intended to console or to punish him, Malik didn't know.

Algensio had been sitting in a corner, happily sharpening his knives and probably contemplating the Vamir version of a good time, which was anyone else's version of mayhem. Now he glanced up questioningly.

"The search came back on the girl. Raeyn Banks. As in Nel Banks. As in the *Sunslayer*—a pirate rig. And not just any pirate rig, but one that had a bad reputation even with other pirates. They followed a strict no-survivors policy. They would come in, fire on a ship, and open as much of it up to vacuum as they could as the most efficient way of killing everyone on board. Then they would board the ship, shoot anyone who might have made it to an envirosuit in time, and take away anything of value."

He didn't add that they'd exchanged a few shots with the *End of Time* on one occasion. The *Sunslayer* hadn't been above showing up in the midst of a raid, after another ship had subdued the target but before they'd had time to unload. They looked upon that window of operational confusion as the perfect time to blow both to hell, giving them the bones of two ships to pick at their leisure.

Algensio let out a low growl.

"Exactly what I thought," Malik agreed. "I assumed she couldn't be up to any good here. I even found a warrant out for her—she's wanted for an assault that occurred in Connie space.

"Then...I read the warrant. It's for injuries caused while escaping her legal owner. She's a slave."

The manacle scars on his wrists seemed to ache, and he rubbed at them absently. "They sold her. Her own parents sold her to cover their gambling debts. That was almost a sintinz ago. And now she's come close to killing her owner, escaped, made her way here, and expects me to find her a job. I should've known when she showed up with Tau that it would be complicated. Damn boy can't do anything the easy way."

Raeyn carefully finished setting the final seal on the battered envirosuit and sat back to inspect her handiwork. Her neck ached from holding it in one position for too long, and she absently rubbed it as she ran the last check on the seal. It held.

Finally. I thought this shift would never end. She stood up and stretched, then yelled towards the front of the shop. "I'm going home, Mrrow!"

Her new employer, Mrrow-Gumg, poked his head around a pile of second-hand clothing, some of which bore very suspicious-looking holes ringed with bloodstains.

"You see that thief Tau, you tell him he steal from me again, I chop him up and sell leftovers to Vamir." Mrrow seemed to consider a moment, licking his eye contemplatively. "But he get good trade, he come to me—I give best pay on Rock!"

Raeyn barely suppressed a snort. *I'll keep that in mind if Tau ever wants to be swindled.*

"You come early shift tomorrow—I got good stuff on way! Maybe a little broken," Mrrow added as she went out. She waved without comment, slung her tool satchel over her shoulder, and left.

The new job didn't pay much—and she'd had to threaten Mrrow to keep him from cheating her out of any wages—but it was enough to rent a tiny pod down on LevSix. She stopped by just long enough to pick up a small object and drop it in her satchel. She'd found the item amidst the insane maze of junk that represented Mrrow-Gumg's livelihood and had haggled him down to a price she could actually afford. Fixing it had been relatively easy; now it was time to put it into operation.

Tau found her before she'd gone far. One moment she was walking alone through the crowd that thronged the tunnel in front of the Blender; the next, he was striding along beside her as if he'd always been there. She wondered if he'd memorized her work shifts, then chastised herself for assuming he would even want to do such a thing.

"Heyo," she said, "can we go to your hide?"

"The one with the lake?" he asked, and she realized that he probably had half a dozen bolt holes that she nothing of. "I guess. Why?"

"I'll tell you when we get there."

It was a long walk, and the arduous climbing and crawling that accompanied it left her breathless by the time they finally got into the cavern. The last stretch of tunnel still made her limp with fear, although it wasn't quite as bad as it had been the first time.

She'd had to push her satchel along in front of her, but it had been worth it. She'd tucked dinner in there, and they ate first. She told him more about her new job, particularly about her insane employer, and managed to actually get a rare laugh out of him.

When they were done, she took the object out of her satchel and carried it to the lakeside. He followed, looking puzzled. "What's that?"

"A surprise. Sit down."

He did as she asked, and she settled in by him, both of them facing the beautiful, poison water. "Now," she said, "we're sitting on the beach on Hestia 12. The sand under us is soft and comfortable. We've just been swimming in the ocean, and a warm wind is drying our skin. The waves are breaking on the shore, and the sound is like the breathing of some huge, friendly animal. Behind us is a big house, and maybe later we'll go up and have something more to eat. But for right now, we're going to sit on the beach and watch the stars come out."

She pulled the cloth away from her prize. It was nothing more than an obsolete, globe-shaped light that hummed to life when she threw the switch. But as the gentle, directionless radiance spread, it caught in the crystals on the hidden ceiling. They blazed forth from the shadows, thousands of them, perfect as diamonds in the blackness.

"Stars," she said, pointing up.

Tau smiled, a gentle, unguarded expression that made her feel warm inside.

"Stars," he agreed.

~END~

MANIFEST DESTINY

Jim Johnson

"Well that's a new one," giggled the Halsan female. "You weren't that pretty when you got here."

Octavio Vexus brushed his black hair back and looked deeper into the mirror as the reflection of the woman behind him. She lay naked on the bed, half covered by the rumpled coverings. His gray eyes roved the long graceful curves of her exposed, lavender colored flesh and he debated how much he had to spare.

She patted the mattress as though reading his thoughts. "Come on back to bed," she grinned, then coyly added, "I never knew Humans could be so much…fun."

So far so good. Time to bump it up a notch. "Sorry, sweet thing," having no idea what her name was. "I'm running late as it is."

"Oh come one," she actually implored. "I was good, wasn't I? Look, this round is for free, just for kicks, my treat."

Octavio grinned like a Bansnict drowning in credz. "Maybe later," he lied. He plucked up the small empty vial from atop the bureau and, though the contents were odorless, sniffed it.

It had definitely proven itself worth every cred he had paid for it.

"Oooh, what's that?" the Halsan asked excitedly, sliding from the bed to press herself against his back. He could feel the tempting warmth of her skin through his clothing.

267

What the heck, he though and handed her the small polybdalloy container. "Here. Something to remember me by."

She held the vial reverently, a blend of happiness and sadness in her dark violet eyes. "I'll keep..." her musical voice cracked. "I'll keep it forever."

"You do that," he advised. He turned and wrapped her in a hug; it seemed the polite thing to do. Then, without the slightest twinge of guilt, he left her alone in the room. She would get over him—he checked his chrono—in just about ten minz.

Octavio left the Blender, this lev's inter-species brothel, behind and head for the nearest sub-trans station. He boarded the conveyance amid a crush of Port Nowhere's diverse population. Pressed like sardoveets in a tube, Octavio found himself squashed between two Bansnicts on his left, a Nicovan on his right, a Talseen who reeked of brine and an L'Talton behind him. The beak of the latter jabbed into his backside.

"I hate the sub-trans," he said to no one in particular.

When the tube train made its end of the line stop on LevSix, in the Gamma sector, Octavio debarked and stretched his limbs. He looked around, trying to remember the name of the Bansnict merchant he had purchased the vial of synthesized Halsan pheromones from. The name of the small shop escaped him, but as he recalled, it was situated between a bar and yet another of the Rock's innumerable inter-species brothels; one he had opted not to patronize given the particularly seamy quality of working girls-n-boys.

The brothel's sign caught his eye down the left esplanade: *Madame Shooki's House of Thrills*. He passed the brothel, and there, tending his wares was the Bansnict, Mrrrow-Gumg.

"Hey, remember me?" Octavio asked as he approached the diminutive fur ball.

"Ah! Captain Vexus. I never forget customer, never," beamed Mrrrow-Gumg. His long tongue flicked out for no discernable reason then returned to the Bansnict's jagged-toothed mouth. "I guess you try out purchase, eh?" He winked conspiratorially. "Worked just like promised, yes?"

Octavio, nodded. "I'll need at least four more vials."

"Oooh, you be in big lust. Four vials. That's gonna cost you major credz, friend."

"I wouldn't be here if I couldn't afford it."

The sudden glint in the Bansnict's dark, beady eyes made Octavio regret the comment. The price had probably just doubled on him.

"Well, this way, this way."

Mrrrow-Gumg led him deeper into the densely laden shop. Octavio waited at the back counter while the merchant disappeared through a curtain of dangling beads. When Mrrrow-Gumg returned he placed four vials, identical to Octavio's first purchase, on the counter top.

"That be one hundred twenty-five credz... each." The Bansnict smiled pleasantly.

"Five hundred! You little thief, the first one only cost fifty credz."

"Heyo, you go try down at Mook's shop...but he not have what you want since I make the stuff myself."

Octavio had expected a higher price, but not more than double. For all Octavio knew, the little crook was telling the truth. Even though the Bansnict couldn't have known, Octavio had scoured dozens of shops like this one in search of the stuff. The little crook had him over a barrel.

"Fine. But if this stuff fails to do the job, I'll come back here and vaporize your sorry hide." He tossed the cred chips on the counter and swiped up the vials. He left the shop to the sound of Mrrrow-Gumg gleefully counting his plunder.

"Well," he admitted as he stuffed the tiny vials into his flight jacket pocket. "Once I get what I'm after, five hundred credz will seem like pocket change."

Now back up to LevOne and the Starview Lounge. If he was going to go broke he may as well do it in style.

Besides, he had some making up to with Sherveena. She had been against his 'testing' of the pheromones, but he had to know that they would work and how well, if he was going to bet everything on their use.

<^>

Octavio reached the docking platform where his ship, *Sherveena's Beauty* was berthed, strode up the ramp and entered the vessel's hatchway. The first thing he saw was the real Sherveena, but it wasn't her beauty that met him, it was her wrath.

"You boveen!" She cursed him as she threw a utility wrench at his head. "You actually did it, didn't you?"

He ducked the projectile, barely. "Sherveena…"

"How could you?"

"Heyo, I thought we came to an understanding."

The lame excuse hung suspended between them as the Velantran woman squared her graceful shoulders and burned holes through Octavio's head with her electric green eyes.

Try again, Octavio ordered himself. "Listen, sweetie, you know I had to test the stuff. Everything we've ever dreamed of depends on knowing how well it works."

"Your screwing some Halsan whore was never a part of any dream of mine!"

In spite of himself, Octavio knew that Sherveena was right. It hadn't been necessary for him actually have sex with the Halsan woman, but…

"Sherveena, listen. I…"

"No, you listen, Octavio. I know what's at stake, what we stand to gain…"

Octavio noticed the encouraging *we*.

"…but from now on, I'll be watching you work. That's right. When you start working on the next Halsan slut, I'll be close enough to kill you both if you take it too far."

"Sherveena, be reasonable. I can't just…"

Sherveena's lovely golden face turned hard stone. "Oh, but you will. You don't have any choice in the matter."

And with that, she turned and stomped deeper into the ship.

If only they could start the final phase of their plan now, instead of having to wait unit tomorrow, Octavio thought. He sighed and picked up the wrench. It was going to be long night.

The next day was no different than any other in the Gamma sector as Octavio and Sherveena made their way through the

270

cosmopolitan throngs. They had waited until early evening to set out. Sherveena had said not a word all night and, though she had yet to speak to him all day long, Octavio was a least grateful that the ice in his her eyes had thawed somewhat. And while he wished that she would start talking before they arrived at their destination, he knew better than to make the first move.

All at once they found themselves at a standstill. An amorphous group of the multi-species citizenry had, for some reason, congregated just ahead of them.

"What's going on?" Octavio wondered as he wedged a path for himself and Sherveena through the gaggle of onlookers. As they reached the forefront of the crowd, Sherveena finally spoke.

"A Red Publican priest."

"A whatchmawho?"

"...again I warn you; beyond the galaxy lies eternal damnation! And again, I warn those who seek to venture there... the order of the Red Publicans is watching you!"

The speaker was Human, pale skinned and bald headed. He wore what looked to Octavio to be a pair of red quartz goggles. Hi angular face was striated from forehead to chin by four blood-red lines. Tattoos, paint, or...something else, Octavio wondered?

"We are watching," the priest reiterated one last time before drawing the folds of his crimson cloak about him and disappearing into the crowd.

"What was that all about?" Octavio wondered aloud, chancing a glance at the still aloof Sherveena as the two of them resumed their walk.

"They claim to be a religious order," she volunteered, the interruption in their trek apparently pretext enough to drop the silent treatment. "But how an aversion to extra-galactic travel factors into a religious belief system is apparently something only the Red Publicans know."

"I've been all over the galactic rim. I don't think I've ever heard of them before and I'm sure I'd remember a religion named like a pub owner?"

Sherveena arched a slender eyebrow. "I can think of two reasons for starters, my dear. First off, the Red Publicans seem to be unique to Port Nowhere. Secondly, you never bother to view the infovids the customs people give at every starport we've ever been to."

"Oh, those," Octavio waved dismissively. "They're usually outdated and inaccurate anyway."

"Hmmm, that's odd," said Sherveena, almost to herself.

Octavio saw that she was flicking through her personal data-pad.

"Says here that the Red Publicans were founded as far back as Port Nowhere itself. They used to meet in a spacers' tavern called the Red Publican."

Octavio sniffed. "That explains the name. Is this pub still around?"

Sherveena flicked through the index. "There's no reference to it."

"See? Out of date, inaccurate information."

"Funny," she said, returning to the Red Publican entry.

Just by the way she'd said *funny*, Octavio knew that he'd been bested, but he stuck to the familiar script anyway. "What is?"

"It says here that the Red Publicans have been increasingly active for the past three strechiz. And the last update to this file was four cyks ago."

"We're here," Octavio said, thankful for the chance to change the subject. "Keep your gorgeous eyes open," he reminded her.

Here, was a middle class rec-club called the *Second Shift*. It was located two doors down and across the promenade from the scandalously swank Starview Lounge.

Scanning the after-work rush, Octavio began to scowl. The minz whiled away, as did the number of beings on the street as they entered into the various hot spots.

"I don't see her. Are you sure this is where she comes to after work?"

Sherveena gave him a withering look. "Overeager, are we?"

Octavio drew a long silent breath.

"I've set up my part of the plan, so yes, this is the place. Just give her a few minz."

Just then a bubble-cab glided to a stop in front of the Second Shift and Captain Eversyn's Halsan secretary, Lisolia, got out.

In spite of himself, in spite of Sherveena standing right next to him, Octavio felt his jaw slacken. Whatever might be said of Captain Carle Eversyn, the leader of Port Nowhere's Consolidated Guard had an impeccable eye for beauty. The lavender-skinned woman was utterly stunning.

A sudden, worrisome thought occurred to him. What if Eversyn had hired the Halsan woman simply for her looks? Would an office ornament actually be expected to perform secretarial work? Would she have access to the information he needed?

As the Halsan entered the Second Shift, Octavio felt the weight of Sherveena's glower hit him like a meteor. He transferred his stare from the joint's entrance back to Sherveena.

"That was her, eh?" He hoped he sounded indifferent.

Judging by Sherveena's taut features, he hadn't succeeded.

He tugged at his flight jacket, patted his breast pocket and felt the small vials therein. "Well, I guess this is it." He started toward the door but was brought about by Sherveena's iron grip on his elbow.

"I'll be watching. Don't screw up," she hissed, and then added: "You know what I mean."

He did. "Jealously does not become you, my love," he said.

Then in a more business-like tone, "This stuff," he patted the vials, "works fast. I'll have her singing like an L'Talton in ten minz."

Inside the Second Shift, Octavio looked around for Lisolia. It bothered him that Sherveena had entered just minz behind him, to keep watch. It bothered him also, that she would be so distrustful of him. She knew what he was like. He was a lady's man; it was an important element in how he made his way in the galaxy. Had she forgotten how they had met?

His eyes fell upon Lisolia sitting at the bar. Perhaps, it was time to cut Sherveena loose, to move on to someone else.

Maybe he should first approach Lisolia without the synthetic pheromones, try his natural charm. If he could win her over that way, there might just be a chance he could get what he wanted... and her as well.

He glanced around. He couldn't see Sherveena amid the milling patrons; nevertheless, he could feel her laser-like gaze upon him. He shrugged t off and moved to the bar, insinuating himself between Lisolia and a hulking Coriliun. The two meter tall bug chittered its annoyance but shifted slightly aside.

The Halsan woman seemed not to notice him as she twirled the straw through the foam of her already near empty drink, something yellow with a thick foamy head.

Octavio caught the bartender's attention and ordered two more of the same.

She must have had a rough day to down her drink that quickly.

The gray-furred Vamir barkeep set the twin concoctions on the bar before Octavio, who slid the obligatory cred into the nearest bar-top pay-slot. A quick glance told Octavio that Lisolia's attention was elsewhere at the moment. He hesitated. If he was going to use the pheromones, this was his chance. As much as his ego cried otherwise, Octavio knew that he couldn't afford not to employ the chemical. He also knew that Sherveena was watching and that any deviation from the plan would only inflame her jealousy.

Guardedly, he poured the contents of one of the vials into the second drink. He was pleased when it disappeared into the drink's thick head. He cleared his throat and Lisolia turned in her seat to face him.

"I noticed that you were running low there so I took the liberty of ordering you another," he said in his most sincere voice.

The Halsan woman's plum colored eyes seemed to analyze him, as if, Octavio thought, searching for a motive. He could play this off quite coolly. With a smile, he nodded and slid her the pure drink. He caught a glimpse of surprise on her face just turned away in seeming indifference. He took a swig of the pheromone-laced drink and surveyed the crowded dance floor.

And waited.

"Thank you," she said, in her naturally melodious Halsan voice. He noticed that she was now perched on the side of her seat nearest his.

"Don't mention it," he said. Then, to get the production started, he added. "A woman as lovely as you should never have to pay for her own drinks."

As lame a line as there ever was, he admitted, but the effect of the pheromones all but guaranteed that he could call her the crusty end of a boveen and she would think it a sweet, poetic compliment.

"You're very... kind," she said, leaning still closer. "Not like the rest of these bov-brains. They've only got one thing on their minds."

He smiled slightly; he knew what was on her mind. "And what might that be?"

Her delicate features lit up mischievously. "Well, I could show you if you're interested."

Finally, he turned to face her. By the Sylmet Nebula, she was beautiful!

And if he thought so, Sherveena would too.

"Hmmm. You know, I think I am interested at that."

She beamed at him and took hold of his arm. As she quite literally dragged him toward the door, Octavio quickly chugged the remainder of his drink, not wasting a drop of the precious supplement.

In the back of his mind, he could see Sherveena following like some deranged mole-bot. It was obvious that Lisolia was taking him to her domicile, or to some other suitably secluded place.

Hopefully Sherveena had enough control not to overreact.

The young Halsan woman hailed a bubble cab. As one of the small, spherical vehicles drew up to them, Octavio chanced a look around and saw and beryllion-faced Sherveena catching a ride of her own.

He also caught the look of vengeful warning she shot him.

The next instant, he found himself being drawn into to the cab's cramped interior, a fact Lisolia seemed to relish as she practically entwined herself around him. Had he used too much of the synthetic pheromone? Or had that Bansnict fulfink, Mrrrow-Gumg, deliberately upped the potency?

"Where to?" queried the automated cab.

Without lifting her eyes from Octavio's, Lisolia absently giggled an address. A moment later, the cab was underway.

"Uh, say," began Octavio. He was suddenly, uncharacteristically, feeling flustered. "Say, I didn't catch your name?"

"Lisolia." She buried her angelic face in his neck.

He drew away, pressing himself against the curved wall of the cab. "Lisolia. Th-that's a nice name."

She pressed toward him again.

"Um, say, don't you want to know my name?"

This wasn't going as planned. The pheromones were intended just to loosen her up, get her in a friendly mood, to get her talking. If she jumped his bones now, Sherveena would know and he wouldn't have time to devise some excuse or alibi, and then the grand plan wouldn't matter.

At best, if he was lucky and Sherveena went easy on him, he'd only end up dead.

The window! If he opened it, would the pheromones blow away? Could they? It was worth a try. It was an older model cab. If it hadn't been upgraded, it would still have control buttons. He reached behind his back and fumbled for the panel as the Halsan woman locked lips with him. She had completely turned the tables on him.

"Mastre," said the cab. "Please do not tamper with the controls."

Octavio tried to explain what he wanted, but all he could manage to speak past his shanghaied lips was "Mmmumba-Mmmphul."

"I am air-conditioned," the cab informed him. "If you are too warm I would be happy to lower the temperature."

"Mmmuma-Mmmmphul!"

"I regret that I am unfamiliar with your language. I will have to consult the home office's database for the appropriate upload. In the meantime, if you do understand Basica, please refrain from tampering with the controls."

Octavio redoubled his efforts even as Lisolia redoubled hers.

The bubble cab came to an abrupt halt. The doors swiveled open and the cab promptly ordered them to get out under threat of calling the Connies.

"Ah, air," gasped Octavio as he stood on the slidewalk and peeled the lavender woman from him. A second cab drew to a stop several meters back.

Sherveena.

Octavio gripped Lisolia by the shoulders and held her at arms distance. She giggled like a schoolgirl. Ah, that was it, she wasn't just affected by the pheromones, it was the drinks. The girl couldn't handle her liquor. She was slopped. On what, not even two whole drinks? Well, who knew what someone, not to mention a Halsan, of her size could handle.

He looked around, and realized that they were actually quite near the address she had provided the cab.

"Good, good," Octavio muttered at her as he guided her along. "We can walk your buzz off... I hope."

Several paces on, Octavio was forced to pry Lisolia from around his neck. She only laughed her bell-like laugh and wrapped her arms around him more tightly.

"Silly Human. Where are you taking me?"

"Home," he grumbled as he peeled her arms from around his shoulders. By the Core, she was wasted. And was he imagining it or was she actually getting more sloshed by the minz?

"Yourrrrr home?"

He stumbled over her feet and, for the first time became aware of the passersby taking notice of them. They were predominantly Halsan, indicative he was in the right sector. It boded well that she had recalled her actual address.

"No," he snapped. "You wanted to go to your place."

"You know where I live? Oh I knew you were smart."

"You told the cab where you lived."

"And you have a smart cab too? Oh, you're just so..."

Octavio let her babble on nonsensically. He was now scrutinizing the pod numbers. Ah, at last.

"We're here," he said.

"Here?"

"Your pod," he said as he propped her up next to the door. He looked around for observers, making certain that no one would see as he raised her delicate, lavender hued palm to the identpad.

"My pod?" she asked, oblivious to Octavio applying her palm to the pad. "Oooh. You are one lucky boy."

"How's that?" he muttered doubtfully as the door irised open.

"You'll get to meet my sisters."

"Your what?"

With a sudden, unexpected alacrity Lisolia propelled him though the open door with a shove.

He stumbled inside, and heard several distinct cries of alarm as he tripped over the doorframe and landed face down on the floor. There came the sound of breaking eggshells, followed by wetness in his tunic pocket.

The last three vials! The thought had barely struck him when he found himself set upon by Lisolia and, judging from the number of hands, her three sisters.

Much, much later, the door to the pod irised open with a crackling flash. Octavio pushed a lazy Halsan arm from his face. Streetlight poured in around an all too familiar silhouette. The next thing he knew, Sherveena was yanking him to his feet. Exhausted, purple forms fell to the wayside.

"Get dressed," hissed the furious Velantran.

Haggard and disheveled, Octavio stumbled from the den of Halsan werecats. With an iron grip on his arm and a blaster in her free hand, Sherveena was directing him to an idling bubble-cab.

"Listen, sweetie, it's not what it looked like. Honest. I can explain."

"Get in."

Get dressed. Get in. What was next? Get out?

"We had a plan, Octavio. We knew what we wanted and we knew how to get it. We had even wanted the same thing."

"Sher…"

She silenced him with a nudge of the business end of the blaster. "But apparently our *wants* have taken divergent paths."

"Sher…"

"All you had to do was get her talking and to get you the manifest… but instead all you managed to do was…"

Octavio pushed the barrel of the weapon aside. "I did get her…or rather one of her sisters, to talk."

Sherveena eyed him skeptically. "That Lisolia whore is Eversyn's secretary. Her sister's not."

"Yes, but, as it runs out, the sister in question works for the Dome Seven's Port Master. I didn't get the manifest…but I got the info we need just the same."

Beneath the enormous polybdalloy bubble, the population of Dome Seven bustled about its business. Up on the rim, at true surface level, Octavio and Sherveena waited to board a public ground shuttle for the short ride over to Dome Seven's spaceport.

This was it. Octavio could already smell the credz. As a shuttle alighted at the platform, they boarded it along with a dozen other travelers. But just as the doors were closing, a slender lavender arm snaked through the gap. Octavio watched in growing horror as the arm pried the doors apart and the dreadfully beautiful Lisolia forced her way onto the shuttle.

"Whew. I almost didn't make," she gasped. "Ah, there you are, Octavio! I was hoping to find you here."

Sherveena's blue-green gaze ran a slow circuit from Octavio to the Halsan and back. "And why might that be?"

Octavio delivered an honestly mystified shrug. His hand went to the front of his shirt. Three vials was a lot, but surely he had washed all of the pheromones from his chest. But why else would Lisolia be here now? No, that wasn't quite right. He hadn't seen her, much less been near her, since Sherveena had extricated him from the Halsan's apartment. Whatever had brought her here was something else.

"Well?" he asked, hoping to divert Sherveena's focus back to the purple girl where it rightly belonged.

"Octavio, you silly Human, don't you remember? You said that you could take me away from this gods forsaken lump of beryllion, that we'd be rich on some high-class inner-system world."

With a worry-widened eye on Sherveena, Octavio automatically stammered. "I never said such a thing."

But had he? It sounded like one of his lines. And hadn't he toyed with the thought of dumping Sherveena for Lisolia? The Halsan definitely had the sort of dazzling good looks a man of means should surround himself with. No. No. No, he would have remembered saying it, surely, had he actually dared to.

For as big as Port Nowhere was, it was far too small and far too remote a place to evade Sherveena's wrath.

"She's crazy," he added.

"How much does she know?" Sherveena demanded.

Lisolia stepped closer. "Oh, I know all about Octavio's plan to pirate one of Jaxsin Deshti's outgoing ka'frindi freighters. In fact I know everything about the plan, except you and how you fit into it."

Sherveena's golden complexion turned ochre as she took a step in Lisolia's direction.

Octavio stepped between the two women. He leaned toward Sherveena's ear. "Not here, there are too many witnesses. We're almost to the spaceport; I'll shake her while you tag Deshti's ship."

"Why don't *I* take care of her and *you* tag the ship?"

"Because if she's with me, she won't be causing a scene, and the last thing we want is for port security to take an interest in us."

Sherveena peered over his shoulder toward Lisolia, then seemed to weigh the options. Finally, she dug a small device from her satchel.

"What's this?" Octavio asked as she began to tuck it into his tunic pocket.

"A personal tracker."

"What? You don't trust me?"

"Lets just say that if you go anywhere near the *Beauty* before I get back to you, you're a dead man."

280

Octavio scowled. He gave the tracker a second look. It had a disintegrator tab on it. As long as he was within a meter of the gadget, the tab could be tripped to reduce him to molecular dust.

He wanted to say something, to lay down the law, but they were too close now. Sherveena had become so distrustful of him; should he consider again dumping her in favor of Lisolia? After all, the Halsan was not only devastatingly beautiful; she was well connected to the Connies. Teaming up with her had its distinct advantages.

But it was now too late to change the plan. He was committed to seeing it through.

But...afterward, afterward was a different story.

A fleeting mental image of Sherveena's lifeless body tumbling among Port Nowhere's surrounding asteroid field flitted through his thoughts.

Yes, Sherveena had been fun, but like all good things, she'd reached the end of her line.

The ground-shuttle was coming to a stop inside the port dome. Octavio smiled charmingly. He lightly patted the pocket and the tracker/disintegrator inside.

"Don't worry about me," he said. "Just make sure you tag the right ship."

For Sherveena's benefit, when he next spoke to Lisolia, he made certain his tone was purely no-nonsense, aloof. "Follow me, and don't interfere."

The Halsan blinked from Sherveena to Octavio. She nodded and, as the groundshuttle doors opened, fell in step with him as he exited.

Octavio glanced back over the thronged platform, assuring himself that Sherveena was well away in the opposite direction. He turned to Lisolia.

"Why are you here?" he demanded.

"What?" she stammered. Octavio noted the deepening lavender of her cheeks. Was she blushing?

"You heard me."

"I...I think I'm in love with you," she blurted.

Impossible, thought Octavio, and then he repeated the thought aloud.

"It should be, yes, but it's true."

"The pheromones don't last that long nor have that much of a lasting effect."

"What are you talking about? What pheromones?"

"Nothing." There wasn't time to explain, and he wouldn't have anyway. "Come on, we need to get closer to the *Beauty*."

"And who is she?" demanded Lisolia. Her tone was so similar to Sherveena's, it sent a shivering down Octavio's spine.

"*Sherveena's Beauty*, my starship," he said as he lead her along.

"You'll have to re-christen that ship if I'm going to be your partner."

Octavio came to a dead stop and spun to face the Halsan.

Was she telepathic, empathic, or just overconfident?

"Even if I wanted a new partner, this is not the time to get one."

"Oh, the *job*, I almost forgot."

Octavio jaw tightened. "Yes, the *job*. I'm not going to blow the take of a lifetime for change of partners."

As soon as he'd said it, Octavio realized that if she felt left out now, Lisolia could bring the Connies down on him in a half a minz. Sherveena would have simply led her down some side passage and killed her. But Octavio knew he couldn't do that. Not even on the most desperate of days: and certainly not to Lisolia. He honestly wanted the Halsan woman as a partner, for both business and pleasure.

"Look. You want to partner up with me?"

She nodded emphatically.

He nodded back. At the very least he had to convince her not to call the Connies when he left her behind while he and Sherveena pirated Jaxsin Deshti's freighter.

"Look, the plan is fixed, solid as beralloy. I can't change it now, but the way it's going to work, I'll be back on the Rock in a matter of owerz."

"You mean you aren't going to head for the galaxy?"

Her tone gave Octavio pause. Was she only interested in him as an avenue away from Port Nowhere? It was what the less than privileged seemed to want—why would a Connie secretary, however highly placed, be any different? Well, if that were her motivation, he would have to play this carefully.

"For a short while, anyway, at least while the Connies comb the asteroids and the likely in-gal space-lanes. After that... who knows?" He was pleased to see the accepting look in her eyes.

"After that," she said, "we can deal with the Velantran?"

Octavio nodded and they resumed their way toward the *Beauty*. They stopped several berths down.

"Which one is yours?"

Octavio pointed to the small, Gaverinal picket ship—a forty sintinz-old remnant from the Gaverin-Simbolsia wars—which he had purchased on the cheap...stolen, in other words...and then retrofitted for his own purposes.

"How can I trust that you'll ditch the Velantran and come back for me?"

Thinking quickly. "You've seen how she is. Why would I subject myself to her company over yours?"

That seemed to mollify Lisolia's suspicions. "Now then, you're going to have to hang back, out of Sherveena's sight until after she and I launch."

"And after that?"

Octavio seemed to ponder the idea. "I won't be gone but a few owerz at the most. Meet me back at your place. By then I'll have dealt with Sherveena." He grinned. "And more important still, you and I will be free to begin a—literally—rich new partnership."

Just then, Sherveena's voice crackled over Octavio's personal communicator. "It's done, Octavio. Meet me back at the *Beauty* in fifteen minz."

Octavio noted Lisolia's wrinkled nose. "At your place in a few owerz," he reminded before heading alone for his ship.

The Port Authority cleared the *Beauty* for take off. Octavio powered up the lift-thrusters and piloted his ship up through the many-tiered docking bay. Sherveena sat next to him, in the co-pilot's seat. Her mood had lightened considerably, now that it was just the two of them again.

She had shed her confrontational attitude like an Ophidian shed it skin. But, thought Octavio, just like an Ophidian, Sherveena would turn on him in an instant the next time another woman caught his eye. There was already Lisolia and, just as certainly as they were about to plunder Deshti's automated freighter, there would be others after her as well.

"We're almost through the final lock," she offered as though her recent mood had never happened.

Octavio checked his screens. There were half a dozen ships in transit at the moment within the spacious facility. Which one was Jaxsin Deshti's was anyone's guess...but Sherveena's.

"Are you sure the tag is in place?"

She smiled. "Octavio, my love, have I ever failed you before?"

She hadn't. In fact, it was precisely Sherveena's proficiency in all things piratical that had kept the two of them together these past three sintinz.

Three sintinz? By the Core, that was practically an eternity!

He nodded. "As soon as we clear the dome, activate the tracker."

<^>

Gravity had not compressed the asteroid field surrounding Port Nowhere into a conveniently flat ring. Instead, galactic forces that had flung the errant planet to the outermost edge of the galaxy had shattered what many planetologists surmised to have been at least two, and quite possibly four lunar bodies, and sent the debris dragging like a comet's tail with the runaway planet.

As a result, the asteroid field was oblong, tapering to a point back toward the galaxy. The bulk of the field, dense and restless, cloaked the planet like a swarm of petrified insects.

Octavio checked the scanners again; there were several ships in the vicinity, each represented on screen by a green icon. One, though, was red, the reading not of the ship, but of the tag Sherveena had attached to it. Octavio studied its movements made a guess as to the tagged freighter's probable course and then had the *Beauty's* computers do the same.

Both conclusions agreed.

Octavio maneuvered the *Beauty* into close proximity to a large asteroid, registering a high beryllion content, along the freighter's projected path. The beryllion would effectively render his ship invisible to scanners.

"Anchor us," he said.

Sherveena released the grappling tether. They both watched as the powerful claw-hand snaked forth and then sank its claws into the asteroid.

"We're secure," she said.

And so they waited. And plotted, not just on taking the automated freighter, but as far as Octavio was concerned, against one another as well. As soon as the ka'frindi haul was secured, he would send Sherveena on a one-way spacewalk, without a 'virosuit of course. In spite of himself, Octavio shivered. But killing Sherveena was the only option. Alive, he would never be free of her. And if he left her for another woman…if he left her period, he knew that she was quite capable of killing him.

She's brought you both to this point, he told himself. *She's chosen her own fate.*

"Here it comes," Sherveena announced, snapping him out of his thoughts.

He looked to his screen. The red blip was almost on top of their position.

Show time.

The freighter cruised on past their concealing asteroid, oblivious to their presence. Octavio retracted the *Beauty's* grappling claw and then, matching the freighter's speed, he piloted his ship in a slow pursuit.

"That looks like a good one," he told Sherveena, pointing ahead of the freighter to a cluster of smaller asteroids. "Ready on the thrusters."

"Just say when."

Gauging the freighter's proximity to the cluster, Octavio watched and waited several minz as the gap narrowed.

"Now."

Sherveena flicked a switch and the two of them watched as the old-fashioned solid-body projectile—chosen since it would not be as easily detectable as a normal energy weapon—flew from the *Beauty's* launcher. The missile screamed through space and into the thick of the clustered asteroids where it detonated, dispersing the lunar fragments toward the unsuspecting ship.

As the asteroids began pelting the freighter, Octavio used the diversion to take the *Beauty* in close. The freighter's automated systems would not be able to differentiate between the *Beauty* coming into contact with its outer hull and the impacts from the small asteroids.

As soon as Octavio felt the *Beauty* touch the freighter, he activated the magnetic grips, securing them to their prey like Quamarin remoras.

Several more tense minz ticked by as the freighter continued on its path. When it was clear that the *Beauty* had not been detected, Octavio got up from his seat.

"Let's go shopping, shall we?" he said as he and Sherveena headed for the airlock.

As he suited up, Octavio considered the fact that this was the scariest part of pirating. Not the boarding of an automated freighter; true, that could be a bit creepy—especially on freighters belonging to such races as the Rewtem, or the Coriliun—but what scared him in the general sense was the trust.

He had to trust Sherveena one hundred percent.

As he ran down his suit's checklist, testing the air supply, the seals, the boot magnetics, he looked to Sherveena. Better test the waters.

"This'll be a big haul, sweetie, the biggest of our careers. What do you think we should do to celebrate when we finish here?"

Sherveena smiled. "I know it sounds silly, but I'd like to settle down in some quiet world and raise a family."

Octavio managed to keep his face from splitting with a mocking grin. It was *silly*, and not just because she had never hinted at such a future before now. It was ridiculous because Sherveena was as greedy and plotting as he was.

He could not come up with a placating lie quickly enough so he just nodded, and stepped into the lock. The door sealed between them and he moved to the outer hatch.

He clamored out, making his way to the hull of Jaxsin Deshti's freighter. "Which way?" he called back via his comlink. He hated space walking. The sooner he found an access point the better.

"It doesn't matter," Sherveena replied.

"Come on, Sherveena. Point me to the nearest hatch." As he spoke, he turned back toward the *Beauty*. His eyes popped wide open as he saw the ship's magnetic grips retracting. "Sherveena! What are you doing?"

"So long, you unfaithful bastard."

"Sherveena!"

The *Sherveena's Beauty* drew away from the freighter, and pivoted back toward distant Port Nowhere.

"Sherveena!"

In utter dismay, Octavio watched as the primary thrusters glowed to life and the *Beauty* abandoned him. It was still in sight when his earphones crackled to life once again and Sherveena's voice filled his helmet.

"Have fun with your new friends."

What? Then, as if in answer to his unspoken question a section of the freighter's hull cracked open, spilling red-orange light into the blackness of space. What was this? Shapes emerged from the fissure, humanoid and otherwise. There wasn't supposed to be anyone onboard this ship. Deshti's freighter was automated.

The half dozen beings advanced up him. He would have shot at them had he been armed. Instead he could only watch their approach. Their suits were black; black or blood red. He couldn't be certain in the near nil lighting afforded by the vessel's hull lights.

A cold shiver ran up his spine as the foremost crewmember came close enough for Octavio to view the face within the helmet. It was Human, bald, adorned with red-crystal goggles and marked with four vertical red slashes.

The Red Publicans.

~**END**~

AIR FOR AN ERR

Richard C. Meehan, Jr.

The flutterpod ride back to Dhamu's Place was uneventful at best, especially after a meal at the Starview Lounge. Even the troublesome Lt. Baranin at the LevTwo airlock seemed distracted, ushering them through with barely a glance in Crila's direction this time.

Charlie couldn't decide what to talk about. After Rudof Dyll had announced that Benita Frohmyn's envirosuit had failed, perhaps causing her death, he could think of little else. To top it all, Captain Eversyn had shown up just as they were leaving the Starview. Or, were they being ushered out? With Rudof Dyll, you never knew exactly where you stood. Charlie felt uneasy with the whole thing.

"You know, I had a really good time, Charlie." Crila snuggled against him. "No one has gone to so much trouble over me in a very long time." She kissed him on the cheek.

Charlie's misgivings evaporated instantly. By the time the flutterpod arrived at Dhamu's Place, he had managed to find his hands graciously full of Human/Halsan female.

"WHAT GOES ON IN THERE?" roared someone outside the pod.

They ignored the intruder.

The flutterpod tilted violently sideways, spilling its occupants out on the hard rock of the cavern in front of blocky webbed feet. Its former passengers were left to untangle themselves on the moist stone.

"Dhamu, what are you doing—you—you big scaly oaf?" Crila had leapt up almost instantly, but her yellow dress was covered in blue-green mildew.

She did look like a bruised banana, mused Charlie, as he was lifted from the ground and shaken like a rag doll. But, she probably didn't even know what a banana was.

"I told you *NOT* to harm Crila!"

Lights sprang behind Charlie's eyes as his head connected with the cavern wall. In fact, he added to himself, she probably didn't even know bananas were the staple food of half of her ancestors.

"Heyo, Dhamu! He wasn't hurting me, he was *kissing* me!" Her voice held an edge of fear overlaid by anger.

"Oh. Sorry."

Charlie's feet suddenly found his weight, which of course they refused to support. He slid down the cavern wall next to the bar's entry portal. Scaled fingers tried to dust his gray suit off, but only managed to smear the grime around.

"Dhamu, just look what you've done," said Crila. "Help me get him up! Can you stand Charlie?"

Whether he could or not, the salesman was standing in the next instant, pinned against the wall by powerful Modajai arms.

"You can have a drink on me," prompted Dhamu.

"Can I take a rain check on that?" Charlie rubbed the back of his head, feeling a lump already.

"What's a *rain check*?"

"Later—may I have one later?"

"You off-worlders. You don't speak so good. Have the feeking drink anytime you want!" The Modajai lumbered through his portal shaking his head, leaving Charlie and Crila alone.

The barmaid soothed, "Dhamu means well, Charlie. Sometimes he gets a bit protective. He's gotten me outta a few tense encounters with customers over the years."

She encircled his waist and reached up for a kiss. Despite the throbbing of his head, he gave her a good one.

After they had had their fill of each other's embrace, Crila said, "I have to go back to work now. Thanks again for the great time. And Charlie," she touched his cheek with her real hand, "don't you think it would be a good idea if you kinda laid low for a while? It isn't everyday a Connie dies inside a fish while wearing an envirosuit, you know."

She had a point.

Reluctantly, Charlie kissed her a last time before folding back into the flutterpod. A few voice commands later, the pod lifted away, heading for the Wayamr Commercial Quarter and his Protectaire retail outlet.

Charlie was relieved when the flutterpod arrived. Traffic had been light from Dhamu's, although several Rewtem had blocked one tunnel for nearly twenty minz while performing what appeared to be an unsuccessful attempt to merge. The gelatinous creatures kept bumping against each other until one finally popped, thus opening enough space for the flutterpod to squeeze by. It was revolting. Smelly glop was everywhere. Whoever said those things didn't have internal organs?

He sent the rental pod back to its owner on LevThree. Turning, he nearly slammed into another Human coming out of the Protectaire booth with a new envirosuit.

"Watch it, buddy. This suit cost me a mint!" The large man scowled and trundled away with his new Mark II Humanoid. It would serve him well.

After checking the status of the Vend-A-Suit, noting the number of envirosuits sold lately, their types, and their profit figures, Charlie used his omnipass to enter his private domicile. The tiny apartment, carved into the stone cavern wall at the back of the booth, had served him well over the years. It had a shower. That was the main thing next to a toilet. Come to think of it, it was nice to have a sink and a bed too. He made use of them all.

Waking refreshed, Charlie ate a quick meal of reconstituted chicken salad in his cramped kitchenette. His first experience with the product had been on a backwater planet called Terra, where the aboriginal Humans claimed it was made from a fowl

closely related to the L'Taltons. A bite of chicken went down
the wrong way as he tried to arrest his laughter at his own
conjured image.

Hacking to the point of tears, Charlie recalled his last visit
to the L'Taltons. It had been a totally wasted trip. After much
negotiation with one Assemblage, he failed to open that market
simply because the bird he had been negotiating with was too
low in the pecking order. He briefly wondered how roasted
L'Talton would taste.

He packed his duffle bag with sundries to last several
strechiz and donned his own Mark V Humanoid Class I, top of
the line. It would be prudent to get on with his sales route, give
some time and distance to the death of that Connie. No use
tempting the Beryl.

In less than an ower, Manus boarded a geo-glider for Dome
17, the L'Talton abode. Those birdbrains were hard to work
with, but they bought a lot of envirosuits from somewhere—
probably Nykee. At least his omnipass was still working;
perhaps all this was for nothing. Well, it was about time he
cracked some eggs over there anyway. If Eversyn wasn't going
to renew the Connie envirosuit contract, then maybe new
business from an L'Talton Assemblage would placate his
Protectaire superiors.

His first-class window seat offered an external view of the
Rock, which he took advantage of. All too soon he would be
stuck in some dank hole surrounded by squawking bird beaks
for the next strechiz.

Despite the desolate, moonlike appearance of the planetoid,
Charlie felt a rush of freedom. Crila had once told him others
were jealous because he could come and go as he pleased.
Hang them all; he was glad to be traveling again!

A pleasant scent of an unidentifiably exotic perfume wafted
over him as the aisle seat was taken by the lithe form of a
Halsan woman. For an instant, Charlie's heart swelled at the
thought Crila had decided to join him, only to deflate when he
realized from the smaller, more elfish physique, that this
woman was pureblooded. Her ears were more prominent and
sharp-tipped, and she appeared childlike by Human standards.
Stupid too, since she was not wearing an envirosuit on a

surface trip across an airless landscape full of potholes, canyons, rock spires and mountain ranges. He decided to ignore the fool.

Like the flutterpod, this inter-dome geo-glider used electromagnetic levitators to offer a smooth ride across the rough surface of the planetoid. However, the noise level far exceeded the smaller pod. As the geo-glider lifted off, its sub-harmonics thrummed through Charlie's body with the beat of an electro-percussive concert band. It was going to be a long trip.

<^>

Owers passed. The broken gray surface flickered past in the wane light of the Galactic Arm. Charlie was sipping at a rum neat when a sudden bump caused him to slosh most of it into his lap. More than a few spacer epithets strung from his lips as he sopped the liquid from his envirosuit-covered knees with his napkin. Of course, the rubber-like fabric of the Mark V was impervious to such things, but it kept his hands busy. That had been a bad jolt.

"All beings fasten your restraints!" The words blared from the comsys.

Just then, a series of jolts caused Charlie to drop his glass entirely and struggle to get into the seat restraints. He glanced at the little Halsan woman as he snapped his buckle in place. Her skin was nearly purple with fear.

"We're going down. Brace for impact!"

"Put your head between your knees," Charlie yelled over the increasingly offbeat thump of the electro-levs. He did so himself.

The Halsan yelled something back that Charlie couldn't make out. He wondered fleetingly if they were going to die. Damn Protectaire for making him come to this forsaken lump of feek in the Void!

The salesman smashed headlong into the folded serving tray of the seat before him. His vision went red—cleared. The Halsan woman was folded over like a snapped Sloygat.

Everything was shaking. Rock fragments whizzed between the seats.

Air sucked away.

Darkness...

Clank...clank, clank...screech...shuffle.

One breath; another. Thank the Beryl—air! Charlie Manus gulped and sputtered in the total darkness, sucking air into his depraved lungs. The cold rock upon which he lay seeped through his envirosuit. Something was wrong there; the suit should warm him.

But he was alive!

Something shuffled near his head.

"Who—who's there?"

~END~

WAKING UP WITH SHA'ZREEN

Jim Johnson

Broose, the muscle, stood in the studio shadows within arm's reach of his boss, the one and only Mastriz Sha'zreen Glowberreez. This cyk's edition of her early morning talk show, *Waking Up With Sha'zreen*, had just wrapped; Sha'zreen stood just off stage, her lush, deep lavender lips pursed in an unintentionally alluring pout. Her gold-flecked purple eyes, however, were green with envy as she glared vibro-blades into the human now before the vidcams.

"Good morning, Port Nowhere, and welcome to 'The Rock Chipster Ower'," he beamed over the uplink.

Sha'zreen snorted daintily and spun away from the travesty. "Come along, Broose. We need a drink."

Broose fell in behind her as she stormed through the studio like a hothouse flower on a rampage, the pronounced sway of her hips radiating shockwaves of attraction to all she passed.

"How does a poo-head like Rock Chipster wind up with the cyk's prime time slot?" Sha'zreen fumed aloud as they headed down to the lobby.

"It's beyond me," Broose said as always, half listening to his boss, half lost in the flowery fragrance she exuded. So he almost walked right over her, literally, as she came to an unexpected halt. It wasn't easy bringing his hulking, Govarian frame to so sudden a stop but, when he did, he found Sha'zreen almost pressed against his chest.

She glanced up, flashing that gazillion-cred-smile of hers. "You know what I was thinking, Broose?" she asked with a gleam in her eyes.

"No, Mastriz. Not exactly, that is."

She reached up and patted his right biceps which, for the record, was nearly twice the diameter of Sha'zreen's whole body. Well...except for her trademarked bazoombas, he thought involuntarily.

If he was blushing, Sha'zreen either failed to notice or simply didn't care. Her beaming smile became a soulful, reflective one. "I was just thinking how tragic it would be if Rock Chipster's face had an accident."

Broose felt his brow furrow; this whole moment was a break from their usual early cyk routine. "Uh, are you asking me to...you want me to pun..." He fell silent as Sha'zreen's delicate fingers covered his broad mouth.

"Of course not, silly boy," she said with a follow up giggle that tinkled like the high notes of a somasar. "It just occurred to me how tragic something like that would be, even for someone like Rock Chipster; poo-head that he is."

With that, she turned and resumed her exodus from the studio.

Still wondering if she *really* wanted him to arrange for the Chipster to have a run-in with his fist, Broose followed Sha'zreen through the lobby, out the front doors, and down the corridor toward the Starview Lounge.

Their morn routine had resumed the instant that they stepped onto the public ped-way. Broose expertly registered everything, ready to pulverize anyone or anything bov-brained enough to cross the line where Sha'zreen's personal space or safety was concerned.

Sha'zreen, being Sha'zreen, was oblivious to it all. For example, she didn't seem to hear the multiple crunching of a flutter-pod pile up caused by the drivers she distracted. Nor did she notice the enraptured Fwazek who fell from a second story window and onto the arc of the force field barrier while trying to catch a glimpse of her.

The energy barrier, a one-way force field, had been erected by studio security to hold the ever-present fans, the autograph seekers, the impersonators—and the stalkers—at bay.

Sha'zreen flashed all of them her famous smile and blew all of them purple kisses. She even reached through the invisible barrier to sign a few autographs—all the while making steady progress down the line toward the Starview.

At the end of the block, and the end of the force field, Broose followed Sha'zreen down the side alley to one of the private entrances of the Starview.

The Starview Lounge was *the* place. Certainly the only public place Sha'zreen cared to be caught dead in. It was the Quiet Hour. Even so, the place was half filled, though the crowd was essentially yestercyk's leftovers.

Sha'zreen led the way toward the floating dining platforms above the dance floor at the lounge's center. Broose's pitch black eyes darted everywhere. From across the cavernous establishment, he caught the yellow-eyed scowl of Bharstus Bhogani, the Starview's head bouncer. Broose watched as the Modajai shook his scale-plated head and subtly signaled the other bouncers on duty.

Broose shrugged; he sympathized with Bharstus. Sha'zreen's presence always meant trouble. On one occasion—after a particularly lively brawl inspired by Sha'zreen's having blown a kiss to an inebriated Nicovan while ignoring the advances of an equally wasted and much deadlier Vamir—Bharstus had banned Sha'zreen from the lounge all together.

But Banastre Caravello, the Starview's owner, had, not surprisingly, succumbed to Sha'zreen's charms. As a result, Bharstus and his staff simply had to deal with the inevitable consequences of Sha'zreen Glowberreez. End of discussion.

Just then a loud voice called out.

"Sha'zreen darling. Welcome to my humble establishment."

The voice belonged to Caravello. The squat, round Human approached from the right. But Broose was paying more attention to the rest of the sentients alerted to Sha'zreen's presence by Caravello's greeting.

"Silly boy," Sha'zreen gleamed as she bent to lay a lavender kiss on Caravello's bald scalp. "You said that very same thing

296

to me just yestercyk, and the cyk before, and the cyk before that and…" she let out one of her stock giggles and Caravello giggled in kind.

Giggled, not laughed, Broose noted with a roll of his eyes.

"Come, come, darling," Caravello said, taking her by the hand. Broose noted the contact but let it slide. Certain circumstances and certain people, like 'em or not, were permitted. "We were just about to have breakfast."

"We who?" Sha'zreen inquired as the lounge owner led her up the steps to an idling dining platform.

"Rudof Dyll, at your service, Mastriz Glowberreez," answered the ornate Human now visible across the table as Sha'zreen, Caravello and Broose reached the platform.

"Oh stop, you silly boy," gushed Sha'zreen with a wave of one hand. She had dined with Caravello and Dyll more times than Broose cared to recall.

While Sha'zreen and Caravello seated themselves, Broose exchanged curt, businesslike nods with Dyll's Vamir bodyguard, Algensio.

Caravello summoned a waitress. "What would you like, darling?"

Broose saw it coming.

Sha'zreen sighed. "Oh, an ice water, I suppose."

"And?"

"That's all," she replied dramatically. "I really don't feel too well."

At this Rudof Dyll, eyelashes sparkling, jewelry jingling, leaned forward in his seat, his painted face draped in concern. "Are you ill, Mastriz?"

Another, more drawn out, sigh. "It's just…work. You know how the biz can be."

"Not us," said Dyll. "We can imagine, but we couldn't possibly know. Show business; acting and performing. Well, it's beyond the likes of us," he said, nodding to Caravello.

Caravello shooed the waitress away as Sha'zreen's glass of water, like all beverages, rose up from the tabletop dispenser. Sha'zreen took a gingerly sip.

"Well, you can ask Broose," she said, though not even Broose expected to be questioned. "The day started off well enough, my guest today was some up and coming new chef, I forget who…"

Caravello piped up. "Jule Emryll. After watching your amazing interview, I'm even thinking of contacting him to work here."

Sha'zreen arched a graceful eyebrow at the interruption. "Anyway, let's just say that by the time that poo-head, Rock Chipster, goes on the air, I've all but delivered him a ratings-clinching audience."

Caravello and Dyll exchanged a quick, sidelong glance.

The longest sigh yet. "Silly boys. Rock Chipster has the number one show because he has the number one timeslot. And as long as he keeps riding on my coattails, he'll always have it. It's just all so dreadful. I'm doomed to second best because I am the best. How can I possibly be less than…well, than perfect? It isn't my fault. I can't be something that I'm not, can I? But as long as that poo-head has my audience to snatch up, he'll always get top ratings."

At that point, Sha'zreen sniffled pitifully. Broose, Dyll, Caravello and Algensio all produced tissues—they were prepared for such Sha'zreen moments—and with genuine concern offered them to her.

She accepted Broose's by habit. "Silly boys; you're all such gentles. Not like that poo-head Rock Chipster."

After a moment, Rudof Dyll said, "You've said 'poo-head' several times and, while that isn't the strongest word that comes to one's mind, it certainly illustrates your feelings regarding Mastre Chipster."

"Rudof, you silly boy, that's because it isn't the word, it's how one says it. And no one says 'poo-head' quite like me."

"I'll drink to that," cooed Caravello.

~END~

⊙DD ⊙∩ϵ ⊙UT

Charlotte Babb

Crila dropped to LevFour and made her way along the spiral tunnel to the entrance to the public temple of the Sisterhood. It was open to the public, but almost no one ever entered without explicit directions. Two warrior Ophidia kept guard at each side of the temple opening, a simple round hole in the native rock with serpentine inscriptions for decoration. A statue of three Ophidia, a healer, a dancer and a warrior, stood inside, just past the opening. It took a bit of courage to pass the guards and face the statue.

Inside were various curtained openings, some lighted and others dark. Smoky incense added to the mystery of the place. Beyond the statue on a platform were a group of dancers, perhaps a class as no one seemed to be watching except the musicians who played wind, string and percussion instruments Crila had never seen before. The music was hypnotic, as was the dance. She forced herself to look away from the dance to find the pod where Heart of the Core and JayRand would continue her training. She passed several Ophidia, all about 3 meters long, but in various colors and mode of dress. Each nodded to her and sent her a mental greeting: *Sister Gives More than was Taken.*

Crila had learned to pick up their names as she passed: Beryl Scales, Speaks with Many Voices, Bites First then Asks. As yet Crila had seen no males, but she supposed that they were kept in some kind of harem or stud farm, whether managed or enslaved, she did not know. She saw JayRand's crest emerge from behind a curtain. She wondered again why an L'Talton would pair with an Ophid—L'Taltons always had pair-mates. But JayRand's mind was too different from the Ophid's for Crila to read, or it was not open to her. Yet he would mind-speak with her when he wished.

A little mystery keeps things interesting, Crila thought, ruefully.

Then you must be completely engrossed, Heart thought back, with the warmth of emotion that accompanied a smile.

That her thoughts were like loud conversation to the Ophidia still embarrassed Crila. She pushed the dark curtain aside and entered the pod. It held only lounges for her and Heart, and a roost for JayRand. Heart was coiled on one lounge, her upper body draped in a silky yellow shawl.

You'll learn. Perhaps today. Heart's thoughts carried a smile. The best thing about the mind-speak was that the emotions carried through the thoughts had to be genuine. The Ophidia were known for telling the truth, even if not the whole truth. How could they lie to each other?

False-telling is easy enough if you believe what you are thinking, JayRand added. He nodded to her, raising his crest in salute. *All sentients are capable of it if they are capable of deceiving themselves.*

Crila sat down on the lounge and curled her legs under her. About two meters long, a meter wide and less than half a meter off the floor, the lounges had one arm and a back which slanted down to meet the foot of the other end. An Ophid could coil or stretch out, dangling her tail over the side while she rested her humanoid body on the arm. This one was very soft, with a suede leather covering. Crila didn't ask what kind of leather or if was synthetic.

Clear your mind, Sister, as you have learned to do. Heart said. *Do not concern yourself for the animals whose skins made up the covering of your lounge. They did not suffer in their life or death.*

Crila took a deep breath and drained the thoughts from her mind into her body and into the floor. Grounding, Heart called it. Crila stared ahead, practicing seeing what was around her without analyzing it.

Well done. Now close your eyes and wait for our next question. JayRand's voice had a different texture than Heart's.

Crila let the thought pass on without considering it. As she closed her eyes, she heard sounds of someone slithering by. The sound stopped. Crila felt that someone had joined them in the pod, although she could not hear anything. She stopped herself from asking, even mentally, but continued to listen. She resisted the urge to look. She felt a mental touch from Heart, as if Heart had put her hand on the back of Crila's head. Then Crila knew that four beings were in the room. She could almost see the shapes of them, shadowy figures modeled in the fuzzy gray of her mind's eye...herself, JayRand, Heart and another Ophid, one she had not met, smaller and different.

Open your eyes, Sister Gives More. The thought-voice was male, young, almost like Tau's except without the edge of long-term distrust, fear and working the angles. His name was Plays Deep.

Crila opened her eyes but held onto the psychic vision she had of the room, looking at Plays Deep's face, but taking in all the detail around him that she could. He was brown with geometric markings, not as large as Heart, perhaps not fully grown, but with serious eyes in a face full of mischief. He wore a tunic that closed beneath his waist, covering his genitals. Crila did not look down.

Excellent! JayRand did not smile, as his beak did not allow for that expression, but the others did, with that wide but closed-lip grin of predators that do not show their teeth as a sign of friendliness.

Heart nodded. *Brother Plays Deep is an adept of trance. He is quite young, but he has the gift. He is in training, much as you are, to teach what he knows.*

"Wh..." Crila started to ask, the control of her thoughts and curiosity taking away from her control of her speech. Embarrassed, she tried again. *What is the need for trance? How is it used?*

You remember the trance state of the initiation?

301

Yes. Crila had never experienced that level of belonging to the group, but while she seemed to be treated as one of the Sisterhood, the feeling had faded.

It was necessary for you to be in mental contact with the Sisters for you to survive, Heart explained. *Now you learn how to transmit messages across the planet.*

We are here to protect you, JayRand added some ruffling of feathers to his thoughts, *and to guide Plays Deep. When you are to report to us, you will need to go into deep trance because you will not always be able to come to us.*

Crila pushed a stab of fear from her mind. *Have to close your mind to be open-minded...*She blushed again, looked at the floor. She had always been able to think what she would, whether or not she expressed her thoughts. Now she felt stripped, vulnerable, helpless.

Yes, Sister Gives More...Crila, Plays Deep sent her a warm, hugging thought as well as his smile. *We have many minds, all with doors we learn to open and close. All of us have to learn this, even we "gifted" ones.* He pulled the edge of his tunic away from his neck to show Crila the scars of fang marks, the ones that matched Crila's.

So do I call you Brother or Sister? Crila's upbringing did not include a male who could enter the women's inner circle.

All of them laughed aloud, the noise startling after the quiet thoughts. They weren't laughing at her, though they found her unstated assumptions about the differences between male and female funny, and they even felt some of her sarcastic tone of voice.

JayRand's trills in particular were so piercing that another Sister, one of the warrior guards, jerked the curtain aside to see what caused the ruckus. She clamped off her thoughts as soon as she saw Crila, but the emotional content slipped out almost as an odor.

Some Ophidia were not happy about having out-species as sisters—or brothers.

Thank you for that teaching, Sister. Plays Deep bowed to her. *I will strive to be a true brother as well as a sister to you. Call me Plays...or call me Deep, but call me!* His double entendre came across as well as the joke.

Crila met his eyes. They were all mischief this time, as much as any young human male.

Some jokes do cross cultural lines. JayRand commented. He preened, settling all his feathers into their normal immaculate state as he settled his mind. He too raised its crest to her by way of bow. *Though heart-fasted to Heart, I too am your sibling—though neither brother nor sister…*

Crila felt too many emotions to trust herself to speak or to think. She felt she had asked a stupid question, one they had taken as a joke. She pressed her human side into its niche, and settled herself into her Halsan training, focusing on what she could sense physically to make herself more present in the moment.

Yes, very good, Heart thought. *You already have this skill you desire, to close the door for a private space. Now you will learn to build a space for the private thoughts as well.*

Crila nodded, still separating her conflicting selves. She breathed deeply, stared at each one for a moment, and then let her breath out, feeling where each one stood, feeling a connection with each one. *Shall we start the training now?*

Two hours later, Crila and Plays Deep were exhausted. He had taken her by the hand, mentally, and led her into his own mental construct for reaching the deep kind of trance necessary to send and receive thoughts across the planetoid, and perhaps even into space. He showed Crila how to build her own mental rooms for separating her private thoughts, using the metaphor of her human self shoved into a dark closet.

Don't be so cruel to yourself, Plays Deep chided. *Each part of yourself is beautiful, even if it needs to be protected from a cruel world.*

What would you know about that cruel world? Crila's scorn came through with more intensity than she expected.

Because I can't experience it? Plays Deep sent her a wry smile. *Just that—because I can't experience it. To go out of the Enclave, I must learn to be a warrior, to be the killer we are rumored to be, just to save my own scaly skin from becoming someone's aphrodisiac.*

Crila shuddered. Her revulsion from the idea of someone grinding up Plays Deep to a powder for sale on a LevSix bazaar shelf pushed her out of her body. She hadn't done that since she was a child, her consciousness floating above her body as it lay inert on the lounge beside Plays Deep. The others turned to look at her and beckon her to return. They did not seem upset, only a little surprised.

Welcome back, Plays Deep thought. *It is time that we go back to the mundane world, as your spirit can tell.* He again offered a mental touch to help Crila walk back up the ramps she had imagined into the depths of her mind.

Crila became aware again of the lounge beneath her body, and the Ophid beside her, though her body still retained some of the feeling of the paralysis of sleep. She opened only the door of her public mind, the one she and Plays Deep had constructed as she opened her eyes.

Someone had brought in a pitcher of liquid and glasses. She realized that she had not seen the Ophidia eat, and that she might not want to. But that thought stayed obediently behind her private door, and she got no reaction to it from anyone, not even Plays Deep.

~END~

MASTRIZ MEREDI REGRETS

K.G. McAbee

The shuttle had finally reached the docking airlock; she could hear the series of snaps and pops and clangs as they echoed throughout the craft. There was the usual flurry of announcements and the shuffling of feet, tendrils and various other appendages as the passengers got ready to disembark.

A willowy Neek handed out information vids and repeated warnings in a burbling voice: "Remember, visitors! Port Nowhere is currently under the control of the Consolidated Guard. Please keep your ID-badges in full view at all times. Have a pleasant stay, and it is strongly advised that you never go below LevTwo without proper authorization and hired bodyguards. Boomboom's Rent-a-Guard is a most reputable firm; so is Gweedo's Strongarms. Visit their kiosks in Alpha Corridor."

Maryn Meredi, ignoring the hubbub that murmured and whispered and trilled about her, stretched her long legs forward, kicked the seatback in front of her, then leaned back. The Sloygat that had perched in front of her for the last ower, with few apparent signs of life, now turned its stick-like upper torso and glared over the back of its seat.

Five eyes can produce a lot of glare, she thought in amusement as she grinned back at the 'Gat.

"It is of the rudeness utmost to extend lower appendages and disturb this one," it said, in a clipped and precise accent. It was showing off—many 'Gats were linguists—and its voice was pitched so high as to make visible shivers run down the back of a portly Bansnict that sat across the aisle.

"Sorry." Maryn pulled her legs back, on the way kicking the 'Gat's seat again just for fun. It gave an irritated whine that faded away into supersonics. The Bansnict growled in agony and its long tongue shot out to lick an ear.

Maryn slid down further in her seat and propped both booted feet on the back of the 'Gat's seat.

LevOne. She hadn't been on LevOne since…how many visits to the Rock ago? She hadn't been to Port Nowhere for…well, way too long. The Rock was so much more than these voids and offal around her would ever know. But still. It was going to be…interesting to visit with some credz in her pockets for a change, after all the times she'd hit the Depths running, with little more than a Mark Five at her hip, a list of people to rob, and a deadline.

Too bad Mal couldn't be with her. Those had been some times.

Yah. Times when we'd almost get killed from one cyk to the next. Don't miss 'em. Better now.

But she wasn't so sure it was. Life could get pretty boring when nobody was trying to murder you. And being alone wasn't as much fun as she'd thought it would be. Sometimes she missed the rough and tumble of the old *End of Time*; the crew hot-racking, sharing sleep pods, half on duty while the other half slept as they raced from one score to the next, with shore leave a distant dream.

Yah. Those were some times.

Too bad every last one of her old crewmembers was dead.

Piracy could be a dangerous way to make a living.

Maryn drifted through the lines at the reception pod with a handful of credz prominently displayed in one hand. Her expression was a careful blank, as if she had no suspicion that the credz were there, nor that the wad decreased in size with each step she took.

A tribe of youngling Bansnicts clustered around her at one point, tiny hands reaching smoothly for her pockets. She snapped at them in their own language, calling them 'offspring of toothless z'darrownnnn', and they recognized one in their own vocation, gave up on her and headed for a more likely target—a fat Human female with two husky attendants who looked to be all gonads and no brains.

At the end of the final line—most of the passengers who'd ridden down with her were still stumbling through their retxams—she lost the last of the wad to a Connie with a small head and a large blaster. He handed her the single case that he'd just that minz closed.

"Welcome to Port Nowhere, Mastriz," he said, offering her a stiff bow that showed how unaccustomed he was to any sort of formal courtesy. She grinned at him, remembered how rich she was and changed the grin to a sneer, then wandered through the last set of doors in the containment corridor into Dome Seven proper.

Another corridor. Around her, species from all segments of the galaxy—those who were O-2-breathers, anyway—swarmed past, coming and going in every direction. And the throng wasn't limited to O-2-Bs, either, she saw; a pair of methane-breathing Szigitzizes rolled past, both in the latest style envirosuits; Protectaire brand, no less.

Szigitz with credz. What a concept.

But unlike inside the reception pod, with its utilitarian off-white walls in smooth polybdalloy, this corridor was a vibrant kaleidoscope of colors running off in both directions, blending and changing and morphing without stop. The shifting images were dizzying, forcing the eye away from them and towards the opening across the corridor.

"Blazing Core," Maryn whispered, then grinned at the Rock oath coming back to her so aptly. She stepped over to the window, gazed up, up, past buildings and restaurants and domiciles and pod-clusters, to the top of the semi-transparent dome almost half a klick above her head. On the other side of the dome, ice crystal stars clustered in swirls deep inside the galaxy, or danced alone on its edges.

"Hard to believe all of this sits on top of nothing but piles and piles and piles of—"

"Welcome, welcome!" The soft, seductive voice came from a vid-screen that took up several square meters on the corridor wall just beside the window. A purple-skinned female, all gleaming smile and enhanced mammaries, continued, "I'm Sha'zreen Glowberreez and I'd like to extend my personal welcome to Port Nowhere! Nothing like it exists in the rest of the galaxy. Welcome! We're so glad you're here!"

"Yah. I'm sure everyone here will be just delighted to see— my credz." Despite speaking in little more than a whisper, Maryn saw that several passers-by had caught her words. One, a male Neek with aqua-and-black bandings, allowed a small grin to illuminate his flat face before he offered her his throat in submission stance. A janipod and squeegee clanked in one web-fingered hand as he disappeared down a ramp a heartbeat later.

Neeks seldom hung around after exposing their throats for cutting; kinda took some of the sincerity away from the offer, Maryn had always thought.

The caster on vid-screen was listing points of interest. "Visit the stunning Starview Lounge, where all tastes are catered to and all species welcome. Drop into the shops that line Dome Seven's Alpha Corridor, and buy the most elegant wares available in this arm of the spiral. Stay at PodRoyale, the most luxurious pod-cluster on Port Nowhere, for a strechiz or your expected life span, and rejuvenate all your senses after your journey. Buy…"

"Yah, yah. Buy, spend, buy, spend. Zantz. Like I got nothing better to do."

She shifted her case to her other hand, comforted by its weight. She wasn't on the Rock for fun. She was there to find a man, kill him, and leave.

Simple. Quick and easy. At least, she hoped so.

Although there was certainly no reason why she couldn't enjoy herself in the process. Mal would have wanted her to have some fun…even while she was offing his genetic double.

That was all she needed to do; then she would be all caught up, all debts paid. She could shake the Rock dust off her feet and blast for a place with air and a sky. Maybe settle down; get some rest; count her money. Take it easy.

Without knowing it, Maryn sighed at the dismal prospect.

Then she shook off the almost unconscious images and headed down the corridor.

Had to find a place to crash for a few cyks. And the booming voice had recommended the Royale...

The PodRoyale wasn't just the best podcluster on the Rock; it had to be the best in this arm of the galaxy. And when she'd passed her right wrist, with its subcutaneous cred-chip, over the viewer, the desk clerk had metaphorically dropped to his knees and kissed her boots—would have in actuality, no doubt, except Rentoveens didn't have knees. Instead his long neck curled into a loop and all four of his eyes blinked in rapid succession.

Two bell-Neeks fought over her case; the one that lost motioned her to the drop and they both ushered her into a suite that cost, per cyk, more than she's once spent on a crate of Mark Sevens, *with* charges. Maryn dismissed the Neeks, both happy with their handful of credz, set the door lock, and wandered around the pod. Zantz, it was bigger than Hold Nine on the old *Time*. She cast an eye over the pod-service holoscreen that took up a large chunk of one wall; whatever she had a taste for, in food or drink or other pleasures, was listed, in seventeen gaudy colors and blaring opti-sound...plus quite a few things she had no taste for at all, and was pretty sure she never would.

She waved a hand over the controls, and the screen blanked. The sudden silence beat loud against her ears. She sighed, caught herself doing it, and snorted.

"I sound just like Mal did when he remembered his time in the cage."

She grabbed her case and tossed it on the sleeping platform. A snick of the lock—a very simple, innocent, easy to pick lock—and it fell open. A few personal items, tunics, a robe— the case of a woman who was on the Rock to do some serious shopping.

Maryn dumped everything onto the plat and manipulated the hidden compartments in the oddly thick walls and bottom of the case. In a few minz, she had assembled a tiny Zintero blaster, no bigger than a Bansnict's ethics; it had a clip that she could attach to her hair, though she'd had to let it grow out for that very purpose.

Irritating. She liked to keep her hair short. But she didn't have to worry about firelice or podbugs, not in the Royale.

And it wouldn't be for very much longer anyway.

Now. She was ready.

She strode to the opposite wall, and activated the window controls. The cloudy gray faded to sharp transparency, and she gazed out over a large chunk of Dome Seven, spread out before her like the holoscreen goodies she'd just dismissed.

Across a wide cluttered expanse of shops and corridors and open esplanades, almost directly in front of her window, sat the iridescent dome that was the Starview Lounge.

Maryn grinned the grin of a predator. If any of her unfortunately deceased former crewmates had seen that grin, they would have recognized it.

Guess it was just about time for supper.

<^>

Malik Blayne huddled down, making himself as small as he could in the hollowed out opening too small to be called a cave. His knees hurt as they dug into the rock beneath him, and his shoulders ached as he tried to hunch them down even more. Beside him, Tau—apparently boneless—perched on his heels, comfortable and at ease. The boy's eyes glinted in the muted light as he peered through brown, dirty tangles of hair into the larger cave beyond.

"How much longer?" Mal hissed. The hiss turned to a faint gasp of pain as his arm jerked spasmodically and banged an elbow against a jagged crystal that stuck out of the rock at his side.

"Long as it takes," the boy replied, and gave a fluid shrug that just rippled his twenty-times-handed-down coverup.

He's enjoying this. Blazing Core, wait'll I get him back up-lev. I'll...I'll...what the feek?

A single—word?—spoken as loud as a shuttle engine revving for liftoff. It tore through the cave, reverberating into endless echoes that piled atop each other like a wall of sound.

Malik saw Tau tense. They both hunkered down further.

Don't know what that was...don't know if I want to know what that was...but if I have to do this much longer, I don't know if I can stand it. Too much like being...in a cage. He took slow, long breaths, his eyes focused on the floor beneath him. A layer of grey sand. A single firebug trundling across the uneven rock, jaunty antennae waving; it marched into a crack and disappeared.

Another...word?...softer this time; just loud enough to send the pale sand nuggets pirouetting across the darker rock surface. They danced for an instant then collapsed in a pattern of swirls.

A third sound—they *must* be words—but spoken from what vast mouth?

Tau gave Malik a comforting pat, nodded towards the opening of their makeshift hiding place, and disappeared through it in a smooth and almost soundless slither of arms and legs.

Malik followed, cursing silently as joints popped and tiny pains cut into stiff muscles like shards of glass.

It was such a relief to stand up straight—out of the cage at last—that for a moment Mal reveled in the feeling. Then he saw what was spread before them, on the shores of a dead and deadly sea, and his breath stopped in his throat.

Row after row after serried row of small figures, barely taller than a youngling Bansnict, clustered on the grey sands. Their masses reached as far as Malik could see in the dim light—he made a mental note to never visit again without his lumilenz—and stretched from the very edge of the poisoned sea into the dim distance, and he had no doubt far, far beyond.

An expectant hush filled the huge cavern. Even the silent, tideless sea seemed to stop its restless motion and grow still, as if holding its breath in anticipation.

Then Tau grabbed his sleeve and tugged. Mal followed the boy down a rocky slope and ever closer to the silent, motionless beings. The grate of the Humans' booted feet on rock and sand sounded like a sacrilege, an intrusion on an almost holy moment, but none of the figures made the slightest sound; no fur-covered head turned, no yellow eye flicked sideways.

They reached the first of the ranks, and Malik at last could see what the beings were. Uffas, the wedge-tailed amphibians that swarmed in the deep lakes. How did they get here, on the shores of this lifeless sea, a sea cut off from all the other subterranean bodies of water on the Rock?

The small Uffas opened a pathway for them, a path that closed behind in eerie silence. Tau stopped a meter from the waterline, and Mal stumbled into place beside him. They turned to face the amphibian ranks.

As if it had been one single appendage instead of thousands, the right arm of all the creatures rose, in astonishing unison. A heartbeat later, the left followed. Mouths opened—Malik could see those closest to him, round holes that housed tiny forked tongues and row after row of blunt teeth—and again, a single word poured out in a single sound, as if uttered by a single mouth.

Again, the word, in a shout that loosed small rock fragments from the invisible ceiling far above. One hit Mal on the top of his head.

Malik could feel the blood rising in his face. "This is embarrassing, Tau. How much longer?"

"You saved their leader, their king, when you sent the medz. They want to give you thanks. This is their way." Tau grinned, his white teeth bright in the gloom.

"Yah. Blazing Core, I just shipped in some supplies; it was no big. They didn't have to go to this much trouble."

"The Uffa are an honorable race. They return thanks where it is due. Enjoy. How often does someone tell you thanks?"

The boy had a point.

Malik sighed and plastered a grin on his face. He nodded in what he hoped was an appreciative way, instead of one embarrassed to the Core.

Good thing Crila wasn't there. She'd never let him live this down.

"All right. But I can't say long. Got a meeting set up."

"Won't take much longer. Just look like you enjoy the attention."

Attention: that was the last thing Malik enjoyed.

Now his alter ego, on the other hand…

<^>

Malik stepped out of the huge shower pod in his private quarters of the Dyll Dome. He'd had to take three separate showers, with different sofsoaps for each. The dead sea sent out dangerous poison fumes; that was taken care of by the first soap. The Uffas smelled like rotten fish; the second soap took care of that little problem. The third one deposited time-release scents on his skin. Rudof Dyll always reeked of perfume.

He glanced up at the iridium-plated chrono on the wall.

Late. He was going to be late.

Good. Everyone expected Rudof to be late. Rich citizens had their own schedules, and those who served rich people set their chronos to match.

Malik cursed under his breath as one of his jeweled eyelashes stuck to a finger. He got them all on at last, and slid into tight orange breeches and green shirt with ruffled breast and sleeves. He yanked his hair, now a brassy yellow, behind his head and jabbed a ruby-studded comb into it.

Had to remember to get some more red dye.

Malik stared into the mirror.

Rudof Dyll grinned back at him.

"Time for supper. And I'm starved."

<^>

The Starview Lounge. It was huge, gaudy, pretentious, loud, overpriced and full of an assortment of richer-than-they-should-be Rock denizens, all having a Core of a good time.

Maryn loved it.

She'd reserved a table on one of the floating disks. Wasn't sure now that it had been the best idea. The preprogrammed 'random' patterns kept the disks—there were only seven that she'd seen—fairly far away from each other.

Not the best situation, if Dyll occupied a floater too. But if he was at a ground-lev table, that would work. She'd already

313

mapped out the disks' orbits; each drifted over the lower fixed tables in set patterns and within easy jump range of the floor.

And occasionally, she was glad to note, of each other.

But she hadn't seen Dyll yet. No problem about recognizing him, natch. He was Mal's genetic double, but she was certain he wouldn't dress like Mal, in handed-down coverups and battered boots. Not a man as rich as Rudof Dyll was. He'd no doubt be the gaudiest one in the entire Starview, not even excluding the pride of Galavanz that occupied a table in one corner; their iridescent shells glowed in ever-changing rainbow hues.

The thought of Dyll made her reach up to pat her elaborate hairstyle, a gravity-defying upsweep miraculously created by one of the Neek dressers at the PodRoyale. When a single finger touched the tiny Zintero, Maryn smiled. She reached out a hand and activated the holoscreen. A drink; she could use a drink. Hmm...Draught of the Gods, with Adonis nectar. Just the thing.

She punched in the order and settled back in her chair. She looked relaxed, a bit bored. When any of her old crew had seen her look that way, they'd check their blaster charges and strap into safety harnesses. But the Human waitperson who floated up on an agrapad showed no concern when she delivered the drink. Just a rich woman enjoying a drink at the Starview.

Time, as is its wont, passed. Maryn watched the dancers in their groups of two, three and more move to the soothing sounds of somasar music, while her mind mapped and plotted each disk's precise trajectory and route. Her own disk was one of the smallest, seating only two at its onboard table. Most of the others were filled with diners.

All but one, indeed. It was the largest, and flew the highest, and had the most elaborate pattern.

And it was set for two, though the table was big enough to hold many more. Maryn had learned—and had paid good credz for that little bit of information—that Rudof Dyll was never seen without his Vamiri bodyguard. There were other Vamir about the place, but save for a pair on the dance floor, the others appeared to be simply employees.

Maryn yawned in boredom. If he didn't show this cyk, it made little difference. She'd keep coming until he did.

Then her mouth snapped shut as she swallowed the last of the yawn. The largest disk had paused at the highest of the three mezzanine balconies and two figures were taking their seats. She couldn't be sure, from this distance, that one of them was Dyll—he was humanoid, at least—but the other was certainly a Vamir, four armed and covered in brown fur. She couldn't make out its clan stripes, but she knew that Dyll's own particular Vamir was of Clan Snrl'Pau.

She watched as the disk hovered, waiting to enter the pattern. While it waited, Maryn checked back through the disks' routes, trajectories and relative speeds, all stored in her head. Sintinz of navigating through the galaxy, often without the benefit of nav-comp or nav-bot, had made her almost as fast at calculating, and easily as accurate, as any machine.

She would reach within leaping distance of the disk—the disk that was at this instant entering the flight pattern—in fifteen-point-seven minz. Three-point-six minz afterwards, the disk would be skimming over the dancers' heads.

Maryn dragged her eyes away from Dyll—she hoped it was Dyll—and the Vamir. She could feel her heart speed up. At last. The final debt paid, the slate wiped clean.

Only a few more minz...

She shouldn't, mustn't stare. She settled back into her chair, heard the nanobots whine as they matched it to her mass and form.

Plans marched through her mind. Point-four minz to make sure Dyll was dead. Three-point-two minz after she blasted him, she'd drop to the dance floor, head for the kitchens. Her route was mapped out; a new subcutie already under the skin of her left wrist, so credz were no problem.

Calm. Stay calm.

Think of something else.

Memories...the first time she'd seen Malik, squatting naked in a cage...he'd looked up at her, brown eyes into green, and asked her not to kill him. She hadn't had to think twice; she knew he'd be useful to her, even before she knew who he was.

315

Useful. Yah, like a 'virosuit was *useful* in high vac. He'd made XO in less than a strechiz, right after she'd had to space Vezmir Zad's fat ass for stealing. Pirates stole for a living, but the code was clear; you didn't steal from shipmates. Mal had been her right hand for three sintinz. She'd held him in her arms a hundred times after one of his dreams of being back in the cage.

And when they'd lost that final battle and watched the *End of Time* blow…when they ended up in the bohralinite mines on the prison planet of Golgarno…when they'd plotted the mass escape that had gone so terribly, horribly wrong…she'd known then that whatever Mal asked of her, Maryn would do.

Well. Mal had never had the chance to ask her to do anything. But this was something she was going to do for him on her own. She was going to kill that feeker Rudof Dyll, and enjoy doing it.

And if she didn't manage to escape? The way Maryn saw it, it didn't much matter. Not any more.

Not with Malik dead. Not with all her crew dead in the escape attempt from the mines.

Didn't much matter.

The disk was close enough now for Maryn to be sure. That foppish dandy had to be Dyll. Besides, under the makeup and jewels and fancy clothes, he looked enough like Mal to be his brother. Zantz, they were clones.

Maryn watched as the disk drifted closer. She followed it, her eyes tracking the trajectory. No use not watching now; it was Rudof Dyll, the richest man on the Rock. Everyone else in the room watched too.

The chrono in her head sent adrenaline rushing through her veins. Just a few more minz…

Maryn drew her legs back, sat up straight, pushed her chair back. She turned sideways, bent over as if looking at the dancers below.

The Dyll disk was two meters away. Maryn gathered her long legs under her, leaped, her chair not even disturbed. She landed easily half a meter from the edge of the Dyll disk's table. It was larger than hers had been, but there were only two chairs, opposite from where she'd landed.

The Vamir—a tiny segment of her brain noted that yes, it was a male of Clan Snrl'Pau—snarled out a deep-voiced *Throob!* but she ignored the threat. The Zintero was in her hand, the tiny but deadly muzzle trained on the ruffles over Rudof Dyll's heart.

For half a heartbeat, green eyes stared into—green eyes. Dyll's eyes widened so far that one lenz popped out, the true brown exposed. Light sparkled on his jeweled lashes as his mouth opened in an incredulous—smile?

Maryn tightened her finger on the triggerpoint...just at Dyll raised his hands and she saw the manacle scars that encircled his wrists.

The same scars she'd seen so many times on Malik Blayne.

She tried to stop the reflex of her hand, tried to keep from pressing the triggerpoint, but it was too late.

Too late.

Too late.

The words beat in her head as the blaster's minute powerplant shot out a jagged beam of energy, enough to blow a gaping hole in anything made of flesh and blood...

~ΠOT THE ƐΠD~

GLOSSARY

Chrono: Clock.
Cykul or cyk: Day. The Port Nowhere 'day' is divided into 25 **owerz** containing 50 **minz**; each **minz** has 50 **sekz**.
Strechiz: Ten cyks.
Quintin: Five strechiz.
Sintinz: Ten quintinz.

Credz: The basic monetary unit.
Mini-cred: Half a cred
Micro-credz: A quarter-cred.
Mega-credz: A mega-cred is akin to a thousand bucks.
Google-credz: We're talking Bill Dyll here.

Void: An insult, referring to the space between a human's ears —or relative spots in other species—being empty; i.e., calling someone too stupid to live.

Mastre: An honorific or term of respect to an adult male. The female version is **Mastriz**.

Feek: Pure excrement of most species. Slang word used as an exclamation of frustration, or as a substitutive noun in the place of the actual noun, i.e. "Look at that feek!" or the popular "I'm not taking this feek any longer!"

Ka'frindi: A fungus that grows on sewage in only one place in the galaxy—in the reclamation plants on Port Nowhere. Valuable as an export, due to its flavor-enhancing qualities, it is also used, during its fifth cycle, in the creation of straz. Stage three is the very valuable ka'frindi, which is edible for about twenty minz after being placed on prepared food. The fourth stage is inedible and poisonous. The fifth stage is straz, a very addictive and psychoactive drug.

Throob: If you have to ask…

ARTWORK (C) 2004 J. A. JOHNSON

GET A CHUNK OF THE ROCK!
VISIT THE WAYAMR COMMERCIAL DISTRICT
VIA THE WEB
FOR FREE DOWNLOADS...

Including The Complete
PORT NOWHERE
Compendium

If you enjoyed your first visit to the Rock, be
sure to look for further adventures at the edge
of the galaxy in volume two. (December 2004)

WWW.THROOB.COM

WWW.MYSTICTOAD.COM

Copies of PORT NOWHERE are available at our secure
website. If you'd like to order by mail, send check or money
order for $15.00+$2.00 s/h to:

MYSTIC TOAD PRESS
PO Box 401
Pacolet, SC, 29372-0401

MYSTIC TOAD PRESS

Coming soon from the Toad...

ESCAPE THE PAST by K. G. McAbee
Winner of the Dorothy Parker Award of Excellence

SOL SYS I by Jim Johnson

THE THING IN THE POOL, sequel to the bestselling THE THING IN THE TUB

PORT NOWHERE, VOLUME II: MORE ADVENTURES AT THE EDGE OF THE GALAXY

Visit ***www.mystictoad.com*** for more information.